I0615757

Iliya Englin

Convergence

A Novel

1983-2015

All struggles,

Nightmares and terrors,

Desolation and emergence,

Desperation, combat with fate -

Sentenced, in time, to convergence.

I remember the faux promises from the first round all too well - and stare back sternly.

"Radiation?"

He shakes his head with a sad smile.

"No one has ever shown that radiotherapy works with this subtype," Wilkins replies, drumming his large fingers on the mahogany desk in thought. "No, look, a few cycles of jungle juice should do it. Let's not make it more of an affair that it need be. Relapses are common with this tumour."

I nod, grappling with a tightness in my throat.

"I'll be there," he says, gripping my sweaty hand across the desk. "It will be done before you know it. Are you working on anything at the moment?"

"Looking into body corporate fraud," I reply automatically. My mind is somewhere far from this airless office sixteen floors above the traffic, somewhere on the windswept beach, my feet sinking in damp shingle. There is an incoming tide, and a Turneresque sunset. I took a picture like that, once - with a seagull crossing the break between the brilliantly lit clouds. My editor asked whether I was religious.

Am I?

"I have to run along," says Wilkins from somewhere far. "Margaret will be in touch."

We shake hands, and I blunder out of the office, nodding at Margaret automatically. She is an old dragon neatly disguised as a middle-aged Maori lady who wears exclusive black suits. It's been some time since I became eligible for free visits, and she nods at me with prim disapproval.

The lift doors open, and a young woman waddles out of the lift, her head encased in a scarf. She is still ample in figure, but yellow circles surround the sunken eyes. I know that state well and look away, stepping aside to let her pass.

Outside the lobby I am assailed by the sea breeze struggling to dispel engine fumes, and I am glad I didn't drive myself in, feeling dizzy and unwell all of a sudden. I suppose the denial phase is over - the awareness of the illness is washing over me like an incoming tide. It is time to confront it head-on.

I think of the cancer as an army of crude, witless marauders that need to be destroyed using superior intelligence. They are many, and I am one - but they are primitive, mindless savages, and I happen to be a technological man, the pinnacle of evolution in my world. Nothing can displace me from the top of the food chain.

I stride down the dowdy city pavement, a faded strip of bitumen decorated with dubious stains. It is a left-over from the old days before Independence, when this part of the world was a mouldy, windswept backwater. But it gives me comfort that even in the olden days the pavement was laid down with a laser-guided precision.

People around me hurry about their business; they are

listening to personal media players that contain entire libraries of film and music. Their mobile phones are connected to a state-of-the-art telephone network, not to mention the globally ubiquitous Internet. Why, I can extract my rather dated unit and send a message to an astronaut hundreds of miles above the Earth - and if the latest round of chemotherapy succeeds, who knows, I could even live long enough to send email messages to men on other planets. That is not too far in the future.

I study the passers-by, deriving comfort in their purposeful movements, the neat casual attire, the bland, well-groomed appearances - no one too young or too old. All the signs say that I am part of a solid, all-powerful world, in which my tenure is not threatened but merely trespassed upon.

Just a neighbourhood mishap, I tell myself - and the authorities are on the way to sort it all out.

There are many spare tables at my favourite city haunt, and I choose one near the window, with a view of the sea. The ample waitress nods curtly and shouts something into the kitchen, then begins to work her magic with the coffee machine.

Eggs hollandaise and a vienna thus on the way, I extract my phone, unroll the soft keyboard on the scarred table.

As never before, I am driven to write. But somehow, I am not motivated to commit it to a keyboard. On impulse, I rise and walk up to the counter.

The young lady looks at me with some surprise as I

ask if I could buy a few fresh notepads, of the kind they use to take orders. She shrugs her shoulders and hands me a wad of these, waving off my offer of payment.

{}{}{}

There is too much noise outside to get back to sleep, and I roll over, feeling a gentle but insistent throbbing in the base of my spine. It's been a great nuisance of late, the damage I sustained rolling down a steep embankment, carrying a' wounded soldier who died in that fall. The throbbing always comes when the cold of the night is laced with icy drizzle. As is the case today.

Nellie shifts in her sleep and presses a warm backside against me. I feel dampness that remains from our vigorous coupling and smile in the darkness. She is the only woman in Grey who would treat male seed so carelessly, letting it ooze from her replete tunnel. Everyone else goes through all manner of contortions to ensure that the seed stays put.

Conception is a hard, unlikely thing that is precious not only in feeling but in material terms as well. Mothers of surviving babies are well-rewarded by the town with food and firewood, and they get the best of vacant housing.

Not that my seed ever made a woman swell - and Nellie is well past the age of child bearing. She did more than her share before she came to Grey, pushing out three lusty babies who greedily slurped on her rich milk, even as they grew breasts of their own. Her milk is an acquired taste - she made me try it - but the girls grew into fine, healthy women like their mother. One, sadly, died on a sea crossing, but the other two are alive and well, with many children of their own. May they survive and thrive.

I caress Nellie's hip fondly. We couple often, the plump innkeeper and the grizzled soldier. Our age is mightily defied when we rush at each other, grunting and heaving our scarred and worn bodies until we are spent. I seldom lie with local women, who are an easy temptation to resist - hard, bony bodies with tight faces and pasty skin that comes from living off fish.

It is not much of a diet, our average meal - it's been some years since we had the resources to guard fields or hunt animals on land. We have cowered behind the wall for longer than I care to remember.

There are muffled noises outside, moans and muted laughter. It is something of a tradition: women flood the barracks the evening before a convoy departs, to couple with as many soldiers as possible. There are many more fertile women than men, and the ladies drink the juice of the purple berry, rushing around wearing nothing but loose frocks that can be simply lifted. They roam the barracks wild-eyed until hot seed begins to ooze down their thighs. If a lady is lucky, some soldier seed will strike its target, and a swelling will gladden her flat, underfed belly. Sometimes, if luck holds, the baby will stay alive in its warm, silent refuge and even survive the bloody passage into our cold, savage world.

Most of these babies will eventually regret being born - but that story is for another wasteful, sleepless night full of miserable thoughts.

The noises grow louder as the woman urges her consort with hungry, insistent gasps that resonate through misty darkness. I frown, thinking that the happy time has long-ended, leaving the busy soldier with little sleep for the long day ahead. Maybe, I tell the stern disciplinarian within, the labouring warrior is not assigned to travel tomorrow. If anyone looks tired on the convoy, I will have him clean latrines through the entire journey - the disciplinarian accepts this bargain and recedes into a dark corner, leaving my agitated and disturbed mind.

Indeed, one is reminded, it is high time I get to sleep myself. There is not much to do in the morning, but it's poor form to look as if I was up coupling through the night before the departure. Nellie should not sleep with me, that is so - but it has been a long-standing breach of protocol, and I always look tired anyway. The scarred middle age does not agree with me.

I turn over again and reach into dark corners of my much-used conscience. Something is not right - I know that much. Wish I could grasp what that is - but it won't come to the surface.

The moans outside cease abruptly, and I hear muffled giggles as the woman finally releases the soldier from his mighty labours. Her receding footsteps creak on the wooden pavement as she makes her languid, replete way to the gate.

I go over a few last days in my mind. Sometimes it

works that way - a thing that bothers me can be lost some place, letting me attend to something more important. It later festers, keeps me awake and irritates until I remember.

No such luck now. As always before the convoy's departure, everything is checked according to a list we hold sacred. This has been carried out, and nothing untoward has been found. There were no great discipline problems of late, and the cargo is of a modest, mundane nature - metal ingots, painfully heavy, but nothing like transporting explosives.

Much as I try to avoid it, the mind slips from productive thoughts about problems at hand to the general picture, which is not reassuring. The population is not increasing - the number of empty houses testifies to that.

A burial detail roams our town, knocking on doors when alerted by concerned neighbours. Occasionally they are answered by a disgruntled owner, hobbling to the door with a curse. More often, alas, they encounter a stony silence and break down the door with axes. They float corpses in the river, tied to a log. The current carries them out into the heaving sea, and our fishing fleet makes a point of not trawling nearby. Empty logs wash up on the beach, still trailing ropes torn up by powerful jaws. The fishermen are commonly accused of lying when they speak of giant beasts that leap out of the water, snatching men and equipment from the deck. Having seen the torn ropes, I don't think that all of these stories are drunken lies.

Empty houses are cleaned and boarded up, taking great care to keep out the rats. Mind, the rats of Greytown lead short and precarious lives - they share the streets with vicious packs of cats, feeding whom is strictly forbidden. As a child I was bitten by a rat on my foot. There was an awful swelling as I shook with fever - Father dropped everything to sit at my bed until the fever went down. It is the only time he ever cried in my presence, and I harboured a reverence of cats ever since.

Empty houses are assigned to women who give birth to live babies, but the number of empty dwellings keeps creeping up. Occasionally the council men demolish something that leaks or threatens to fall down, but one suspects that the main purpose of such demolitions is to hide the dismal truth. Our population is shrinking, and the enemy's population is increasing.

I can see the first hint of dawn in the window and sigh with resignation. The sleep is no great loss - as soon as the convoy starts moving, I can lie down and rest aplenty. But such failure to sleep after a good meal, much gin and exhaustive coupling is a sad reminder of my age. That too is a senseless train of thought. Nothing can make one younger.

I sigh once more and roll over to place a suggestive hand over Nellie's rump. She doesn't react, breathing softly in her sleep. I slide my fingers into her damp middle, feeling her thick flesh that is parted with such pleasure. She turns over onto the stomach and opens her large thighs, arms languidly stretching to grasp the head of the bed.

"It's too early," she rebukes me sleepily.

"It is time," I reply firmly, intensifying the pressure of my fingers.

She catches her breath and pushes into my hand slightly.

"How long is the convoy?"

"Eight days, maybe nine," I say absently, working on the hooded knob that swells under my touch. She moans softly as I bring her to, the first of many times before cruel dawn forces me from the warm, tussled bed.

What follows is as inevitable as dawn itself.

{}{}{}

I scroll through the emails absently - they are mostly from various editors, offering me stories. According to Margaret, the hospital is likely to call me in the next day or two. I type a few polite rebuffs without giving reason. After staring out of the window - the sea is calm and green this shadowy afternoon - I send the latest draft of the body corporate story to the magazine, as is. They haven't yet paid me and will be happy to receive most of the article gratis. I type a few words to explain the reason - giving away three weeks of work is unusual behaviour, and I don't want them to suspect insanity.

A few drops land on the glass as black clouds drift over from the sea. Shutting the laptop, I get up and walk over to the window to watch as the storm makes landfall. The guardian angel was looking when an elderly aunt decided to mention me in her rather lavish will. Otherwise a merry freelancer like myself would never own an apartment overlooking the water.

I can see the wind shake the wide pane of glass, which makes me feel somehow protected and cosseted. As luck would have it, a neighbouring apartment block had been built with a shopping complex on the ground floor, and a hard-working Chinaman leased the back section to open a cosy Cantonese restaurant. It is easily my favourite haunt - his glassy-eyed daughter brings me a carafe of house white, and I down it with dishes of the chef's choosing. It is up to me to call a halt to a parade of entree-sized portions of things mysterious, each tasting better than anything I ever tasted before. No drunk-driving either - unless one counts the ride in the lift.

With the spectre of chemotherapy looming, one may question whether I should start boozing. The sensible part of me loses that argument soon enough, and I raid the wallet on the table in the hallway. The Chinaman prefers to be paid in cold, undeclared cash. Glacial is his greeting to those who pay with plastic - and congealed is the sauce on their dishes should they make the mistake of coming back.

Just as I step out of the front door, my conscience forces me to return and set my home phone to divert to cell. The people in the hospital have enough to do without having to play hide-and-seek. They probably won't call today, but if I don't take the phone to dinner, it is entirely certain that they will call. I am sure that makes sense in the dismal game of cosmic dice, where human lives are tiny, contemptible chips.

When I reach the door, I turn around again, this time to stuff the notepad into my pocket. Writing feels good, and an experienced wordsmith never stops when on a roll.

{}{}{}

My stomach is still struggling with breakfast as I heft the kitbag over one shoulder and the harness with weapons over the other - then trudge down the short flight of stairs with the weight that gets heavier every year.

I nod to Trevor, my old batman. When he was a young man under Father's command, he fell off a moving transporter, and it was a sheer miracle that his broken bones mended. Sometimes Trevor regrets surviving that fall because of the pain in his mangled joints, but such moments are few and far in between - mostly he values being a useful, independent and much loved soldier in my command. He walks slowly and painfully, but speed is not required in his duties. My house is spotless, and my uniforms are perfect. I regret putting them on in more ways than one.

He salutes and wishes me well for the journey, casting a brief glance of disapproval upstairs, where Nellie is still ensconced in the rumpled bed.

"Let her sleep, Trevor," I implore in a loud whisper. "She works long and hard."

"Sure she works hard," rasps the old soldier. "Elbows

down, arse up - they can hear her rattling your house all the way to the port."

"Be fair," I reprimand him lightly. "She runs a good inn, you have to admit that much."

Trevor waves his hand in contempt and turns away.

"I will get that bed cleaned up by the time you return," he mutters sourly. "Why you never take a proper consort is beyond me."

"Maybe I am happy just so," a hint of steel creeps into my rebuke. "Take care, old soldier."

The open door admits a blast of cold air liberally anointed with drizzle. The wind almost wrenches the door from my hand, and I stagger to regain balance, thankfully before old Trevor feels obliged to hobble over to help me.

I cross the barracks yard, icy drizzle needling my face. The convoy is assembled at the far end, transporters gleaming in the rain. I always revel in the sight of squat shapes painted dark green, cleats of the tracks tightly sprung on the sprockets, gun barrels upturned into the grey sky, as per regulation, to avoid accidents in a built-up area.

I heave my gear inside the lead transporter and begin the final inspection. It's my last hope - I am deeply unhappy about something that cannot be named, yet has to be found at any cost.

After climbing up and down, under and over, inside and out of every transporter, I raise a copper whistle to my lips and blow it three times. Men rush out and line up outside their machines in the thickening sleet.

Redmond, my master sergeant, marches up to me and salutes, snapping to attention. I salute back.

"What is it, Commander?" he asks urgently.

"That's the thing, Red," I shake my head in annoyance. "I know something is not right, but can't say what."

"You mean you don't want me know?"

"There are no secrets from my men. I don't know myself."

Redmond sighs, knowing that what follows is inevitable. He salutes me and turns on his heel, extracting his own whistle. It is not the first time I do this on instinct, and lives have been saved every time.

"Emergency inspection!" he thunders across the yard. "On my whistle, begin!"

He blows a shrill note, and the soldiers begin to scurry around their transporters, shouting urgently. Redmond turns to me for more instructions, but I can only shrug and smile apologetically.

One of the merchants, a short man with heavy shoulders and a scraggy blonde beard that cries for a sharp pair of scissors, approaches me resolutely. He is somewhat new at this kind of thing, I recall quickly. It is best to keep things low-key.

"What is the meaning of this delay?" he stabs an

angry finger at the frantic activity around the transporters.

Redmond heads him off.

"It means trouble, good sir," starts the sergeant placidly. "It means that we are about to cross three hundred miles of forest, and something is wrong. So we won't be going anywhere until we find it and put it right."

The man is now truly puzzled.

"You know that something is wrong but you don't know what?"

"More or less, sir," replies Redmond with an air of perfect patience. "The rest will take too long to explain."

The merchant stares at us with a hurt, nasty expression of a thug denied a chance to scrap. I am about to step forward and tell him what I think, order his cargo to be thrown off into the mud - but Solly runs towards us and salutes, requesting attention. I push past the merchant roughly and face Solly, inviting the man to attack me from behind - knowing that if he tries, Redmond will tear off his arms.

"Permission to report," barks Solly, my best new sergeant.

I nod resignedly, knowing that whatever Solly has in mind, it's not what I am afraid of.

"My transporter has a cracked spring," says Solly. "I am sorry, Commander - but it was invisible until we loaded the rear."

I nod again and turn around. Redmond gives the merchant a superior look and stares past me at the culprit. I follow his gaze; with an eye of faith you can see a slight sideways tilt.

"We have plenty of springs," says Solly. "Why, there are two in the lead transporter."

"There you go, my good sir," says Redmond with elaborate courtesy, staring at the merchant with a predatory smile. "If we hadn't found it now, we would have to change that spring in the forest. You would have to sit in the snow, with hungry eyes staring at your smooth bottom from the bushes."

I wave my hand in the direction of a stricken machine. Solly and Redmond run off, arguing whether the rear end can be jacked up fully laden.

I walk towards the lead transporter and trudge up the ramp. The lead machine does not carry cargo, and everything in it is built for speed and agility. There is no one inside - it's all hands to the massive jack used to lift the damaged transporter - but I notice, with gratitude, that someone has hefted my gear into the turret.

Once upon a time men flew around in vast aircraft - they even landed on the Moon. The planet was criss-crossed with giant roads, railways and bridges, and more than one nation had weapons that could destroy every living thing.

I clamber up the ladder into my compartment, happy

that no one can see the awkwardness that comes of ageing joints creaking in the damp cold. Such debility does not become the most powerful man in the land - and possibly the most powerful man alive. I say that because a desperate search of two generations failed to detect traces of civilized life further out. We inherited the knowledge of radio making, and other survivors should have passed it on elsewhere. Yet the last ship to arrive from afar came in when my great-grandfather was a little boy. There may be others - but without radios and other technology to protect them, they are doomed to extinction. I am therefore certain that we are the only survivors.

Sadly, that makes sense. We think that we know why our ancestors survived the scourge. It seems that whatever carried off the ancients falls apart too quickly in cold and wet weather. The sunrise side of our land is surrounded by tall mountains, and the poison never took hold where we live. Animals do not appear to carry it, and stricken people collapse within a few days, before they can cross the mountain passes. We never travel to poisoned areas without special arrangements.

Occasional expeditions are mounted when we run out of arcane supplies such as books: transporters, men and cargo are quarantined in tents at the top of the mountain pass. They are encouraged to spend their time drinking - a good way to pass what may be the last of their young lives. If they are alive and well a week later, the cordon at the bottom of the valley is lifted.

Sometimes no one travels down from the camp to

challenge the cordon. When that happens, an airship is sent up to spray fuel over the tents, which are ignited with a phosphorus round from a safe distance. Airships burn expensive fuel that we distil from woodchips with a great deal of trouble, but a few containers are always on hand in case someone brings the poison over the mountains.

I unroll my bedroll on the floor of the turret, taking care to lay it over a well-worn spot away from the gun. Below that spot, under the round sheet of steel floor, is an exhaust pipe from one of the engines. I, the most powerful amongst the descendants of men who walked on the Moon, enjoy the reckless privilege of sleeping above that pipe - which affords me some respite from the ever-present cold.

We spend most of our time and resources in an effort to keep warm. The ancients believed that burning their fuels made the planet warmer - perhaps. All we know now, when humanity is reduced to a few cowering dregs of its former multitude, is that the world is unbearably cold, at least where we survive. It takes all of our measly know-how to avoid freezing to death.

Bare survival is not, of course, enough - women seldom give birth to live young, and small children die like flies. The cold may have kept out the poison, but it is killing us as well. I suspect that all remaining populations have shrunk in that manner until they became extinct. Without copious supplies of fuel it is but a matter of time.

We, for a fact, do not have a copious supply of fuel.

We run most engines on wood, however dry we can get it – and heat our homes with the green stuff that barely catches fire. Both are threadbare and tiresome means of survival: the trees take forever to cut down, to transport and to split; the firewood takes forever to dry in a place where rain falls twice a day without fail. We get cut off whichever way we turn, and I cannot see a way forward.

That thought doesn't leave me in the best state, and I am glad that no one can see that: slumped like a rag doll, pressing my burning forehead against the icy wall of the turret, all of life's blood drained from my body and all hope drained from my soul. At least I can truly hide by sitting on the hatch. The turret is the only place where I can safely be alone with desperation.

The sole consolation comes from the turret's other occupant, a heavy-calibre hopper gun. I had that made according to a design I especially liked - the ancients used such guns to shoot down fast-moving aircraft. Men laughed when I told them - the only aircraft we know today are floating ships that fly in low wind with flimsy motors driving propellers, and you can bring them down with a single shot. The motor's hot exhaust is fed into the sackcloth impregnated with resin to keep the airship afloat; it is best to use them close to sea in case they spring a leak. The monsters that lurk underwater are infinitely preferable to what lurks on land.

Mounted horizontally, the hopper gun provides highly accurate fire with a lot of power. After being laughed at by Trevor, I used the first gun to cut down a moderately large tree. Each bullet tearing out a large chunk of green wood, a short volley simply slashed it in half - the trunk did not even have time to crack before it was severed in two.

Machines give me strength. They are valid, concrete reminders of what is possible. A rational world is one in which guns project unstoppable power; engines only stop on command and men with the right qualities triumph over a vile, disorganized enemy whose only weapons are hunger and malice. I do not live in such a world, but the gun reminds me that it is still possible to build one.

The floor shudders as the lead piston, the front left one, puffs into life. The command transporter has the largest boiler, designed for maximum speed.

Our machines had survived much refinement to become as simple as possible. We kept paring down ancient designs until we ended up with two tracks, driven by one or two pistons each. Steering is accomplished by running one track faster than its opposite member. There are no gears - steam-driven pistons provide enormous power at low speed. We do not travel fast - it only erodes ancient roads we have few means of maintaining. Instead, the engines drive the track sprockets directly. The platforms are mounted on the chassis with hard springs that serve as a primitive suspension. Each engine is a simple unit that can be easily lifted by two men once detached from the sprockets, only held in place by four bolts.

The burners suck air from inside the cabin, forcing more air to come in from outside: an effective ventilation system with no moving parts.

The fuel is more of a problem – dried wood, chopped to fine wedges and stacked with utmost regard for precious space. The water is bad enough – we have to stop every few hours to replenish the tanks from the roadside streams, but dry wood is nowhere to be found and has to be lugged with us. At least we are warm inside the machines and run the furnaces through the night – it keeps men warm and allows the engines to be pressed into service without delay.

Electrics are run on a small generator we engage instead of brakes when going downhill. They are restricted to bare essentials - intercom and radio. Making acid batteries is a recently rediscovered art, and they do much to ease our discomfort. We seldom use lights because shining them in the darkness strongly attracts vermin. It is entirely possible to outrun the moving transporter, and it took little time after grandfather's first convoys to determine: at night it is better to find a defensible position, turn everything off and listen as hard as you can for the first sounds of an attack.

There are windscreen wipers, rotary brushes that are turned from inside by a spare pair of hands. The windscreens are thick glass, concealed for good measure behind a fine grate of hardened steel. That glass is easy enough to crack, but even bullets cannot make it fall apart.

Three generations of trial and expensive error had seen a transporter evolve into a box with sides sloping inwards towards the bottom, a near-flat roof and a round turret, whose gun is encased in a thick metal sleeve woven from sharp metal ribbon. The barrel gets very hot with firing, but that doesn't always act as a deterrent. Handling the ribbon, however, is an error you only make once.

The boiler forms the roof of the machine at the front, with the bottom twice as thick as the top – my grandfather lost many men to boiler explosions, until he designed the unit to explode outwards. The main door of the transporter is its rear wall, which is cranked down to the ground to become a cargo ramp. There is also a hatch in the floor that we use for stealth. Simplicity and absolute reliability are required of any piece of machinery that leaves the town perimeter for use in the forest.

All space above the drive train is cramped with people, weapons and cargo. This is what I do - my company, grandly known as The Regiment, escorts civilians to three remaining towns outside Grey. Two have poor sea access because they are set in rocky bays with violent seas, and the third is inland, built to take advantage of a large lake. That is where we go now.

I shake my head as I remember Rina's last words. My thoughts turn to her, the fiery redhead with whom I've had many explosive liaisons. When all is said and done, we live in two places separated by days of dangerous travel, and that is probably just as well. Our rapturous couplings and lacerating fights would probably see the death of us had we lived within the same walls.

But I often feel her tender touch on my scaly hide and recall the way moonlight glows on her honey-coloured cheekbones. I wonder whether she ever thinks of me in her quieter moments. I wonder whether she feels the same regret at our parting. I wonder whether she will choose to see me in three or four days, when the convoy reaches Brana.

I wonder whether I should ask to see her first. Then I wonder if I have the courage. Well, I do - but in the end, I am lost for what I would want to say.

I stare through the porthole above the gun and sigh as the transporter begins to move. Whatever it was that alarmed my senses, I had failed to identify or fix it. Now it will simply have to take its course, and the consequences will simply have to be survived.

{}{}{}

The chopsticks sink into delicious and nameless contents of my bowl as I glance at the phone compulsively - but its display remains dark and silent. In a few days I will be unable to even think of food. I will lie on a plastic mattress covered with disposable paper sheets, hugging a vomit bag. A wide intravenous line will snake into my rib cage, and I will feel it drip venom into my system. There will be violent shakes, dizziness and headaches straight from hell, and if I am really lucky I will also get gout that sets joints on fire. The latter is sort of good news - it does mean that a whole lot of cancer cells had died, although it doesn't mean that they cannot return with a vengeance.

But that is not the worst part by far. I would bear being cut in half if I knew that it would end the entire business one way or another. Alas, such luxury is not available to cancer patients - we suffer all manner of hurts during treatment, but real torture begins when doctors pat us on the back and tell us to go home. Every ache and niggle immediately triggers panic - maybe the cursed thing had come back for the kill. Sometimes, more often than we care to admit, we wish it would kill and be done with it - just to put an end to the terror.

The phone lights up.

I snatch it before it rings, rushing away from the table into a little alcove next to the kitchen. I don't recognize the number, and it doesn't look like it's from the hospital network.

"Nick, I hope I hadn't caught you in the middle of anyone," says my ex-wife drily. "I just heard. Helen is crying her head off, and I got it out of her. Hope you don't mind."

"No, that's okay," I tell her absent-mindedly. "Just make it quick, I have three naked women panting and slavering on all fours."

She laughs with relief. Sandra never got over the fact that I am no longer her possession, and others are free to share my bed - which, on occasion, they do. But I never brag about it - which she knows.

"I am sorry that Helen is upset," I tell her. "She had to know - I couldn't just leave her hanging with that body corporate thing."

"Please tell me everything will be all right," she pleads. "You should not have given that story to her for nothing - she thinks you are about to die."

"It won't be for nothing," I reassure her. "She will have to throw me lots of work once I get better."

Sandra is now sobbing into the phone. I sigh in resignation - my dinner is getting cold, my ex-wife is endangering her marriage to a wealthy man by crying over a relapse of my cancer, and Helen, a long-time friend to both of us, is probably distressed beyond words.

"I'll call her as soon as I finish eating," I tell Sandra suggestively. "I am just across the road from the high-rise."

"It will be all right, won't it?" asks Sandra again.

"I will see to it," I tell her menacingly. "I look forward to frying every one of those little fuckers. I want to hear them squeal as they pop. All right?"

"That's the spirit," she tells me in a choked voice. "I better go now. Take care, Nick."

"You too," I reply, meaning it. Jesus, Sandy - I hope your second husband wasn't within earshot. Heaven be my witness, I am not much of an expert on relationships - but common sense suggests that if your ex-husband still matters that much, it is best to keep it to yourself.

The Chinaman appears as if by magic, carrying my

remaining dish back to the table.

"I gave the pippi another burst in the wok," he tells me in his clipped Hong Kong English, setting a bowl with steaming spirals of marine flesh in front of me. I nod in gratitude, and he retreats to the humid bustle of his kitchen. Which is not a bad place to be - it's going to be a decidedly cold night.

I finish eating and leave the cash under the soya sauce dispenser, nodding to the Chinaman's daughter in thanks. She nods back vacantly and returns to her phone, spindly fingers with pink nails tapping an intricate dance on the screen. No doubt, some young buck is staring at his display in hope, awaiting her reply. I opine that his chances look reasonable after the eatery shuts - he might get to take the princess for a short spin and an ice cream. She might brush his shoulder as they walk to her front door, but that is where the boy's luck will end. Her slender thighs will only part on a rich man's bed - after her position as a rich housewife is secured.

I cross the empty road, shivering in the tearing wind as I traverse the short distance to my apartment. Heavy drops of rain begin to pelt my forehead, but it is reassuringly warm inside. The glass lift gently raises me away from the ground as I dial Helen's number.

She doesn't pick up, and her answering machine is off. I have a fairly good idea why - poor Helen has probably fallen off the wagon. All signs point to that of late - crude spelling errors creeping into her email, light tremor in her broad hands and a blotchy redness of the cheeks that no make-up can conceal. My news would not have helped one bit.

I return the phone to its cradle, frowning. But airlines have an excellent saying: please fit your own oxygen mask before assisting others. It is time for a hot bath and an early bed, listening to the pelting rain that is going to rage through the night. I take the notepad into the bathroom and pour a hot bath, to reread what I had written today, immersed in the make-believe comfort of hot water.

{}{}{}

I stare blankly through the narrow porthole, covered with a cleverly arranged plate of glass that slides up and down with the gun, along the sloping wall of the turret. The transporter clatters over the cobblestones as we begin our journey.

I make one final effort to identify the problem. It still eludes me.

"Tannis, proceed," I order into the intercom.

"Order to proceed acknowledged," his voice croaks in my speaker. I really should replace the old headphones - Sandford has been boasting about his new design for some time. I generally work on the principle of "not broken, don't fix", but my hearing is not what it used to be. Firing a hopper gun in a metal turret does nothing to improve it.

The convoy stops at the gate, where the sentry stands to arms. I unwind the lock and push open the top hatch, allowing the heavy lid to drop onto the roof of the turret with a loud clang. It is all tradition.

The sentry steps forward to challenge the convoy, and I recite my name and rank, as if these are unknown. He demands the destination, and I loudly announce:

"Brana, return in nine days."

He salutes and steps away from the gate to wind the crank. The heavy gate slides open, and I can hear the frantic hiss of escaping steam beneath me. The sprockets engage with a loud hiss, and the transporter surges forward, nearly sending me off my feet. It's an art to accelerate without producing this surge, and Tannis is not in good form this morning. I wonder if it was he who laboured on a woman outside my window before dawn. If his act doesn't improve, I will have to find out.

The street is busy with vendor carts - ageing ladies selling dry fish, seaweed and lobsters in the narrow alley. They move their carts out of harm's way as our beasts of burden clang past, within inches of their rickety stalls. I smell the sharp reek of stale seafood and sigh. Beer and smoked meat await in Brana - her intrepid men roam the land in packs, shooting deer. Unlike us, who rely on weapons and armour, they resort to lightness and speed. They run through the forest armed only with crossbows and big knives, which they use for butchering their kill. Whenever possible the meat is retrieved by airship, which makes the entire exercise difficult and expensive. Even in Brana the diet is mainly fish, caught in the safety of its vast lake.

We cross the market square and approach the town

wall, transporters thundering on the cobblestones and filling the air with steam. I wonder if one of my engines is coming up for replacement - that much steam often means that rust has eaten the piston. Water, alas, does that to metal. Thankfully, our engines are simple to make, and the foundry recasts old blocks with very little loss of precious metal. We do not have the fuel to smelt iron and scavenge it by melting down the rusting remains of ancient machines.

At the main gate the ritual is repeated, but with a longer formula.

"I am obliged to advise and warn," drones the sentry from the town guard, staring at me with importance. "Exiting town defences presents an extreme danger to life."

"Your warning is gratefully acknowledged," I tell him. It's a ritual utterance.

"I furthermore advise that the town cannot be held responsible for your fate nor does it have resources to attempt any kind of rescue," declares the sentry.

"Acknowledged," I reply with less patience. Fuck your sorry bitch of a mother, we are the town's resources, my men and I. Without us the wall would be breached within a day.

"I therefore release the gate at your own risk," concludes the sentry, turning towards the ladder of the watchtower.

He scales it and makes a show of scanning the outside

as if anyone would attempt lying in wait for the gates to open, then begins to wind the handle. The gate rumbles sideways on rusting rollers until its outer edge slams into the stops and comes to a noisy rest.

I quickly drop inside the hatch and wind it locked. Out of habit my heart quickens as I scan the horizon through the porthole. Engines puff and hiss with the effort, pushing the great machine past the safety of the wall into a hostile expanse of the outside world. There is nothing to worry about just yet - the open space near the wall is fervently denuded of vegetation all the way to the river.

The path we use as a ford is a pile of large stones, which we occasionally have to repair after the spring melt. We take the ford at full speed, and I cling to the gun handles to avoid being slammed against the walls. At least it is now warm inside the turret, thanks to the exhaust pipe that runs beneath the floor.

The forest awaits on the other side of the river - a menacing ocean of lush green, whose bottom we traverse along what remains of the ancient road. Vast mossy trees block most of the light and drop cascades of raindrops with every breath of wind. The forest does its best to obliterate the road, young trees sprouting in its surface after mere moons of our absence. The tracks of our machines mash them to pulp, but deep in our weary hearts we know that they belong here, and we don't.

It appears, in fact, that my kind is no longer welcome on this earth. Our survival becomes more precarious each day.

Exhaustion overtakes me, and my eyes blur. I leave the sentinel duties of the convoy to those formally assigned to that task and unfold my bedroll. The rocking motion of the transporter soon merges with the gentle see-saw of the engines - just like being in your mother's belly.

Sadly, the best part of existence is in the past - for I am already long-born.

{}{}{}

In the morning the clouds are still thick and replete with drizzle. I sip a tepid coffee and stare out over the beach, the aches in my body a subject of certain alarm. They advised me to watch for fever, as the immune system never really recovers from chemotherapy - in addition to which my bloodstream is full of cancerous cells. I get out the thermometer, drink a little water from the tap and check my temperature. It's normal.

The day is all mine as the hospital hasn't called in the first few hours since breakfast - that makes a free bed unlikely. I decide to take a spin around Lake Brunner and have lunch at the fine café next to the railway station, where they still serve the best chips on the planet.

That will do me for breakfast and lunch - I am not hungry, and there is little point in feeding the cancer. It surprises me that I have this much energy with a relapse - but then again, it's early. If I didn't have a test for cholesterol at the behest of my hard-working GP, this would probably go undetected for another three months, until the oncologists saw me for a routine review. As it is, my brother-in-law had a heart attack, triggering a panic of cholesterol-mongering in the family.

I take the lift down to the garage, where the GTO is gleaming in semi-darkness, its menacing profile concealed in the corner behind large 4WD trucks of the people one floor above. Having more money than sense, they have two of them - his and hers.

I get in, dropping the window to get rid of the musty smell. Sadly, this masterpiece of suicide engineering sees little action - I get around town on an electric bicycle. My tools of trade are increasingly confined to the smart phone plus a small saddlebag with wet weather gear.

The antique engine turns over a few times and comes to life, shaking the garage with its angry growl. My machine craves speed, and it knows that today its hunger will be fed.

They recently sealed the road at the southern side of the lake, once a challenging route through superb native bush. I take the corners with vengeance, hoping that the patrols are busy on the main highway. The GTO slides a little on wet corners, but that's all part of the fun. I am not overly afraid to die in a fiery crash - no one who has been through chemo would fear such an end.

I get around the lake in record time and by eleven I am sprawled under the awning of the railway café, chewing on the chips and admiring the panorama of the lake before me. The wind is whipping up white-topped waves in dark-blue water, and the mountaintops behind the lake are tipped with snow. I revel in this scenery - no idea how I lived my life before I moved down to this part of the world.

The chips are gone with surprising speed, and I return to the sleek black beast poised in the gravel car park. The fuel consumption is a little high, I note as I restart the massive V12. This is not surprising given its age, but I write down the mileage and the fuel gauge. If she begins to burn more fuel, that's a bad sign. I don't look forward to changing this car, but all the same, I hope to outlive it.

Which is not at all a given.

I return home in mid-afternoon, but the answering machine is bereft of news. It is both a relief and an anti-climax.

I check my email - nothing bad there either. Helen wants to pay me for the truncated article and is asking for an invoice. She wants me to have a drink with the crew before I go in. I dial her number, but it's engaged.

My sister is planning her brat's thirteenth birthday, and that is a serious occasion. I take my duties as a mad uncle seriously, doing my best to push my eldest nephew to his full potential instead of becoming trapped in the middle class. I do hope I will be out of hospital for his birthday - and, all being well, no longer barfing from chemo. I type a hopeful reply that I will play my part to the hilt.

After that I succumb to sudden fatigue. I did nothing

physical and slept well - it's the cancer, and I need to lie down for a few hours. My appetite is definitely gone - the bowl of chips had killed it stone dead, and I cannot see myself wanting a substantial dinner. There is no desire to drink whatsoever, which leaves only one thing to do - run a hot shower and get into bed with a large plastic tray, sturdy enough to rest the notepad. I am getting used to writing with a pen, even if the wrists still hurt. Still, it feels like being a real wordsmith. Anyone can peck keys.

{}{}{}

The awakening is a jolt, and then it takes some time to recall where I am.

It is dark, and the fingers of my raised hand strike cold, bare metal. I am dismayed to have slept so long - we must have made camp a long time ago.

My state, however, is entirely acceptable - refreshed, and none of my joints are aching. I slide down the ladder like a young man, landing on the lower deck with a nimble crouch.

The soldiers crowded around the furnace turn and salute without rising, as protocol permits - leaping to one's feet is a perilous thing to do inside transporters. I salute back and smile as they shift, freeing a place near the fire. Someone hands me a metal mug of thick fish broth, and another soldier, whose name I can't quite recall, throws another log into the furnace. It is entirely warm and comradely.

Solly toasts me with what I hope is berry tea. On past precedent there is reason to fear that his mug could be laced with gin, but he knows better than get drunk on a convoy, and the rest is up to his experience and wisdom.

"We made a decision not to wake you up, Commander," he says with deference. "Rumour has it that you were kept awake for much of last night."

He winks obscenely, and the transporter erupts in laughter. I am slightly embarrassed, but at my age that can only be taken as a compliment. After a little contemplation I nod acceptance of the toast, tipping back my mug. The broth slides down my empty insides in a very timely manner - I now feel ravenous hunger.

"Another night of rest, and I will be almost recovered," I remark between sips. The laughter erupts once more, and I wait for it to die down.

"When you boys grow up, you too will discover women instead of poking each other."

There is much shouting and laughter, mugs jostling to be toasted to mine. I smile a rare genuine smile, feeling warm and calm inside as if I had drunk a considerable quantity of gin.

No. Not all hope is gone for my kind.

We sit around for a while, then the sergeants order everyone to bed. The time before dawn - that's when it happens. One needs to be ready – and, if still alive at sunrise, the traveller must get on his way as soon as it is light enough to move.

I waddle to the latrine to relieve my throbbing bladder. Our latrines are round cabins at the back of the transporter, consisting of a simple seat suspended over the ground. The entire assembly slides up and down on a ratcheted rail. Once we stop for the night, we lower the latrine cabins until they are firmly rammed into the ground. They are not much of a joy by morning, but wildlife cannot make its way into the cabin.

I emerge from the said assembly, regrettably much used whilst I slept, wash my hands and face, then trudge across the cabin, responding to calls from various well-wishers. I am generally admired by my men on the account of well-known adventures - which, alas, don't seem to have come to an end. My authority as a leader is hard-earned.

I clamber up the ladder, doing my best to look nimble and powerful - and largely succeed, thanks to the spirit of the occasion.

Lying in my bedroll on cooling metal, I listen for outside noises out of habit. There was a time when there weren't enough men to stand sentry duty through the night, and we simply relied on the transporter defences to survive a surprise attack. Anyone who remembers those times will never just shut his eyes and fall asleep on the floor of a transporter deep in the forest.

The noises from the hull are gradually dying down - crackling of rapidly cooling metal, rustle of bedrolls, muffled whispers, clang of weapons stowed in readiness next to sleeping men, a little snoring.

As my ear gets used to this racket, it begins to let in the sounds of the forest - cooing of night birds, the rustle of wind in the leafy trees, water dripping from their branches onto the sheet metal of the roof. After a while I am no longer hearing any of that either, listening for something more significant, like the soft crackling of twigs in the undergrowth that heralds a malign presence.

I cannot listen all night - I need rest, and there are other men assigned to stay awake - but I always establish a connection with forest sounds before going to sleep. Listening for an ambush is an art - you must breathe slowly and through your open mouth, head held slightly forward. Much concentration is required to filter the innocent sounds from the cabin and from the forest. It is all about periodicity - the sounds coming from someone creeping through the undergrowth are regular, no matter how much patience they have. A good engine maker can hear the slightest impertinence in the beat of the piston, and an experienced sentry can always tell the difference between a possum blundering through the forest and a predator crawling towards his transporter.

There is an expectant anxiety that comes with listening for an ambush in the dark. It cannot be helped - a thin layer of metal is protection enough, at least until the guns come into play, but it is hard to feel secure in something that cannot even keep out the night's cold. It is not impossible to burst the rivets by denting the sheet metal - depending on how much time it takes to break the first wave of the attack.

I lie on my back on the cold metal floor, insulated by

the thick wool of my bedroll, my hand on the anchor of the hopper gun. The solid, heavy rod is reassuring to touch in the darkness.

The convoy only stops on whatever open ground we can find, transporters forming one or another geometric pattern selected to fit the circumstances. Sentries sprinkle broken twigs around the perimeter and sometimes string up lines attached to metal bells. There is no sense in making it easy.

In the event of an attack the hopper guns cover the convoy from above and shred anything that climbs onto transporters. The rest of the attack is mowed down by fire through side portholes. That is usually enough to secure a retreat, although there have been some dismal exceptions, with survivors lucky to tell the tale afterwards.

We use a few cheap tricks - the roofs are studded with spikes and razor-sharp metal ribbon. We cover the sides of the transporter in slippery paint and do our best to ensure that nothing can crawl underneath. Sharp grates have been devised to be lowered between the tracks - one at the front and one at the back - on levers operated from inside. Everything must be done from inside - leaving the machines is considered a measure of last resort.

I roll over to my side, feeling quite awake. I could stay up for a while, but had prohibited myself to read on a convoy. It's either sleep or listening to the outside - despite my age and relatively poor hearing, I am better than the young sentries, for I understand the task better than they ever could.

The forest is full of sounds, but none indicate danger. There is a bit of movement below as some poor soldier has to get out of his bedroll and creep to the latrine in the darkness. I hear him fumble with the door, trying to make as little noise as possible, and I hear the rush of his water on the latrine sides. His atonement for an excess of berry tea accomplished, he makes his way back, trying not to trip over his comrades.

After the rustle from his bedroll subsides, I am again alone with the sounds of the night forest, which I pride myself on knowing. There's a weka scratching at the soil for worms. There's a night hawk settling on the upper canopy - you can tell by the way other creatures scatter for cover. There's a breath of sea wind - it blows in longer blasts than the wind from the mountains. There's a crackle in the undergrowth - too light for a large animal, it is probably a bush rat. I wait for the sound to repeat, but the rat must have reached its hole.

I hear water rumble in the brook - perhaps we are too close to running water. It does no good to contaminate streams with our waste, and there's always a problem with trying to listen for other sounds...

{}{}{}

On the third day of waiting I give the apartment a good clean. There is a morbid undertone to my mood - I don't want anyone to see my mess if I don't get to come back. I know that's melodramatic and unlikely, but I want my things to be in order in case my sister and her kids have to come down, even to look after me.

I make a few trips in the lift, getting rid of unwanted things into the dumpster downstairs. The place doesn't quite sparkle as a result of my efforts, but looks respectable. All my clothes are clean and more or less folded in drawers or hung up in the closet. My kitchen looks far less cluttered without the magazines that covered every available bit of space, and my bathroom looks almost new without the shaving gear and other grooming aides cluttering the bench around the sink. I even tidy my bookshelves - a more monumental task than the rest put together. My large book collection is a source of great wonder and pride. I also use it as a shibboleth when it comes to women - any prospective bed mate who doesn't stop to admire my books is relegated to a one-night stand. Harsh, I know, but it saves so much trouble in the long run.

It is only lunchtime when I am quite satisfied with my efforts, and the rest of the day is mine. I go out onto the balcony with a toasted cheese sandwich and stare out at the valley. Urban sprawl does not become the West Coast, but the split between North and South left over a million people with no choice except to come here. The government departments now located in Greymouth provide work for most of the refugees from Auckland who chose not to live under Australian management, and the water supply is coping for the time being. Nevertheless, seeing the coastal strip crammed with new housing that stretches all the way from Blackball to Kumara is a shock to anyone who remembers the Coast as a wild, moody place that could be painted in many shades of solace. I shut the balcony doors and decide to go for a walk on the beach.

What used to be the main highway is now a four-lane street with numerous traffic lights. Houses are crawling up the mountainside, and the waterfront is crowded with "false teeth" of multi-storey apartment blocks such as mine. The only thing that remains unchanged is the shingle beach - still lonely, hostile and wild. Its moody surf remains untamed, and the sunsets over the ocean are as stunning as I ever recall. The port now includes a naval base, and there is forever talk about building a vast wave break that would make the beach more swimmer-friendly. Nothing came of these proposals yet.

I cross the busy road and reach the loose shingle strewn with driftwood. I used to light fires on this beach as a younger man, the driftwood catching fire from the first match. We used to drink cheap wine and watch the sun sink behind the dark-grey ocean, and we would bet on the timing of storms that drifted onto the horizon from the south-west. None of that is possible - now that Grey is a large metropolis, sacrifices have to be made. Overall, the secession was a good thing - the rotten mess that was the North Island was amputated from the Mainland, leaving a largely healthy body to regenerate the necessary organs in comfort.

Aotea is one of the smallest nations in the Pacific, but it is also the cleanest. We are doing our best to live up to the reputation as the Switzerland of the South Seas - ten percent tax on income, twenty percent tax on consumption, universal military service, citizen-initiated referenda, a tiny government with a part-time public service. Oh yes - every bureaucrat has to have a real job, usually in the area of relevant expertise. I, for instance, am an editor of a national parks' publications, for which I get paid a modest amount - but cannot fatten my arse at taxpayers' expense.

Unlike the previous effort at making things work, we have every chance and every show of success - a clean, fair legal system, health care that is the envy of our mega-rich neighbours, a zesty drone air force, a brand-new spanking navy that is admired by many larger countries and a tourist industry that makes Sydney weep. Aotea is a tax haven whose banks make feverish amounts of money, but they are not allowed to lend home loans that are likely to cause hardship to borrowers. That killed the city real estate bubble stone-dead. Hence the growth of previously uninhabited places and industrial decentralization. I am one very proud citizen of this new nation.

My life used to be pretty good. I lived well on little money, paid my bills without having to check my bank balance and spent on life's necessities without care. I had saved a very tidy sum doing what I enjoy at a comfortable pace. I had lots of fun - driving, wind-surfing, skiing the glaciers, walking in the mountains and kayaking in mountain lakes. The wine kept getting better and better; more and more single women roamed the streets in hungry packs.

All was well until my bloodstream filled up with tiny insurgents that would have me turn into a bag of leukaemic cells.

I bend down to retrieve a piece of driftwood that looks just like a Picasso figurine, feeling the unfamiliar stiffness and pain in my spine. Hopefully the next few weeks will change all that. Enjoy your last few days on this planet, little bastards - the pest controller is coming, and your days in my body are numbered.

{}{}{}

I awaken in the tentative light of dawn and take time to peer out of the porthole without making a sound. We were obviously not attacked during the night, and it is pleasantly warm - well, not as icy as mornings can be in the mountains. I take great care to clamber down the ladder in silence and creep to the latrine, urged on by a bursting bladder. Then I tiptoe back past sleeping men, doing my desperate best not to steal the last precious moments of their peace.

Despite my efforts, Solly rolls over and stretches lazily towards the furnace, feeling its ribbed side for warmth. He flips over his enormous body with a single movement and opens the cast iron flap to throw a log into a glowing interior with one easy flick of his forearm.

He looks around and sees me, then salutes from his bedroll. I reciprocate and bring a finger to my lips - it is just a little early. He shakes his head in disagreement, pointing to the light coming through the porthole. I nod in acquiescence.

He clambers out of the bedroll and fiddles with the

controls to make the wood catch fire. We try to get the most out of our miserable wood.

Solly turns towards me and makes a drinking gesture. I nod. It's time for hot berry tea.

We boil water on top of the furnace as it crackles to life, consuming the near-dry log in its iron belly. Men slowly stir awake around us, with Solly crashing and banging metal mugs.

The same sounds begin to emerge from neighbouring transporters. We are in a star formation - machines lined up with their tails towards each other. That gives the convoy maximum firing power from the side portholes. Redmond must have had concerns about our camping site.

On the cusp of that thought I clamber up into the turret and mount the gunner's seat. I lower the gun so I can look through the porthole and rotate the foot pedals to traverse the turret. It's a fine enough skill, to control both the gun and the turret at the same time, but one manages to acquire it after repelling a few attacks in total darkness. Terror is a wonderful teacher.

Redmond seems to have chosen a flat outcrop of rock next to the road. I almost approve, except that the sides of the outcrop fall away, making it eminently possible to conceal a close approach. Admittedly, the undergrowth is quite far.

The intercom crackles, and I lift the headset.

"Commander, good morning," says Redmond

respectfully. "What do you think of my spot?"

I tell him about the overhang; he admits that it was invisible in darkness as they stopped.

"I teach sergeants to drive around the prospective site," I remind him without anger.

"The men were very tired," he confesses. "We drove a long way before we stopped."

"Where, pray, are we?" I ask irritably. "I don't recognize the place."

"Past Mossy Gully," he tells me.

I whistle - that is more than a third of the way to Brana.

"I didn't want to go over the ridge in the dark," explains Redmond.

I agree. The ridge is the highest point of the trip, and it is often slippery with snow - when not completely buried under same. It is not an unknown location for ambushes - nothing is easier than to roll a few rocks onto the road. The ancients did not have a care in the world when they built the highway with their fabled machines, but clearing rock falls is a different matter in our miserable epoch.

"We need to get going," I tell Redmond. "Give the first warning."

"First warning, acknowledged," Redmond rasps in reply. I remove the headset and stare out into the porthole as Redmond blows his whistle loud enough to wake the dead.

Solly climbs up the ladder with a full mug of berry tea in one hand - no small feat of acrobatics. I rotate the entire turret to take it from his hand.

"The first warning has been sounded," Solly tells me redundantly. I nod. There is plenty of time to drain the tea before we begin to shake the meat off our bones.

I hear workman-like noises from below as the weapons are stowed, the latrine is raised, and the first lazy movements of the piston grow into a hissing frenzy. As it merges into an angry clatter, the turret fills with coarse vibration. I toss the empty mug into the bedroll as the other piston strains to crank the right sprocket. The driver coaxes both sides for a few moments with small bursts of steam, then takes off. I hold on to the gun as sprockets engage and the machine surges forward.

Tannis is much smoother this morning, controlling the starting speed as he should. He leads off slowly, then the rear engines engage with a rhythm that is higher in pitch. The noise is now quite loud, and I fit the intercom headphones.

"Lead transporter proceed," orders Redmond. By convention, the convoy sergeant commands from the second machine.

We do proceed. There is much mist clinging to the mountain, reducing visibility to a dangerous level. Tannis cannot go fast, and he maintains just enough speed to keep the tracks turning, showing considerable skill for one so young.

I rotate the turret idly, scanning the forest on both sides of the road with little effect. I can only just see into the undergrowth - which is particularly dense on the lee side of the ridge. It is most beautiful, with vines dropping from tall trees to enmesh with vast ferns below. But I appreciate this beauty all too little, for I know what it conceals.

We clamber up the mountain, air getting markedly colder. My breath turns to vapour and becomes laboured as we gain altitude. The residue of the warmth in the cabin is long-gone, the furnace only just keeping up with the cold that blows into every gap. I peddle hard to rotate the turret for exercise.

The first patches of snow appear soon enough, and I sigh in resignation - we are nowhere near the saddle of the pass. Tannis cannot drive any slower, and we continue to rattle on the broken ancient surface. We try to keep the road in reasonable repair, but at this altitude we allow ruts to remain - they increase traction. It makes for an unpleasant ride.

"Redmond, how are things in the cargo transporters?" I ask.

"Like a box of bullets, Commander," he replies happily. "With that weight they will sink through anything."

A large tree lies across the road, and I hear Tannis swear all the way from the turret. It may not be possible to push it out of the way.

The convoy halts some distance away, and the lead

transporter clatters up to the tree, pushing into it with the front guard - a heavy slab of steel, mounted on springs to lessen the impact of such collisions. Sadly, nothing happens: the machine remains in place, its tracks impotently scraping the broken road.

"Ambush watch," I order into the intercom.

"There is much noise below as weapons are removed from cradles and readied. It is not quite time to put on armour, but an attack is a distinct possibility.

I cannot see the left side of the road - it happens to be a steep drop; if an attack comes from that side, it will, sadly, come from above, and none of us will be able to see it. I therefore concentrate on the right side, where I can only just see past the ferns into the mist.

Tannis revs up the engines to execute a reversing manoeuvre. The machine rises as the left track catches on the fallen tree. Tannis backs off and reverses the action - now the right track has just enough clearance to turn past the gnarled trunk. The machine rotates in place to face away from the tree, and I turn the turret in the opposite direction. What happens at the back of the transporter is now vital.

The main hatch opens in the rear, and a sturdy chain is thrown over the trunk. A pole is passed underneath the tree to catch the anchor at the end of the chain, then I hear it clatter as men heave the anchored end inside. With both ends of the chain secured, Tannis pushes the engines and takes off towards the rest of the convoy. I brace for the impact.

The chain snaps tight, but the tree shifts only a little. Tannis lets out the throttle for all it is worth, filling the air with a deafening hiss and sooty smoke. The front of the machine is nearly airborne as tracks scrape the road. I see clods of soil flying from below and shout for him to stop.

"We need another transporter," I explain in ensuing silence over the intercom.

A second machine uncouples its trailer and takes off towards us, executing an about-turn just short of scraping our side. Another chain is passed from its rear to my machine, and we try once more, with four tracks and six engines now engaged in the task. The tree begins to shift, and I study its lower trunk. It appears to have fallen with roots intact - that makes a planned ambush unlikely.

There is a loud crack as we break off large branches stuck in the undergrowth, then both transporters begin to crawl forward. I order them to slow down as the tree edges to the side of the road, its root system now hanging in the air above the steep ravine.

The chain is released and reeled back inside, after which the rear hatch is cranked closed. The most dangerous moment behind us, Tannis reverses the transporter again and rams the tree with the front bumper, pushing it off the road's edge. This time it cooperates and drops down the steep slope with a thunderous crack. A cheer goes up as the lead machine drives on, grinding the remaining branches into the road.

There is a little less mist as we rise further, and Tannis gathers a little speed. The rattles are not too bad, with a layer of snow now continuous and thickening as we gain altitude. I listen for the characteristic squeal of spinning tracks, but traction remains adequate for the time being.

I find myself in an elevated mood that comes from sitting in an armoured transporter moving forward at relentless speed, grasping the mount of a powerful gun. I almost wish they would come - this morning is as good a time to unite ammunition with the enemy.

There is even a bit of sun breaking through the mist. It is not yet fully clear, but the air takes on a yellow hue. Why, we may even have blue sky further on. I almost smile.

The convoy is nearing the saddle, which I can tell by the height of the trees. No longer the proud giants of the rainforest, they are gnarled trunks used to battling mountain winds and blizzards. I stare into the boiling mist, looking for the remains of the ancient village that lies in the pass. We are not quite there.

Below decks Solly starts a boisterous marching song, and the men catch on as a choir - even I hum the tune in my turret. The words are about a soldier about to leave for the forest, but his legs ache from labouring on maidens hungry for his seed, his head is heavy from berry gin, and his stomach is bloated from the feast the night before. I suspect all of that resonates with Tannis even this morning.

The first remains of the ancient village come into

sight - soot-covered piles of brick and remains of wrecked machines used by the ancients on what must have been velvet-smooth roads. My favourite is what must have been a black speed machine now deeply embedded in a crevice between two vast boulders. Little remains of its front end, but it is hard not admire the beautiful lines of its rear, and I can make out the ancient letters stamped into the metal below the remains of its rear bumper:

"GTO"

I wish I knew what that stood for. I wish I could drive one. I wish I lived at a time when such beasts prowled the roads. I wish many things, none of which will come to be.

I am here, and I am now.

We travel past the ancient ruins slowly. Like all ruins within our reach, they had been blown up and burnt to prevent them from offering shelter against the elements. Shelter means survival of young vermin - if they can hide from the cold and from predators, they thrive and grow in numbers. Nevertheless, you never know what lurks in the ancient ruins, and we stare in all directions with devout attention as we pass.

We pass the ruins without incident, with only a hawk rising from a pile of moss-covered bricks. Otherwise a sad, replete solitude reigns in the narrow valley. It is still possible to see where the ancient iron road ran beside the highway on a raised ramp that protected it from flooding. The iron tracks had long rusted in the harsh climate, their remains just visible on top of the ramp.

The convoy crosses a river next to the collapsed ruin of the ancient bridge. We rattle over loose stones of the ford as fast as possible - it's a deep river, and if traversed at low speed, too much water seeps into the transporters. A little bit is tolerable, and there are special valves on the floor to drain it. Any more than that eats into the longevity of the metal, and that is not to be encouraged.

The lead machine emerges from the stream and labours up a steep bank, engines heaving and belching acrid fumes into the crisp air. Holding on to the gun for dear life, I feel the tracks spin a little and make a note to level that approach when we have spare time. If we can organize a convoy at the height of summer, it may be possible to camp here overnight and do some roadwork during daylight.

Then again, who knows when we return. The drive to Brana is safe enough, but its council has been playing a strange game. Not all is well with their heads, I fear - my grave suspicion is that the good men of Brana had taken to sneaking into rotted places for supplies, rather than trade with other towns. It is not unacceptable to go to rotted places, but quarantine rules make it unprofitable to rummage for ancient artefacts instead of buying from the living.

I had seen Brana's zest for trade lessen for some time, and so far I said nothing. They don't need me to understand that Brana is doomed without the rest of us. They have no access to sulphur and hence cannot make powder. Their transporters are monuments to the pathetic old men who had not been to the forest in years - they are wise to keep them in the sheds. They can barely pour crude window glass - and hence cannot make reliable radio valves. Their only fuel is peat that they cut and haul into Brana by hand. To perish, all they need to do is lose our trade. Which they are close to doing - smoked meats are wonderful, but they are hardly a reason for my merchants to haul a great weight of metal over the mountains. If I had anything better to do, my company would not accept commissions to escort anyone here.

Yet the leadership of Brana behaves strangely. There was talk about damage to the drawbridge and taxing my convoys to pay for the repairs. In response I decided to keep my transporters outside the city and ordered a construction of lightweight carts. We camp on the other side of the moat, and my men pull the carts with goods from Grey to the market. They return to spend the day in the transporters, rather than loll about the market and its lusty taverns, and they return at the end of the day, to haul the trolleys laden with Brana meats back to the convoy. We load the cargo as light grows dim, camp outside the city wall as if we were in the darkest forest, and at dawn we begin the return journey without any acknowledgement from Brana.

It takes no great mind to see that good will had gone, and sooner or later I expect the arrangement to break down altogether. But in the end of the day, the good people of Brana will either cut their throats or they won't. I did more than my share to prevent it from happening, and my reward was Rina turning on me as if

I gave her the dripping sickness.

Our final argument was about the future of her town, and she lost her temper when I told her one home truth too many. It is not that she likes her uncle, a brooding, vicious mutt who has been a head of Brana's council for longer than anyone can recall - but Rina would not have him criticized by a stranger.

I ended up being evicted from her bed, having to stagger to my convoy through unlit, filthy streets. In those days we stopped near the market, and I managed to evade the night patrol prowling for the breakers of the curfew. But sneaking past them took much of the night, and when I finally arrived to hammer my fist on the armour of the transporter, I was numb from the cold and wet to the bone. I got lung rot a few days later and was lucky to make it to Grey alive.

Rina and I had not spoken since.

We reach the end of the valley and begin the long descent that runs all the way to Brana. Someone strikes up a song about the long convoy that winds its way through a sad, despoiled land. That is entirely appropriate, I feel - we are indeed travelling through terrain devastated and left desolate by annihilation of her former masters.

We are but pathetic remains of the defeated world, rattling past crumbling monuments to its glory in our crude machines. My belief in future survival is tattered to shreds as I am confronted with what we had become, for even in my contemptibly short life things used to be much more acceptable than they are now.

That much is true. What I don't understand is why anyone would take such trouble to undermine their survival even further.

{}{}{}

I listen to the message the second time. It is not a very comfortable thing to do, as I need to press many buttons on my virtual keyboard to replay the voice mail on my mobile.

"Nicholas, this is Margaret here," says the prim voice. "I am so sorry we could not accommodate you until now, but Dr Wilkins' registrar will be calling you in the next day or so regarding your admission. Thank you for your patience. Be well and God bless."

I nod sadly. I don't know whether God will bless, but I know that I won't be going in today.

I disconnect the call and lie back on the couch, where I fell asleep over a book. It is now mid-afternoon of day six, at rough count. In one way I am relieved that an ordeal is postponed for another day or two. In another, frustration is beginning to build. I am a little worried, you see, that the delay is in no small part a reflection of my prognosis. Maybe Great White Wilkins doesn't consider it a priority because I am unlikely to be one of his successes.

"What fucking rot," says the street-smart, savvy journalist.

"Preen your feathers, prim and proper," replies the

gutter-wise captain of the Home Guard. "Just don't forget Aceh, or have you done that already?"

The civilian is a little lost for words. I spent just on a year in a sewer even I cannot describe in words. Our young nation, you see, was ever so keen to fly its flag. A tiny contingent of the new citizen army went with Australians to Aceh, to keep peace and distribute a few food parcels after a devastating earthquake. The Indonesian army, if one could call it that, was stretched beyond belief on other islands. That's what they said - in reality they knew better than show up in Aceh, a province overrun by hardy and experienced rebels. The so-called Indonesian soldiers are no good against people with guns.

It was a very ripe mess, in which we spent more time shooting at shadows than distributing supplies. I am proud of my military service, but that was one senseless mission, and I am glad that only fifteen from our unit came back in cardboard coffins. We did much better than the Australian contingent, most of whom were Ikamaua - North Islanders, to old friends.

We were used like toilet paper, all of us. Aussies jumped in to remind the Indonesians about a few home truths - like "one of ours is worth a battalion of yours". There are ten hungry Indonesians for every sated Australian, so that reminder is never wasted.

But the Ikas pushed to be chosen to show their worth to their new country. Less than ten years into Australian rule, North Islanders bent backwards to make a point. Maori demigods, huge males with mounds of totally

57

natural muscle who moved like ballerinas, they made stunning footage for the HD cameras. Clad in extra-large uniforms of their new masters, they made a very impressive sight. Whatever was left of the old North Island died right there, and the Ikamaua Territory was truly born. New Zealand ceased to be even a memory. I mean, who remembers that New Amsterdam was once the name of New York.

We southern rednecks just had to go along or get left out, as the old saying goes. Most of my unit were rugby players too - massive lumps of blonde meat clad in the distinct olive and brown camouflage of Aotea. My boys could not quite dance like Maori, but they were impressive in their own way, spit-polished and moving like a drill band when everyone else was covered in mud and half-dead in the humid hell of Aceh. We took some rough placements and claimed a good share of enemy corpses. Most observers had to concede that the new nation is punching well above its minuscule weight.

Aceh was where my freelance career was born. I never worked for myself before Independence, but my job as a press officer in the Defence Ministry disappeared when Australians took over. After that I emigrated south on principle, doing odd jobs for local advertisers. Once the new constitution was ratified, all live males were conscripted into the new citizen army, and Aceh came on the heels of that just as soon as I finished officer training.

I began to take snaps and scribble for the army news website, and this is how things work in a small nation:

the editor of a large metropolitan daily saw my efforts, then a little commission came my way. It had to go through the ethics committee, but - small nation again - that took all of two days, and a freelance journalist was born.

I clear the answering machine's memory and sigh for the fourth time since hearing its unhappy contents. It looks like another free day, and I am running out of things to do with my freedom. It is, I guess, a sign of happy middle age that I have no backlog of activities I would do in my time off. Well, there are a few things one could always do to pass the time, says the infantry captain wickedly - but one does not embark on them whilst full of leukaemia and awaiting treatment.

Riding or walking seem like wrong things to do, as I am dizzy, sore and tired. Not sick-tired, but end-of-day tired - and it is only ten in the morning. There is no point in shopping for shiny things because I don't know how long I have to live, and there is no sense in buying food when you don't even know when they will let you loose from the chemo ward. I decide to stroll through a few bookshops and try to enjoy a leisurely coffee on the beach promenade.

Beginning with my favourite bookshop, I scour the history shelves, looking for books on Independence. It's a bit of a blood sport of mine, reading about salient events from only a few years ago - to see how even after such a short time and plenty of living witnesses, history is completely and hopelessly distorted. It makes me want to burn books.

One can have quite a time of it, arguing what is more harmful - burning books or allowing utter lies to be printed en masse.

We did not, as newly-minted school materials allege, secede to protect our clean and green way of life. Australia was way greener and cleaner, and being taken over by a vast, wealthy country actually meant that we no longer had to rape our land for the final iota of agricultural worth in each parched, polluted paddock. Australia could afford to put our farmers struggling with the drying climate on welfare, purchase their farms and let nature reclaim the land that the old government heavily subsidized anyway.

No, we seceded to stop vastly superior financial interests from taking over a nation that we cherished for six generations. It was as simple as that - we wanted to do it our way. The move never carried great risk - we could have joined Australia any time and can still do that now. But Aotea was a runaway success that defied all imagination. We are an Israel without war, a Switzerland without Nazi gold, a Bhutan without theocracy. Broadly speaking, our secession had achieved its goal with very few downsides - the main is possibly the expansion of the population into regions which looked much better without people. Secession quadrupled the population of what used to be known as South Island - there were many who abandoned the North Island to its Australian fate to remain with their own. It happened to be a bloodless secession, too - one referendum saw the birth of a provisional government, and away we went.

I don't see any new books on the subject today - which makes it a rare month. Academia is utterly fascinated with our act of nation-building. As mentioned, most of what they write are lies, some well-meaning and others with a nasty racist undercurrent. It is true that most Maori went the other way. It is true that some deliberately chose a happy-go-lucky melting pot, Aussie-style, over a relatively monocultural population of the south. But most had no ideological motives - they merely went north with their family, and many went with the money, thinking that Aotea will remain lonely, cold and poor. Time certainly proved them wrong, especially the last bit.

I cross the road to my favourite coffee shop, whose vast wooden deck abuts the beach promenade. It's a wonderful local institution which serves great coffee and poppy seed cake, Vienna-style. It is located at the end of a long path heavily in favour with rollerbladers, and few middle-aged singles like myself would pass up the view. Not five minutes passes by without a young, perfectly proportioned goddess in tight lycra made even more suggestive by sweat, heaving her way towards the outside counter to command an iced coffee.

My phone rings as I order a long black. It's Helen.

"I am just at the beach," I tell her happily. I missed Helen's company.

"There in five," she says shortly and hangs up.

I order a macchiato, to come in ten minutes, and find a table facing away from the rollerblading path. Helen is not a model, shall I say as inoffensively as possible, and young ladies in tight shorts are not what one should poke into her eyes.

My timing is perfect - just as the ageing waitress with utterly historical brow piercings emerges from the counter with the second coffee, a dirty mid-sized jeep screeches around the esplanade curve, sliding, more than slowing, to a halt at the kerb. Helen jumps out of the car; she is wearing a plain black robe over baggy black pants. True to form, there is no jewellery, shoes or even a watch. She leaves the keys in the ignition and pointedly fails to take her handbag. She is a powerful woman, and it is not for the likes of her to worry about carrying small change for coffee.

{}{}{}

We leave the snowline just after midday, beginning the steep descent towards Brana Lake. The weather is most clement - it is almost warm, and the wind is but a light mountain breeze. Every now and again the sun peeks from heavy clouds - an extraordinary sight this late in the year - and I even crack open the top hatch to let in a little breeze.

In mid-afternoon the third transporter breaks its track. Thankfully, this happens in the widest part of the valley, with a long expanse of space covered with low tussock. I look with considerable pride as the machines are stopped in a correct defensive formation without any orders, and men emerge from the transporters to begin repairs. Fortunately, the broken machine is a cargo unit built in the worst times. It has enormous jacks at either end, and, provided the ground is not too soft, the entire transporter can be lifted by cranking the jacks from inside.

Our machine turns around to retrieve the broken track. Tannis drives over it and stops. Someone drops out of the bottom hatch to hook a tow chain onto the broken metal ribbon, then we rotate in place and race back, dragging the track behind us. As we assume our place in the defensive formation, the track is uplifted, the broken joint removed and the track is strung under one sprocket, then another. The ends are brought close to each other, hooked with a clamp and pulled together, then bolted. The men run back to their transporters with their tools. The clang of rear hatches tells me that the operation took less time that to boil a pot. I am proud of my men.

Tannis guns the engines on Redmond's order, and we resume our descent, the sun now drifting towards the mountaintops on the other side of the valley. It's a bit colder and windier, and I close the top hatch with a little sadness. Goodbye summer - may you not be my last.

That unhappy thought heralds the first glimpse of the lake, a vast, shallow depression occupied by water since the scourge. The ancient dam has long burst, but a vast quake brought down a mountain, filling the breach and building up the dam even higher. The lake greatly expanded in size, burying most of the ancient structures that once lined the shores - their roofs were still visible in Grandfather's time, and I remember seeing them on his old maps that were framed above his bed. I remember staring at that map through tears as he lay dying.

I was eight, and he was over seventy, a powerful, swarthy man who succumbed to a rotten wound. A boiler explosion seared the flesh to the bone in his thigh - the burn was showing promise for more than a moon when it went rotten. I remember holding Father's hand and looking at the dead man's face - it showed the agony of his oblivion, pale blue eyes still staring with hatred from red-rimmed lids.

The ancient road disappeared under water when the lake expanded, and we had to cut a new track through virgin bush. It was a painful joint effort between my father and Brana's council. Symbolically, this is where the journey gets rough. The vegetation was easy enough to bulldoze, but the resultant path turned into a muddy creek with the first autumn rains. It was hastily filled with large stones and logs - anything that may stop the tracks from sinking into soft, sucking mud. Transporters have to be tied to each other with chains - which we do on the open meadow near the water. Then we open the throttles, racing over the muddy track as fast as we can go.

I hold on to the gun as Tannis rattles us on the mud-covered timbers. Laden transporters behind us slide and slither, but appear to maintain traction through the swampy part of the track. Then we reach a rocky outcrop where stone surface provides relative safety - so long as there is no ice. It is a mixed blessing, that outcrop - it keeps our tracks turning in the summer, but makes the entire journey impossible even in the driest of winters.

With that happy thought I see the first glimmers of Brana - flame-like reflections in the windows that face the sunset. A short time later I can make out the grim wooden stockade that tops the defensive wall. I never agreed with using wood for fortification - eventually it must dry and become a fire hazard even in the absence of a real enemy. But the good men of Brana know everything and won't be told otherwise by clever outsiders. They had cut down the neighbouring forest to build their wall - which, they argued, enhanced its defensive value as it created a vast open space around the town. It is true that Grey's earthen wall is easier to climb, but it cannot fall down, and it cannot burn.

The convoy is close enough to see blue-green flags that fly from the watch towers on either side of the massive drawbridge. They dug a moat that connects with the lake when the wall was built - it is not the cleanest of water courses, but the fish from the lake keep it in reasonable shape. Giant eels slither in its muck, eating the fish that eat the weeds that eat the filth from the town. That's right - we are no longer at the top of the food chain. The eels take people too.

We fire an incendiary mortar round over the lake, and it arcs a fiery path in fading light, slapping into the placid surface of the water. We use white phosphorus that is lighter than water, and it emerges from the dark depth, catching fire as soon as it is back in the air. The tiny, vicious flame continues to burn in the middle of the lake as we round the contours of the shore, approaching the town slowly and inevitably.

The wall guard of Brana signals back, flashing a powerful light on and off three times. Ammunition is scarce at Brana, but they have no shortage of electric power - the shores of the lake are rich in peat, which is stored in massive amounts within city walls.

I can feel Tannis race a little towards destination, seeing it in plain sight. It's a bit hard on fuel, but I keep my mouth shut - I too look forward to a roaring fire, a mug of black Brana beer and plate stacked with smoked meats and dried berries.

I think of Rina. Will she come? She will know of our arrival - that will be the biggest news to any resident of Brana for the past three moons - that is how long we had been absent. Irregularities in the rules of the trade and minor infractions upon good will had disrupted the convoy schedule to dangerously low levels. Any more trouble, and I will be looking for other work - and the good people of Brana will be looking at extinction. Reality is a harsh place where you get eaten if you stop paying heed to the consequences of your behaviour.

Rina... Our last coupling was a wondrous occasion in her soft bed with candles lit in each post. I remember the peat fire glowing in the grate in the corner of her bedroom, and I recall the silky feel of her pale skin. Her green eyes shone like stars in the candlelight whenever I rose above her to stare at her red cheeks, framed by the long red hair that lay scattered over her rumpled pillow. I remember that bright shine that bespoke her adoration more than any words. All of a sudden, it became just a surreal memory.

My hands, clad in rough gunner's gloves, tighten on the hopper gun.

The reality fails to improve as we near Brana. The drawbridge stays up: there will be no welcome and no plates laden with smoked meats.

I turn to the radio with anger and twist the dial to the town's frequency.

"Grey convoy calling Brana. Grey calling Brana. Brana, reply," I intone into the headset, keeping my voice free of the anger I feel.

There is no reply.

"Brana, we are a merchant convoy from Grey. We request hospitality."

The radio remains silent, and my jaw tightens with anger. Rina or no Rina, I am close to doing something everyone will regret later.

I wait a little and turn the dial back to convoy frequency. I know that Brana is listening.

"Redmond."

"Yes, Commander."

"Halt the convoy."

He shouts the order, and the engines spin down. I get thrown onto the breech of the gun and swear loudly.

When I recover from the fall, I dial back the town frequency.

"Brana, I know you are listening," I rasp with anger. "We are a trade convoy from Grey. If we do not receive hospitality, we are turning around and travelling back to Grey at first light. Repeat, if you don't start acting like decent hosts, we are turning around, and we will never come back."

"Grey convoy, stand by," I hear an immediate response. "We are seeking clarification."

"Of what, I pray?" I ask with acidic courtesy.

There is no response.

"Brana, this is the Commander of the Grey convoy," I say as calmly and as slowly as I can under the circumstances. "You will be given a short time to wake up, then we are turning around. Fuck me for a moment longer, and we will not even stop under your walls."

After what seems like a very long time, I am about to switch frequency and order Redmond to turn around. Almost as my patience runs out, the voice from Brana is back on the air.

"Grey convoy, please accept our apologies for the delay," says a rich male voice coldly. "You may stop near the wall, but we cannot lower the bridge after curfew. You will be able to enter town after dawn when the curfew is lifted. By order of Brana Council."

So there it is. No smoked meats, no roaring fire, no

Rina - just another cold night in the damp turret. I grind teeth in anger - the insult is substantial, but accurately calculated to be insufficient for an expensive reaction.

"You heard them," I rasp into the headset, still on the town frequency. "That's our reward for crossing the mountains to bring them their metal, my comrades. Very well, set up a camp and stand down for the night."

"Stand down and camp, acknowledged," replies Redmond without switching frequencies. "Commander, are we going to come back here after this?"

"Time will tell," I reply coldly. "Before I plan another convoy to Brana, we will do the sums on fishing vessels. Perhaps there is better luck to be had at sea."

{}{}{}

Helen marches over from her car gingerly, toes curling on the hot bitumen of the path. She sees me and changes direction slightly, not acknowledging me at all, but when she levels with the table, she throws her arms around me even before I stand up, presses me to her muscular body and sobs.

I swallow hard and give myself a few seconds to compose. It's a little hard to console friends when I know their grief may well be justified. But that is just one of many small obligations to fulfil as we travel our path.

"It'll be all right, Hels," I tell her, squeezing her forearm with affection. "You know me - I am hard to kill."

She nods, still sobbing.

"Don't worry," I tell her. "My middle class experience is far from over."

She chuckles, lets me go and sits down, wiping her face with a sleeve. Then she lifts off her sunglasses and throws them on the table, revealing swollen eyes.

I point to the coffee, and she nods mechanically, lifting the cup to her thin, pale lips for a token sip.

"I paid for that story," she says absently, setting the cup down. "It was nearly complete - one of the cubs just had to chase up a few numbers."

"I thank you, kind lady," I bow and tug my non-existent forelock. I shaved my head yesterday, in preparation for chemo. Otherwise, the hair makes a mess of the bed.

She smiles and shakes her head.

"You are a tough son of a bitch."

"One has to be," I tell her with a little sadness. "It's not like the world brims with random kindness."

"When they... fix it, I want you to do something," she says resolutely. "I want you, Sandy and Tama to go to Bruce Bay with me."

I whistle appreciatively. Such journey would recreate much happier days, when the world was, well, a little younger. We all just moved to the Coast, and back then I had long hair, secured by a black bandanna. I used to drive an ex-army jeep with a flag of Aotea flying from a tall aerial. Its silver fern unfolding against the blue sky became a symbol of much that was good and new in our once-stale lives.

We drove to Bruce Bay to swim in the tepid surf, drink Otago whites on the beach at sunset, gorge on seafood and retire to our log cabins. Sex was random - by mutual and unspoken consent the lights remained off, and the ladies roamed. That was how Sandra and I ended up together - she fell asleep after a long, exhausting session and we woke up with each other at dawn. She roamed no longer - and the rest, as they grimly say, is history.

"I don't know about Sandra," I say gingerly. "That husband of hers is not going to wear it."

"We will take him along," she tips the rest of the coffee down her throat and sets down the cup, looking around to the waitress. "I will not be denied."

I smile, nodding at the good memories.

"I'll be there."

"How long is the treatment?"

"Six weeks, if all goes well."

She frowns as she calculates dates. "It will be in the middle of bloody winter."

"Maybe we will start with a trip to Fox. Do the spas."

"You are on, boyo."

She glances at my watch and curses under her breath.

The waitress brings us a refill, and we wait for her to walk away.

"She has a pierced clit," says Helen absently.

"How do you know that?" I marvel.

"Never reveal sources," chides Helen playfully. "Mutual friends, shall we say."

"How on earth can someone do that to themselves? I mean, I've had my share of piercings in the chemo ward. Couldn't think of a worse way to assert my identity."

"Tut-tut," says Helen, wagging her finger. "The ring is to heighten pleasure. Makes for a much more powerful female orgasm."

"Female what?" I ask in amazement. "You mean you have them too?"

She laughs and drinks the rest of my coffee. "Not today, sadly. I have a meeting with the CEO. Our great white father is flying across the mountains to minister to our spiritual needs. Better put on some shoes."

"You better be there, too," I tell her with alarm.

"Neh, don't worry. That's his plane coming in now."

I stare across the water. Helen is right, as usual - a silver streak is banking steeply and makes a circle over the bay. A private jet - but of course.

"Well, it's time," Helen tells me grimly. "Take care, love."

She stands up and hugs me to her stomach, holding

me for a few seconds in silence, then she marches across to her car. I wave as she guns the engine and takes off with all the speed her poor truck can muster. She never had a single accident, reputedly, but I don't ever get in a car when Helen is at the wheel.

I check the phone and set it down next to bereft cups, then take out the notepad and fidget a little, getting more comfortable in a hard chair. I notice such things of late - I must have lost weight.

{}{}{}

It's good to stretch my legs and breathe fresh air. Well, as fresh as it can be this close to the moat of a large town.

It is not often that we leave our machines outside town walls, but today is a clear day, and the cleared land that surrounds Brana offers no opportunity for a concealed approach. The turrets remain manned, and any vermin that becomes visible would be shredded long before reaching the convoy.

I walk around the machines lined in a defensive formation just next to the drawbridge, whose massive frame is resting on the muddy earth a few feet away from my transporters. The soldiers are busy unloading the cargo and helping the merchants cart it to the market square.

High clouds are racing across the sky, and the wind is blowing steadily this morning. For once it is not cold, and I hope that the warm spell is not about to end with a blizzard. That is not uncommon in late autumn.

There was no explanation of last night's outrage, and I am still seething. In the entire history of convoys run by three generations of my family, there is no instance of such dereliction of hospitality. Small town survival depends on trade - only Grey has everything it needs to survive, if one uses the term loosely. It is widely accepted that we risk our lives by traversing the forest along predictable routes at slow speed - which, alas, is all the landscape allows. Flying is out of the question - enough men died trying to set up air bridges - and water is not practical, especially in the case of Brana. It is possible to navigate the streams from the sea to the lake, but only during the wettest time of the year, and the narrow rivers are even more vulnerable to attack than our transporters - at least we can afford the weight of armour.

We are therefore not used to ingratitude, and earlier this morning I heard a few rumbles that made me cringe. I can expect perfect obedience from my men when it comes to their duties, but they are not to be trifled with. Every weapon, Grandfather told me, has a safe end and a deadly end, and my men are each a fearsome weapon.

I suddenly become anxious to see how they are faring in Brana's mean streets and decide to end my stroll, marching up the drawbridge into town. The sentries eye me with distrust and fear, and I walk past them with my mouth curved in contempt. My joints are up to the job in relative warmth, and I build up a marching stride, hoping to catch up to the carts before they reach the market. I am unarmed, apart from a dagger that I never part with, but that will not matter as soon as I catch up to my unit.

I begin to breathe hard and to sweat, which annoys me. After three days on the road I smell bad enough as it is - and the opportunity to bathe and refresh had been denied to me in the rudest fashion possible. If I run into her, I will have to stay upwind.

Not that it will happen. I brush the thought away from my mind, as there are more urgent things afoot.

The streets of Brana stink even worse than I do. They never bothered to build proper sewers, leaving it up to frequent rain to keep the town clean. Their forefathers did have the wisdom to construct streets with a slightly raised middle, and it is possible to walk without treading in filth - but a few days without rain makes the place quite vile. There was once talk of running water down their streets first thing in the morning, but a few wet years made the project seem unimportant. Now that the locals are even poorer and sicker, there too few healthy men to cut extra peat to power the great pumps which draw clean water from the lake. It is done only when the reservoir at the top of the hill runs low, and wasting water on cleaning the place is not a possibility any longer. Such are the rewards of being small-minded.

The windows in Brana are also small and mean - the local glass makers were never up to the standard of Grey's wizards, who make vast window panes that withstand ocean gales. But even small windows that face the main street cannot hide a bitter reality - the dwellings are damp and coated in soot of peat fires from both sides. Faces that stare at me from these windows are pale and drawn. It is clear that things are getting worse in Brana.

My pace quickens as I feel increasing unease. The feeling I had at the start of the convoy is back, but this time it feels as if I am close to the answer. I see a column of smoke rising above the sagging roofs of wooden shingle - that is the smokestack of the great meat works next to the market - and I am almost running uphill, breathing hard and dripping sweat on my tunic, my eyes fixed on the path ahead. It is more than my life is worth to slip on the filthy path and sprawl on the excrement-streaked cobblestones before the good people of Brana.

The narrow street turns a final corner and I drop back to a walking pace as the market square comes into view. It is full of stalls and shoppers with small handcarts, children with crude backpacks, women in black dresses and woven baskets. My men are busy unloading the metal ingots, and all seems well.

I wipe my forehead with my sleeve and march up to them, breathing hard through my nose. I do all I can to disguise the strain of the climb, which is not easy. My heart thumps against the ribs, and a dull discomfort builds in the left armpit, making me nauseous and dizzy.

I slow right down, pretending an interest in the stalls I pass, returning polite greetings with a wave of the right hand, controlling my breathing as best I can. The dizziness slowly lifts, and my left armpit begins to recover. It is time to look like the part.

I stroll up to my men, nodding approval at their effort. Solly turns to me and salutes, sweat dripping down his low forehead. He is at least a head taller than I, and I need to rise on my toes to take a twig out of his short blonde hair. Then I return the salute.

"Any problems this morning?" I ask casually.

"It seems not, Commander," he replies, shaking his head in disapproval. There is a lot of ill feeling after yesterday, I see that clearly. Something unpleasant will have to happen to Brana once we leave, and my only concern is to defuse the situation for now, preventing anything we may regret later. Perhaps I will raise passage prices or refuse to come here for a full year. Maybe Brana should be blacklisted altogether until they send a convoy of smoked meats to my men. I will consider such ideas at length, and it will bring me pleasure on the return journey, for I am greatly angered.

"Where are the merchants?"

"They are all in the council house. Negotiating a bulk purchase."

I shake my head ruefully. Something is about to happen, I can feel it - it is now close, yet I still can't quite see what it is.

"Come along, Solly," I lead him away from the men, and we walk into the middle of the square, towards an empty space in front of a low stone platform. This is where they execute people, those who break the rules. Brana was built by a commune of believers, fervent adherents to the ancient faith. There are a few such people in Grey, and they are largely respected for their hard work and honesty. Their women stay at home and go out to shop in pairs. They wear long dresses and bland scarves to cover their hair, which they keep short. The men don't couple with women other than their consorts. Some break out and live a normal life - if our life can be called normal - but find themselves shunned by their relatives.

It is touchingly quaint, but in Grey we teach all newcomers to mind one's business and leave others to mind theirs. Our town cannot work any other way - everyone makes very personal choices about survival, and everyone else has to respect them, unless there is trespass against someone else. We do not care how someone dresses, whether their roof sags more than it should, or whether their children eat rats. There is help for those who ask, but we live and let live until asked for assistance.

Not so in Brana, where the law comes straight from the books of the ancient religion. Here each man is his neighbour's keeper, and each neighbour is the enforcer of ancient laws. In Grey we do not have executions - murderers are expelled. If there are witnesses to an unprovoked killing, we escort the guilty out of the city across the river. They are not allowed back, ever, reducing their choices to walking into the sea to drown, or to stagger into the forest and brave what happens after dark. Lesser crimes attract fines paid with work - there are plenty of dirty and dangerous jobs in town and at sea. Property damage and bodily harm are punished by restitution, which is a harsh penalty for most.

Survival is hard enough without having to do extra work for someone else, and an obligation to so much as provide firewood for a second household can prove fatal. Each day of work under the cold rain can become your last. There is little crime in Grey.

But in Brana a mere curse can see you beaten with sticks or even killed by thrown stones. Women are dangerous business in Brana - one unwanted touch can result in a savage beating by the town guards. Women who live alone are free to bestow attention on fertile men - that is nothing if not a necessity - but approaching them is severely punished. Drunkenness is also against the law, and there is no gin or weed in Brana. The locals brew wonderful beer, but it is diluted with water prior to sale. Men who couple with men are burnt alive. It's a dull town.

We stop next to the stone platform bearing the scorch marks of recent fires. I can almost smell the stench of roasted human flesh - it is probably imagination, but the locals avoid the platform, passers-by making an evident effort to detour around it.

"Solly, I have an order to relay to the men," I tell him in a whisper. "It is to be done very quietly."

Solly nods in expectation.

"Something is very wrong," I explain. "I am not sure what they are up to, but something is happening."

"No doubt, Commander," Solly tells me. "They have been very strange since we arrived."

I stir at his words as my fears are instantly confirmed.

"Finish unloading as fast as possible," I tell him. "Escort the men outside. I will get the merchants."

Solly eyes me with fear.

"Commander, I do not understand what is happening. Where are the merchants? How will you get them out on your own?"

"I don't understand anything either," I tell him curtly. "Not since my Grandfather's day had civilized men turned on each other, and I cannot guess what they are thinking. But we cannot use force in town, so one mouth is as good as a squad of men."

"What do we do if they attack?"

"Run."

He opens his mouth to protest, then thinks a little and closes it once more, nodding agreement. The stakes are very, very high, and no living man had played this game. We simply don't remember the moves.

I pat him on the massive shoulder and walk away, resuming my inspection of goods for sale. I slow down where they sell weapons and admire the quality from afar - powerful but simply made crossbows that fire sharpened wooden quarrels. The bone tips are weighted with small stones, secured to the shaft by strings that began life as fish guts. It is simple, cheap and made from materials that cannot run out.

The next stand holds long hunting knives. These are

even more impressive - gleaming blades that look like good metal, heavy handles of wood with thick metal pommels. Smithy is clearly alive and well in Brana, unlike firearms manufacture. They had not ordered sulphur for some years, and I am reasonably certain they cannot find it locally.

I have an idea that the ancient religion is something to do with reluctance to use anything they have to obtain from us. I am rather willing to bet that such madness is behind all their sinister self-harm. If so, it's truly time to leave town.

I hear raised voices and wheel around, realizing that my enlightenment had come a fraction too late. Solly is surrounded by four men of the town guard, who point long knives at his chest. Another of my men is on the ground, holding his stomach with an agonized expression, and a third is held down by three more town guards, whose faces and grey uniforms are liberally anointed with blood.

I run towards them as more guardsmen come from all corners of the market, drawing their knives and crossbows. We are about to be heavily outnumbered.

"What is the meaning of this outrage?" I thunder, hoping that all the participants will sober up at the sound of my voice.

"Town business, old man," tosses the town sergeant over his shoulder contemptuously. "Stand aside or you will get some as well."

It's been some decades since anyone spoke to me in

this manner, and my men's mouths fall open. They look like they expect lightning to rend heaven asunder at this sacrilege. Alas, that is not within my power.

My anger turns cold as I begin to study the new reality. It is clear that my men and I need to get to the main gate, and our chances of doing this peacefully look bad. At the back of my mind I mark that once we are all safe, Brana will be made to suffer like no one remembers. Simply put, any other outcome will destroy my good name.

I suppose there was a warning that I should not have disregarded. When they refused us hospitality, we should have turned around and left. But then my merchants would have eaten me alive in never-ending claims for compensation, and I could never have proved what was about to happen.

I dismiss these utterly untimely thoughts with an angry shake of the head and finish my sprint by slamming both elbows and both knees into the town sergeant's back. He is flung to the cobblestones, and I complete the manoeuvre by slamming a boot into his ear. He roars from the pain of the burst eardrum and curls into a ball, hands around his ears. I pick up his blade and weigh it in my hand.

My men burst into life, and the rest of their captors are instantly on the ground, alive but unwell.

"No killing!" I cry, snatching the small cargo trolley. It takes all of my arm's strength to raise it off the ground and swing it in the air, but the effect is most rewarding -

two more town guards are felled like matchsticks, and the rest scamper away.

We all drop to the ground as a hail of crossbow quarrels whistles harmlessly above. Accustomed to shooting sprinting deer, the locals aim high out of habit.

The bad thing about crossbows is that they take some time to reload. We use this opportunity to form a wedge, and my men crash into the line of guards, laying about with blunt edges of the long knives taken from their would-be captors. There is confusion and screaming, with the second wave of attackers rendered harmless in a most satisfying manner: they simply run away.

I quickly scan the square for an escape route. The entrance to the meat works is a short distance away, and that is where we run, shutting the heavy gate just as more crossbow quarrels begin to whine their deadly song and drum on the timbers outside.

"Barricade it," I order hoarsely. There is a lump in my throat I never felt in combat before. The fate of the town is in the balance, and I cannot stop thinking that I must get to Rina. I resist the thought and focus on the miserable reality.

Solly and two other men lift a large wheelbarrow with four long handles and throw it against the gate, then pull up loose cobblestones to fill its metal belly. There are men heaving against the gate on the other side, but between the bolts and the wheelbarrow we look like we bought ourselves a little time.

We run through the cavernous building of the meat

works, past the deer corpses on hooks and past the stinking pits containing offal. We cross the vast smoke house where peat beds glow red in darkness, and Solly unerringly spots a wide, low window made of small, sooty panes set in a light metal frame. He begins to kick at the frame, sending shards of thick glass all over the floor. The frame buckles, then begins to loosen.

Solly throws off his battle tunic over his head and wraps it around the middle of the frame, pulling at it with all his enormous strength. He succeeds in tearing it out of the wall and sends it flying into a dark corner with a loud heave.

We scramble through the empty window, finding ourselves in a dirty alley filled with wooden crates. I quickly get my bearings and point down the hill. Solly throws down the tattered remains of his tunic and stares at his hands, covered in deep cuts.

"Later," I shout angrily, running in the indicated direction. I hold the blade at the ready - regrettably, it is more or less time to use lethal force.

But no one stops us as we run down a narrow, curved street towards the lake. We pass a few locals who scamper out of our way, making their gesture of the cross in our wake. I see the main street at the bottom of the alley and increase my pace. The bridge keepers will soon be warned, if they haven't been already. It takes some effort to wind up the bridge, and we have time to get across, provided the town guards didn't have the wits to set up an ambush at the main gate.

We reach the end of the alley and run into the main street, nearly colliding with a pursuit party.

"Don't fight, just run!" I shout with all my might, zigzagging in the middle of the street, just in case someone had the presence of mind to bring a crossbow.

My men follow me downhill. The pursuers are middle-aged thugs, and we are able to maintain a healthy gap without getting exhausted. I look back briefly - there are no crossbows in evidence, and that gives me hope.

We reach the main gate, where the guards stare with utter amazement. Then they realize what they must do and begin to move. There are not enough of them to be a problem, I note with relief - and even fewer when four out of six decide to run away. The others rush up the ladder of the gate tower with the clear intention of raising the bridge. They do not have time to do that either, I realize with relief, fighting dizziness and gasping for breath. Just so long as there are no crossbows, all we have to do is keep our legs moving.

There is not enough strength to think anything else as we streak across the small square adjacent to the wall. We rush through the gate, and our boots drum a furious rhythm on the timbers of the bridge. Its chains tighten as it begins to rise, but there is plenty of time for us to race its full length and leap to the ground on the other side of the moat.

Engine whistles scream as the convoy guard spots what is happening, and I see frantic movement around the machines. Running on the last of my endurance, I hear engines being cranked into life, then the lead transporter jerks away from the camp and races towards us. I change direction slightly, allowing to have a direct line of fire on our pursuers. Just then I hear the heavy thud of their boots on the bridge and marvel at the stupidity of chasing us out of town and into the guns of my men.

The lead transporter clatters past us, swerving to block the pursuers' path, its piston straining against a cold start, with dense soot belching from the exhaust. I slow down, then stop, gasping for breath. Bracing myself with both hands on my knees, I look around. My men have all made it little worse for wear, and we are now safe behind the machine. The man who was winded in the initial altercation is heaving bile, but Solly's cut hands appear to be the only genuine casualties so far.

I see the town guards stop at the end of the bridge as it continues to rise. They stare at the lead transporter that blocks their path across the bridge, its hopper gun pointed right into their faces.

They backtrack towards the gate, and the bridge begins to rise faster. Soon all we see is a mossy expanse of thick timbers as the bridge keepers heave it upwards. It continues to rise and slams into the towers on either side of the gate.

Brana has closed its defences, leaving me outside and Rina within. I raise my hand in an involuntary protest and open my mouth to shout, but my throat is in spasm, and what comes out is an incoherent, angry gurgle.

I let my hand fall and regain my senses. The merchants, who handsomely paid me to protect them, are trapped inside. Now they will no doubt believe me and will be grateful to get home alive, but there is a small chore to perform before all is well.

I must get them out.

We run towards the rear hatch, crouching in case someone decides to shoot. But nothing happens, and all of my men reach safety alive and well, diving into the transporter and dropping onto the deck, still gasping for breath from our run. Someone frantically winds the rear hatch closed - and our immediate plight is over.

I grasp the hand of the soldier next to me, and we laugh, prostrate on the cold metal. The engine hisses as the machine turns around and backs away from the moat.

Someone touches my shoulder, and I roll over onto my back, letting my left arm flop on the deck. It's Tannis, who offers me a flask. I reach for it and gulp greedily, choking on the strong gin. It is too precious to spill, so I struggle with the desire to gag, then force the remainder of the mouthful down the throat. The dull pain in my armpit disappears.

Sitting up, I nod in gratitude and pass the flask to the other survivors, patting Tannis on the shoulder. He should not have the drink with him, but we could not be more grateful.

"Commander, Redmond wants you to come up front," he tells me deferentially.

I take his hand and rise to my feet, doing my best to walk to the cockpit without swaying or gasping for air. Redmond is at the controls - he is wearing undershorts and nothing else. My flight from Brana must have surprised him in his sleep.

"What a ride, Red," I tell him lightly. He shakes his head in wonder.

"What is happening, Commander?"

I pat him on the sticky shoulder.

"A world has ended, my friend. Ours and theirs."

"Why?"

"That I cannot know."

We stay silent as he drives the transporter back to the camp. The other machines are in battle formation, two pincers veering out towards the city wall. Redmond steers around the convoy and stops in the centre to complete the formation.

I lift the radio headset from its cradle.

"All sergeants meet me at the back. Radio silence from now - I am sure they know our frequency."

There is a short period of silence whilst they digest my order - then the thought sinks in. Our enemy has radios and guns. We have never been there before.

I hear boots on the decks of transporters nearby, then the great rear hatches begin to creak open. I leave the cockpit and march through the cabin, slapping men on their shoulders with a reassuring smile. I am not reassured in the slightest myself - the situation appears to be sliding out of control, leaving me with little choice but to open fire on fellow human beings.

The sergeants await me at the rear hatch, and I lead them out, away from the earshot of the men within the transporters. We stare at each other for a short time.

"That was madness, Commander," says Tancred, a short man with dark skin and narrow eyes. I respect his opinion, as he is one of the oldest men in my employ.

"Agreed," I tell him ruefully. "But what choice was there?"

"I don't know," replies Tancred, frowning. "What did happen in town?"

I turn to Solly, who stands beside me with fresh bandages on his hands. One is leaking blood, and he holds that hand at shoulder level.

"They began to harass Hollis," says Solly. "They asked if he had any weed. He said no, but they grabbed him and began to search near his private parts. So he struggled, and their sergeant kicked him in the stomach."

"Did Hollis have weed?"

"No, Commander. He didn't even smell of it. They attacked him because he was the youngest. I would say they were there to pick a fight."

Tancred shakes his head at the insanity of it.

"If they didn't want us around, why didn't they just say?"

"Maybe whoever wanted this is not fully in charge," I say slowly, racing through the possibilities in my head. "I suspect it was Josiah, acting without agreement from other elders."

Everyone thinks that over for a while. Rina's uncle and one-time guardian is a dark, towering figure - a bull of a man who stands a head taller than I. He has been a dominant figure in Brana Council for longer than anyone can remember, being the owner of the fishing fleet that plies the vast lake.

He never concealed his hatred for Grey, for our merchants, for my soldiers and for myself in particular. He would almost break his teeth, grinding them in anger whenever Rina appeared at my side. I never bothered to ask what exactly drove that hatred - presuming that it was envy.

Not that I consider anyone in Grey lucky or even especially safe, but for the time being we are many, and we have most of what we need. Brana, in contrast, has been a mistake from the day when a convoy of crackpots wound its way out of Grey, up the great river and onto the shores of the lake. Once they isolated themselves here, it was only a matter of time before their enterprise met its doom. Which, in all likelihood, looks very much as if that happened today.

"Maybe we can talk it over," rumbles Tancred. "No one got hurt, after all."

I smile and shake my head sadly.

"That won't be possible after what they did."

Tancred stares at me with disapproval but says nothing. Other sergeants nod vigorously.

"We need to squash these fuckers," says Solly forcefully, brandishing his bandaged hands. "No one does that to us and lives to boast about it."

Tancred rounds on him with visible hatred.

"Your pride got hurt," he shouts, dark skin turning a shadow of purple. He spits on the ground. "Fuck. These people upset us. Let's burn their town."

"Be fair, Tancred," replies Redmond gravely. "We came here in good faith to trade. First they denied us hospitality, then they attacked us. I can live without hospitality, but I cannot allow an attack to go unpunished. You know the law."

"Fuck the law," hisses Tancred. "There are five thousand souls in there. Do we feed them all to vermin for calling us names?"

"Gladly," replies Solly, turning sideways, his massive bandaged hands balling into fists. I am beginning to worry that their dispute will turn to brute force. A scrap between two of my sergeants - that would be even worse than what happened in town.

"Enough, both of you," I say under my breath. "The men are watching."

Both of them step back and loosen their postures.

Instinctively, Solly and Tancred glance over their shoulders at the rear hatches, where the crews look at us with intense concern.

"There is no harm in asking what's going on," I tell the sergeants. "We can wait until morning before we do anything that cannot be undone. You wait here."

I return to the lead transporter and unwind the cord of the headset, twist the dial to Brana's frequency and turn up the volume, then return to the sergeants, twisting the ear pieces outwards so everyone can hear.

Tancred stares into my eyes as I hold my hand over the microphone toggle. He nods.

"Grey convoy calling Brana," I say in a neutral voice. "Grey convoy calling."

There is a long silence as we stand in the sun and sweat our anticipation. I feel a welcome breeze, but black clouds are visible at the sunset side of the lake. I sigh in resignation - there will be snow, as sure as night follows day, and we will have to cross the mountains in a blizzard.

"Grey convoy calling Brana," I repeat with sudden anger, turning away from Tancred. "Listen, vermin's children. This is Commander Ritter. I demand my merchants back, safe and sound and with compensation for their stock. You will acknowledge this transmission right now or I will take it to mean that you have declared war between us."

After a few moments the speakers crackle to life.

"This is Brana town guard, acknowledging your transmission," says a young voice that strains to conceal fear. "We are discussing the situation."

"I want my merchants released right now."

"We are discussing it."

"They better be unharmed, if your town is to be here next year," I thunder, now shaking with anger. "Discuss that!"

There is no further communication from within the walls, and I stare at the gate, clenching my fists. I fear that we are continuing to tumble down a steep slope, and the bottom is nowhere near in sight.

"Brana, I am giving you until dawn," I tell them in a calmer tone. We have clocks, but people of Brana reckon time differently, and there can be no confusion today. "At dawn if my merchants are not back on the convoy with fair compensation for their goods, I will attack."

With that I take off the headset and sit down on the ground, feeling and looking despondent. In truth I am more than a little dizzy, and there is dull pressure in my chest. Sitting down appears to make it better, and I remain on the ground, the sergeants joining me one by one with reluctance. Tancred remains on his feet the longest, then shakes his head angrily. He drops on his knees and sits opposite me cross-legged.

"This is altogether frightening, Commander," he tells me as if I am a child. "Think of all those people. I know

93

their elders are fools - but we cannot be a part of whatever sick intent they have."

"Screw the town," I reply bitterly. "How about us, old soldier? Like, you and me? What are we going to do without convoys?"

The younger sergeants open their mouths in horror - they just realized what the stakes are for ourselves.

"But we have Bruce and Karito," protests Solly.

I shake my head with a sad smile.

"No, my young friend," explains Redmond gravely. "They are tiny compared with Brana. We cannot maintain a hand cart on what we would earn from the other settlements."

Solly looks at us with a hurt expression, and I realize that he has never been to the smaller places. That's right, he only came to us in the winter. His people always fished.

"They are just little lagoons where you can drag the sea for shellfish," I tell him. "There is also green stone in Bruce, but no one cares about that any more. If they weren't on the water, they would not survive. We go there to keep them alive, just because their ships are not strong enough for open sea. It is not possible to make a living off their trade."

Solly nods in comprehension and stares at the bloody bandages ruefully.

"It's not over," I pat his shoulder with a heavy hand.

"We have until dawn, and we live in hope."

I get up and begin to wind the cord of the headset, working my way back towards the lead transporter. Just as I near the hatch, the headphones crackle back to life.

"This is Josiah speaking," says a low, relaxed voice. Even in the tiny speakers I can hear its rich, heavy tone. "Answer me, Ritter. Can you hear me, servant of Satan?"

I raise the headset to my mouth as the sergeants rush over to listen.

"I don't know any Satan, and I serve nobody," I reply in a cold, metallic voice.

"Well, Satan knows you, all right. You have committed a final outrage in our town, and you are not coming back."

"I will be back one final time unless you release the merchants," I tell him heatedly. "And it will be the last day for your people, I promise you that."

"The merchants broke our laws."

"That is no concern of mine. We do not answer to your laws, and I will deal with you as I wish unless you release the guests who were under my roof, safe and sound."

"Well, that cannot be," replies Josiah with what sounds like a belly laugh. "You see, we executed them before noon."

I lower the headset and stare at my men in horror. The

slope down which we are tumbling just got steeper - indeed, it feels as if we now slide into freefall.

"That better not be true," I say into the headset.

"It is entirely true," replies Josiah defiantly. "You might as well go home, devil spawn. And don't come back - your heathen stink is not welcome here any longer."

"I want the bodies," I say mechanically, feeling very dizzy. "That is the least you can do."

"Help yourself," says Josiah. "You may find them in the lake. But you better hurry - those big eels are always hungry. Once they get to the surface, there won't be time to salvage anything. Oh, and take care swimming - their snouts are bigger than a man's head."

I throw down the headset and stare at the sergeants, trying to think calmly despite bubbling rage. I look at the skyline of Brana in search of a target, guessing in vain where Rina might be on this evil afternoon.

The town is defenceless before our guns. They may have a little gunpowder, but I doubt that it will fire more than a few rounds. There are no large weapons like catapults or mortars.

"We ought to go, Commander," says Redmond respectfully. "We can spend the night on the flats across the lake, but it's better if we go further and higher. The water might rise overnight."

I stare at Redmond as if I just met him.

"Go we will," I tell him harshly. "After we offload some ammunition."

"We don't have a lot of that to spare either," says Solly with fear in his voice. "There's the return journey, and it looks like snow all the way."

"Snow, you say?" I look at him with triumph. "Then we won't have any need of incendiary rounds. No sense trying to light the undergrowth in a blizzard, is there?"

He looks down at his feet.

"No, Commander. There is not."

"Redmond," I look away from Solly, computing the angle of the sun. We still have plenty of daylight.

"Yes, Commander."

"I want to burn a big hole in that wall."

"But Sir, that will endanger every man, woman and child in Brana. Surely they are not all to blame for the murders."

"It won't endanger them. It will simply mean that every man, woman and child in Brana will be very busy for the next moon. They have what it takes to rebuild it - I just want them to lose that moon out of their lives. It is surely better than killing a lot of people."

Redmond thinks it over.

"You know the law, Red," I tell him in a conciliatory tone. "Killings must be avenged. Those merchants were in my hospitality, and that makes me liable for their deaths. I cannot go back to their widows and orphans and say that we just climbed into transporters and drove home. Can you?"

"No," he admits. "Something has to be done, and clearly they are not open to any talk of compensation."

"We need to think twice before we do something we will be ashamed of for the remainder of our days," says Tancred. "Is there no other way to seek retribution?"

"I am open to suggestions," I tell him earnestly. "Truly, Tancred. I don't want to do this either. But... Does any man here understand what actually happened? I mean, why?"

I stare at the sergeants in silence, and they stare back. One by one, they shake their heads.

"It was either some sickness related to their faith or robbery," says Solly.

"What?" Tancred stares at him in amazement. "Sickness I can see, but robbery? What on earth for?"

"They need metal," I tell him quickly. "They asked for this convoy, and they specified the cargo. But I bet they had nothing to trade. I bet they provoked a fight because we brought them the goods, and they couldn't pay."

"Surely not," says Redmond, shaking his head in disbelief. "How could they think they would get away with it?"

"Probably by killing me," I reply grimly. "They

would lure me to negotiate before I understood what they were up to. And I would probably go."

Tancred sighs and holds up his hands in surrender.

"It sounds very likely, Commander," he says gravely. "If so, a terrible crime has been committed, and it must be punished."

"Yes. We do not need the incendiary rounds for the return trip. Let's use that and a few bullets to loosen the gate. Where the chain is threaded through the timbers - everyone aim at that. Avoid firing on people if possible. Radio silence until we are done."

We turn away from each other with no further words and march to our machines. I clamber up into the turret as the rear hatch is closed, leaving Redmond on the lower deck to explain the orders to his men.

No one has done this for five generations, and I grit my teeth, getting ready behind the hopper gun, checking that the magazine is secure in the hopper, and there is plenty of water in the canister above. I run water through the outer sleeve of the barrel and into a canister below. The water is hopefully cool by the time it reaches the bottom canister, and the canisters are swapped to keep the gun from overheating.

"Approach the moat," I order Tannis, sliding the feeder handle of the gun towards me. It makes a chilling, rasping clang - the gun is now just a touch away from dispensing mayhem.

Engines hiss as Tannis traverses the short distance to

the moat. He drives slowly, and I approve - it certainly adds to the effect.

When the transporter stops near water's edge, I stare at my target for the final time, as if to remember Brana as I would have liked it to remain.

An ancient bronze bell begins to toll above the gate. I watch it sway back and forth for a few moments and nod my acceptance of the challenge.

A stream of evil orange sparks rains from the barrel as the gun jerks in my grip. I walk the fire to the bell and let the bullets ring a wild, agonizing song on the dark metal. Then I go a little higher, and bullets tear into the support beam. The bell jerks and falls away, dropping to the ground on the other side of the wall with a short, thunderous note.

At a guess, it cracked on impact and will never ring again.

I stop firing and sit still, breathing hard. There are shouts coming from the other side of the wall, but they all stay out of sight.

"Concentrate on the left bridge anchor," I rasp into the microphone and commence fire.

The vast timbers of the bridge take time to splinter, but the outcome is inevitable. Heavy bullets slam into the mossy underbelly, each tearing a chunk from the wood. There is a loud crack, and the left anchor comes loose, the bridge now sagging on its remaining anchor.

"Right anchor," I say into the microphone.

"Stop, heathen filth!"

"Ah, Josiah. I see you found the convoy frequency. Hope you like what you created."

"Stop what you are doing now! The bridge is about to fall!"

"That's the idea," I tell him harshly.

The bullets take even less time to tear up the timber around the right anchor, and the bridge collapses, smashing into the ground on our side of the moat. Many of its beams crack and splinter on impact, rearing up like broken teeth. It is seasoned totara - I can see that from here.

"Prime the mortars with phosphorus and report," I order curtly. There is no purpose in maintaining radio silence now.

There is movement on the deck below as men ready the mortars. Our incendiary rounds are sealed shells filled with white phosphorus, a viciously dangerous substance that burns white-hot once it finds itself in contact with air. The shells have a hollow nose, and a revolver cartridge is inserted into the nose just before firing. It explodes the shell on impact, spilling phosphorus to coat the surroundings with sticky gel that instantly catches on fire.

I stare at the bridge as mortar crews report readiness one by one. I listen and wait.

"This is for you, Josiah," I say into the microphone. "Mortars, aim for the bridge. Fire at will."

There are loud pops from my left and from my right, and mortar shells whine through the air. They land and explode in the middle of the bridge, which instantly disappears behind a curtain of white flame. Other rounds are evenly distributed around the gate, setting the towers ablaze.

"Josiah, make sure no one comes near the gate," I tell him evenly. "We will shoot anyone we see."

But it's not as if anyone can put out that fire - the gate is now a raging wall of white flame with mesmerising whirls that suck air into the blinding white glow. Burning phosphorus consumes all air around the flame. If enough incendiary rounds are dumped in one place, they will create their own draft that whips flames into an even greater frenzy. It won't be long before there is a wide, charred hole where the gate used to be - and I am willing to bet that the downed bell is now a puddle of molten metal.

I take my hands off the gun handles and lean back in the seat, soaked in sweat. My nose and eyes sting from powder smoke, and I reach up to crack open the top hatch. The armoury is owned by relatives - my great aunt's descendants - and I am limited in my criticism of their "smokeless" powder. It does at least do the main job - that much can be said without dishonour.

It is very hot - the heat from the fire is making it quite uncomfortable inside the turret. I am almost ready to issue an order to move further back, but broken timbers are almost burnt through.

I let time wash over me as flames exact my revenge. When the burnt remains of the bridge sag and drop into the water, I lean towards the hatch and call out.

"Red, come up here!"

He takes a few moments to leave his battle station and climbs up into the turret.

"Pray, who is that Satan?"

"Lord of the underworld, according to Old Faith."

"Ah, I recall now. In charge of hell, is that he?"

"That's right, Commander."

"Also stalks men and encourages them to do evil on earth?"

"So it is said, Commander."

I nod my thanks, and Redmond disappears in the well.

"Therefore, Josiah," I toggle the headset. "It is time for us to part. Give my regards to Satan when your people cut your throat."

"Why should they do that?" asks a deep, mocking voice.

"If any other townsman of Brana can hear me, I want them to say so now," I say coldly.

There is no reply.

"I want someone to reply now, or I will burn another

hole in your defences."

"I hear you," says a young voice I heard earlier. "I am Samson, the day sergeant."

"Very well, Sergeant. Kindly log my message: I demand that the good people of Brana collect compensation for myself and the families of the merchants you slaughtered. You will take it to Grey using your own means because I don't ever wish to come back here. You will come to us by mid-summer, otherwise I will return with great numbers of men and weapons before winter. You will not see another summer if I do."

"I have entered your words in my log," replies Samson neutrally.

"Then I leave you to ensure that all your townsmen know," I tell him with sadness. "Kill that son of a whore Josiah - before he kills all of you. Then appoint a proper leader and begin to repair the damage you have done. Brana cannot survive without outside trade."

There is no reply, and I stare at the ruined wall one last time.

"Cease hostilities," I order my men. "Convoy, set course for the pass."

Engines hiss and tracks clatter as our empty machines turn in place and follow the lead transporter. I turn the turret to take one last look at Brana. Its window are lit by an afternoon sun just like yesterday, but dirty smoke fills the sky - the peat is being piled into the town's water pumps. They will need much water to put out the fire on the wall, something they will begin to do as soon as we are out of range.

I stare at the wall beneath the smoke-stained sky. Forgive me, Rina, for I had fulfilled my promise. You and I will never meet again - that much is clear. I made that vow in anger, but both of us hoped to break it.

The convoy rolls on, and the burning wall is but a small speck of fire in the vast horizon. Then we turn abruptly into the forest, and I see it no more.

Redmond climbs into the well noisily, and I turn towards him. He completes the climb and kneels next to me on the floor.

"The men are wondering," he says softly. "We have a favour to ask."

I nod.

"What we want is to spend the night on the flat near the shore," says Redmond apologetically. "Where we can see the town."

"Explain."

"We will only be a short ride away from Brana," he tells me. "If it's attacked before tomorrow, we may be able to help."

I nod again.

"By tomorrow they will have enough rubble to block that hole," he continues. "They don't need to rebuild the gate until next summer - the wharf is more important to them than the gate onto land. But if they are attacked before tomorrow, they may not be able to repel it."

I know it to be an irrational thought, but I am hoping that his concerns will come true. If Brana is lapped by a tide of vermin, I may see her. Maybe more.

"Veer formation, double sentries," I tell him. Redmond nods his acceptance with eager relief. "Everyone in armour, light dinner only. Anyone who drinks gin or even thinks of weed, I will cut off their manhood myself."

"You would have to beat me to it," says Redmond with a grateful smile.

"If it begins to rain or snow, we move uphill," I add. "Also, there are dead trees on that flat. I want the firewood stocks replenished as soon as we arrive. We could be stuck on this side of the range for a few days."

"Surely, Commander," Redmond lowers his legs into the well. I nod, and he drops down to the lower deck.

I listen to the sparse sounds of approval. No one is happy, even with this rather large concession to our new, vile reality. We should really travel as high as we can get before the storm - if one must get stuck in the snow, deeper is safer. Vermin are less of a threat once it gets to waist height, and if the snow reaches the roof of the transporter, it is much easier to stay warm in the bitter mountain winds.

But these are small things compared with the whirl of guilty thoughts that none of us can help thinking. The good people of Brana will not be there by spring - I suspect that rather strongly - and what happened today means that they will live what remains of their lives without hope. If a convoy of refugees turns up at Grey's gate, they will be allowed to settle, and I would even feel a little better if they did. But I suspect that they have no means of making the trip. With no transport and with no firearms they cannot survive one day outside the wall.

With that bitter truth acknowledged, I feel truly depleted of strength and lie on top of my bedroll. I bring my arms to my sides and squeeze my legs together to trap the stench of my body. It must be the fifth day without a shower, and the desperate run through Brana did nothing to improve things. It is quite warm, and I would kill for a dip in the lake once we stop - but such a bad example cannot even be contemplated. Nevertheless, I fantasize about the transporters stopping next to the shore. Just a few moments in the water... Then maybe dry the uniforms on the armour...

Out of the question. The forest will be a short distance away - it is possible to run across the flat lakeside meadow in less time that it would take me to undress. I pull the bedroll about me and turn over for good measure. It feels good to close my eyes and give in to the rocking motion of the transporter, moving over sunken logs as slowly as possible. We should be there quite soon.

I awaken in dim light and realize that dawn is upon me. I should be hungry and annoyed at such a display of weakness, but all I feel instead is gratitude - Redmond broke the protocol and let me sleep without armour. It is his job to ensure that everyone, myself included, obeys my orders - and I am ever so glad he chose not to fulfil the letter of his contract.

I rise from the bedroll and stare through the porthole. We are indeed near the lake, which had not started to rise. The black clouds are too dense to let through the tones of sunrise, and it is clear that our passage through the mountains will be slow and hard. That cannot be helped, and it is far too late to regret anything now, but our trip is likely to endanger our lives. Had nothing happened, we would have stayed in Brana and drunk beer until the snow melted.

I turn to look across the water, but dense mist blankets the placid surface of the lake, totally obscuring Brana. That is that, I think sombrely - I will never see it again. It will be possible to travel to the ruins, but I cannot think why we would risk lives to do that.

I rise with my back against the cold wall of the turret and fight the wave of nausea and sweat. My hand on the latch in case I begin to retch, the dull pressure takes over my chest. It passes slowly, and I gulp cold air, willing it to pass before anyone hears me and comes to check on my well-being. I let go of the latch and sink back to the bedroll.

I worry needlessly - the men are deeply asleep, and Redmond is clearly not in a hurry to wake them up. Who would want to leave the warm oblivion of their bedroll for the ugly reality of this dawn - we are returning with in a humiliating failure, spattered in the blood of our customers, and my soldiers are likely to starve once our resources run out some time in the summer, unless we find new ways of eking out a living. It is hard to imagine a sane man who would want to wake up to that a moment earlier than he must.

I look up on sheer instinct, and my gaze meets a menacing pair of yellow eyes that stare at me through the porthole. Mesmerized, I stare back, my will sinking into the oval darkness of its pupils. There is an unfathomable hatred in that stare.

It's a very large male - I see that by the size of the hand that is clamped around a huge wooden club. The sparse hair around the snout is flame-red in colour, and the skin is pale, almost white. The mouth is half-open, and I can see the vicious fangs with dark markings near the gums. It stares at me, and there is no doubt whatsoever about its intentions.

We both move together - I dive for the charging handle of the gun, and it slams a massive heel into the sharp grate that protects the porthole. Then it lets out a scream as the porthole turns crimson with blood. The grate protecting the glass is made of old knife blades, painted to look like blunt metal bars.

I recover my balance and jerk down the breach of the gun, which raises the barrel up, away from the roof of the transporter. I swing the turret sideways, forcing the creature to hang off the metal sleeve around my barrel, dripping blood from the cuts.

"Vermin on the roof!" I scream at the top of my voice.

There is much movement all around me in response. I cannot see what is happening outside but hear many feet, much growling and yelping. Something smashes against the side of my machine below, but it appears to land harmlessly. Then the guns awaken at last.

I hear heavy bullets slamming into soft bodies and the agonizing screams of the dying. I rotate the turret frantically, trying to move the blood clinging to the porthole. It is of no avail - I turn the turret in the direction of the sounds of heavy footsteps fleeing the convoy and let out a long, veering volley.

After the gun runs dry there is silence, and I scramble to put on the headset.

"Redmond, report."

"A fair few corpses, Commander. I recommend that we leave quickly."

"Concur," I break open the magazine and throw a new box into the hopper. "Let's ride."

Engines begin to hiss into action, and we are soon enveloped in soot as the drivers throttle the machines hard. We move up the slope, slight bumps indicating when we drive over bodies - of which there are gratifyingly many.

I get out of the seat and work the rotary handle of the porthole wiper. There is enough mist to get the dry blood off the glass within a few cycles. I wait until more mist gathers on the porthole and wipe again, running the prickly brush back and forth. After that, I can see.

"Did anyone get the mutt that hung onto the gun of the lead transporter?" I ask.

There is silence.

"Anyone seen what happened to him?"

"I did," says the young sergeant from the third transporter. "He ducked under the firing line, and I think he escaped. His left foot was bleeding."

"With luck it will go rotten," I mumble to myself, more than the men. It will be a while before I stop seeing those yellow eyes in my nightmares.

"I hope so, Commander. I am sorry I wasn't fast enough."

"Next time," I tell the boy placatingly. "There is always a next time."

The convoy speeds away from the lake, where much dead flesh awaits its undignified fate. The vermin always come back for their dead, and it is not a good idea to remain near the kill.

I rotate the turret, but the mist is still thick over the lake, and there is nothing but white in the direction from which I hoped to catch the last glimpse of Brana. I curse under my breath and rotate the turret to face forward, scanning the misty horizon for the enemy. The visibility is quite appalling this morning, and the sticky warmth is bad too. We can expect snow some time soon.

"Red, let's race for the pass," I say gruffly. "I feel we

have until midday before the snow starts in earnest."

"We must do that, Commander," he assures me tonelessly. "I am just checking how much wood we have."

I nod in the loneliness of my turret and lean back against the seat, wiping a sweaty brow with my sleeve. The good news is that I am no longer aware of my body odour. The bad news is that I need to visit the latrine. It would have done much business this morning, and there was no time to hose it off.

I straighten my clothing and slide down the ladder, nodding to the men - most of them are half-dressed and still packing up their bedding. There was no meal either - all of this will begin to add up before the day is a lot older. Maybe the snow will force an early stop, and we could line up in a square formation and do some washing. Oh, the temptation of that thought.

The latrine could be in better condition, and I make my visit as short as possible, holding my breath. Using the latrine when the machine is in motion is, of course, nowhere near as offensive as when we are stationary. I get out and rub water on my hands, then throw some over my face and neck. The run-off is murky, and I do it again until it turns clear.

"Commander, we failed to recognize you," says Redmond lightly as I come past. "But now that you cleaned your face, we know it is you."

I exhale, wiping my forehead with a sleeve.

"Yes, it looks like I made one clean spot," I reply in the same spirit. "Red, we have to organize showers when we stop. We will begin to go mouldy otherwise."

He nods.

"We will stop at a stream, Commander. About mid-morning, I would say. Then we push on until the snow stops us."

"Yes. Tell the men to get their spare clothing ready. We won't wash clothes today, but there may be nothing better to do tomorrow."

"There is no problem with fuel, either," says Redmond. "We are a little worse off for food, though."

"How much?"

"Three days, then we are down to emergency rations."

"It will do," I tell him. "No one will starve to death. Just stay alert - that was one ugly surprise."

"I am sorry, Commander," says Redmond. "We did not prepare the stop properly, and the mist did the rest."

"No blame," I tell him. "The whole thing is insane, Red. I should not have agreed to your plan either. And I should have stayed awake."

"Every man's endurance has a limit, Commander," says Redmond, waving a stern finger. "No harm done, and let us be thankful for that."

"We got a few while we were at it," I add, feeling a

sudden release of tension. "Good work."

"We should announce that later," says Redmond. "Once we stop."

I nod and leave him to his many duties, climbing into the turret. In truth, I could easily go back to the latrine - but my quivering bowels will just have to settle down. I have to admit that I got a fright staring into the merciless, inhuman eyes.

I lie down on top of the bedroll and stretch my legs. It will be honest to admit that I feel great guilt. I know that the monster will survive his injury, and I know, as night follows day, that he will live to probe the torn defences of Brana. That makes me feel very small.

There is a lot of noise and a heavy stench of soot - the drivers have their orders, and they are speeding away from the lake as fast as we can go. There is less mist further away from the shore, and it becomes clear that the sky is a pregnant shade of dark-grey. The wind picks up as the morning cold gives way to stuffy warmth that always precedes a storm from land's tail. These storms are usually merciless.

There is a simple gear-driven indicator at the driver's console which shows how many miles we travelled since it was reset. I can tell speed, in miles per day, with relative accuracy after a lifetime of commanding convoys. At present we are doing about fifty miles a day - we could return to Grey by nightfall tomorrow if we keep up that speed. Of course, the ancient road is not up to it in the mountains. We will need to find a defensive position and make the rest of the distance when the snow melts.

I pull back the charge handle and check the firing pin. It seems in working order, and there are just a few specks of residue in the firing chamber. I crack open the top hatch and toss water over the outside of the porthole, then drop back to run the cleaning brush over the wetted glass. The remainder of dried blood seems to come off; not that it was in the way, but still a reminder of an annoying and frightening incident I cannot put out of my mind - knowing, as I do, that its consequences are far from over.

I close the top hatch and consider another sleep, immediately rejecting the idea. Last night was more than enough, and I am embarrassed to appear so frail. It is not an image that already demoralized men need.

Tannis appears in the access well and knocks on the wall for permission. I nod.

He clambers into the turret and salutes. I return the salute and motion for him to sit down. Something is clearly on the boy's mind.

"I am on a break, Commander."

"Surely. Are you very tired?"

"Could be a little better," he admits, leaning back against the wall of the turret. "Redmond actually told me to have a rest. He is driving now."

"I hope he remembers how," I reply lightly.

"He cannot do worse than a fledgling like me," says Tannis with a smile. "I want to ask you something while I rest. May I close my eyes?"

I nod. He closes his eyes and rubs them with dirty fists. I resist the urge to take his hands and stop him, as one would a sleepy child. But Tannis is two hundred pounds of steely flesh and long past his twentieth birthday. He had grown up seeing men die at sea.

"I understand that I hadn't been with you that long, Commander. But... what will we do now? Can we ever go back to Brana?"

"We can go back," I sigh, stifling a yawn of genuine fatigue. "We can go back and forth every moon. Apart from snow, nothing can stop us. But there won't be any trade, and we will just risk ourselves for nothing. Brana is finished, take my word for it. One winter, then maybe one spring - no more."

"Will they be overrun?"

"Of course."

"Can we stop it?"

"Only if we invade," I reply grimly. "Only if I station all my men and all my machines and have them fire at anything that comes close to the wall. Like we do in Grey."

"Why don't we invade then?"

I consider the question. Why not indeed - no one can stop us.

"Brana is not mine to invade," I reply at length. "They have a council, and that council made decisions. I can punish them for what they did to us, but I have no right and no reason to save them from themselves over and over."

Tannis opens his red-rimmed eyes and studies me at length.

"What will happen to us? Please, Commander. I have to feed my children and their grandmother."

"I have to feed many more than that," I reply tartly. "As soon as I have an idea, I will share it."

"But what happens if you don't have one?"

I smile and shake my head vigorously.

"Tannis, my friend," I lean forward and grasp his shoulder. "All my life I had fought for survival like my Father and his Father before me. I am not frightened when my survival is on the line. That is entirely usual. So long as I am not fighting alone, I fear naught."

"May I make a suggestion, Commander?"

"You know the answer to that," I tell him irritably. "What did we tell you on your first day? I do not want men I have to drive like machines. Speak."

"Except you may find it foolish," he says apologetically.

"Or it may save us from starvation," I rasp curtly. "Speak your mind."

"I wondered about fuel."

"I am listening."

"Well, it seems to me that on land it is all about fuel. At sea we have our spinning sails, and we can move forever, in any direction, just as long as there is wind. When we don't move, the sails make electricity. Even when we run out of electricity, we can burn whale oil in furnaces."

"That is so."

"On land everything is so hard because we have no fuel. There is not enough warmth, not enough light, not enough fuel for engines, and the men at the mill have to drive their saws by hand because they cannot fire up their boiler most of the winter. There is not enough firewood."

"That is so."

"But the ancients took fuel out of the ground before they decided to make electricity like the sun does."

I stare at him sharply. So much for the ragamuffin boy growing up on a fishing barge offshore.

"You have been reading," I tell him with approval.

"The captain had a lot of ancient books, Commander. He didn't lend them out, but I was his favourite."

I choose not to think about his early life on the barge.

"You are right," I return to the theme at hand. There are fuels to be found in the ground. Solid, gas and liquid. Fuels beyond our imagination. Fuels that burn so hot they could set fire to wet firewood and even melt metal. But there are none in Grey, and no one knows how to find them now. The ancients made special machines to see what is under the surface."

"Sometimes on the surface, Commander. "Not far from Grey."

I study him sharply.

"Might you know where?"

"Possibly, Commander."

I make a gesture of irritation, and he nods hurriedly.

"I think I have seen this in one book in captain's cabin."

"On the barge where you grew up?"

"The very one, Commander. You see, the old captain - he was a book lover. Once we landed at Karito, when the locals were desperate."

"They are always that way."

"That is the truth, Commander. It was a foolish place to build a town."

I nod, deciding not to distract him with the story of Karito. In ancient times it was a tiny hamlet built on a shallow lagoon, little more than a puddle on the edge of the forest where people came for a rest. After the scourge the forest streams became surging rivers, and they created the peninsula of Karito - a wide tongue of land surrounded by water. The vermin don't like that - anything deeper than waist height is an effective barrier against them. Karito was a refuge to which panicked farmers flocked when the first vermin crossed the mountains. No one planned it that way.

"So we moored our longboats at Karito with the supplies they needed. They traded everything they could for us to unload, and that's how the captain got the town library."

"Did he read it all?"

"He began. Then there was a storm - the one my uncle died in."

I lower my gaze to hide what I feel. I know Tannis still honours his uncle, who saved the young boy's life from starvation on land - only to sell him to fellow sailors. Our laws prohibit such things with abhorrence, but that only applies in town. Men aboard barges - vast platforms built on top of assorted flotsam that never come too close to land - obey no law.

"The captain was knocked down by a huge wave to the deck. He broke his skull and lay unconscious for many days afterwards. When he awoke, his left arm didn't move properly, and his vision was very poor. He could no longer read."

I stare at Tannis with increasing intensity.

"I knew writing, and he made me read his books out loud," says Tannis. "Every night. I was glad of this because men left me alone. The captain's wick became useless after his head was damaged, and I was safe at last. It was so for a few years, and I grew tall and strong."

When Tannis grew tall and strong, men began to disappear on the barge. I approve - revenge is a sacred principle in our law. But when the dimwits began to discern the pattern - and they did, for Tannis was young and impatient - he had to escape with his life, rowing to the shore through a foggy night. An act of a true hero, given the dangers he braved to get to Grey in a tiny boat.

He rowed up the river and asked for me in person. Intrigued, I walked to the wharf and heard what he had to say.

He reminded me that I once visited the barge to bargain with the captain about whale oil. My relatives use it in gunpowder manufacture - they worked out the ancient way to make smokeless powder. Not even the ancients did it so well - they used chemicals that took all the might of their society to manufacture. We need just four ingredients – wood, urine, ash and whale oil. Our powder is not entirely acid-free or smokeless, but it works - as vermin can attest.

My company has an interest in the powder works, and I was delegated the ugly job of flying to the barge. I climbed down from the airship and spent the entire morning - that was how long it took us to drink the flagon of finest gin I could find - in the stink of the captain's cabin. I do remember many books, most of them covered in soot and grease from the oil lamps.

Tannis came to serve us snacks. I refrained, wondering about the cook's hygiene on a vessel where entertainment meant drinking and coupling with other males.

Tannis studied me with curiosity as the captain excused himself and lumbered outside. I remember holding my breath as he came past my chair.

"Are you Commander Ritter?" asked the gangly boy with deference.

"I am he," I told him with a smile. "How do you know that?"

"I heard many stories about your convoys," said the boy with a touch of sadness. "It's all so exciting."

"It is all so dangerous and hard," I corrected him sternly. "Men die from that so-called excitement."

"Men die here too," replied the boy sadly. "But it is just unfair. One of our boats capsized the other day because the rudder failed in high wind. Six whale men went down, and they never had a chance. The monsters got them before we could even come close."

"In that case, the forest is better," I told him. "On land we can fight, and we usually win."

"One day I want to serve under your command," young Tannis told me.

"Come and see me when you are ready," I replied. The old captain returned at that stage, walking the relieved walk of an old drunk who just emptied a bursting bladder.

Some years later I stood on the wharf, reminded of that conversation as the fog rolled in from the sea. There was little time to reminisce.

"I did tell him to come and see me," I told the guards. "Boy, your boat looks like it belongs on the bottom of the sea. Do you much care for it?"

"No, sir," Tannis told me. "I am afraid I bumped into the reef in the fog. I doubt that it is worth repairing."

"In that case, set fire to some flotsam inside it and let it float back towards the sea," I ordered. "I want no trouble with the men from your barge. I want it to burn down to the waterline, and waves can do the rest."

I smile at these memories now as I look up.

"Then you grew tall and strong," I repeat for emphasis. "You think the old captain is still alive?"

"I saw him in the market this summer. He did not look like he will be on this earth for much longer."

"Then we need to see him soon. Tell me, have you ever spoken of this with anyone else?"

"No, Commander. I gave it no thought until what just happened in Brana - and then you explained how we lost our livelihood."

"Very well. Do not discuss it again - with me or anyone else. When we return... Say, do you think the men on the barge would recognize you?"

"No, by the memory of my Father. They cannot. I am twice the size from when they last saw me, and I have a beard."

"Shave your scalp and eyebrows for good measure. That always makes men look older and meaner. I will need you to come with me."

"As you command," he says gladly, running his hand through the short hair. "Might look better anyway."

"I am grateful," I tell him. "But keep your mouth shut. If the captain realizes what he has, we will not be able to buy it."

He nods with a wicked smile.

"If you are right, Tannis, we will both die rich."

He waves a derisory gesture.

"I just want to have enough to eat and a warm place to sleep."

"Both of which we barely have now. What you say may change many things."

He bows respectfully.

"I will see if Redmond is ready to be relieved."

I nod with a smile, and he climbs down from the turret.

I lie back on the bedroll, going over our conversation. I am pleased that my reaction was low-key - yes, a worthwhile project, but one of many. I did not let Tannis know that he just said the most important thing I ever heard.

I let my mind drift, and the swaying motion of the transporter takes me away into oblivion. When I come to, I am thrown against the metal wall, and the cold feels worse than the impact.

I brace myself to rise, but realize that we had merely come to a halt. The engines are still running, but there is excited banter from the lower deck.

"I can't see a fucking thing, Red," I hear Tannis shout from the steering seat.

"I am taking a look outside," I hear Redmond's reply, and I hear his feet stomping up the turret ladder.

"Sorry, Commander," says Red - and I can see that he means it. "It doesn't look like we will be going any further today."

I nod as he winds open the top hatch and squeezes through it. He stares at the landscape for a few moments, then drops back and winds the hatch closed.

"We will be here for a day or two, Commander."

I rise on both elbows and twist my hips to rise in the turret. There is nothing to be seen out of the porthole - except huge, wet snowflakes that splash against it in the thick fog.

"Convoy formation?" I ask Red.

He nods and climbs down into the lower deck.

I stretch, listening to the rasps of engines and

thumping of the pistons as machines arrange themselves into a square, rear hatches facing inside. We have arrived.

With Red gone, I wind open the top hatch and raise myself to look outside. It is not at all cold, but the snow is coming down thick and fast, and the visibility is indeed zero. The transporter's tracks are now completely under snow, and soon it will reach to the bottom of the turret. We are not home, but we should be completely safe.

My thoughts turn to showers, and I lean down to shout the necessary orders.

"We are onto it, Commander!" shouts a familiar voice I cannot place. "There is a stream right next to the road!"

I close the top hatch and wipe the snow off the floor. My hands turn red and throb, but it is a pleasurable sensation that brings back childhood memories of throwing snowballs at other boys at school. My gloves got wet during snowball fights, but I never took them off for fear of losing them. Coming home without gloves always earned a thrashing - a child who removed his clothes was yelled at by all passers-by, for a cold child soon became ill, and a sick child was but a few fevered days away from death.

I sigh at the memory, then climb down and spend some time inspecting the transporters. The men are busy clearing out the dirt, tossing whatever will burn into the furnaces and the rest outside. We are taking stock of the madness of the last two days, and it is beginning to feel almost normal - until I see a stack of bags in the corner of the large cargo transporter.

"They are the merchants' belongings," Tancred says sombrely. I place a hand on his thick shoulder, and we stand in silence, looking at the bags. I am thinking of visiting the families - something I had not had to do for a while, not since a soldier fell in a battle with vermin some six years past. To my shame, I cannot even recall his name.

"I wonder who gets the first shower," I say to Tancred, removing my hand from his shoulder. He turns and nods gravely. It is clear he is not in the mood.

I leave him be and return to the quadrangle, where the first of the men is already standing naked in the snow, rubbing his muscular body with soap under tepid water. The others are counting loudly - every man is given one hundred counts.

I join the counting chorus, and when I am two men away from the end of the queue, I strip off the tunic, undo the boots and stand in the snow barefoot. When the man in front of me runs under the water, I pull down the uniform pants, remove the long underwear and roll it up into a ball.

"Ninety-eight. Ninety-nine. One hundred!" shouts the chorus.

The soldier in front of me runs out of the shower, retrieves his clothes and boots from the snow and runs into the cabin, steam coming off his bare back. I toss my boots and clothes into the snow and run under the feeble trickle of warm water - which feels like the most luxurious of showers I ever had.

I rub my body with soap and rinse it off, leaving before the chorus gets to eighty. The men cheer, and the next soldier takes my place as I run inside the lead transporter to stand next to the stove.

It feels ecstatic to rub down the skin with the rough towel, and I climb into the turret stark-naked. I sit on the bedroll and slide a spare set of clothes over my body, then climb down and retrieve what I discarded. The boots can wait - I throw them as far as I can - and roll my dirty clothes into a tight bundle to trap the smells until we return to Grey. The steam laundry can take care of the problem.

Once warm and dry, I think over what Tannis said. The steam laundry - well, that is the name. It can manage steam on most days, but frequently it is barely capable of generating enough heat to wash clothes. Damp timber is hardly fuel.

But coal... I read of grand factories powered by coal, of vast metal foundries and power stations, all made possible by coal. It would need a few trailer loads of coal to power Grey for a moon, with warmth in every home, with safely lit streets, with clean drinking water and power for a fleet of ships. With coal fuelling our metal works we could make real weapons, fell the forest, grow grain and farm animals.

I hear good-natured insults coming from the

quadrangle between transporters, where the last of the men take their turn under tepid water. Who knows, maybe that is the last such shower they are forced to take. I shake my head in wonder.

We then have a long evening of entertainment. Each man has to tell a joke or sing a song - there is little room for anything else, with all four crews crowded into the freight trailer, sadly empty of goods. I tell a few old stories that most of the younger soldiers have not heard. I leave them happy, then sneak out of the trailer through the side hatch.

It stopped snowing, and the wind has died down, leaving the air so cold that it makes me gag when I breathe, and I place my hand over my mouth. The stars are now visible through the thinning cloud, and that bodes poorly for the nights ahead - but for now, the soft snow is too thick on the ground, and nothing can get through it for the time being. As it melts during the day and hardens tomorrow night, it will be a different story, a race between being able to extract the convoy from the pass and the vermin moving on the crusted surface. But that is for tomorrow, I sigh as I knock on the rear hatch of the lead transporter, and tomorrow is not today.

I swallow a few poppy seeds and wrap up tight within my bedroll. The ceiling of the hatch spins, rather happily, in the starlight as I dream of fuel, furnaces and molten metal, full plates, fat children and warm houses.

Then morning gently intrudes upon my drugged sleep, with voices in the lower deck, clang of metal, the crunch of footsteps in the snow outside and odour of slightly burnt broth. I stretch sweetly, taking care not to protrude from the bedroll. As I roll over, I hear someone climbing the ladder, and Redmond shows up with a bowl of steaming gruel and a mug full of berry tea.

"A very good morning, Commander."

"Same to you, Red. How was the night?"

"Quiet and peaceful, Commander. We are just watching the sun now."

"Any chance of starting today?"

"None that I can see, Commander. We would use up all of our fuel trying to get through that stuff."

"Let's hope it is not too warm then."

He nods. Our best chance is for the snow to melt from underneath, heated by the still-warm ground. If it melts from the top during the day, it will freeze overnight, and the frozen surface will sustain the weight of footsteps but not machines, leaving us immobile and bare to an attack.

"This is a good position," he tells me. "No approach is possible from two sides, and there is a nice slope elsewhere. Provided we have enough moonlight, a surprise approach won't be possible. That's as good as it gets out here."

"That is so," I sit up and study the ground through the porthole. "Nothing on two sides, as you say, and a clear killing ground elsewhere. Have the men rest as much as they can - they will be coming tonight. I can see the melt already, and it is not even mid-morning."

"Nothing else for them to do, Commander," Redmond pushes the bowl closer to my bedroll, reminding me to eat whilst it is still hot. I nod with gratitude and gulp the first spoonful. Every autumn we harvest the oats from the fields where they grow wild since ancient times. It is the best meal of the day, a respite from dried fish.

"We will clean the weapons during the morning and go to sleep after lunch," says Redmond. "Wake up at dusk and stay up till maybe midnight. Then the night watch can take over."

I nod in between spoonfuls of hot porridge.

"We need to sight the hopper guns," I tell him. "Set up the range of fire, otherwise they will waste too many rounds."

He nods acceptance. Our quadrangle is not quite aligned with the killing zone, and moving transporters is not worth the trouble. The less noise we make today, the more likely we are to sleep through the night.

I finish the gruel and scoop the last grains from the bottom. It is warm enough to leave the bedroll, but I am in no hurry today.

"What are the men saying?"

Redmond looks up at me sharply.

"What about, Commander?"

"Brana."

"They are still dismayed, Commander. As am I."

I nod.

"No one can understand, Commander. Why?"

I reach for the mug of berry tea.

"I can't understand it either. The best thing I can say is that we did not commit this crime. We are its victims as much as the merchants."

His face sinks at the mention of the dead.

"Commander," he says hesitantly. I stare at him and nod my permission.

"What will you say to their kin?"

"I will tell them the truth, Red. I will take responsibility and pay my respects."

"What if they demand compensation?"

"I will make them a reasonable offer. There is not much to bargain with - it is not as if anyone wants the barracks, and the transporters are hardly of use to anyone but us."

"What if they want you to go back and make war on Brana?"

"I will consider it. Maybe it is best that we do."

"Could we take it?"

I sip my tea and stare at the snow glistening in the sun through the porthole, thinking. Then I nod, just once. Redmond frowns.

"Would many die?"

"There are a few different ways to do it. But yes, a few will die - and there are a few that should."

He sits in silence, but I volunteer no more of my thoughts.

"Look, old friend, we cannot return until spring, and there will be more urgent matters to attend to. Let us not soil our day of rest with such thoughts."

He nods his acceptance, still frowning.

"Brana may not fight back," I explain. "They may crave rescue, and it may even come to pass that we won't get there in time."

I awaken at dusk, staring at the blood-red sun as it drifts towards the mountaintops on the other side of the valley. It is nearly time.

The snow had melted during the day, exposing rocks in the wide riverbed that divides the valley. The water winds its way between steep walls of rock swathed in lush vegetation. We are in the middle of the bend, and that is wise - it will help to channel an attack into our guns.

There is no noise from below-decks after dark, and I will my bladder to be silent, for I don't want to make any sound and wake the men. The moon is already visible in the pale blue sky, and it promises to be a busy night.

I lie on my back, trying not to think about Rina. I

have this feeling that she is watching me from somewhere nearby, maybe even inside the turret - an ageing man with very wide shoulders and spade-like hands, sheltering under a woollen wrap, separated from certain death by a thin layer of metal.

I close my eyes and feel her sitting astride me in her white nightshirt, long red hair flowing into the fold between her breasts. I smile, feeling the light perfume of her skin, revelling in the warmth of her touch as she caresses my forehead, her long, soft fingers lingering on the ragged scars.

"All will be well," she tells me softly. I reach up and place my hand over hers, throwing back the edges of the bedroll.

"It can only be well now," I tell her, feeling the soft caress on my face. "We cannot lose if we are together."

She continues to caress my forehead, and I drift away as if full of poppy seeds, floating above the frozen dusk, somewhere above the soot-stained turret. I can feel the cold air, but it does not offend me. The light playing on the mountain peaks turns snow from pink to deep purple. Golden rays pierce the pale winter sky as the sun rolls behind the jagged tops, plunging the world into fear.

Then I am alone on the side of the ancient road - except I see its black surface clearly, and it is new and smooth. I am sprawled on back, my right leg throbbing with severe pain. I clutch the ancient rifle - no, I cradle it as if my life depends on it, even though it no longer looks as if it does. Although I hear distant shots, they somehow don't matter to me any longer.

I jolt awake and sit up, staring ahead until my eyes adjust to the darkness and begin to distinguish shadows in the soulless light of the moon. The river is now a dark gash amid the snow-covered valley, but I can make out the expanse of snow that surrounds our position. As I stare harder, I begin to see dark shadows moving in that expanse.

Fire erupts on all sides, spraying the snow and raising whirls of powder where bullets pierce the ground. I hear unearthly howls as vicious silhouettes rise from the snow and rush towards the convoy.

Hail of bullets meets them head-on, black blood spreading through the pristine whiteness of the valley. A few make it far enough to climb onto the transporters, and I swivel my turret to confront them, firing short bursts to cut each in half. There is sporadic fire from the gun ports below, short barks of revolvers whose solid, heavy slugs can blast off heads and limbs.

I replenish the hopper and wait for another wave, but it never comes. The fire dies down, and I sit inside the smoke-filled turret, sweating and holding on to the hopper gun with numb hands.

The full moon now rules the dark sky, and its light is unbearably bright on the snow. I see many dark heaps that lie still in snow stained in dark blood. There are many tracks that were made by escaping vermin on the hardened surface, and there is steam coming off my face, my arms and the barrel of the hopper gun. The eyes sting from the smoke, and I crack open the top hatch to let it drift into the night breeze.

We stay up for the rest of the night, but the attackers never return. The consensus, enforced by the darkening sky, is to take off without breakfast.

Each man makes a loop of rope, and we spend the early morning dragging the corpses into one pile. The hard, smooth snow makes light work of latching a sliding knot around the throat of each creature and pulling the grim load towards the pit filled with dead flesh. By the time the sun is over the tops of the mountains, we finish the job and toss ropes into the hole filled with grey bodies torn by hopper guns.

The lead transporter takes off towards the woods and returns, dragging a large dead tree, which it neatly parks over the pile of corpses. Tancred emerges from the side hatch and unlatches the tow chain, his dark eyes glaring hatred. He spits at the pile before signalling to the driver to roll forward, pulling the chain away from the tree.

Tannis tosses a few rags into the pile and douses them with fuel from a small canister. We board our transporters hurriedly, wiping hands on whatever snow is free of bloody streaks. As the convoy begins to roll away from the camp site, Tannis fires an incendiary round into the pile and runs to catch up with the machine.

I stare backwards, watching the greasy smoke fill the valley - a vile job well done.

We make good speed towards the bottom of the valley and make hard ground as the snow returns, filling the air with a myriad of flakes, obscuring the view. The drivers do their best to keep up the speed - the rest of the day is a race between snow covering low ground and reaching the coast.

The plunge into the river catches me by surprise amid my grim thoughts, and I stare through the porthole. The visibility is down to a few yards, but I can see the lights of Grey above the earthen wall. The lead transporter sounds its siren briefly, and gates begin to roll open.

I shake my head in resignation and begin to roll up my bedroll as the lead transporter rattles on the cobblestones. I hear the greetings at the barrack wall and begin to heft my bag towards the ladder.

It is snowing so hard that our tracks are already obscured as I emerge from the rear hatch, staring down at my feet. I lift my gaze to see a crowd of women whose eyes are piercing mine.

I merely shake my head and drop my bag on the ground. Someone will attend to it, for what I have to do next sickens my heart.

I take a long time to tell the story to the relatives of the dead men, doing my best to ignore their desperation and tears. I don't stop until it is done, and I conclude by dropping on my knees in the snow to ask their forgiveness.

Somewhere in the fog I see Nellie. She stands next to an ageing woman with faded blonde hair, and they lean into each other. Belatedly I recall that one of the merchants was Nellie's cousin.

It becomes too much at just that instant, and I bow my head, kneeling in the snow in front of the small crowd. Snowflakes sting my forehead as I stay still, trying to gather my thoughts. I feel the cold through my wet knees, but the shame burning inside me makes the rest of my feelings remote and worthless.

A heavy hand lands on my shoulder, and I look up. Redmond stands over me, his face creased with sorrow. I turn away and see that the women are gone.

"It is done, Commander," he places both hands around my shoulders and pulls me upwards. "You must go inside and get warm."

I nod numbly and clamber to my feet. Redmond leads me towards my quarters, where Trevor holds open the door with a look of utter disdain.

"Fuck the lot of them," he mutters. "As if these parasites didn't grow fat for three generations, sitting like kings inside your transporters. While we bled and died to keep them safe. Well, it doesn't always work out, and they fucking well knew that, young Ritter."

"That may be," I am somewhat taken aback by his vehemence. "But fire and water, Trevor - they were my customers, and they died under my protection."

He staggers towards me and crushes my wrist in his enormous hand, bringing his broken face close to mine.

"You did everything right, young Ritter. I do not

know the details, but I know that you did. You always did everything right, from the day you stopped wearing nappies. There was bad luck, and men died."

I nod, and he brings his face even closer, snarling.

"So fucking what? It's war."

I open my mouth to say that we weren't at war with Brana, but close it firmly. Brana was at war with us.

"Shut your fucking mouth and get inside," Trevor pulls me towards the door.

I lapse into silence, moving like a machine as I am led into the warmth. Trevor drops to the floor to untie my boots, and a sharp blow to my thigh tells me to raise my foot whilst he holds the sodden leather to the floor.

He makes me leave my clothes in a wet pile by the door and pushes me between shoulder blades, aiming towards the bathroom. I tread on the cold floor still dazed, opening the heavy door to be met by a cloud of steam.

The bath is so hot that I need to climb into it gradually, wincing from the sting. Once in it up to my waist, I splash water on my face and torso, gradually warming up.

After I lie back into the steaming depth, Trevor brings me a glass of berry gin and some dry fish. I let my body float in the wide bath, listening to the gurgling in the pipes that take cooling water to the furnace and return it steaming hot. The bathroom ceiling is draped in ferns, growing in wide pots suspended from the ceiling, and a single candle plays on my glass of berry gin, still full after a few mouthfuls that I don't really care to follow up on.

A very long time later I finish the gin, blunder upstairs and collapse into my bed, staring at the fire that glows in the grate. There is a thick layer of snow on the windowsill, and I can feel the cold coming off the glass. I hope, staring at the blizzard that rages into the night, that the sentries on the wall are not fooled by the silence - but there is little else left of me.

I slide under the thick blanket, and merciful darkness takes me away from my fears.

{}{}{}

The next morning I am awakened by Trevor. His cold, bony hand clutches my shoulder and shakes me awake hard enough to hurt.

I open my eyes and stare at him expectantly. He takes away his hand and shakes his head with disapproval.

"You need to get dressed and come quickly, Commander."

I fulfil that instruction with drill precision, and Trevor gives me a cup of warm tea on the way out the door. I drink as he ties my laces to save time, then gird myself with the pistol belt and hang a dagger around the neck. Trevor checks my uniform with a jaundiced expression and opens the door after satisfying himself that I am dressed as befits my position.

Redmond is at the wheel of a small truck we use to

get around town. I step over its low side, and he releases the steam as soon as I am seated.

"When you are ready," I tell him as we roll through the gate. He is headed towards the wall, and I know precisely what he is about to tell me.

"There's been an intrusion last night, Commander," says Redmond heavily. "Two killed that we know of."

"How was it repelled? I didn't hear anything."

"It wasn't repelled, Commander," I now stare at Redmond as he crouches towards the dashboard with fury all over his round face. "They came and went pretty much as they pleased."

I open my mouth in horror.

"The sentries were asleep in the tower," he tells me through clenched teeth. "But as if that isn't bad enough - they were killed in their sleep."

"So they opened the doors?"

"They did, and they did so silently, Commander. "How can animals do that?"

I stare ahead for a few moments, then shake my head in disapproval.

"We are all animals, Red. Never underestimate the enemy. Remember what the ancients said about pride."

"Whom the gods set out to destroy they first make proud."

"That's right, sergeant. Let's call things by their right

names - they are no more animals than we are."

He nods and concentrates on driving, and I ask no more, lost in thought. We soon reach the wall, where I nimbly clamber over the side of the truck and survey the scene.

There are many tracks in the snow, and it is no longer possible to see where the vermin had been - but one hopes, after a little reflection, that they did not enter any houses as no tracks lead that far. That much would have been obvious to those who first arrived on the scene at dawn, trudging to accept a change of guard through deep snow.

I climb onto the wall and march along the parapet, its snow coating also trampled beyond all salvation. There is better material to be seen beyond the wall, where a wide swathe of footprints leads towards the river. I study the long furrow in its middle, made by crouching and crawling through the snow by at least four heavy bodies. The came in precisely like I would have done it.

The interior of the guard tower is crimson with blood. I study the line of streaks - it looks as if one of the dead men had his throat bitten out, and he spun down, spraying blood high up the timber wall. There is a large pool of congealed blood in the centre of the platform. There are a number of footprints around it, made by feet that trod into the blood.

"What do you make of this, Red - four, six attackers?"

"I say four," he tells me gravely. "But that is not all. I brought you here for another reason, Commander. Let me assure you, I did not interrupt your rest just for the bad news - that could have waited upon your awakening."

I nod shortly, my bowels tightening into a ball. That's the longest speech Redmond ever made, and I have a feeling that he is about to tell me precisely what I fear.

I follow him to the corner of the platform, avoiding the bloody stains on the floor as much as we can. He crouches down to point at the floor near his feet.

I crouch down beside him and see a large print of a naked foot with a high, graceful arch and a broad spread of toes. The heel is narrow and long, and it is not hard to see that it is lined with parallel scars, which are clearly visible in the print on the timber.

"Left foot..." I whisper in horror. "Red, this is the one who kicked at my grate..."

Redmond nods appreciatively.

"I heard you were a mighty tracker in your day, Commander - and I am not disappointed. Yes, that is what I think too. Well, there can't be much mistake about it. But just to be sure..."

He removes a patch of cloth from the breast pocket of his tunic and places it over the footprint, rubbing it with the heel of his hand. When he lifts the cloth, I see that the blood had soaked into the material, making an exact image of the imprint.

We leave the tower and ride back to the base in silence. I wave my hand with impatience as the sentry at the fence salutes me instead of cranking open the gate. He rushes at the task, and we drive past him, spraying his post with dirty snow.

The lead transporter is parked at the end of the hangar, and Redmond walks to the tool rack to return with a short ladder. He places the ladder next to the turret and climbs. Gingerly placing his boot over the spiked surface of the roof, he leans close to the porthole and holds the cloth against the sharp grill made of old knives.

Even from the ground I can see that the two patterns match. Redmond climbs down slowly, and such is his agitation that he neglects to replace the ladder. I heft it up and place it against the wall. No one is to know what we know - for now.

"Then it's true," I say ruefully. "His pack followed us all the way from Brana."

"So it appears, Commander."

"Is that something they are known to do?"

"Not to me, Commander. One of the old hunters may know, but we cannot trust anyone outside the Regiment."

I nod.

"Whether or not they have done this in the past, the fact is, they have done it now," I say slowly. "They not only followed us, but came through the defences with great skill."

"Such as they are - the defences. I don't wish to speak ill of the dead - but they did not fire a single shot. Both must have been deep asleep on guard duty."

"We must reinforce them with our men from tonight," I say curtly. "As soon as possible I will meet with the Council and ask them to string bell lines along the wall and cover the approaches with dry branches, as we do on convoys. They are not to learn the true reason, Red - there are enough townspeople who hate us as it is."

"Could we follow them?"

"We can and we won't," I respond instantly and with force. "Look, they are a formidable enemy, Red. For all you know, he will set a trap. I don't want to lose men like that."

"You say 'he'!" Redmond smiles, folding the cloth.

"I did," I remove it from his hand and stuff it into my pocket. "I have seen him."

"And you say he will set a trap?"

"Someone who has planned all this will easily know how to rig an ambush," I reply irritably. "Run in a straight line down into a gully, then double back, wait for the pursuers on either ridge and attack from each side. It is child's play."

"What about an airship?"

"If one takes off in this weather - you go."

"I will make the arrangements, Commander," says Redmond stiffly.

"That was a joke, old friend," I place my hand on his shoulder. "You will do nothing of the kind. I cannot stand the thought of an airship dropping into a forest when that thing is lurking around, hatching plans."

"Are you just letting him go?"

"Yes. He will come to us himself. You and I need to think how we can make that come about."

"Very well, Commander. I still think we should chase him before anything else develops."

"Your advice is noted with respect, but we are not up for another excursion at the moment. Questions will be asked, and we would be blamed for stirring up another disaster."

Redmond thinks about this for a while.

"We are both soldiers, Red - but I am also the public face of The Regiment. As a soldier, I agree with you. As the owner of a business, I cannot afford to draw attention to what we just found."

"What then?"

"Let's not speak of strengthening outer defences. Let's just reinforce the night watch with our men and make sure we are ready for them when they return."

"Your orders, Commander."

"Two men for each guardhouse every shift. Four more in a machine - use the lead transporter and stop near the southern wall. That is where they are likely to try next time."

"Lead transporter?"

"Fully fuelled and loaded with ammunition, Red. Rounds and mortars. Anything that comes over the wall should be incinerated."

"Consider it done, Commander. Anything else?"

"Call the airship pilot. I need to speak with him."

"Are you going over the forest?"

"No, Red. I must get to the whalers again. Family business."

He nods with a quick glance in my direction.

"Will you go alone, Commander? It is not safe any more."

"I will take Tannis. He knows his way around that flea paradise. Any more would disrupt the negotiations."

"I thought we won't be using whale oil any longer."

"We were less than successful, Red. Corpses do not have enough fat on them. We got so little glycerine from boiling them down that it wasn't worth the firewood - and I am thinking of a long winter ahead."

Redmond bows slightly out of respect for my wisdom, which makes me feel even worse. I detest lying to my men.

"I will have the pilot call around immediately, Commander. You should get some rest this afternoon."

"Is something happening tonight?"

"There is a children's concert, Commander. We are providing the band."

"You are right," I tell him with a smile, but fatigue overtakes me just at that moment, and I yawn. "Tell the pilot to see me tomorrow morning. I will want to sleep now."

{}{}{}

A morning breeze tugs at the long anchor lines. The metal tower is creaking and swaying slightly as Tannis and I climb the steep staircase towards the landing platform.

The great engines are roaring above, filling the air with acrid smoke. The vast hull of the airship is now tight with hot air, and it pulls at the tower, threatening to tear it out of the concrete foundation. I am glad to complete the climb and squeeze into the tiny door amid the resin-lined canvas.

The interior of the machine is no better - noisy and bitterly cold, despite the exhausts blowing hot air into the double hull. The crew greet us with sullen smiles and motion towards the front, where a spiral ladder leads into the gondola.

I know the pilot well - he is nearly the same age. That is quite an achievement for both of us - I, who spent a lifetime in the forest, and he, who spent a lifetime flying sacks of hot air above vermin-ridden land and monster-ridden sea.

As soon as we are seated, the airship slips its

moorings, and the wind carries it away - inland, of course, in the wrong direction. The engine noise becomes overwhelming as the pilot strains to bring us back on course, and we pass over Grey slowly, gathering speed despite the steady ocean breeze. The vibration steadies as we reach cruising speed. I glance across at Tannis - he stares straight ahead, vast jawline set in a tense grimace. I form a fist and hit him quite hard on the shoulder.

"It will be unpleasant," I explain as if to a child. "But I need you to act. It would be much better if you are not recognized."

He swallows and nods grimly. I say no more and turn away, staring at the green sea. It's very rough this morning, with white-topped waves stretching across the horizon. I find myself wishing that we flew higher. I always wish that when I am in an airship.

The flotilla is easy enough to locate - a thick pall of greasy smoke drifts from its power plant over the rough seas. I look over the pilot's shoulder, noting that it hasn't changed in size since my last ignominious visit to this ramshackle archipelago, made up of large disused ships, their hulls half-filled with rocks for ballast and sealed against the elements. They are welded together to form a rather large and stable structure, which drifts a few miles offshore. The currents seem to prevent it from going too far - which is, in many ways, a pity.

The inhabitants of this creation are just a step above the vermin of the forest - violent, filthy men with barely intelligible speech. They live from one drink of rough liquor to the next, fishing and whaling to sustain their wretched existence. They do not, of course, live very long, and there are few women here. The numbers are replenished by renegades from the settlements - escapees from justice or personal revenge.

There is only one law on this floating den - the word of its captain, who is chosen from their number by a crude ballot. Most disputes are solved with boning knives on the spot, and the captain's time is mainly spent on commandeering men to deal with engineering issues.

The present captain has proved something of a survivor, despite the prodigious amount of liquor he poured down his throat in between acts of governance. Perhaps that was the secret of his survival - he made too few decisions and hasn't yet stumbled across anyone who would translate a grudge into action. Ordering half-animals to drop whatever they are doing to stop something leaking or sinking is not conducive to a long life.

The airship slows down and drifts towards the flotilla on minimal engine power, the crew readying the rope ladder. A young airman with bulging shoulders stands at the door with an unhappy look - I surmise that his job is to climb down to the rank platform beneath us and find suitable anchorage. There are no towers for airships here, and we make do with whatever looks stable on the day.

Some moments later Tannis and I gird ourselves into harnesses, which we latch onto the proffered ropes. The airman who mans the door unwinds the capstan as the climber descends, preventing it from paying out freely. Then I grasp the rails, turn and find the first rung on the ladder.

Climbing rope ladders has to be my least favourite adventure - the cursed thing twists and shifts away from the climber, making it hard for my ageing and aching body to complete the climb with the aplomb that goes with my reputation. Even Tannis has trouble, losing the footing a number of times and taking advantage of his enormous strength to hold on. In the end, he gives up wrestling with the rungs and simply climbs down arm-over-arm.

We straighten our tunics and march across filthy decks, up and down slippery ramps and past half-naked savages, who mainly lie on the deck, soaking up the rare sun. The cold breeze does not seem to concern them, even though most of them look drunk.

My revulsion with the stench of rotting fish, sewerage, whale oil and acrid smoke just about makes me turn back by the time Tannis stops and points at a shack-like structure surrounded by a crude fence of metal and wooden stakes entangled in barbed wire. I nod, and we approach the two thugs who guard the entrance in lock step.

"Commander Ritter to see your captain," I bark at them as if my presence is their fault.

My voice and name still have an effect as belligerence dies in their eyes. The thugs exchange a look of uncertainty and one glances at the shack as if to ask for approval from its invisible occupant.

"I do not have all day," I bark in the same tone. "Report my presence instantly, or I will ask the captain to have you both flogged."

One of the thugs turns without a change of expression and shambles into the shack without knocking. He emerges quickly.

"Wait here," he rasps in a voice that sounds simply disused.

A little while longer, and I see the captain at last - a shrivelled, stooped man with a scraggy grey beard below a naked skull covered in scars and dents. The bulbous nose sits in a nest of bushy moustache, and the blue eyes are hopelessly marooned behind sacks of wrinkled skin of his cheeks. He walks with a meandering gait of an old drunk, and there is no doubt that he is heavily intoxicated.

"Ritter, you old bruiser," is all he says, stopping just behind his guards. "Be careful with this one, boys - he can kill both of you with one little finger."

I stand still, looking at him coldly.

"And who is your apprentice?" asks the captain, stabbing a dirty, trembling finger at Tannis. "Looks like a worthy successor to you, anyway - do you eat those you kill, boy? Has Ritter taught you by now?"

"We would not start here for fear of poisoning," I reply calmly, stepping forward to conceal a warning to Tannis - I bump the knuckles of my right hand over his forearm. "If you are quite finished with small talk, dear captain, there is business to discuss."

He turns without a word, jerking his thumb for us to follow him inside. That is not something I relish - an animal enclosure at the end of winter is a paradise of sweet smells compared with the evil stench of the captain's quarters. Thankfully, the captain is smoking weed, and the smoke from his pipe dulls some of the contenders for the worst I am likely to experience.

He motions for us to sit down, lowering his backside onto a greasy sofa which barely sags with his weight. Tannis fetches a wooden bench from the corner, its ancient surface seemingly free of dirt. I sit down, with Tannis standing next to me, his trunk-like arms hanging loosely by his sides.

I scan the cabin until I locate the book shelves. There are indeed quite a few books, and they seem to be free of dust.

"I came to ask that you render us assistance," I tell the captain, watching an ugly smirk spread over the yellowing face. "Something of mutual benefit - we wish to construct another port, which will benefit your enterprise as well as mine."

"How can I participate in this worthy venture?" he relights the pipe and billows out a cloud of rancid smoke.

"I wondered if you have any ancient charts in your library," I point at the shelves behind him.

"Oh," the captain's eyes are half-shut as he sucks on the pipe. "Charts of the coastline?"

"Yes, and maps inland. We need to think through a new transport route."

"I may do, Ritter. I may - but that is not what you are after, is it?"

I feign irritation.

"Kindly explain yourself and remember whom you are about to insult."

He smiles wickedly and waves the pipe in censure.

"You are a dangerous animal, Ritter," he says sternly. "A killer with brains - why, there is nothing more lethal in creation. But you made a mistake bringing my old bum boy here. Little Tannis - how you have grown."

Tannis jerks slightly and grows perfectly still.

"There are so many aching, hungry pricks who miss little Tannis," muses the captain, revelling in his exposure of our game. "And more than a few who would slit his throat. You see, Ritter, Tannis did not say his proper goodbyes when he ran away to become a land rat."

"I have something to say," Tannis suddenly comes to life and approaches the sofa, and a look of fear infiltrates the captain's features as the giant stands over him, blocking most of the light that seeps through a dirty window.

"What may that be, Tannis?" the captain forces

himself to smile as he sets down his pipe.

"I have a message to you from my brother," says Tannis softly.

I am just as startled as the captain when Tannis rams his fist into the captain's midriff. It doesn't look as if a lot of force went into the blow, but the captain collapses like a rag doll, sliding onto the floor where he loudly exhales, doubling up at Tannis' feet. His body jerks once and grows still.

I leap to my feet to flip the captain on his back, but the trickle of bright blood in the corner of the mouth says everything the wide-open eyes do not - something fragile must have burst inside, killing the wretch instantly.

I look up at Tannis, who stares back, statue-like. He is not in the least remorseful.

"This is not very convenient," I mumble, thinking very quickly. "Fetch one of those bottles."

Tannis reaches over without looking and hands me a bottle of foul liquor brewed from fermented fish guts on the flotilla. I twist the wax seal and wrinkle my nose at the smell.

"Put him on the couch now that you have already touched him," I tell Tannis. "You are a messy boy."

He smiles, realizing that I do not hold his actions against him.

"Wipe off the blood with that blanket and cover him.

Oh, and close those foul eyes."

Tannis complies. Now the captain looks very peaceful - as if in a deep, drunken sleep. It is almost enough to make me envious.

I pour the liquor over the face and into the half-open mouth, douse the front of my tunic, then set the bottle next to the sofa and look up at Tannis.

"Find that book of maps."

Tannis rushes over to the shelves and looks through the titles. I can see that he is unsuccessful and motion for him to slow down, keeping a wary eye on the door.

"I am very sorry," says Tannis after a while. "I remember the book well, but it's not here."

"Hmm," I manage in reply. "Look again."

After a little while we walk out the door. I manage to look a little drunk, waving to the sentries in a light-hearted manner. They stare at us but make no move in response.

Once we are out of their sight we begin to walk as quickly as we can without drawing unwanted attention. I have a little trouble getting my legs into the harness, and the airman at the bottom of the ladder has to help.

"We need to leave quickly," I tell him as he pulls to tension the ladder. His eyes go wide, and he opens his mouth.

"Don't speak and keep calm, or we are all dead," I tell him with a smile, then begin the climb.

As soon as all three of us are inside, I tell the pilot to run for our lives. The whaling guns have great power, and the only thing that can give us safety is height - their projectiles are heavy darts that cannot sustain much of a vertical rise.

The wind carries us away from the flotilla as the engines are started, and I feel great relief once we are too far to be fired upon. Mind, that is not the end of the matter, I tell Tannis - but with any luck the captain's death will be put down to ill health.

Tannis stares at the breakers on the water as we approach land.

"I am sorry, Commander," he says simply.

"I am too. He could have told us where the book was."

"No, Commander. He would have done no such thing. I am not sorry I killed him - but I am that he died with the first blow."

I contemplate his statement.

"Under our law you have that right," I tell him pensively, suddenly overtaken by fatigue. "From what I know, you had more than enough cause to kill him."

"Yes."

I avoid looking at Tannis, who sounds as if he is sobbing, staring through the window towards Grey and its wall - how small it looks from the air. Well, it is small - anyone can climb up its steep bank, provided he is not shot by vigilant sentries.

"Where do you think the book is now?"

"I would say it's gone," says Tannis. "He probably used it to light the fire on a cold night - after all, there was nothing to read. It was all maps. He would not have wiped his arse on it."

I smile at his certainty.

"Why not?"

"The whalers never wipe their arses, Commander. It is not their way."

"Box of bullets," I mutter in disgust. "It's just as well you killed him with one punch. Do wash your hands before you eat."

The airship cuts its engines and drifts towards the tower on the wind. I study the sad landscape below - sagging roofs, dirty, cramped streets and chimneys that emit tepid wisps of smoke as the afternoon turns to cold. Even the smokestacks of the Regiment are bereft of decent smoke.

We tie up, and I stroll onto the tower platform, grateful for feeling something solid under my feet. The engine fumes make me nauseous, and I hurry to climb down a steep stairwell, where I see Redmond next to a small truck.

He asks no questions as he drives us back to the barracks. Our dejected expressions tell him all there is to tell.

"Come in for a drink," I order them, signalling to Trevor. He nods and disappears inside the door to lay out some refreshments.

We sit down next to the fire licking a few logs of green wood and click clay goblets brimming with berry gin. I drink mine in one gulp, and Tannis does likewise.

"Not a success?" Redmond asks at last.

"We had to fucking kill him," mumbles Tannis. I do not elaborate on his statement, and that is now an official truth.

"Long story," I add at last, cutting off the obvious question. "And here we are, empty-handed."

"Very sorry," says Redmond.

"No need - I am not," I reply gruffly. "What I am sorry about is that I had to mislead you, Red. This was not my cousins' business at all."

I fill him in on what Tannis told me.

"You would have insisted on coming along," I explain apologetically. "I wanted to keep it simple."

Redmond massages his grey temples and finally nods forgiveness.

"I am sure it was for the best, Commander," he says tactfully. "What of it all now?"

"We are back to square one," I tell him. "No book, no coal, no work."

"We have enough provisions to last the winter," says

Redmond, raising the goblet to his lips and wetting them with gin. "Something will come up by then."

"Yours is always a voice of good hope, Red."

"No, Commander - something will truly come up."

"What might that be?"

"Think clearly, Commander. We live in a world of killing and rapine. Yes?"

"Without a doubt."

"And we are the best cut-throats left, are we not?"

"That is so to my knowledge."

"Then how can we run out of work?"

We stare at each other and laugh. I refill the goblets and we drink again. This time all three of us drain the gin to the last drop.

{}{}{}

Old Manfred, the president of the town council, stares at me with frank distaste. I stare somewhere above his head, signalling my contempt for his proceedings and his purpose.

They call him old, but he is actually younger than I by some years. Life has not been kind to him - he nearly died of lung rot as a child, and that left him weak and mean. He is not my only enemy, but he is probably worth all of the others combined.

"You know, Manny," I tell him, using the childhood

name he detests with a passion. "I like my enemies."

"Please entertain us with an explanation, Commander," rasps Manfred, wiping his blue lips with a sleeve. His jowled face is brimmed by long, grey hair. The beard does not grow so well, and he shaves it to perfection each day.

"You see, my enemies are out to hurt me," I tell him with a smile. "They brandish their weapons and make faces. I see this and get ready to fight back. It keeps me strong and full of purpose, for which I am grateful. I can even go so far as to say I enjoy my enemies."

Members of the council ready themselves for one of my famous ripostes. They are not a healthy crop, the current guardians of public order - weak, pudgy men whose pale, soft hands had never known the cold, hard feel of a weapon. They have slack and glassy eyes that never frightened anyone apart from their servants. I grow angry - being able to order a kitchen maid to lift her dress does not qualify a man to be my adversary. That is an insult in itself.

"The ones I fear call themselves my friends," I finish my explanation. "See, I don't have friends. I have weapons, and I have subordinates. Understand?"

They stare at me as I rise to my feet, resplendent in my dress uniform - black trousers in knee-high leather boots and a long red tunic with braids of gold. I wear a pistol in a large leather holster, and my combat knife hangs from my neck. I hold my fur hat with the family crest in my left hand, stiffly bent at the elbow. The sight is meant to intimidate, and I wear it for that purpose.

"You fuckers just get in the way," I thunder at the council bench. "You snipe behind my back, spin webs and tell lies. For no better reason that being scared of me and my men."

"It is right that we should be scared of you, Ritter," rasps Muldon, the council elder. He is huddled in a fur coat and hat, his long, pointy nose being the only prominent feature.

"My family has served this town for three generations without fail," I shout back. "For fifty years your town has hosted the last real fighting force left on this earth, and we are yet to run over a rat in this town - that's how much of a threat we are! What people should be scared of is this Council - I have never seen a less disciplined horde in charge of our affairs, and that frightens me more than what is in the forest!"

One of the men in the audience raises his hand, and I turn to stare. He is a large, handsome fellow with a mane of red hair - a blacksmith, judging by tiny holes in his tunic that has seen too many washes and hangs on his mighty shoulders like a sack.

"The council recognizes honourable Otto, son of Johann," drones Manfred. I do recall the name - he is one of the men from my cousins' works.

Otto stares at me without fear, and I nod to him with the respect that deserves.

"It seems to me that there is no good explanation for

what happened in Brana," says Otto. "We have no choice but to take the soldiers' word for it, but it's a great mystery to me - why a town would cut its own throat that way."

I nod - just once. Otto is now a little out of his depth - he expected a gushing explanation, but instead there was only the acknowledgement: yes, it is a great mystery - what now?

"I therefore believe that we need to go back," says Otto in a stronger voice. "We need to find out what happened."

"Do you have relatives in Brana?" asks Manfred acidly. "We expect all who speak at this assembly to declare their interests."

"I do have relatives there," replies Otto tartly. "My first woman's sister and her surviving children. She wanted to lie with me when my woman was still on her deathbed. I threw her out of the house, and that is why she went to marry some poor madman in Brana. We have never heard from each other since. I wish her nothing but warts and miscarriages."

There is a thunderous laughter in the hall.

"The assembly will come to order," shouts Manfred. "Silence, damn you!"

I allow the merriment another few poignant moments, then raise my hand. There is instant silence, which brings a pained grimace to more than a few faces on the council bench.

"Please continue, honourable Otto," I say quietly, just to rile Manfred. It is not my place to chair the assembly.

"I care nothing for my so-called relatives," replies Otto. "But Brana is a town of five thousand souls, and it is also our last remaining trading partner. The others count for nothing."

"Your sentiments are excellent," says Manfred. "What do you say, Ritter?"

"Take care how you address me," I smile at him dangerously. "What am I to you - a rat from beneath the boardwalk?"

"I beg forgiveness," replies Manfred with an oily smile. "Commander Ritter, please comment on the proposal we just heard."

"Very well. Do you want to find out what happened in Brana?"

"We do!" I hear a woman shout from the stalls. There is murmur that seems largely supportive.

"Then go." I sit down and rest my hands on my pistol belt. "I will be pleased to give you directions."

"You seem to mock this assembly, Commander," hisses Muldon, leaping to his feet. "That is unbecoming."

"I do mock you," I reply without standing up, which is a grave discourtesy in the assembly hall. "All I will do is mock - for I will surely not risk my men to return to Brana. That would be very foolish, and I never make the same mistake twice."

"Even if the town paid you?" asks a young voice. I turn to see Simon, the priest of the old faith in his black robe, a large metal cross hanging from a heavy chain on his chest.

"Payment is not the issue," I explain patiently. "Danger is not the issue. But senselessness is - I will not go there and back just to hear the same drivel from Josiah. Now, if someone puts up the goods for an invasion - I will consider it, but not before spring."

There is a lot of muttering in the stalls as people discuss my statement.

"In fact, that is all I have to say," I tell Manfred. "As you know, The Regiment does not take orders from the Council."

"That is outrageous, Commander," shouts a rotund councillor with a bald head, whose names escapes me just now. As I recall, he was a tax collector in his youth, until we abolished taxes and money. He now sells what passes for firewood.

"I'll tell you what is outrageous," I stand up and stare at him, a thin smile playing on my lips. "You make young mothers lie with you in exchange for wet logs that smoulder instead of warming their children. If one of them was my daughter, I would challenge you to a death match. I suspect you would burn better than your wood."

He recoils at my words, colour fading on his face.

165

"A cheap thing to say, Commander - knowing as you do that dry firewood is not available for love or gold. I burn wet wood in my own grate, as do you in yours. Now, back to business at hand - the council does have the power to compel you."

"You have the power to order," I rasp, resisting the urge to shout. "But I remind you what the law really says. Any citizen who is given an order by the council has a choice - to obey or to leave Grey unimpeded, with all possessions, within one moon."

Deathly silence now reigns in the hall.

"Are you suggesting that The Regiment might leave Grey?" asks Muldon incredulously.

"I am not suggesting it. I state it for all to hear. We are free to leave any time we want. It would not be our first choice, but yes, we can do that if you so prefer."

I pause and stare around the hall.

"We can stay or leave, but what we will never do is take your orders! Spend thirty summers in the forest, and then I may care what you think! Until then - I and my sergeants are the only ones to whom my men will entrust their lives!"

My shouts echo around the hall and die away. I sit down and stare at the wall above the Council bench wearily.

"We do not mean to order you to do anything," says Muldon carefully. "You are the present Commander, and no one questions your record at this post."

"As Commander, only I make decisions. I will decide whether I will invade Brana. Furthermore, there is no law outside the wall."

"But the Council..."

"You have powers to make laws about what happens here, in Grey," I circle my hand in the air, tracing the directions of the town wall. "You have the right to disregard my recommendations about town security, and it is within your legal power to get men killed on the wall for nothing. Yes. But you cannot order us to do something outside the town gate. That is for us to decide at our own risk, and the law is on our side."

"I don't think this is right," says Manfred, staring around the council bench.

"Then read what the law says. The council has powers over town. All laws pertain to the town boundaries."

"With permission," says the young priest. Manfred nods.

"The council recognizes the Honourable..."

"Father Simon."

"Proceed."

"Commander is entirely correct," says Simon. "I have studied law, and that is exactly what it says."

Manfred looks around the council but finds no useful support for either assertion.

"Let us assume that you are right, Honourable Father. What now?"

"We need to abandon all talk of compulsion and overriding the chain of command," says Father Simon, fingering his cross for support. "If Commander Ritter does not find it in his conscience to help, we need to look past him."

"Just stop right here," I leap to my feet. "You are talking about traversing one hundred and fifty miles of forest each way. Also crossing the mountains. And vermin following you all the way, just waiting for you to make a single mistake."

"Some of us have faith," replies Father Simon earnestly. "We believe that we are not alone, and that God in heaven loves us and cares for us."

"Certainly, you can see his love every day," I tell him vehemently. "His love wets our firewood and kills our babies with cold. That is love indeed."

The young priest colours, and, in truth, I feel a little pity. He doesn't know how many of his predecessors had drunk gin from my goblets, arguing this very dilemma from a gloomy winter's dusk to a hangover-ravaged dawn of the next idle day.

"I regret what happened in Brana," I tell the assembly. "It is my livelihood, if nothing else. But I did not cause it or contribute to it in any way. The guilty are those who govern Brana and hence the people who elected them. I have no pity for anyone but our merchants who were robbed and killed in cold blood."

"How do you know that the leaders were elected?" asks Otto. "Commander, our people had so little to do with Brana lately."

"Not many moons ago I saw Josiah go to the latrine," I tell him. "He went alone."

There are a few ribald remarks whispered out aloud, and islands of uncertain laughter erupt in the hall. I thrust my hand high in the air, and silence ensues once more.

"In our times life is worth very little," I explain, scanning the hall with my gaze. "Men who govern without popular acclaim need to be guarded. We are most vulnerable when we excrete and when we couple. A hated leader requires at least four men to guard his visit to the latrine."

There is a little laughter in the murmur, but it is subdued and respectful - trust old Ritter to think of something like that. I can see the consternation in the faces on the council bench, who are a bit of blur just now. I feel tremulous in the pit of my stomach and breathe deeply to keep control of my voice.

"I have no idea what came over the leaders of Brana," I add, holding up my hand to silence the hall. "But they had signed their death warrants when they killed men under my protection. I say that I have cause to seek revenge against them."

There is silence in the hall - it is not often that I declare a target for my revenge.

"Why don't you invade then?" I hear a shout from the stalls.

Manfred turns to the speaker and asks him to identify himself.

"I am Rutger, son of Holger. I am a builder of houses - or was, before our numbers began to shrink."

I turn to him and recall the man as much younger - his face is now an unhealthy red and bloated by gin. He sits next to a slight, grey-haired woman who holds his hand as he lumbers to his feet.

"We recognize Honourable Rutger and look forward to his wise counsel," says Manfred. There is a respectful murmur in the stalls - anything Rutger had built still stands - and stands straight.

"It is time to correct a great error," says Rutger in a deep, calm voice. "Founding Brana was foolish. This is an age when we should bring together what little we have left, not scatter it to four winds."

He pauses, allowing everyone to absorb the full weight of his words.

"It makes sense to invade Brana and force them to return," he says next.

I shake my head in silent disapproval, and the hall erupts in argument. I can hear people argue the proposal with something approaching fury, and I simply shake my head a few more times.

"Very well, come to order," shouts Manfred. I leave

him to his devices this time, and he leaps to his feet as his order is ignored.

"Come to order or clear the hall!" he shouts at the top of his voice. The noise dies down with some reluctance.

"We require a military opinion," says Muldon, staring at me. "Commander, let us have your assessment."

I take a deep breath and think momentarily.

"Let's assume that I agree to lead this mission," I begin slowly. "I would require most who can bear arms, and the armourers would need to arm them all. Whilst the Regiment is in Brana, the town guard would need to be strengthened."

"That would make for a busy winter, but the armourers can do that," says Rutger. "The soldiers can help make their weapons."

I nod in agreement.

"I would need to scale Brana's wall with an assault force and drop the bridge - assuming they rebuilt it. Otherwise we would need to mount a direct assault on the wall and probably sustain a number of casualties, despite superior fire power."

"You can do that," replies Rutger.

"Yes, indeed. But all that is a simple combat mission - the difficult part comes next."

I look around the faces in silence and continue a moment before they begin to call out.

"We then need to overpower ongoing resistance and persuade the population to move to Grey. How do you propose to do that, Honourable Rutger?"

"Simple. Burn the town."

I nod in thought, assessing the reaction in the stalls. It does not look as if that proposal has offended many people.

"Afterwards we would need to hold Brana whilst we run convoys back and forth. We may be able to use water if the rivers are high, but this cannot be counted on."

"Sounds fine to me," Rutger tells the stalls. "If we are lucky and build a few more transporters, we can manage before winter."

I close my eyes and think hard. Burning Brana will mean the end of my convoys, for sure and forever - but that seems to have happened anyway. I will be able to feed my soldiers for another season - and then, as Redmond pointed out, something is certain to crop up to keep The Regiment in business.

"The town would have to come up with all resources to keep my men fed and equipped," I tell Manfred. "We have to replenish our food stores, and if we go to Brana, we cannot fish."

The council men huddle towards the centre of their table, and their body language seems to suggest that they anticipated the proposal. I turn to stare at Rutger, who stares back at me with a wily expression. I sigh -

politics is repulsive.

Muldon stands up and raises his hand for silence.

"We believe that it can be done."

I clench my fists and increase the pressure until my knuckles begin to ache. Last words, and the matter is sealed. Or so they think.

"I am not going. Don't even bother voting on this."

"What the citizens vote on is not for you to decide, Commander," smiles Muldon thinly, and I can see that they think they have the deal in hand. It no longer matters how they will swindle the ballot - but it is clear that they will.

I sit down to indicate the end of my interest in the matter. There is loud murmur in the stalls, then Manfred stands to declare the assembly concluded.

As everyone trickles out of the hall, I sit back and watch the flow of bodies through the door. Mostly young, mostly thin, mostly pale. We can burn Brana and haul its people back here - but that would simply mean more thin, pale citizens who don't live to grow old.

I rise. Redmond and Tannis rise and follow me outside. The air is rank with acrid smoke from wet wood. We stroll towards the gates of the barracks in fine drizzle, icy breeze biting our cheeks.

"One more thing, Commander," says Redmond from behind. I stop and turn towards him.

"Something I noticed in Brana," says Redmond. "It

was at the back of my mind, and I just realized what it was."

I nod sourly, entirely familiar with that state of mind.

"As we were getting ready to leave, they were stoking up their electricity plant," says Redmond.

I nod, recalling the smoke pouring from the chimney.

"They were preparing to pump water on the fire."

"Yes, with electric pumps. Now, you went inside the turret, Commander. I stayed outside to check the tracks."

I nod, this time in gratitude. Redmond had not forgotten, despite the confusion of that day, to walk around the transporters for a final check - an obligatory procedure before each departure.

"The wind changed, and it carried the smoke towards me, Commander. I smelt it."

My eyes narrow, as I stare at him.

"It wasn't peat, Commander."

My heart begins to thump. I think I know what he might say next.

"I think they were using the black stone of the ancients. It has a strong smell and leaves a bitter taste on the tongue."

"Are you sure it was that?"

"I saw a large pile of it in Brana. I understood what it was after you told me about your hunt for the ancient maps."

"Where did you see it?"

Near the market, just where we helped the merchants unload."

I nod thoughtfully.

"That is why they wanted metal - they were probably going to forge weapons. That's another reason to meet up with Josiah. Probably the best reason of all."

"What do you think the weapons were for?"

"I would not be surprised if he is planning to attack us."

I turn and walk to the gate slowly. Redmond and Tannis level with me instead of marching behind.

"Can they succeed?" asks Tannis.

"No," Redmond shakes his head vigorously. "They are just a rabble. You saw that when we ran - a properly organized force would have stopped us within moments."

"I am tired of discussing Brana," I tell them with finality. "Simply, it is all about the fuel. Either we get it and live in warm houses, or we don't, and Grey dies out in another few generations."

"Yes," says Redmond. "It is that simple."

"The ballot will be held in a few days," says Tannis. "Do we tell them?"

I walk ahead, concentrating hard. We almost reach the gates when I turn around and shake my head. No one would believe us if we came out with this now. It would only discredit me.

"We say nothing. I am not going back."

{}{}{}

I awaken, savouring the soft warmth of the bed. The light coming through the gaps in the thick drape indicates that I had slept until mid-morning, and I bolt out of bed, ignoring the protesting stiffness of my joints.

I open the window and attract the attention of the sentry.

"Call Sergeant Redmond to my quarters."

Some time later I am downstairs in my dressing gown. Redmond comes through the door and removes his boots on the mat. I hand him a steaming mug of berry tea, and we sit next to the fire.

"No."

I nod and stare at the flames. The good people of Grey voted against Rutger's idea. There will be no more talk of invasion.

"We need to think of another way to look for coal, Red."

"Yes, Commander. I thought we could take two airships when the spring winds settle. You know, explore around Brana. What would a coal mine look like?"

"Could be a big open pit in the ground that is easy to see. But it could be just a little hole, like an entrance to a cave. They could cover it up, and you won't see anything even if you stand next to it. "

He wags his finger.

"The stuff is heavy, is it not?"

"Like limestone, maybe."

"Then they would have to transport it with something, Commander. That means a well-worn track somewhere."

"Or a pier on the lake."

"We should be able to see it from above."

"Yes. Now it is time to rest from all this, Commander. I ordered the men to stoke up the baths. We must celebrate the end of the travelling season, no matter how it ended."

I pat him on the shoulder.

"I don't know what I would do without you, Red. Have you spoken to Nelly?"

Redmond's features crease apologetically.

"She didn't pull a knife like you predicted, Commander - but she doesn't want to see you again. With that cousin of hers killed in Brana, his wife lost a roof over her head. She and her children are now living with Nellie, who is not happy."

I sigh.

"That is sad but of little account - I am an old man."

"Should you change your mind, Commander - there are women aplenty."

"I know. It doesn't matter, believe me."

He smiles a secretive smile as he sets the empty mug on the low table and stands up, drawing to attention.

"Permission to go, Commander. There is much to organize - there is no dry stuff in the store whatsoever."

"Then use a little wood from the transporters to stoke up the fire, Red. It is an embarrassment when our baths aren't hot."

He nods and leaves me to my thoughts.

{}{}{}

I am actually awake.

That is not good news, as there is a tube in my throat. I raise my hand to pull on it, and a few moments later there is a rush of voices around me.

"Mr Tanner?"

I open my eyes and try to focus. The bright lights are very hurtful, and I blink hurriedly. Some kind soul turns off the ones over my bed, and I can see.

There is an older woman with kindly dark eyes and a mop of dyed blonde hair who gently restrains my hand, pulling it off the tube. I nod and let my hand drop. She smiles.

"We are glad to see you, Mr Tanner."

I try to form words with my lips, but the damn tube is in the way. Strangely, it does not irritate my throat like you would expect. It must have been there for some time.

"I will be back in a moment. We will see if we can get that horrible thing out of your airway."

I nod weakly and close my eyes, running my hand over my face and down my neck. They inserted the Hickman's line when the lights were out - I would love to know how long I had been unconscious, because the line site doesn't hurt either.

The bladder and bowel are thankfully empty - I missed these grand occasions in what must have been a long period of coma. I wiggle my pelvic floor experimentally and feel a slight drag from a urinary catheter. Small mercies.

The nurse returns and tells me the good news - I am to be extubated. I feel a tug and resist the urge to gag as the tube is pulled out of my throat. Then I open my eyes a moment too soon and see a long piece of plastic with a deflated balloon, covered in blood-stained mucus, being yanked out of my mouth.

I dry-retch, but there is nothing in my stomach.

"One more," the nurse tells me. I really gag as a smaller tube is slid out of my stomach, up the entire length of my gullet and out of my nose. This time I keep my eyes tightly shut until I hear her step away from the bed.

I try to speak, but only croaking sounds come out, as if I have severe laryngitis. She hands me a glass of water with a straw, and I drink a little. It feels wonderful in my parched mouth.

"You had a small stroke," she tells me. "They had to break into your flat."

I nod, awash with understanding. This is, of course, intensive care - as they say in the infantry, welcome to hell.

I look around and find hell not too bad - pastel colours, neutral temperature and a large spaceship-like central station bedecked with screens. I feel remarkably well, except that my legs are a little numb. I move them experimentally.

"It's the drugs," says the nurse, throwing back the sheet. "Hang on, I will secure the urinary catheter. You don't want to pull that off with the important bit."

I smile, feeling the world return to its rightful place. She performs her manipulations at the foot of the bed and then resurfaces, patting me on the shoulder.

"Take it slowly, soldier. You've been away for a while."

"How... long?" I still have to force out the words through my parched throat.

"Six days," she leans over and monitors me for a

reaction.

I shrug. Six days or six weeks - it's all the same to me. More importantly - I now have a bed.

"Have the oncologists been?" the words come a little easier now.

"They sure have. It seems that they need to get cracking - your blood has started to clot because of the leukaemia. They think that's what caused the stroke."

I nod and lie back. So - my next few weeks look spoken for. I run over things in my mind - everything was pretty much ready, and I presume they secured the flat after they found me. Too bad I can't please Helen - I so wanted to take her away for a surprise weekend with the gang. There would have been no shaggathons, for we are respectable, middle-aged citizens and some of us are even married. Well, so goes the euphemism. To call things by their real names - some of us can no longer get it up.

I smile at the memory of nights in Bruce Bay. My pulse must have sped up at some of the recollections, because my nurse is back, checking whether I am okay. I am, very much, I tell her.

She pats my shoulder, and I see moisture in her eyes. She probably read my story, and it is hard not to feel its pain - a still-young, well-to-do man with everything going for him. He should be playing beach cricket with his admiring kids, casting loving glances at his still-pretty wife. Instead, he is on his back in intensive care, and the latest threat to his survival is just a walk in the park compared to the real battle around the corner.

I sigh and reach out to touch her arm.

"How bad?"

"The stroke? You are missing some occipital cortex on the left side."

"We shall overcome," I tell her hoarsely. "So what does it mean in English?"

"It's the part of the brain that handles vision. You may not be able to see anything on one side. Maybe it will recover fully. We don't know yet."

I stare from side to side experimentally. Maybe I am not yet awake, but there seems to be no problem with my vision, I tell her.

She nods, her mouth tight with emotion. I am guessing she hasn't worked in this awful place for very long. There are only two ways to go in intensive care - in perpetual pain, punctuated by moments of triumph, or glass-eyed and numb to the suffering one sees each day. I guess it's no different to being a soldier - reality either pushes you towards insanity, or you burn circuits that feel pain and horror and become an extension of your weapon.

I ask if I can speak to the ward clerk. A mousy woman with dark brown hair and a huge bum waddles over, smiling reassuringly. I dictate some phone numbers and ask for her to make the calls.

My sister has to be told at once - if I ever get to the

nephew's party, it will be as day leave. I ask her to check with the building supervisor to ensure that the flat is all safe. I cannot remember going down and guess it must have happened as I was asleep. The paramedics often leave the scene untidy, and I hope that the building supervisor has been around afterwards.

I also tell her to call Helen and ask her to drop by. I had to think that one through - it will hurt her seeing me like this, but if she doesn't come, it will bother her more. The unseen is always far more frightening than reality.

These Herculean labours see to the last of my energy, and I feel utterly exhausted. Now that I have been back for a while, I am aware that anything in the right bottom corner of my vision is a blur.

I close my eyes. The guess is they will move me to another ward shortly, maybe in a few hours - and it is time to rest.

{}{}{}

The baths are wonderfully hot, and clouds of steam envelop the cavernous building which we built over the swimming area two winters ago. The lights shine dimly in the ceiling, and candles light the dark alcoves that make for wonderfully private bathing.

I stand at the door in dress uniform, welcoming guests. The Regiment is not as popular as it used to be, but there are plenty of ladies, all dressed in flowing capes with hoods, flowing through the doors. They wear nothing underneath. It is strictly prohibited to wear any clothing in the water.

The guests trudge into the baths past Solly, who ladles out gin into wooden mugs. They drink those whilst still in the queue for the dressing room and showers. Given the cold, the citizens of Grey avoid bathing, and anyone who enters the baths is required to wash all grime off their body before getting into hot water.

The soldiers are already in the tubs, sitting in the churning water up to their shoulders. The winter celebration is a rare opportunity to get warm, sitting in the water until eternally cold bones begin to throb with heat. We can only afford this extravagance once a year - it hardly makes a dent in our supply of gin, but the wood needed to heat the baths for a mere day is quite another matter.

As first stars begin to shine in the late autumn sky the flow of women begins to lighten, and by the time the sun sinks into the sea, I have stood outside all by myself for a good mug of gin and then some. I turn to enter the baths when I hear hurried footsteps on the barracks square and wheel about to face them.

"Father Simon, this is quite a surprise," I tell the priest with courtesy I do not feel. "You are most welcome all the same."

He stops next to me, breathing hard, and I stifle the next barb in my throat. Simon is a short, pudgy man with soft features and large brown eyes. He is clean-shaven, as attempts to grow a beard resulted in his chin being enveloped in childish fluff. The blonde hair is receding from a tall forehead that gives him a look of an older man, but there is something else, something that tells me not to demean him - the young man has a backbone. That much is evident from the penetrating look he now gives me.

"I am not here for your heathen orgy," he tells me in a precise, clipped voice. "We need to talk."

"That is not the best time, Father," I chide him gently. "My guests and my soldiers await me."

"Your cut-throats and your guests can drink themselves into madness and engage in fornication without your help, Commander."

"That is true," I smile politely. "Neither are strangers to such activities, my guests or my soldiers."

I nod to the sentries, and they salute, then turn on their heels and disappear into the darkness.

"I will not detain you for long," says Simon acidly. "But you would have heard by now."

"The ballot said not to go," I chime. "Of course, Father. I've heard."

"That is appalling. Thousands are in peril in Brana, and nobody wants to help them."

"It looks as if you are the only one who does."

"By God, yes," he whispers fervently, grasping my arm. I can smell something on his breath - it is not gin, no - it's the juice of a green berry that increases confidence and endurance.

"I want to put a private convoy together," he tells me.

185

"I know you won't go, but will you at least help us set up?"

I stare at him with new interest. Well, well. Josiah would have to watch his back if this one ever got to Brana. Too bad it will never happen.

"You must abandon such thoughts at once, Father," I tell him very firmly, pulling my forearm out of his grip. "It takes a lifetime of training and experience to survive a trip through the forest. Whatever you try, without me and my men you will be risking almost certain death."

"I am not afraid of death. A better world awaits me on the other side of it."

"Doesn't your faith prohibit suicide?"

"Of course."

"Then it commands you to stay put. But if you decide on suicide, it is best to cut just here," I point at a big vein on my neck. "Much nicer than dying in the forest."

"You are heartless, Ritter!" he shouts, stepping back. I hear heavy footsteps, and two sentries materialize from the twilight fog with guns at the ready. I wave them away, staring at the priest without anger.

"We've been over this in the assembly," I reply tiredly. "Neither you nor I have the means. The entire town has to support such a venture, and its people have spoken - they have no such wish. In any case, I am not interested."

"Do you know about the last transmission from

Brana?"

It is again my turn to be surprised.

"What transmission, Father?"

"There was a radio transmission from Brana today. They are under siege."

"Stop right here. What transmission?"

"High-frequency radio," he explains patiently. "A lot of my parish have relatives in Brana. That is how we stay in touch."

I shake my head in disapproval. The men of the old faith have been working on technology they chose not to share with the rest. It is never a good way to win good will when the truth eventually comes out.

"What siege?"

"The town wall is surrounded and besieged by vermin. They have failed to breach the defences so far, but there are heavy casualties."

I begin to feel my heart thump, and a heavy feeling returns to my left armpit.

"Besieged by vermin? Is that what I just heard you say?"

"Why does that surprise you?"

"Father," I sit down on a ledge near the doorway and rub my face with snow to ease the discomfort in my chest. "Vermin do not besiege. They are clever and nasty animals, but a siege is a military operation. They cannot do that."

"Don't be a fool, Ritter. Spread these lies if you want to, but spare me. I know the truth."

I look up and study his face - gone is the pudgy softness. The thin mouth is now set in a tight curve, and his wide, dark eyes bore into mine. The men of the old faith have chosen their leader well.

"There are many different truths..." I begin tartly, but the door flies open, and a giggling young girl rushes outside, her large breasts jiggling with her stride. She slips on the snow and falls face down, remaining sprawled on the cold ground as steam boils off her ungainly body. Even by the dim torchlight I can see her openings, swollen and dripping seed into the snow. The priest makes a gesture of the cross and turns away.

Solly rushes out with a vast, glistening erection at the ready. He salutes me rather comically and bends down, pulling the girl's backside up into the air. He thrusts to penetrate her, then grasps her under the arms and carries her inside as if she is weightless. I gingerly shut the door behind them and wait until the cloud of steam drifts away.

"That was disgusting," says Father Simon.

I turn to him with sudden anger.

"That is life, as it is lived by those still living. Save your breath, priest. I am not interested in your madness."

"Then you won't help your brothers?"

I round on him and stab both hands at his collarbones. He shudders as my grip tightens on his neck.

"They are not my brothers, Father," I make the last word ring with contempt to underline that he is nothing of the kind. "The people of Brana are murderers whom I owe revenge. If you care for them, pray that they never face my guns."

He stares at me defiantly.

"Your so-called brothers are no better than vermin!" I push him away lightly, but he stumbles backwards and falls into the snow. "Both devour their kind."

Entirely out of turn I realize that he had fallen in the same place as the girl, and the back of his cassock must be wet with Solly's seed. It's a ridiculous thought, and my anger leaves me at once.

The priest gathers himself up from the ground and staggers towards the gate. I wait until the sentries step towards him, then turn around and head back inside the baths.

I vaguely recall what came next. There was definitely a tub full of steaming and churning water. Two older women sat next to me, and I recall one of them say: "Foolish old Nellie, giving up a prize like that!", with her soft hand caressing my inner thigh.

I recall resting my head on someone's knees, staring up between her breasts and raising my hand to stroke the long, hard nipple. That seems to have taken place here, in my bed, and I recall the silky touch of the second woman's hair on my stomach. The recollection makes me hard as a rock, and I stretch out, opening my eyes.

I am still in my bed, and it is almost light. The women are still here, and it looks as if I can sneak out to the latrine before they awaken.

I accomplish that mission, to the relief of my throbbing bladder and with no casualties - the ladies are still in blissful slumber when I return, and I study them for a while. One is a widow of an armourer who blew himself up fine-tuning a new type of grenade fuse. I brush away the memory of his funeral, seeing her in the rain, long black hair draped over the dead man's chest. She had to be held down as the log floated away in the river...

I swallow hard.

The next few years have not been kind to her - there are many lines in the even oval of her face, and her once pert nose is now a little lumpy from too much gin. I can see strands of silver in her long hair, and there is loose skin above her elbow. I slide back the blanket to catch a glimpse of her shapely breast, squashed into the pillow.

The movement awakens the other woman, who looks up sleepily. She is thin and pale, like most of our young women, with short, crudely cut blond hair and piercing green eyes. I put a finger to my lips, and we both settle on either side of the armourer's widow, revelling in the warmth that is so rare in our miserable lives. Still hung over from the long night, I settle back to sleep quite easily.

When I am awakened again, it is with good reason - the ladies had rested themselves to the full and demand my hospitality. I accept a long drink of cold water and then get a mouthful of breast, as the raven-haired woman climbs on top of me. I can feel her friend's fingers on our nether regions, arousing both of us with long, throbbing caresses. Then I feel myself slide in, and the raven lady begins to pump with frenzy. I cooperate until she is spent, but in truth there is no pleasure from her thrashing, and I feel relief when she falls away to the side. The blonde woman shakes her head, saying that she doesn't want to bear any more children. I clamber on top of the raven lady and easily reach climax, thrusting between her buttocks. She barely shifts, still numb from her achievement, as I roll onto my back. Her friend lies on top of my stomach and thrusts into my hand, which seems to satisfy her well.

They hastily pull on their capes when they hear Trevor hobbling up the stairs. He opens the door with an icy stare and makes an impatient sign for them to leave. I hear his heavy steps recede on the stairs, the women following him in silence. Then the front door slams with far more force than necessary - and I hear Trevor struggle upstairs again. I often suggest that we install a simple lift, but he wouldn't hear of it. Personally, I wouldn't mind - my legs ran up one mountain too many a very long time ago - but that cannot be admitted to a cripple who insists on hobbling up and down steep stairs all day. They don't make men like that any more.

"I suppose you heard, Commander," says Trevor, standing over my bed.

"The siege at Brana? Yes, Father Simon told me last night."

"Is that really possible?"

"I would have said not, Trevor. But strange things have been happening lately."

I confide in him, describing the attack at the lake and the footprints in the guard tower. He nods thoughtfully.

"Don't tell anyone," he says gruffly. "There will be panic."

"Yes."

"There is panic enough already," he hobbles to the window and throws it open. "Listen."

I slide my bare shoulders under the blanket and lie back. As soon as we fall silent, I become aware of a distant clamour of many voices, loud and cantankerous, shouting and wailing behind the barrack wall. Judging by that noise, most of the town is gathered in front of the city hall.

Just as I fall back on the pillow, I hear another sound - the bells begin to peal. Both of them, indicating that all the townsmen who are of age must attend the assembly.

"I suppose they will want us to tear off to Brana in full force," I say tiredly. "Today, one presumes."

"Something like that," Trevor hands me a fresh towel. "You better make yourself pretty, Commander. It's going to be a long day."

I nod tiredly, accept the towel and swing out of bed. Trevor turns away tactfully, even though I have nothing to be ashamed of - two hundred pounds of bone and muscle, clad in a scarred hide. I am more embarrassed of the way I move - my joints take a very long time to warm up on cold mornings.

"The water is not bad," says Trevor as I walk into the shower. "I used a little fuel."

I nod in gratitude without turning and open the taps. What comes from the shower head is almost freezing, and I shrink away resentfully. I know it takes time, but surely a little warm water is the least I can ask for in winter.

Shrugging my shoulders and shivering, I slide open the shower window and whistle at the sentry. He turns, startles and runs towards me. I don't know him - he looks like one of the boys who joined us at the start of summer.

"Good morning to you, soldier. Call the duty sergeant."

He salutes, snapping his heels hard enough to send him into the air, then runs off. I wait, trying the shower water once more - it is still as cold as an icy mountain stream flowing through fresh snow.

Tancred arrives from the barracks with the young sentry and sends him away with a careless gesture of the hand.

"Both bells," I yell through the window.

193

"Men are ready," he yells back. "We are only waiting for you, Commander."

I nod and slide the window shut. The water feels just a touch warmer, and I am hopeful. A few moments later it is warm on my hand, and steam begins to fill the bathroom.

Not all is lost.

{}{}{}

I run down the stairs to warm up and stride out of the door, held open by Trevor.

"Good luck," he hisses as I walk past him.

I nod, and his final words are drowned by a thundering cheer. I scan the parade ground, and my heart beats a proud tattoo in my chest.

The entire Regiment has formed up at attention, and it is a sight I should admire more often. Clad in their parade tunics, the men stand before me in long rows - the proudest sight in existence, and what a contrast to the mess outside.

I step forward, snap to attention and bring my arm in salute. The roar rises to a crescendo, yet none of them appears to move so much as a muscle.

"Salute!" orders Redmond. Hundreds of glove-clad arms fly to the visors of fur caps.

I bring my arm down abruptly and remain at attention.

"At ease!"

Hundreds of bodies shuffle into a more relaxed posture - feet apart, arms behind the back. I nod to Redmond, who marches to the front of the formation, then descend from the porch of my quarters and march towards the gate, feeling as if I had never aged.

"Attention! Right-turn! Forward-march!"

We set out for the town hall, the heels of hundreds of boots thundering on the cobblestones in unison. It is a fearsome, rhythmical sound, as if a heart of some formidable animal beats against its stone chest.

We approach the city hall, where thousands of people have already gathered. There is room for everyone inside, but it takes time to seat everyone, and it always looks as if someone will end up having to wait for a vote outside. It never happens.

The soldiers break formation to enter through narrow gates, the civilian crowds hanging back, somewhat fearfully, until all of my men are inside. By tradition, The Regiment sits together in assemblies. Space is made for it at the bottom rows, near the stage.

I march inside last, removing my cap and carrying it on my left arm. There is an empty seat next to the aisle, and I sit down, staring at the stage where the wise men of the Council shuffle behind the table.

I turn to the other side of the hall, and I see the people of the old faith occupy the seats opposite ours. Father Simon has even taken an almost identical seat to mine, on the aisle and a few rows down.

Looking much older than usual, Manfred shuffles to his feet and calls the meeting to order. I stare at my knees, with total lack of apparent interest, as he explains the events in Brana as we understand them. There is a total silence in the cavernous timber hall, lit by powerful ceiling lights.

"As the lives of the citizens of Brana appear to be in grave danger, we have called this urgent meeting," concludes Manfred. "It is understood that the citizens of Brana are outside our law, but we cannot allow the situation to stand without putting the choices to our citizens."

I nod in grudging approval - he is nothing other than right, calling the imminent death of so many human beings to the attention of all enfranchised citizens.

Father Simon is called to the stand, to clarify what the transmission from Brana actually said. Apparently, these transmissions do not get through reliably, and it was not possible to maintain an informative conversation. From what is known, the township of Brana has restored its defences after the altercation with us. Some days after the big snowstorm the walls were scaled by forest people - that's the polite name for vermin. After their attack was beaten back, the vermin besieged the town, staying out of the range of its crossbows, but not allowing any boats out into the lake. The town has enough food and fuel for a few moons, but then it will be on its knees.

I stir at the mention of fuel - that can mean wood or peat as well as coal, but a few moons' worth of peat would form quite a pile, and I recall seeing nothing like that inside the town. My sergeant, on the other hand, recalls seeing a large pile of coal.

I wonder if Josiah managed to keep the stench out of his nostrils long enough to bargain with the old whaler and buy his book of maps. Then Redmond politely taps me on the arm, and I look up.

"Commander Ritter," I hear Manfred's droning voice. "We apologize for having to awaken you."

There is good-natured laughter in the hall as I stand up and march towards the stand. I reach the podium and look around at leisure.

"I forgive you, Councillor," I tell him in the ensuing silence. "Only a soldier knows what it is like, a soldier's fatigue. A man who had never stood beside his comrades in battle - I don't expect him to understand at all."

Manfred stares at me acidly, but he knows defeat well enough when he sees it. His only response is to gesture to the stand, where I make myself comfortable. It will be a long session.

"Commander Ritter, we once again call upon your wisdom and experience," he says grimly, injecting decorum into the proceedings with skill. "We ask you again, not long after our last assembly - what would it take to return to Brana?"

"It would take a very long walk, and I will give

directions to anyone who wishes to try it."

There is a low rumble of voices in the hall. Manfred waits in silence, ever so in touch with the mood of the assembly. He lets the resentment build up until we are surrounded in disapproving murmur.

I look down at him with a sour smile. Then, as the murmur begins to build, I raise my hand. The hall falls silent, and my smile loses its acidity as I stare into Manfred's eyes. He is humiliated completely.

Eyes now closed, I nod repeatedly, gathering my thoughts. I inhale deeply and hold the air in my chest, forming sentences in my head. Then I open my eyes and look around.

People stare at me intently. Thousands of eyes are focussed on my stout figure, clad in a tight dress tunic. I hold up my arm in a conciliatory gesture.

"In any case, it can't be done until the snows melt."

The hall erupts in a roar, and I can hear many shouts of indignation. I catch a quick glimpse of the Council - they sit at their long table in silent resignation to the fact that their presence is almost irrelevant.

I frown and raise my arm. Silence instantly fills the hall.

"We would need the entire fleet of timber trucks," I tell them, looking around into as many eyes as possible. "We would have to reinforce them, but there is time enough for that."

There is a little more applause and less stomping of feet. I nod - that is all it takes to restore silence.

"We would have to go back and forth," I say, drumming my fingers on my cap. "The vermin would see us and try to attack in great numbers. There would be a lot of trouble."

There is now sparse applause, and I let it run for a while, then raise my hand.

"What I would need from the town is food and fuel and labour. My men are enough for the transport, and we could leave in the first warm spell we get. But we are not going."

I sit down. Manfred rises and calls the vote for a censure.

Most hands go up, starting with the men of the old faith, who stare at me with stony, hostile expressions.

Manfred calls the vote against, and a few hands go up around the hall. I sweat slightly, but smile with defiance. This would not be the first or last time.

"With all respect, that was a senseless gesture, my dear citizens. My men and are loyal to this town, but it is within your power to destroy that loyalty."

"Please stop!"

I turn around and that Father Simon is on his feet, holding a wooden cross in his right hand. He kisses it and proceeds to speak.

"I implore you to reconsider, Ritter. What little human

is left within you, I will that last remnant to feel compassion. They are running out of time, Ritter. They are under attack, and they have no firearms. We must get them bullets and guns. It must happen now."

I raise my hand to call for absolute silence. The sound of the heavy rain on the roof becomes very apparent, and I point to the ceiling, shaking my head.

"You won't get through even now. There is no question of transporting thousands of people through winter snow."

Father Simon shakes his head in annoyance, as if dealing with a slow pupil. I feel anger but keep my face still.

"It's not snowing yet. Your transporters can still get through. Now, or it will be too late. I demand a new vote - that we send supplies now and wait until spring to evacuate."

I raise my hands in mock surrender and turn to the chair.

"Mr Chairman, I declare that Father Simon's demand cannot be met. The assembly may recast its vote, but The Regiment is not prepared to accede to this proposal. It is suicide."

"What is a risk to a few lives when we are talking of losing Brana?" shouts a pretty woman. I squint to recognize her - that must be Dinah, Father Simon's new consort. I know her as I knew his woman of many years, who died giving birth to twins a few winters ago. We all grew up on the same street.

I stare at Dinah in a manner designed to cause her discomfort. She is very attractive, even in the formless garb that the women of old faith wear in public. Her light-blonde hair is just visible under a tasteless black shawl, and her determined expression sets off the angles of her shapely face. She ignores the undertone in my stare totally, and I decide to tell her like it is.

"Good lady, I owe nothing to the people of Brana except revenge upon a few of their number. If that revenge is exacted by vermin, even better. If I ever go there, it will be to kill."

We stare at each other until Manfred lumbers to his feet.

"Since Commander Ritter is not prepared to partake in this proposal, there is no sense in voting on it. Father Simon, I suggest you inform the people in Brana of this meeting's decision."

Father Simon rises to his feet.

"I thank the chair for its efforts," his voice rings through the hall. "My brethren will mount a rescue without Ritter's butchers. He can sit in his barracks and stare out of his windows. We will get through the mountains with a load of firearms, and we will save Brana."

I look up with interest, calculating what that would take. It all adds up to the same thing - only The Regiment has tracked transporters, and only they can cross the mountains.

"We call upon all citizens for good will," shouts Father Simon. "We need transporters, builders and weapons. I humbly beg that each and every citizen looks within themselves to see what they can spare to save five thousand lives in Brana."

I shake my head and restore the cap to my head, then bow to the chair and leave the stand, signalling to my men to rise. I stand aside as the soldiers flow past me, hurrying out of the hall. Redmond walks past me and nods. I nod back.

I wait until the last of them exit the hall and speak again.

"About the citizens of Brana."

There is silence. The citizens of Grey study me with incomprehension - but they respect or fear me enough to await clarification.

"They turned on their fellow beings just like the vermin of the forest," I explain, allowing contempt I still feel to enter my voice. "That is why I don't want to help them."

I look around, staring into as many faces as I can, before the momentum of my statement begins to dissipate.

"That is not the reason I refuse to help Father Simon," my voice thunders through the hall. "But understand this - he and his fools will pack their transporters with weapons, and within three days these guns will be in vermin hands. Who of you care to bet that the vermin will not be able to use them?"

I pause for breath and look around again.

"We have underestimated the enemy. We are now caught by surprise, and the fault is ours. If Father Simon cares to die in the forest, that is his affair. But if he arms a thousand vermin, Grey itself may be in need of rescue."

I see consternation and smile again.

"Commander!"

I turn to the back of the hall, where a younger man stands in his seat.

"I am Herman, son of James," he declares loudly.

"The council recognizes Herman, son of James," I let Manfred say.

"Commander, what do you mean - enemy? Are they not wild animals?"

"No, Honourable Herman," I turn to him with a grave expression. "They are no more animals than we. Degenerates, but they are clever, strong and nasty. We always knew that. What we did not know is that they are capable of planning military action on a large scale. That is what is happening in Brana now. I wish the town to vote on another proposal."

Manfred makes a patient gesture with his hand, and I nod my thanks.

"I move that we prohibit the gun convoy from leaving until it is adequately armoured and otherwise equipped," I tell them. "To prevent guns and edged weapons falling into vermin hands."

Manfred nods and gestures to the assembly.

"The chair commends the motion for people's consideration," he declares, rapping his gavel once. "All those for, raise their hands."

A number of hands go up in the crowd, and stewards take some time to count their rows, then communicate the results. Each steward adds the votes from the one above to his tally, and the arithmetic alone takes some time.

"All those against."

It's a close vote, but when the last of the stewards comes up to the stage, Manfred looks at me and shakes his head. The motion is not carried.

There is silence as I look around the hall, drawing to my full height. I take a breath in, to ensure that my voice doesn't break mid-sentence.

"Let me say it again. Those we call vermin have laid a siege around Brana. When they are finished there, nothing stops them from coming here to do the same. That is what we really need to worry about."

{}{}{}

"Are they making much progress?" I ask, looking out of the window at a timber convoy return from the forest. Its lead transporter rumbles across the river, dragging vast trunks of dead trees. The foaming water tries to wrench the logs from the chain harness and wash them away to the sea. The treads struggle on the stones of the ford until the machine's battered nose emerges from the water and clambers up the river bank, trailing a cloud of blue smoke.

"They are ready to leave tomorrow, Commander."

It is snowing despite clear sky, and I suddenly feel the bitter cold in my room. The logs in the fire are spitting and smoking, giving off no heat. I give them a forlorn stir with a poker and add a few small sticks that are hopefully dry inside.

Redmond patiently awaits for me to settle, knowing that my erratic movements represent a rapid succession of thoughts. I throw the poker into the metal basket and straighten, reaching for my goblet of gin.

"How many transporters are they using?"

"They bought the entire spare fleet from the timber merchants. I understand that each machine has been stripped down, reinforced and will be used to tow a sturdy trailer."

I stare at Redmond incredulously.

"Trailers with wheels? Towed through snow?"

"Yes, Commander. That is what they are planning."

I pace the room, thinking frantically. Then I stop next to the map.

"They will get stuck here," I stab my finger at a place I know well. "On the first steep hill they get to."

Redmond nods sadly.

"The lead transporter will get stuck on the slope. Then the other machines will lose traction and get bogged behind it. By the time they understand that they are stuck, the vermin will be upon them. They won't be able to get their transporters into a defensive formation."

"Is there anything we could say to them?"

"Other than to wait for us - no."

Redmond nods again. I give the fire another stir - it does not seem to be giving off any heat. I remove a small ornamental axe from the metal basket and split the log on the granite plinth that forms the base of the fireplace. The wood is green and damp inside.

"I spoke to Father Simon last night," says Redmond. "I told him that wheels won't get them through. He wouldn't hear of it."

I throw the green log into the corner of the fireplace and cleave another, finding a dry core. It catches fire immediately, and I feel comfort from that little success. The other logs continue to hiss and spit moisture from their ends.

"Redmond, they are all going to die."

"That seems very likely, Commander."

"I suppose they deserve it."

"I cannot say, Commander. I would not like to see it happen - deservedly or not."

"I suppose I wouldn't either," I give the fire another stir, sending a swarm of embers up the chimney. There is at least a little heat, which means that damp logs will dry and burn.

"We could get out there and block the road. Out there, remember, there is no law."

"Block it how?"

"Cut down a few trees and drop them across the road, Red," I smile, now in my element. "Then we wait for them to come. Those fools will not bring many saws - and even if they do, it will take too long. Their tempers will cool, and they will turn around. If the vermin come, we will be there to deal with them."

"It's utterly against the spirit of our law, Commander. You know - every man has a right to dispose of his fate as he reasonably wishes."

"Isn't it better that losing those fools? The vermin will become insane if they get their hands on them. Why, they will think they can do what they like to any of us."

Redmond shakes his head.

"The vermin may use your road block as an ambush. What then? We would be in danger ourselves."

I think it over briefly. He is, of course, right – as always. Trying to restrain Father Simon's men could even turn ugly – they are, after all, armed.

"How long before we can leave?"

"Five days at the very least, Commander. There is just not enough fuel."

I sigh, staring at the hissing logs. The drying kilns are not having a better time of it than I, with wet wood barely smouldering in their furnace. We signally failed to recover our fuel stocks. There is probably enough to get two transporters to Brana, but not back.

"I am out of ideas, Red."

Redmond shakes his head with indignation.

"What fools."

{}{}{}

"I do not need your killers, Ritter. We are well-armed and prepared for the journey."

Father Simon strides along the old timber trailer, its heavy frame, now covered with light planks in a vain attempt to protect the occupants. I break into a run to get ahead of him and step in his way.

"This is just not going to work," I pull at a plank, and it comes away from the frame. Father Simon frowns and rams it back in place with the heel of his hand.

"We have plenty of weapons."

"Father, you have no idea what you are up for," I implore him again. "They come at you quickly and in vast numbers - you simply cannot fire fast enough. Guns cannot protect you alone - you need armour to buy time.

Please, Father - we know after doing this for seventy years."

He stops and stares at me with doubt creeping into his stony features.

"What is your proposal, Commander?"

"If you must go, wait for us. The snow is still a few days away, and I can have three transporters ready in five days. I need enough fuel to get them there if not back. I can protect you, and three tracked machines in the convoy will be enough to ensure that it can get through the snow."

He weighs the suggestion, then slowly shakes his head.

"We just can't wait, Ritter. Our brethren are about to be overrun."

"Five lousy days," I shake my hand with outstretched digits. "What possible difference can that make?"

He stares past me, and I become aware of many eyes visible in the gaps within the improvised armour. Father Simon's flock stares at me with mute contempt. He shakes his head for the final time, aware of being on show.

"You hide it well, but you are a good man, Commander," he says tiredly. "As good as a heathen can be, and I will mention you in my prayers. I hope that heavenly light descends upon you one day."

He places his hand on my shoulder and gently pushes

me aside to climb into the hauler. I back away, watching as he signals to the driver and turns to stare forward resolutely. The engine begin to hiss, filling the air with steam, and the ramshackle convoy begins to lumber towards the city gate. I stare after it dumbly.

"Is there no way to stop them?"

I turn to the side and see Tannis standing behind me respectfully.

"Not really," I explain gruffly. "Our law is absolutely specific on this point - any citizen can risk their neck any way they want. It is not lawful to restrain them just because you see untoward consequences, and they don't. Otherwise why, my grandfather would have been restrained from travelling outside city walls. There would be no Regiment."

"I understand, Commander," says Tannis heavily. "They are going to get killed, aren't they?"

"Almost certainly," I bring down my fist on my thigh. "There is no way to stop them from going, Tannis. There is only one thing I can do from here."

"What is that, Commander?"

"Three transporters should do it if we hurry," I tell him. "Go after them and protect them as best we can. We leave as soon as there is enough fuel."

We walk towards the barracks, where Solly is the duty sergeant. My orders appear to have been anticipated, for the yard is full of men rushing around with everything that can burn.

I look up and sigh, seeing heavy, dirty smoke rise from the tall stack of the drying kiln. Father Simon's God does not appear to be on our side.

{}{}{}

We round the last corner before the road points up a steep hill, and hear Solly curse as he throws both throttles backwards. The machine stops abruptly - barely in time to avoid a collision with burnt-out remains of a timber trailer.

I see the hauler further along - it had run off the road down a steep incline, stopped only by a sturdy tree. Other machines of the convoy are in a similar state, their smoking remains littering the road.

I scramble down the ladder and hastily step into the armour held out for me by Redmond. Another soldier bends down to clip the buckles and straps combat revolvers to my forearms. I grasp the trigger levers in my gloved fists, and it begins.

I am the first to run through the open hatch, my boots making a noise I had not made for some years. We race past the ruins, scanning the undergrowth for the enemy. In truth, I would like someone to be waiting there - I have something for them.

The bushes at the side of the road are broken and crushed, but quite empty. There is much blood on the leaves and congealed pools are evident on the road - it seems that the convoy exacted a heavy toll on its attackers.

The lead hauler is crushed by a large tree that looks dry and devoid of all leaves - the vermin must have raised it from the forest floor and dropped it across the road at the right moment. I wonder, staring at the ruptured boiler, whether they realized how effective that was, since the haulers towing long trailers cannot reverse on the narrow road. In other words, I could not have planned a better ambush myself.

To my relief, we do not need to look for weapons. Gunpowder has been spilled from the barrels onto blood-soaked ground, and the guns litter the road. Most seem to be broken - Father Simon's men lived up to their responsibility.

"There aren't any bodies," says a young soldier with a child-like wonder. I frown, knowing what lies ahead. It is best to keep the appalling truth unspoken, for he will see it for himself soon enough.

Redmond finds the trail, and that is not difficult - a great many men, some dragging heavy weights, have trampled their way through the forest. I nod, and he runs ahead with four other soldiers. We follow, making as little noise as we can. The gusting headwind makes it a little easier to hide our approach.

After what seems like forever I see an arm with a sprung bayonet wave from the undergrowth. I stop and raise my left arm. The sound of running feet ceases behind me as soldiers stop, training their guns in all directions.

A moment later the arm waves again, and I crouch,

stepping forward gingerly. The arm waves down, and I drop on all fours, crawling along the redolent forest floor with both guns at the ready. The sentry points in the direction of a flat outcrop of rocks, and I see that Redmond lies in a bed of ferns that cling to the stone.

I crawl towards him, and he points forward. We look over a meadow flanked by a small cliff that rises above the forest. I pull a small bush out of the ground and spread its branches over my helmet, then crawl the last few yards to join Redmond.

He hands me the binoculars and points towards the base of the cliff. I push the branches of the bush away from my face and press cold eyepieces to my cheeks, knowing that I will regret whatever I see.

A large tribe is encamped next to what looks like a narrow entrance to a cave. An elaborate fire bed is studded with large rocks that allow pieces of meat to cook above the embers. My nostrils begin to burn with the smell, a cloying, wicked odour of flesh that is very different from deer or fowl.

Clenching jaws, I swivel the binoculars to count. Mostly asleep, there are nearly sixty in plain sight, and one expects more to shelter inside the cave. I study them with horrified fascination, having had few such opportunities outside the fury of combat.

They have lean, hairy bodies with bulging muscles, proud aquiline noses and heavy eyebrows overlying deep-set eyes. The colour of their skin seems very pale, and they are mostly blonde or red-haired.

A few are awake, and I am mesmerized by their movements - relaxed, graceful and precise.

A mother sits behind her daughter, looking for lice in the girl's hair. The child is no more than ten summers of age, with flat nipples and a long cascade of tangled hair. Her face is not unpleasant, with a hint of intelligence in the eyes that stare into the flames.

A second woman is breastfeeding nearby, propped up against an older-looking man who sleeps on his side. She holds the baby to her long, stringy breast with the right hand and runs the left over her groin absent-mindedly. I can't see her face because she looks towards the cave, but the lines of her posture suggest placidity and contentment.

There is a blood-curdling scream, and I look above the binoculars to find its source. I see two large males striding to the edge of the meadow, and I hear the scream once more.

I follow their movement through binoculars and freeze with a slight gasp. Father Simon's consort sits with her back to a small tree, her arms tethered to the trunk above her head. She is naked, covered in bruises and smeared with congealed blood.

Dinah's left leg is a bloody stump - I can see the startling white of the cartilage that used to be inside her knee. A crude tourniquet made from a strip of leather binds the stump tightly, preventing loss of blood from severed arteries.

As they approach she screams once more, trying to

press her back into the tree in a vain attempt at evasion. One sits in her lap with his back towards her. He grasps Dinah's remaining leg and holds it up in the air.

With what must be the last of her strength she kicks out and brings up her knee, driving it into his face. He is thrown backwards, and his face contorts with pain. She must have bitten him, for he struggles and lets out an angry growl.

Her resistance is short-lived - he thrusts his arms forward, then smashes backwards with his elbows, springing to his feet abruptly. There is blood on his neck and shoulders.

He turns, raises a heavily muscled leg and crashes the heel into her mouth. Her head hits the tree hard enough to shake old leaves from its branches, then it flops, doll-like, to her chest. The male sits astride Dinah once more and holds the leg in the air. The other male binds it with a strap of leather above the knee, then slashes at the joint with what looks like a very sharp flint. Moments later they are walking towards the fire, the butcher holding the severed leg by the toes.

Redmond places a restraining hand on my shoulder, and I sink down, resting my cheek on the cold stone. When my composure returns, I raise the binoculars again and study the scene - this time as a leader planning his attack.

Dinah's leg is cooking on the stones protruding from the embers. One of the assailants sits cross-legged next to flames, rubbing the bite on his neck. The other is running an appreciative hand over the breasts of the woman with a baby. She pushes him away half-heartedly, seeming to laugh. He takes the sleeping baby out of her arms and gently places it on the ground. With what looks like resignation she rolls over and kneels on the ground, thrusting up her lean backside. The male straddles and enters with vigour, causing her to wince.

He seems to satisfy himself after a few forceful strokes and pulls away, slapping her backside appreciatively. He turns to say something, and the butcher then springs to his feet, walks over to the woman and takes his turn with what appears to be some kind of gratitude to his leader.

He takes much longer, and the commotion begins to awaken others. They rise on their elbows, stretch and begin to couple, seemingly with whoever is close. I stare with detached revulsion as the meadow comes alive with writhing bodies.

An ugly-looking youth with what appears to be a club foot is limping around the meadow, his immature erection bobbing with awkward steps. He does not appear to be popular with ladies, being pushed aside by one, then another. He approaches a woman with white hair, who kneels on the ground and rests her face on the earth with an air of disinterest in the proceedings. An adult male kicks him away and mounts her instead. She does not look up.

The youth looks across the meadow.

"Over my dead body," I whisper, dropping the

binoculars away from my face. "Red, tell them to move on my command and bring me the crossbow."

Redmond crawls backwards, his head close to the rock. I look through the binoculars again.

The youth unties Dinah from the tree, and her limp body falls to the ground. He positions her flat on her back and strains to part the mutilated limbs. Mercifully, she remains unconscious.

Redmond returns and hands me the crossbow. It is hard to see at that distance, and the youth makes a small target. His frantic attempts make it even harder, and I decide to move forward.

"Commence the attack on my shot," I whisper to Redmond.

I advance nearly all the way, taking advantage of the commotion in the meadow. The smell of burning human flesh makes me nauseous, but I am as angry as I had ever been, and I gulp saliva behind clenched jaws, crawling towards a fallen tree whose exposed roots provide good cover. Once there, I rise to my feet and rest the stock of the crossbow on a sturdy root.

A few of the vermin have stopped coupling and crouch warily, staring in my direction with their noses held high. I know they can smell me from that distance, but their smelling days are nearing an end.

I fire. The youth shudders, arching his back in an obscene imitation of ecstasy. My bolt protruding above his ear, he drops on top of Dinah, who remains unconscious.

I drop the crossbow and rise to my full height. The meadow erupts in a volley of screams, with vermin running towards me. I let them come close and commence fire, dropping them with calm, almost leisurely shots, until my guns are empty. Then I spring the bayonets and begin to skewer the attackers with short, precise stabs to the heart.

By now the soldiers overtake my position. Gunfire erupts all around me, filling the meadow with acid smoke. It doesn't take long to make sixty corpses, I reflect irrelevantly, bending down to retrieve the crossbow.

It is all over by the time I straighten, and the meadow is littered with bodies. The soldiers wander around, stabbing the wounded. My foot lands on something soft, and I look down.

Father Simon looks up from the earth with torn, empty eyes. His corpse is limbless, and the intestines are carelessly tossed aside to harvest the liver. The back of the head is missing, and I can see the broken edges of the skull, hammered open to retrieve the contents.

I dry-retch, retreating from what looks like a dump of unwanted parts - broken heads and limbless torsos. The vermin normally eat everything except bone and hair, but on this occasion they got more than they could possibly digest. They left the more difficult parts, throwing them into a pit on the edge of the meadow.

I rest my helmet against a tree and dry-retch again,

then wait for the nausea to abate. Then I stumble through the meadow, absently restocking the drums of both revolvers with fresh cartridges from the pouch.

Tannis is on his knees, staring at a puddle of bile amid a bed of blue lichen. I pat him on the shoulder as I walk past.

The attack catches me by surprise, and I only just manage to dart sideways. The young girl who hid under her mother's corpse lunges at me again - huge, sharp teeth aiming straight for my throat.

I manage to knock her aside. The heavy blow from the revolver harness sends her off her feet, but she springs up and attacks again, blood dripping from her cheek. This time I am ready, thrusting my left bayonet into her mouth and forcing it through the bone. She jerks and sags at the end of my arm, rabid anger fading in the wide eyes.

I ease her to the ground as others run towards me, aiming their guns quite belatedly. I pull, but the bayonet is firmly embedded in the girl's skull. Tannis places one foot on her forehead and begins to tug at the my wrist, but his efforts are not crowned with success. I signal for him to step aside, turning away from the girl who lies on the ground at the end of my outstretched arm.

I close my eyes and fire the left revolver. Something wet and warm lands on my cheek, and I stagger backwards, gore dripping from the freed bayonet. I open my eyes, and the retching returns in earnest. I am grateful when someone splashes me with water, flushing the girl's brain from my face.

Dinah still lies under the youth's body, but her eyes are open. I take hold of the greasy hair and heave with all my strength, tossing her assailant out of her sight, then kneel beside her.

She turns towards me, her eyes startling lakes of perfect blue amid a broken and soiled face.

Her arm lies limply on the ground next to my knees. I stroke it, and she begins to sob. Streaming tears make tracks on her grimy cheeks. I tear off my helmet and place it to cover her nether region.

She tries to rise, but moans in pain and stops. I now see that both of her shoulders have been wrenched out of their sockets.

I bend down to examine the stumps of her legs. The left looks as if the tourniquet has been in place for a long time - there are black patches in the grey flesh around a rude strip of leather. I need not sniff - it is hard not to smell the sickly sweet stench of rot. Every soldier knows what that means - unless one can cut away the dead flesh, the victim dies in the worst way imaginable. We have poppy extract back in the convoy, but it is not enough to induce heavy sleep, even if anyone had the skill to remove the dead flesh without killing her. That can only be done in town, a two-day trip through mud and snow.

I weigh all that up, imaging her life afterwards: two stumps, mutilated arms and the memory of the last two days. Our world does not take kindly to those who cannot take care of themselves.

I remove both gauntlets and place my hand on Dinah's forehead. Our eyes meet, and she stares at me mutely. I gently shake my head, just once.

Her lips try to form words, and I wait with infinite patience. After a few attempts, she stops trying to speak with her shattered jaw and lies back, closing her eyes tightly.

I stroke her forehead with my left hand, and she whimpers softly. I move the hand to cover her eyes with my palm and watch her intently.

Dinah appears to make her peace, and her body goes limp - she lies as if in a peaceful slumber. I bring up my right hand to point the revolver at her heart and squeeze the trigger with greatest force, willing the gun into action before my strength falters.

The shot reverberates over the silent meadow. I stand up and retrieve my helmet, spattered with droplets of her blood. Soldiers stare at me with mute compassion as I bend down and roll over the body, to conceal the nether region and the ragged hole in a once-luscious breast. Seen from the side, the curve of Dinah's stomach makes me wonder if she was pregnant, and I turn away with haste.

Solly runs up and touches my shoulder. Still dazed, I become aware of men standing next to the cave, pointing their guns inside. I walk over, the last of the nausea receding deep in my stomach.

I regain control of my breathing and allow myself to only feel fury.

There are muted cries, from what sounds like a large number of vermin who took refuge in the cave. Solly strikes a flare and tosses it inside.

The flare arcs through the darkness, and it seems to light a narrow, down-sloping passage that leads into a cavernous space. I look up at the cliff - such caves are rare in sheer rock, and there is almost certainly no other way out.

"Grenades," I tell Solly through clenched teeth. He nods and shouts the order.

Men run over, hastily removing fragmentation grenades from their belts. We begin to toss them inside the cave, and many shouts are heard from within. Someone even attempts to toss a grenade back at us, and I fire down the passage. All shouts cease.

Last three grenades are tied with one string and tossed inside with their pins removed. We step away from the entrance and count to four.

There is thunder inside the rock, and a cloud of dust scented with gunpowder and blood bursts out of the cave. I wait for it to settle and step forward to listen. There is no sound.

"What's that smell?" asks Solly curiously.

I inhale deeply, driving the stenches of blood, vomit, powder and dust from my nostrils. I smell it too - the sharp, tangy odour that is vaguely reminiscent of rotten fish.

"Back!" I shout, running down the meadow. My men follow me, and we run to the rocky outcrop, where I drop to the ground, panting. Redmond drops beside me.

"What..." he begins to ask. I push his head down to the ground.

We lie like that for some time, and I even begin to think about rising to my feet - when the ground convulses beneath us, throwing bodies, soil and rocks into the air. My ears nearly explode, and I scream in pain. Then I feel, rather than hear, a heavy rumble as if a mountain slides down into the valley.

I stand up, deaf and dizzy from the stabbing pain. I run my hands over my ears - there is no blood, which is hopeful. My hearing slowly returns, and I turn on my feet to avoid turning my head.

"Commander..." gasps Redmond beside me, pointing over my shoulder.

The mountain had truly fallen into the valley. Half of the cliff is gone, blown away by an explosion of the gas beneath the earth.

"Red," I whisper. "I think I know what this means."

I begin to stumble across the ruined meadow, covered in corpses and debris from the explosion. I manage to get across without tripping over and drop to all fours to climb the shattered ruin.

The cave is now an indentation in the face of a cliff.

Nothing is left of its inhabitants - but something else catches my eye. The walls of the cave are stark, sheer black. At first glance they look charred, but closer inspection reveals that they consist of utterly black, shiny rock. I clamber up, Redmond struggling to keep pace.

I spring my bayonet and begin to stab at the wall. The black surface easily crumbles under steel. I chip away a small piece and study it, kneeling on the hard surface. It stains my gauntlet black, like soft charcoal. Redmond kneels next to me and stares at it, frowning.

"Do you know what this is, Red?" I ask him.

He nods his head.

"That's right," I bend down so our helmets touch. "Believe me, my loyal comrade: we'll remember this day as long as we live."

{}{}{}

"Order! Order!" shouts Manfred, rapping his gavel on the heavy tabletop. "Enough!"

He stares at me, but I merely beam a benign smile. In truth, I am here out of good form, not at all interested in what anyone else has to say.

I shoot a glance to the corner of the hall, where the air shimmers with heat. The stove is throbbing with a force it hadn't felt since it was forged, its metal chimney that runs to the tall ceiling now too hot to touch. A while ago I sent Tancred into the building with a truckload of coal, and a few shovelfuls were enough to set fire to the mould coating the chimney. The pungent smoke still clings to my nostrils, reminding me that the town hall has never been warmer - with a bitter midwinter blizzard howling outside.

I smile once more. Manfred sits down and simply waits.

The din of amazement does not cease for some time, and I eventually tire of it, standing up to straighten my tunic. I have a thoroughly heroic look, with bandages over both forearms covering blisters made by wet gun straps. My cheek sports a new scar - I am certain it wasn't the feral girl but something I brushed running away from the cave. At least that's what I like to think - I would not care to be slashed by fingernails coated in excrement and human fat.

"The chair recognizes Commander Ritter," declares Manfred importantly. Silence falls in the assembly.

"It's rather warm in here," I tell them, pulling at the top button on my collar. There is raucous applause, and I acknowledge it with a wave of the hand.

"My fellow citizens," I tell them, scanning the hall. "Mark this day as the end of our dismal struggle for survival. Never again will we shiver in our homes."

The roar of approval is almost deafening in reply. People leap to their feet, applaud, shout - and more than one demure-looking woman raises her skirt and thrusts her nether regions in my direction. That is a very intimate gesture amongst our women, second only to coupling itself. Yet more than one respectable matron now makes it in full view of the town. I smile and raise my hand.

"As soon as the blizzard is over, we will begin to build. We need everyone who can work and all who can bear weapons. I wish to build machines to carry this fuel from the forest. Payment for work will be in coal."

There is no applause this time as the town folk churn over my proposal. A squat, elderly man stands up. I stare at him but cannot place his face.

"The chair recognizes Wilfred, the son of Arthur," says Manfred loudly. Something unpleasant flashes in my brain, but I cannot place that memory just yet. I make a note to drink less gin.

"I ask the chair to consider the following," says Wilfred in a high, nasal voice. "Who really owns the coal?"

Manfred nods as if expecting the question.

"In ordinary circumstances the ownership rests with The Regiment. They found it."

He looks at me and then back to Wilfred.

"Of course, these are not ordinary circumstances."

I wince in anger at sudden memory. Wilfred is the son of a man Father hated and fought with. His idea was for the Council to seize control of The Regiment and incorporate it into the town militia. It was too important to be owned by a single man, ran the argument. Father finally challenged him to unarmed combat and demolished his jaw with a single swing of his fist. The man looked like he was hit by a falling tree and died a few moons later.

"The mercenaries own their barracks," says Wilfred. "But not the forest. It belongs to all of us."

"Is this correct?" asks Manfred in a business-like tone.

"It is, Honourable Chair," chimes Wilfred. "No one holds the title to that land - there are no recognized titles outside the wall. "

I clench teeth, cursing my lack of forethought.

"Sergeant Tancred!"

He jumps from his seat and snaps to attention. I stare at him with a false grin, returning his salute.

"Sergeant, load the remainder of the coal back in the truck and drive it to the barracks."

He snaps off another salute and jumps over the knees of his comrades, runs down the aisle and wheels the barrow full of coal out of the hall.

"My sincere apologies to the Chair," I turn towards Manfred with a mock bow and straighten in time to see a snide smile wither on his face. "We will replace the town's property as soon as weather permits."

"What is your meaning, butcher?" squawks Wilfred behind me.

I turn towards him slowly, as if rotating the turret, and

I stare at him coldly for a few disconcerting moments.

"It seems that we misplaced what was not ours to take," I explain with a metal ring rising in my voice. "I will remedy my error of judgement as soon as I can. The coal must go back to where I found it."

"Are you going to tell us where that is?" shouts a young male voice from the top row. I don't bother looking up, smiling at Wilfred instead.

"I will report in full," I say mildly. "Then, it seems, it will fall to the Council to make arrangements for its lawful retrieval. I thank the people of Grey for relieving me of this burden. It's a round trip of two days through the forest."

"Go back to your barracks, butchers!" shouts someone from the back rows. I stare at the empty space where Father Simon used to sit. The crowd seems to have left it vacant by unspoken consensus.

"Why, we will do that," my voice rings loud with anger, and the hall falls silent. "Except there is a point you are yet to grasp. None but The Regiment operates that far from the wall. No one else has had to fight vermin in the forest. No one but we know how to build reliable machines that can travel that distance. Father Simon hadn't grasped this point either. Look over at his empty seat - that is the penalty for failing to live in reality."

I study the silent faces and stare at the open eyes.

"I am willing to ensure that everyone can afford the

coal - but it is mine, not yours. I found it. You did not pay me to run after Father Simon and his poor madmen. My men and I went out there at great risk to our lives, and that is when we found the coal."

I turn to study Manfred's face - his expression clearly says that he did not expect this turn of events.

"It is in your power to take what we found in the town's name - for better or for worse, that is how our town works. But if you do that, do not expect loyalty. We will retreat into the barracks and drink as you freeze and starve. When you fail to deliver the coal, we will come to this hall and bay for blood like the rest who live off the efforts of others - and if you ask us to solve your problems, we will skin you for all you are worth."

I remember the merchants who died in Brana, and my expression turns savage. I know that because the soldiers tense, expecting a sudden call to action.

There is a loud din of dissenting voices. A few arguments break out in the rows, and two men clutch each other's throats. They are pulled apart by neighbours.

"Vote on this now," I order the town. "I never wish to discuss this matter again, or the coal goes back where we found it, and you can trudge into the forest and risk your unwashed necks if you want it."

The men of the Council confer, then Manfred stands up and drones out the bill:

"We, the free citizens of Grey, propose that any coal

found in the forest remains the property of the finder - all those for raise their hands!"

Many hands rise, and the votes are counted.

"All those against!"

Even without the count I can see that there is no need for a counted ballot. We lost.

I nod to Solly, who runs down the aisle and out the door. He returns with Tancred - they had replenished the barrow from the truck outside and haul it with considerable effort. The crowd cheers wildly as they toss luscious shovelfuls of coal into the stove.

I raise my hand in a gesture of reconciliation.

"Consider my proposal. I will run convoys to the coal and blast it out of the mountain with explosives. Coal will be sold by The Regiment, and it will be priced so all citizens can afford it."

A few cheers are heard in the hall. I look around, noting that women are at it again, hauling at the skirts. It will be a wild night, and few of my men will be any good tomorrow morning.

"The town can build a large generator to supply the town with electricity. There would be no more dark streets, and no vermin would be able to sneak up to the wall. The entire river wall would be lit every night."

There is now a loud cheer from many men. Anyone who has survived their nineteenth summer is a member of the town militia, whose duty is to keep order - mainly, to guard the wall. Deaths are rare, but it is not a pleasant duty, given the consequences of failure.

"We will make better steel and cast it to make better machines. We can make good fuel for ships and transporters out of coal, and we can use them to get proper food from the sea and from the forest."

There is cheer, but Manfred shakes his head resolutely.

"Your proposal has already been voted on, Commander Ritter. You will have to wait until the next assembly to put it to the citizens again, as is your right."

I shake my head resolutely.

"I already said I will not discuss it again. I want an acceptable agreement right now, or you are on your own."

There is total silence in the assembly as an elderly man rises to his feet.

"The Chair recognizes venerable Judge Ivar," says Manfred emphatically. "Your Honour, do you wish to take the floor?"

Ivar stares in the direction of the council table - he has been blind for some years. His handsome, angular face is framed by a neatly cropped beard, and he is dressed in a meticulously neat grey cape.

"I do, Honourable Chair," says Ivar. He makes his way down the aisle slowly, feeling each step before placing weight on his foot. A tall youth pushes out of his row to take Ivar's hand and guides him down to the stage. Ivar turns around and places a hand on the council table, leaning against it lightly.

"Honourable Chair, the Commander is correct in law," he begins slowly. "The leaders of Brana acted appallingly. On behalf of the women and children of those who died on his convoy, the Commander is even obligated to find the killers and avenge their actions."

I sit still, wondering where he is headed.

"However, we cannot involve others in the murderers' just fate. That is what ancient law calls collective punishment. It is a very wrong thing to do."

I remain still, seeing that more and more eyes turn away from Ivar and bore into mine.

"The ancients classified collective punishment as what they called war crimes," says Ivar. "Commander Ritter, consider the following. We, the citizens of Grey, are most fortunate thanks to your courage and wisdom. We are particularly fortunate now, as we are about to regain many necessities of life that our ancestors took for granted. There is no doubt that our children will stop dying, and for the first time in centuries there is reason to think that our kind has a future."

I rise to my feet, knowing that Ivar is about to say something important.

"I ask, Commander," continues Ivar. "Do you really want to begin this good life, knowing that your brothers and sisters in Brana are about to be massacred by savages?"

I stare at his blighted eyes, and the dim light of the hall with its sea of faces becomes a blur. I find myself at another time and place.

A light, cold rain falls on my bare head as twilight stretches shadows over the ruins of Brana. I smell burning wood and burning flesh. I smell my sweat and fresh blood that is drying on my armour. I hear a soldier retch nearby, and I smell the bitter stench of his bile.

I stare at my helmet that rests on the honey-coloured stomach, covering the thatch of red hair matted with alien seed. I smell the sour stink of violation of the only one I ever loved.

Rina's legs are hacked away at the knees, and she lies in the rubble sobbing. Her eyes are tightly closed as I kneel next to her, running my left hand on her forehead. She tries to stay still, but fear of death overtakes her. She opens her eyes just as I bring the barrel of the right revolver to her breast.

I grasp the rail of the dock to stop myself from falling. Two soldiers rush towards me, and strong hands grip my torso to prevent me from swaying.

I regain vision, staring around me with relief. Sweat is dripping down my face, and I am heaving to catch my breath. The vile dizziness slowly clears as I breathe again.

I cannot speak but turn to Ivar and bore into his blind eyes in silent rebuke. He stares back with compassion, and I entirely believe that he knows what I had just seen.

I nod once. The blind judge nods back.

"I therefore wish to propose a compromise," he says gravely. "It does not do for the Regiment and the rest of the town to be at loggerheads, and it won't save Brana. Nor can anyone apart from the Regiment get the coal from deep forest. That is a fact."

He pauses to compose his next sentence in the tight silence of the hall.

"I suggest that the Regiment is given a title to the coal," he says slowly. "In exchange for mounting a mission, with the aid of the town, to save any citizens of Brana who wish to be rescued. Now that we have coal, there should be no difficulty in making enough fuel and weapons very quickly. Is that correct, Commander?"

I swallow hard and clear my tight throat.

"That is so."

"Are you amenable to this idea?"

"I am, Judge. On the condition that I act as I see fit once I reach Brana. I decide what is safe and how to ensure that citizens of Brana can exercise free will, each and every one."

Manfred proposes the motion, and it is carried unanimously - which is historic in itself.

On impulse, I turn and walk down the isle, hearing my men rise from their seats. I turn and motion them not to follow me and walk outside. The snow has abated, and I run to the beach, into the lusty sunset over the water, bitter tears rolling down my cheeks.

Once on the gravel beach, I have a strong urge to walk into the water and, once and for all, gain peace. That is just an urge, however - there are many invisible chains that stop me well short of the roiling surf. I grind my teeth in frustration and kneel in front of a vast log of driftwood that seems to bar my way, staring at the sun behind eternally perfect clouds, ocean spray hitting my face like shards of ice.

I extract the knife and plunge it into driftwood, which proves surprisingly hard. I stab it again and again, finally giving up as my naked hand turns numb against cold metal. I rest on my knees, staring at the sunset behind a much-used weapon uselessly stuck in a piece of wet wood.

Let the inevitable come.

{}{}{}

"Welcome back," says Wendy with a sad smile.

"Could be worse," I reassure her. "I am in good hands, anyway."

She pats my shoulders and adjusts the drip rate on the pump. The first lot of chemotherapy is now coursing into my bloodstream through a plastic tube - the slightly yellow liquid makes me think of snake venom. I saw a snake being milked in Aceh, and that is what it looked like.

I shiver involuntarily, even though it is too early to feel unwell. The great white fathers have held council, and they decided that the best thing to do is go ahead fast, despite the recent stroke. It was, theoretically, better to wait out a period of recovery - but that ran the risk of another stroke.

"How have you been, anyway?" I ask, turning away from the machine. Wendy looks up from the chart she is filling.

"So-so," she replies after a short delay.

"Tell Uncle Nicky," I order curtly.

She smiles and shakes her head briefly.

"Man problems."

"Tell Captain Turner. That's an order."

"Oh, all right," she sighs and pulls up a chair. The ward is not that busy right now, with Wilkins away. Wendy sighs again.

"Tim and I are separating."

"What the fuck?" I remember Tim, a boisterous tradesman who had a habit of bouncing into the ward with flowers for his new wife. "What is the dumb mutt thinking?"

"I caught him with an old girlfriend," a tear runs down Wendy's shapely cheek. "She left her husband recently, and it turns out that Tim was in her sights. Old schoolmates' website - ain't technology grand?"

I shake my head in dismay.

"Is he serious about this?"

"Well, he moved out last week. Staying with his parents."

"Fucking madman," I tell her in my army voice. "The woman could have grown up into anything - he has no idea what she is like now."

Wendy nods and reaches for the tissue box. She is no beauty, with an ample figure that runs to being a little too heavy in the cold months, and she neglects her looks, sporting a simple pageboy haircut and not bothering to dye her mousy-brown hair. Mousy... I don't know why they call it that. Mice are grey.

But she is a kind, honest woman, which to this combat veteran is worth its weight in platinum. She works long hours and enjoys a well-deserved respect of her colleagues and patients. Even Wilkins is a little more human around her, reflecting her warmth subliminally and involuntarily.

"I pegged Tim as the well-hung outdoors type," I tell Wendy with a sigh. Chemotherapy patients have special privileges - souls suspended in purgatory, we are allowed to say what we think.

She smiles through her tears and nods.

"Not the sharpest pencil in the box."

"Yes. So better now than later, when you have kids."

That reference makes her cry for real, and tissues no longer hold precipitation at bay. I reach over and sip some juice from a tall glass at my side, then adjust a few items at the bedside, all to indicate that I am not in a hurry to conclude the conversation. After a while she looks up and wipes her face with the sleeve.

"You are right, of course," she blows her nose loudly and tosses the empty tissue box into the waste bin. "Camping, BBQ, rugby, party. Good stuff, but not really what relationships are made of."

"Yes. The old girlfriend did you a favour - make sure you send the bitch some flowers."

She chortles at the thought.

"Lilies," barks Captain Turner.

Wendy looks up and smiles. She is quite adorable as quiet resolve firms up her features.

"Are you going to do something nice for yourself?" asks the good Captain.

She shakes her head in genuine confusion.

"Go away, buy jewellery, get drunk with friends? Better still - buy a dog."

She stares at me and nods vigorously.

"What a good idea. What kind?"

I look out the window at the bay - there is what I call a bronze light. It's a very special hue, seen only when sun breaks out between heavy rain clouds. It is prized by nature photographers, as it does wonderful things to colours.

"Hmm, what dog... I'd say something large and not too smart. Not quite the ex, but enough to give you a bit of a substitute."

She laughs and slaps her knee.

"Fetch, jump, lick."

I am a little unbalanced by that turn in conversation and restrict my reaction to raising my brows.

"Good security, too."

"Do dogs drink beer?"

"Sometimes. Not their staple diet."

"Well, that would be a pleasant change. Woof."

"Do you need a lawyer?"

She stares at me in fright, then slowly nods.

"I guess I better get one."

"Do it soon. Get rid of all the untidy bits right away. Do you have a joint account?"

"Yes, but there isn't much in it."

"Whose name is the house in?"

"We are still renting."

"Even better," I reach over the leather folder with all my bits and pieces and write a name and a number, etched in my memory, on a memo pad. She takes it and nods gratitude.

"Tell him I sent you."

She carefully folds the paper and stows it away in her shirt pocket.

"I better do some work. Thanks, Captain."

I smile as she leaves. Sadly, that is as much as I will do with vigour today.

I glance across at the drug pump, where a drop of yellowish fluid is forming on the needle inside the chamber. The machine clicks, and the drop falls into the pool below. An equal volume of poison has just been sent down the line into my body.

I lean back on the pillows and take a deep breath, looking out the window. The clouds have moved in to cover the sun, and the bronze light illuminates me no longer.

I stretch out my hand to the bedside draw, pull it open and find the notepad without taking my eyes off the window. I flip it open at the plastic bookmark between pages and take a deep breath before tearing my eyes away from the window to read what I had recently written.

{}{}{}

As the transporter rounds the last corner of the log road, I see Brana once more.

I grip the gun handles tighter as the walls come into view. They repaired the breach, and the gate is yawning with new, glistening white timber. The moat also seems wider - they probably raised the level of the dyke. I would.

None of this seems to be of much use to the townspeople now. The plain before the walls is crawling with vermin, most of whom seem to be just standing still, just a short distance out of crossbow range. They know that time is on their side - or was, until we made the long trip. We approach from upwind, and the vermin don't hear us until they are surrounded.

I stay silent, letting the sergeants act on instinct. Eight machines hurtle out of the forest and veer out to form a wide row, then race at top speed to close the distance. The vermin begin to run as they are overtaken by doom from every direction. It is far too late.

Eight hopper guns open up, shredding the crowd between the machines and the moat. The gunners begin at both flanks and work the stream of angry lead into the bunched middle. My machine begins to pitch as it rolls over the dead, and I loosen my posture to ride the hard jerks, keeping the gun steady and efficient. We slow down as we close the distance to the fleeing crowd, flanking fire driving its ragged remains towards the centre. I shout obscenities as my gun runs dry, snatch a new canister of ammunition and ram it in the hopper, jumping back into the seat to wrestle with the slide, frantic with desire to rejoin the killing.

Without warning the driver lets go of the throttle, and the tracks slacken. We roll to a stop, and I rotate the turret from left to right, walking fire into a mess of hairy backs and flailing arms. I continue until the view of the wall is clear. Only then do I force myself to take stiff, sweating hands off the handles.

There is an eerie silence as smoke drifts out of the turret, leaving me with a clear view. The moat is a short distance before the transporter, and it runs red with blood. The ground is entirely covered with bodies - I guess that we never caught so many vermin in an open space.

I turn the handle on the top hatch, emerging from it amid the smoke. I see many faces on the wall, staring at me with a mixture of awe and horror.

"Drop the fucking bridge!" I shout as loud as I can. My voice is hoarse and harsh, and I see the bridge move at once.

I slide back into the turret and pick up the headset.

"Red, we are going in," I tell him. "Go over the bridge, up the main street and into the market square. Form a defensive perimeter once we arrive."

"Acknowledged, Commander" I hear Redmond's calm voice. "Up main street, defensive perimeter in market square."

I settle back into the gunner's seat as the machine turns, rumbles to the bridge and thunders over the new timbers. There is a feeling as if I stepped out of my body and watch the convoy rattle over the cobblestones of the narrow main street of Brana from somewhere above.

The market square comes into view as I almost succumb to nausea, then the dizziness is gone. I climb down the tower into the lower deck.

The tracks come to a halt as I march down towards the rear hatch. On my signal the soldier whose name I can't recall winds the handle, and the hatch begins to open. I hold out both arms for someone to strap on the weapon harnesses, then step into the dim light of early dusk.

I stand fast, letting light rain fall on my burning forehead, holding out my arms to point the revolvers into the ground just in front of me. I watch the transporters line up into a defensive formation - four sides and the rest in between - as Brana's townspeople rush towards the market square. My gaze is riveted to the plain outside the wall, dark with the dead of our attack, and my mouth is clenched hard with the receding rush of combat.

I await until the square is filled with people and lower my gaze to survey the crowd. I turn away and walk inside the lead transporter, climb into the turret and emerge from the top hatch, climbing gingerly over the labyrinth of sharp metal blades on the roof. I spy a spot missed by the builders and step on it, staring at the sea of faces that now surrounds our machines.

The final moons of the siege have not been kind to Brana - most of its defenders look driven to the edge of starvation.

"It is simple," I shout across the crowd. "You know who we are, and you know why we are here. All who wish to come with us will be taken to Grey. We will carry small precious possessions; you need not take anything other than weapons. The citizens of Grey will provide you with everything you need."

There is much murmuring, and I can see that many in the crowd are breathless with hostility. It is understandable.

"A few other points," I tell them. "Good citizens of Brana, I am well aware of your skill with the crossbow. There are many among you who can take a deer from as far as the eye can see. Mind that you do not shoot any of men."

I pause and stare into as many gaunt faces as distance allows.

"If any of my soldiers are harmed, I will withdraw and burn your town. No rescue and no survival behind the walls."

Without pausing to study the reaction, I continue.

"I have a blood debt against those who had killed my merchants. I will settle for a trial by combat with Josiah. The rest may go free, but they will not come back with me to Grey. I care not what they do or where they go."

I jump from the transporter nimbly enough, crouching right down to the knees and springing up to point the revolvers at the first man I face.

"Take me to Josiah."

The man stares into the barrels numbly. He is heavy-set and middle-aged, with recent scars on his face which look like burns. He carries a heavy knife at his chest and a crossbow is slung over his shoulder on a tattered leather band. His beard is grey, and the small eyes stare at me from beneath hooded lids. He does not change his posture in response to the threat, and I guess that he stood many a watch on the crumbling walls of Brana during the past few moons.

"Now."

Something akin to contempt flickers in his eyes, then he turns on his heel and begins to walk from the square. I follow.

We head down one of the older, crooked streets that leads from the market towards the lake. It looks as if there were many fires during the siege - I make a note to ask about that later. Many houses are charred rubble, with crude wooden crosses marking where someone had died.

My guide walks slowly, to show his scorn for the threat of death. I follow him some yards past, with Redmond and a few others marching a few steps behind me.

We find ourselves in a wide open space that faces the lake. I smell the stagnant reek of the port, a long bay of the lake enclosed by the town wall. It is full of fishing vessels that always plied the lake - they are tied with heavy chains and protected by heavy mesh from above.

I must ask what from.

The shore is lined with crosses that protrude over fresh mounds of earth. It makes sense, I note in a kind of a daze, to bury the dead in the moist soil next to the lake - that is where the contamination will last the least.

My guide weaves among the graves and suddenly stops. He turns, and a nasty smile creases his scolded face. He beckons me with a mocking finger and waits until I stand beside him. He points the finger into the ground.

"I give you Josiah, warlord. May you meet him sooner rather than later."

He begins to walk away as I stare at a large metal cross that is shaped like an ancient sword. I read the old script over and over - there is no mistake.

"Stop him."

There is a short scuffle as my men leap on the crossbowman. He tries to draw his knife, but Redmond slaps away his hand and twists it behind the man's back. I take a few steps to confront him.

"Josiah had a niece. Her name is Rina."

He nods.

"Where is she now?"

He straightens, and I signal Redmond to release him.

As I see the crossbowman turn and walk between the graves, a stream of liquid ice floods my insides.

He points at another grave. There is no cross, just a few withered flowers over a mound of dark, muddy soil.

I run towards him and stare at the freshly turned earth, then jerk the crossbowman by the shoulder to face me.

"What happened to her?"

"As you can see, she killed herself, warlord. No cross."

I stare at him with incomprehension.

"Our faith prohibits taking your own life. We cannot bury these poor wretches with honour, and their souls are condemned to wander the earth."

"Why?"

He shrugs shoulders with an utter lack of interest.

"It was always so."

I slap him hard across the face, and he is thrown off his feet onto the ground. I follow and spring the left bayonet, whose needle-sharp point just touches the grizzled skin of the throat with a needle-sharp point.

"That was your last insolence, knave," I hiss, holding his head to the ground by the ear. "What I asked is why Rina killed herself."

"Who knows," he replies with surprising tenderness in his voice. "A better question is why the rest of us didn't."

I place the point of the bayonet on a stone next to his

face and push to stow the blade, then clamber to my feet and turn away. I hear him rise and walk away with the light tread of the hunter.

I sit down next to the grave and take the withered flowers from muddy soil. They look like mountain daisies, and I place them back with infinite care.

My vision goes dark, and there is a feeling of utter emptiness in my chest. I long to be gone from this vile place and close my unseeing eyes, to lie amid soft grass, mountain daisies swaying in the sky above me. It would be a peaceful end, falling asleep in the warm sun.

Suddenly I am not in a mountain meadow. I am dying all right, but it seems to be a soldier's death. I am wearing a familiar-looking combat tunic and clutch a rifle that I can only dream to have - a slick, light piece with a huge magazine and what looks like a small telescopic sight. I never succeeded in making one of those, but I know exactly what that is. It seems to be the side of the ancient road, but its surface is dark and smooth, not the mossy rocks I am used to seeing. There is a terrible pain coming from my right leg, and I moan in agony as I rise on my elbows to take a look.

When I come to, it is nearly dark. I rise and see Redmond, who sits nearby, his head bowed in sorrow. The other soldiers are sleeping on the ground, and I signal to alert them.

We walk up the hill in total silence. I decide to never ask how or why again. It may be possible to find out more, but even a short train of thought leads to the inevitable conclusion - if I have any chance of sleeping another peaceful night, it is best not to know.

{}{}{}

"This is our star patient," says Wilkins, smiling broadly.

I hastily shut the notepad as my tiny room is invaded by the oncology round. This is a timeless hospital ritual that is part patient care, part communication between different teams, part ritual abuse of apprentices, depending on the personalities involved. Primarily, it involves talking over a patient as if he is a block of meat resting on top of a hospital bed. Any sensitive communication with the patient has to be done later - decent people always refrain from saying much and return afterwards, if much needs to be said.

Wilkins holds out his hand, and his registrar, a small Indian man with a fine moustache, hands him the tablet with my results. Wilkins squints at the figures, holding the device as if it was smeared in faeces, then drops, more than hands it, back.

"Excellent news all around," says he, beaming. "The white cell count is, more or less, gone, which is an excellent response. The uric acid is a bit of a menace at this stage. You!"

Everyone shudders from that violent change in his voice. As a sensible adult, I roll my eyes and stare out of the window in embarrassment. The day outside is the same as for the past two weeks - bright and sunny. I am beginning to hate that - it's like a constant smile of a retarded man. Not that I have anything against retarded people - but smiling all the time is simply inappropriate. Life also requires tears, anger, frowns, grimaces - that is the normal way to behave.

The object of Wilkins' venom has been located - a tall blonde girl with bland features and a short white coat, which is the sorry mark of a medical student. I shift my gaze and examine the victim - frumpy, ill-fitting clothes, a plastic watch and thick glasses in an industrial-size black frame. She instantly earns my sympathy as I backfill her story - brought up on a rocky farm, worked like a tractor, avoided boyfriends with sticky fingers and frisky penises, learned everything a crappy school in an inland town had to offer, probably cried for the first time in her life when the offer from the medical school arrived in the rural mail. Fuck me, give that girl a medal. Not this.

"Uric acid," purrs Wilkins with a dangerous undertone in his voice. "Why are worried about that, pray-tell?"

A dozen heads swivels at the girl, who goes bright-red.

"It is a product of DNA breakdown," she answers in a shaky voice. Wilkins face visibly reflects his disappointment.

"So what?" he asks petulantly.

"Um, Mr... uh..."

"Captain Nicholas Turner at your service," I tell her

in the best officer voice I can muster under the circumstances. To best speak with authority you need to stand up, and all I can do is rise on the pillows. Nausea has been something of a problem today.

Everyone turns towards me, some faces registering annoyance, others surprise - look here, it can talk.

My diversion works perfectly. The girl marshals her resources and rises beyond elementary bullying.

"Captain Turner is losing a lot of leukaemic cells," she says in a loud, clear tone that mimics mine. "This is causing a build-up of cell debris, including DNA, which is broken down to many products, including uric acid."

Wilkins more or less ignores her answer and merely resumes where he left off.

"Two more days in the current cycle?" he asks the registrar.

"Three including today, yessir," replies the Indian quickly, as if Wilkins might change his mind about giving me chemotherapy.

"Excellent, excellent," says Wilkins without turning around. "Have we made discharge arrangements?"

The question is addressed to an intern, a tired-looking youth with a round face and a mop of curly red hair. He is tall and has wide shoulders, but his cheap office pants are beginning to bulge at the waist. Rugby and beer, I think sadly. As people get older...

"Yes, professor," replies the youth without delay. I am

relieved that he was paying attention instead of rummaging in his to-do lists, as they always do. Internship in a teaching hospital teaches little about medicine, but it's a great way to learn self-organization. Your life depends on acquiring that skill.

The discharge arrangements have indeed been made. I am going home on the weekend, and the nurses will visit daily.

Wilkins nods and chooses not to explore that statement. I have to report to the oncology clinic every few days anyway.

"What did the ophthalmologist think?" asks he vaguely. This is, of course, deceptive.

"A very tiny anopia," says the intern eagerly. "They could barely map it."

"That is a good thing," says Wilkins brightly, and he is suddenly a real doctor, genuinely there for his patient. That's what he must have been like when he was young.

He looks at me questioningly. I shrug my shoulders.

"I can't tell. Feels pretty normal in that department."

"But we are going to do a second cycle," says Wilkins, wagging his finger. "I want this to be your last relapse."

I nod without a change of expression.

"It wasn't so bad this time."

He reaches over the end of the bed to shake my left

hand, unencumbered by an IV line, then turns to the door. Everyone files out of the room, and Wilkins strolls down the human corridor, looking as if he was just crowned.

{}{}{}

I pick at a sore tooth with a splinter and wait for the sergeants to finish the count, seated at an imposing table improvised from a charred door and firewood. I am slightly dizzy from poor sleep - everything in my body is aching, and I am restless from grief. It's a warm, sunny day that makes me feel even worse - that is nature's way of reminding humans about their insignificance.

Life has to be lived, and I will have to learn how to live it.

The warmth raises the prospect of snow in the next few days. This is a consolation - I need that river full to the brim.

Solly runs back to my table and dumps eight scraps of paper covered in numbers on the rough timber surface. I toss away the splinter and slam my hand on the paper pile just before it is caught on the breeze. The tooth feels no better for being probed.

He watches as I turn over one sheet at a time, add its total then crumple the lot and toss them over my shoulder. I check the numbers once again, then straighten in my chair with a grimace.

"Eight hundred and ninety so far, and a few more are

thinking it over."

Solly whistles in surprise.

"Call the others. We need to talk."

He runs off, and I drum my fingers on the table, forcing myself to focus on the problem. That is certainly three times more than the number expected. There is no hope of stuffing that many bodies into my convoy - I expected maybe two hundred, with a few more riding in improvised trailers. A thousand refugees will require all of my creativity, if any of us are to get home alive.

The sergeants take their seats around the improvised table. Someone has brought a large container of boiling water, and we brew berry tea.

"There are three ways," begins Redmond, staring at a crowd of people behind the line of soldiers. "We have the road, the river and the sky."

I ready the pencil to make notes.

"By road we can only take two hundred and forty," says Tancred. "I counted three times."

"No more?" I ask with dismay.

"Not in our machines," he replies with finality. "Any more would have to stick their heads out of the hatches."

"Very well," I write down that number. "Do they have any machines we can commandeer?"

Solly shakes his head.

"Street carts," he spits curtly. "They get stuck in a

puddle between cobblestones."

"So that's two hundred and forty by road. Which leaves, say, seven hundred and fifty. What is their airship strength?"

"We can get eight into the air," says Redmond. "Each can lift ten men."

"How much fuel?"

"Plenty, Commander. But it's crude, filthy stuff, and their ships are useless in bad weather. The engines go out in high wind."

Everyone instantly looks up. There are just a few feathery clouds over the highest peaks, and the lake is mirror-smooth, which is rare at this time of day.

"The weather could be anything," I tell them. It's half a day's flight to Grey, and another half-day back - at that rate I don't see the point."

"Maybe they can come later," says Tancred.

"Not a chance," says Redmond without glancing in Tancred's direction. Animosity between my sergeants is not what I need, and I note that for later.

"Why not?" I ask out of curiosity.

"Anyone who wants to leave is considered a traitor," explains Redmond. "Not only to the defence of the town, but as an outcast from the faith. They will never let this happen once we are gone. No, whoever gets to leave has to come with us or not at all."

"That leaves the river," I tell them, marvelling the bewildered looks.

"Their boats cannot go that shallow," says Solly. "Three foot draft, no less."

"It was done in Grandfather's time," I tell them. "He began with river transport until he built the land fleet."

"Was the river deeper in his day?" asks Redmond.

"It was slightly deeper," I reply. "He used flat-bottomed boats with paddle wheels to go against the current. The wheels were sturdy enough to push against the bottom on the shallows. It was hard work, but he managed to get up to the lake all the way from the sea."

"So where do we get paddle wheels?" asks Tancred.

I bite off an impulsive remark - the man is beginning to get on everyone's nerves.

"You are a little slow today, my friend," I enunciate each syllable, and that is all they will see of my irritation. "The hard work was to get the boats up the river. They floated by themselves on the way down."

Redmond nods his head in comprehension.

"Rafts."

"Yes, rafts. Logs in a frame, with around twenty people on each."

"That will be too heavy," says Solly. "They still have to scrape through the rocks and the shallows."

"I have thought of that."

They study my design, which I draw on the back of the tally paper.

"How will they roll?" asks Tancred.

"That's a metal frame," I stab the pencil into the paper. "These bolts will go into the wood and serve as axles. Not precision engineering, but logs will turn in the shallows like rollers. The current is more than strong enough to push them through."

"Where do get the materials?" asks Tancred.

"I believe I know what Commander has in mind," says Redmond. "There are dried logs near the port, and the metal rods are found near coal mine."

Heads turn.

"A coal mine?" asks Solly incredulously. "These fuckers have coal?"

"They found it some time ago," says Redmond. "That is when trouble started."

We all stare at him in anticipation as he sips on his tea.

"Three days before we arrived one of Josiah's henchmen crushed his leg loading the catapult on the wall. He is dying and was visited by a priest. The dying man made a full confession."

Redmond looks up from his tea and looks each one of us in the eyes.

"You need to hear it for yourselves."

We follow him across the square into a squat brick building that serves as the local infirmary. As is custom in Brana, everything is meticulously clean and organized, with the wounded suffering in dignified silence on white sheets.

We cross the infirmary and enter a corridor with many doors. It is clear that most of them open but once for many that are carried through - this is where they put the dying men who can no longer control their cries.

Four of our soldiers stand guard at the end of the corridor, and they snap to attention when we approach. I salute them back and wave for them to open the door. A group of Brana men stands some distance away.

"These are church elders," says Redmond, bowing to them deferentially. "I wanted them to hear this too."

A sickly sweet stench of dying flesh drifts into the corridor from the open door, and the sergeants cover their faces with scarves in disgust. I walk into the room and head for the window, holding my breath.

Cold wind rushes inside, but the dying man seems to appreciate it. His tall, powerful frame is sunk deep into the canvas bed, all of its sheets soaked in sweat. What remains of his leg is covered in a bandage coated with pine tar. Even under the thick dressing it is clear that the limb had swelled to grotesque proportions.

I sit down next to the bed, drawing a pained turn of the bald head.

"What is your name, soldier?"

"Harvey, warlord."

"I came to hear what you want to say, Harvey."

"It began during last spring," whispers Harvey, sinking back into the bed. "Just over a year ago Josiah went to do business with the whaler people."

Tannis and I exchange a look.

"He returned with a great book of maps, and that is how we found the coal. It was right under the town."

I nod with resignation.

"Then Josiah decided that we must attack Grey."

Everyone is startled, myself included.

"What the fuck for?" I ask in amazement.

"Manpower. We did not have enough townspeople to make good on our new fortune. It would take a generation or more, and Josiah did not want to wait."

"But you had no hope," I hear myself say through a haze of dizziness. "You have no weapons, few men and no machines."

"All true," says Harvey, running his hand over the bedside table. I reach over and push the drinking bottle into his palm.

He drinks deeply and opens his eyes, holding the bottle to his burning forehead. I snap my fingers and point to the pillow. Tancred soaks a hand towel next to the wash basin and drapes it over Harvey's scarred forehead.

The dying man nods in gratitude.

"Josiah and I made a treaty with the bush people."

I bolt out of the chair, and it takes all of my willpower to stop. I want to throw Harvey through the window and tear him to pieces outside the infirmary.

"How is that even possible?" asks Redmond hoarsely.

"Just like I speak to you now," Harvey tells him. "Their words are hard to understand, but they are not unlike ours. Even after the scourge we were one and the same people. First Josiah trapped an old male and learned his tongue. Then he made some kind of a deal and released him. A week later he ordered me to come with him across the lake. We landed in a hidden cove and met with the bush people, he and I."

"What were you planning?" I force myself to keep my tone calm, imitating Redmond's cold, precise cadence. "How did you intend to use the vermin?"

"He offered them food in exchange for service," says Harvey, his voice beginning to slip. "He wanted them to attack Grey and told them how. I was detailed to train them in making weapons."

"Better and better," I comment in a state of detached marvel. "And pray, what weapons do they have now?"

"Spears and primitive bows. Not crossbows - they tried, but you need metal tools for that. We did not give them any."

"Have you supplied them with any of your own

weapons?" asks Redmond.

"We have not," replies Harvey hoarsely. "Josiah reasoned that they must use their own resources, rather than rely on ours."

I force myself to sit down and take a few deep breaths before continuing. Harvey seems exhausted by his confession - he lies back on the sweat-stained pillow, breathing through an open mouth brimming with black and broken teeth.

"So the plan was for them to take Grey?"

"Yes. All children and young women to go to Brana. The rest - as the bush people saw fit."

A dangerous smile begins to form on my face.

"But then the vermin realized that they don't have to tramp all the way to the coast. There were rich pickings close by. Am I right?"

"Yes, warlord," whispers Harvey. "You are."

I look up and stare each of the church elders in the eyes.

"They attacked Brana instead," I tell them. "Doesn't it say somewhere that he who lives by the sword dies by the sword?"

"It does, warlord," says Harvey.

"Who else knew of this?"

"Nearly a dozen others, warlord. But they all died in the siege."

"Like Josiah?"

"Yes, like Josiah. He threw himself into the thick of every battle. I don't believe he wanted to live."

A thought startles me, and I touch Harvey on the shoulder.

"What about Rina?"

"His niece..." Harvey opens his eyes and pierces me with a pained stare. "After Josiah was killed she found his diary."

"Was that why she took her life?"

"I have no way of knowing, warlord," Harvey's voice is now a rasping whisper. "But when we found her, the ashes of the diary were still smouldering in her hearth."

I look up to the ceiling and fight a swarm of thoughts.

"I have only one favour to ask."

My mind returns to the stinking infirmary cell, and I look the dying man in the eyes.

"I suppose you want a quick end?"

"No, warlord. I do not."

I raise my brows in surprise.

"I am the last of Josiah's inner circle," whispers Harvey. "There is no forgiveness for what we had done. I know I am going to hell, but maybe it won't be so bad if I suffer before I die. Please ask them to do what they can to keep me alive a bit longer."

I don't recall how I left the infirmary. My next recollection is of retching the meagre remains of my lunch in a dirty alley. Redmond passes me his flask, and I pour it over my head, then rise and pour the remainder into my mouth.

He replaces the flask, staring at me with calm concentration.

"At least that explains many things."

I nod as I gargle, then spit out the fouled water.

"Small mercies. Red, we are in deep trouble."

"We have been for some time, Commander. The difference is that we are now aware of it."

I stare hard, evaluating his statement. He is, of course, right. I nod.

"The only question is how we proceed," says Redmond. "How we plan the counter-attack. What happens after that - well, you know. No battle plan survives the first volley of fire."

I nod again.

"Come and see what our naval engineers have been up to," says Redmond, starting to walk downhill. I follow.

The waterfront has been transformed. All who chose to leave, from children to elderly, have been organized into crews. The logs had been sawn, the frames had been welded, and many assembled rafts line the hill overlooking the water.

I study the end product with doubt. They have to survive nearly a hundred miles of river, the first thirty so shallow that a man can walk across without getting his belly wet. The heavily laden rafts have to navigate this waterway without getting stuck - no doubt, our river escapees will be watched with great hunger from the forest.

"Show me how it floats," I order Solly, who is toiling shirtless, his knotted arms covered in tiny burns from the welding.

He nods and whistles. Twenty men run to the raft and mount its platform of thin planks set just above the logs. They use long poles to push off the shore and launch the raft, the logs rolling exactly like wheels.

The raft drifts away from the shore, its waterline just above the logs - leaving the deck mere inches above the water. It will be a wet ride.

"Overturn it," I shout, and they place long poles to one side, heaving at them with all might. The raft tilts, but shows no intention of capsizing.

I nod, and they release the pressure, polling the raft back to the shore. I kick at the metal experimentally - it seems entirely solid.

"How many more can we build, Solly?"

"Enough for all, Commander. There is plenty of material."

I bend down and sniff the fresh cut of a log.

"What is this timber? It floats so well."

"Black beech, Commander. Very strong and light once it is seasoned. It doesn't grow on the coast."

I nod my approval and count the ready rafts. More than two-thirds are ready.

"Another few days, and we are ready to leave, then?"

Solly nods reluctant approval. He is clearly surprised by his own success.

"It seems so, Commander."

"How do we get to the river?"

"One of these rust buckets will be used to tow a batch of rafts to the first shallows, Commander. From there the current is fast anyway."

I nod. We decided not to stagger the flotilla, thinking there is safety in numbers. If there is a fight on the river, the refugees stand a better chance together. I am hoping for nothing of the kind - the vermin hate water. My main fear is whether the rafts will hold: if they fail, the occupants will be soaked in freezing water, then wade ashore to seek their fortune in the forest.

"Each traveller is to be armed," I tell Solly. "To the teeth."

He nods and points to boxes stored under canvas awnings next to the refugee tents. We made something of an armed camp near the waterfront, to prevent any trouble with those who wish to remain in Brana.

"Brana crossbows," says Solly with awe. "The ones that fire repeatedly. A great weapon - light enough for a child to wield, yet lethal out to fifty yards."

I nod, thinking of the futility of life. We cast guns out of the best metal that neither fatigues nor rusts. We hunt over land and sea to collect chemicals to make gunpowder, then we manufacture and store that substance at great risk.

But the men of Brana somehow discovered the ancient design. They use wood, stone chips, glue boiled down from deer hooves and a few rude nails - to make something just as deadly as a revolver, with barely any weight.

It seems as if all labours of the mind arise from the failure to see the obvious, and I am weary of this life, where the obvious is usually invisible.

I leave Solly to his labours and turn to the cemetery. Rumours travel fast - I see that the sword marking Josiah's grave had been broken off near the ground and stolen. Flies are swarming around it, suggesting that someone passed water on Josiah in the night.

I turn away and find Rina's grave, barely visible behind a forest of hastily erected crosses and crude gravestones. As we approach, I see that a pile of rags lies over the mound of bare soil. I am even curious to see what that is.

At the sound of our footsteps the pile bolts upright

and begins to run. Catching up with ease, I take hold of the filthy cloth and spin the entire sorry package off the feet, holding him to the ground.

My quarry is a boy of seven, maybe eight summers. His thin face is grey with dirt, and the smell coming from the tiny body is less than conducive to conversation. Blue eyes stare at me with resignation and sadness.

"What is your name, ragamuffin?" I ask, shifting the weight off my hand slightly.

He stares at length, then turns his head and spits on the ground.

"I am called boy."

"That's not a name," says Redmond patiently. "You are that, but so is every other boy. You must have a proper name. Mine is Redmond. Do you know who that other man is?"

"Sure," replies the child with contempt. "It's the grand warlord himself. She said you will come here and finish what the bush people started."

I jerk him upright, bringing my face close to his.

"She, you said. Who is this she, rascal?"

"Lady Rina."

I let go of the torn collar and slide to the ground, kneeling in front of the child.

"How do you know her, boy?"

"She saved me from starving after my parents died," says he tonelessly. "I slept in her wood shed and ate in her kitchen all winter until... she was no more."

"So where do you live now?" asks Redmond.

"Here."

I look around and see no abode.

"I sleep wherever there is shelter," says the boy. "Sometimes here, sometimes there."

Remaining on my knees, I grasp his bone-thin shoulders.

"Do you know that she once loved me?"

That penetrates his armour like a bullet. The dirty face crumples, and huge tears make white streaks on the grimy cheeks.

"Come with us, boy. I will care for you like my own son."

He stares at me for a long time, then nods.

"I have to take a friend."

Before I can open my mouth he runs away and dives into what looks like the remains of a cellar amid a pile of charred timber. I rise to my feet and look at Redmond, who shrugs his shoulders.

The boy emerges from the hole cradling something in his arms. As he approaches I see a most unusual cat - white with brown ears and tail. It stares at me with a single blue eye. The other appears to be missing.

"What is that, boy?"

"I call him Rat. He and I are partners - he catches rats, and I cook them. That is how we stayed alive."

I nod.

"You and Rat will be most welcome among my soldiers," I tell him with a slight bow. "Anyone who can survive like that can teach us a thing or two."

The boy stares at me with suspicion but finally nods.

"Where shall we transport them?" asks Redmond.

"They come with me in the turret."

Redmond nods.

"Escort them to the camp and have him shaven, washed and fed."

The boy looks at me with instant hatred, and the cat rears its triangular head. Its solitary blue eye pierces me with a warning stare.

"Also, could you find him a small uniform, complete with a dagger."

The hatred changes to exultation, and I wave them away.

I know - this is the last time I get to be at Rina's grave, and I lie down on the damp soil, resting my cheek against the chill of the grave. I run my hand over the mound of dirt until it is smooth and press my palm into the clay, leaving a trace of my presence the only way I can.

{}{}{}

We stare at the skies, studying the feathery clouds that race across the jagged horizon. It feels like a funeral, for we will never return. In weeks to come Brana will be fighting for survival, and it is not going to win. My final visit to this place has made that certain.

With a heavy sigh I step into the lead transporter and walk the length of the lower deck, grasp the rails of the ladder and clamber up the rungs into the turret. Boy sits in the far corner on my bedroll, holding Rat in his arms. Both stare at me - three blue eyes of Brana's despair.

I nod in silent affirmation and turn the handle to open the top hatch.

"Commander, I would not do that," crackles Redmond's voice in the headphones.

I place the headset over my scalp and adjust the microphone.

"Has to be done, old friend. Has to be done this way."

He does not reply, and I clamber up until my torso protrudes from the hatch.

"Soldiers of the Regiment, once again we depart this sad place. Move out."

There is a loud hiss of steam, and a cloud of acidic smoke belches from the stack. The transporter shudders heavily and settles to a fine vibration.

"Forward."

There is a jerk, then the machine lurches forward, and the air is filled with a deep rumble of the strain. We are towing a long trailer, filled to capacity with people and the few possessions we permitted them to take.

The citizens of Brana line our passage, hard, grimy faces staring at me as I roll past, eyes front, my right hand in a stiff gesture of salute.

That is the only thing I can do now.

We approach the wall, and the drawbridge is lowered without orders. Our tracks rattle over massive timbers as I turn my head to watch the heavily laden convoy exit the town. There is no reaction to our departure, save for the bridge beginning to rise as soon as the last vehicle clears the moat.

"Lord have mercy upon them," says someone over the radio. It sounds like Redmond, but I do not move to identify him. Lord, if there is one, may you have mercy on us too.

If there is mercy enough to go around.

{}{}{}

Boy and I stare at the forest through the porthole, and for once I do not feel tired. I absently note that the sky is turning black by degrees, but otherwise have trouble marshalling my thoughts, noting only that the warmth and the leaden sky do not make for a promising trip.

Rat stirs in Boy's lap, stretching out an impossibly long paw into the air and fixing me with his sole blue eye. He stares at me with no good will whatsoever, turns over and goes back to sleep, pressing his diamond-shaped muzzle into Boy's chest.

"She did love you," says Boy.

I turn to stare at him in surprise, then nod just once.

"I know it hurts."

"Tell me," I start hesitantly, clenching my fists at my sides. "Did she say anything I should know?"

He looks into my eyes, then shakes his head resolutely.

"She said very little, warlord."

I wait, then nod with finality.

"I am sorry," says Boy.

"Thank you," I hear myself say in a choked voice. "It means a lot that you care."

He studies my face, puzzled.

"You are all I have left of her, child. I will make sure that you do well."

Before he has a chance to answer, Redmond's head appears in the turret.

"Commander, I think you should know," he says gravely. I turn to him and raise my eyebrows.

"The barometer is dropping very quickly," says Redmond.

"Did you make up the difference for height?"

"I did, Commander," I detect a flicker of annoyance in his expression. "We haven't gained much height since we left."

"I do not mean to doubt you, old friend. That is bad news indeed."

"We have maybe until midday, Commander. I recommend that we find a defensible position and stop."

I wind open the top hatch and will myself to attend to reality - which I manage with some difficulty. It is very, very warm for this time of year, and I can see the dark clouds obscuring the sky.

"Let's go higher," I reply after some thought. "The worst place we can stop is on this plain."

Redmond nods and disappears back down the well.

"What is wrong?" asks Boy, clutching his cat.

"It's about to snow," I explain, studying the terrain through the porthole. "It means that once we stop, we won't be able to move for a while. "

"Can they move in deep snow?"

I turn to study his face but see no trace of fear - he stares at me with earnest eyes, asking a simple and practical question. I feel pride.

"They can, until the snow gets this deep," I indicate chest height. "Then we become safe for a while. Then the snow begins to harden, and we are in great danger, for we can't move and they can. Then it melts, and we can move again."

"But you have these great guns," Boy points to the hopper gun.

"All very well until night time," I explain grimly. "Then it becomes a contest of hearing. The snow makes it possible to move in near-silence."

"What can they do to your machines?"

I sigh, recalling the last breach of the armour.

"We cannot have thick walls," I tell him, shaking my head. "Metal is heavy, and we cannot make it too thick. It is possible for them to get inside if they are not shot up before they come close."

I can see his angular jaws tighten.

"You have your dagger," I tell him. "Stab anything that comes near."

"Warlord," he says sternly, ignoring my light-hearted remark. "Are we in real trouble?"

I smile.

"I've been in and out of such trouble all my life," I tell him. "I am still alive, and many vermin are not."

{}{}{}

"Mac!"

"Captain!"

We shake hands. My old friend from Aceh is Lance Corporal MacKenzie, my right-hand man in the jungle. Life has not been that kind to him. Or, for that matter, to me.

"I didn't know you were in here," he rushes to pick up my carry-bag. It is full of books, but he jerks it over his shoulder as if it was empty. Mac stands just a little taller than I, and his shoulders are probably twice my width. His broad Maori face with a long, thin nose that sports more than one break from his torrid youth is adorned with a beatific smile.

The uniform of a patient driver bulges on his once-steely frame. He has clearly taken his love of beer to a place one shouldn't go.

He supports me by the elbow, and I am grateful. This is the first decent time on my feet for some days, and the old balance is yet to recover from the chemo.

"Is it the old leuk?" he asks harshly.

I nod.

"You gonna fuck its arse," says Mac with total assurance.

"You can count on it, El-Cee. Looks good right now, anyway."

The lift arrives, and he walks me inside, not bothering

to put down my bag. It's like a feather to him.

We ride down to the car park as he tells me the usual post-war story - an angry missus, feral kids, a string of jobs, alcohol.

"I am now living with my cousin," he concludes. "He is a paramedic, so he got me this job."

"Good for him," I rest my hand on his bulging shoulder with more pressure than I need to remain upright. "Anything you want, just ask. I'll be hanging around, you see."

For all its puffery Greymouth is still not a sprawling metropolis, and we pull up at my apartment block in minutes. Mac takes me up in the lift and waits as I rummage in the bag for the keys.

There is a musty smell inside the apartment, but it is entirely tidy and recently cleaned. A big bottle of southern port adorns the dining table, and there is a drinking straw taped to the bottle. I open the little card - it is, of course, from Helen and Co.

Mac asks me where I want the bag, and I nod at the couch. He refuses coffee, and I hug him before he leaves. I lost some weight, and the hug feels like a cobweb clinging to a tree stump.

I throw open the balcony doors, go outside and stare at the sea, settling down for the lengthy term of imprisonment. I am not allowed to socialize on the account of an immune system still shot up by the chemo, plus I have to follow a strict diet. Much as I crave the Chinaman's art, I can only eat bland, well-cooked food that will not tax the stomach. Guess it will be boiled potatoes and meat... Maybe make a shepherd's pie...

My phone was chirping for quite a while before I even realize it. The ring tone is set for a tiny hospital room, and I can barely hear it above the noise of the surf. I walk back to the kitchen and lift the phone out of my bag.

"Captain Turner?" asks a young female voice.

"Speaking."

"I am Lindy Chalmers, the medical student you might remember from a few days ago, on the ward round?"

I smile in recognition.

"I do. Right. Hello."

"I am just wondering if my colleague and I could come around for an extended interview? This is a project we need to do with someone who has just finished chemotherapy."

I guess they only carry hospital germs anyway. Blessed relief from boredom - I dictate the address and walk off to have a shower and change. They ring the bell from the lobby just as I grind fresh coffee.

Her colleague is a young Chinese boy with a slender frame and delicate features but tall, as young Chinese are these days, nearly my height. He is dressed simply but immaculately, and his long, slender fingers must surely mark him as a future brain surgeon. He is introduced as Harry Kwan - we shake hands warmly and I ask if he is aware of the den across the road. We immediately hit it off, as he launches into a concise but learned, discourse about local eateries. Yes, the lad will go far.

I serve them coffee and order them to eat biscuits with cream filling, for both look like they live on caffeine and air. They attempt to refuse.

"I am not feeling well," I tell them. "If one or both of you collapses from starvation, I will have real trouble doing the CPR thing. Eat, that's an order."

We spend the next two hours talking about my favourite subject - how a man with everything to live for copes with the prospect of dying young, of a horrible disease.

I find the discussion a great reality check, as no one else is strong enough to handle that topic - not Wilkins, not the nurses, not my friends, not even counsellors. Working on the edge of oblivion is too much for any normal psyche. These kids handle it well because they are doing it for the first and maybe the only time -

depending on their paths, the rest of their lives may proceed unsullied by the world of those with one foot in the grave.

They ask me why captain - sea? I laugh and tell them about Aceh. They nod respectfully, being old enough to remember the first blooding of their little nation. Lindy smiles.

"Thanks for what you did on the ward round," she says earnestly. "I appreciate it."

"No problem," I tell her. "I dislike bullies. Hospitals, you see - they are just make-believe places, with their petty hierarchies. Wilkins has no real power."

"Well, he does," says Lindy sadly. "He can give someone a lousy mark for the term, or he can remember a student and make his life hell during internship."

"What if you stand up to him? What's the worst thing that can happen?"

"I won't get placements of my choice."

"Do you know precisely what you will end up doing?"

"Not really."

"Then how do you know that your choices will be the right ones anyway?"

She smiles, understanding.

"I wanted to be an architect when I was a young man. I was into buildings."

"What happened?"

"I was useless at maths."

They both laugh, and I laugh with them.

"What can you do? I can still sketch fantastic designs, but you need maths to see if they can stand through an earthquake."

"So what did you do instead?"

"I got a shit-kicking job in public service, producing glossy brochures. Then came Independence. Then army and Aceh. I began to write about combat, and commissions began to flow. I got loaded with work when I came back. Then leukaemia. You have to make what you can of your life."

They stay until dusk starts to colour the corners of the sky. I grow quite tired and decide not to offer them dinner; they take their cue and thank me profusely as they leave.

I make myself mashed potatoes with cheese and enjoy this simple delicacy as the sun sinks into the ocean.

Today is a perfectly cloudless day, and that makes for a very bland sunset - the fireball simply dips into the water with no effect whatsoever. It is always the most irritating aspect of any human tragedy - nature goes on without a care. The sun rises, travels across the bright blue sky, sets, rises again - oblivious of the misery and pain on the earth beneath it.

Yes. How does one cope with the prospect of dying?

{}{}{}

"I suppose this is the best we can do," I tell Redmond.

We line up the transporters on a long meadow surrounded by the river on three sides. The fourth side is the way we came in, breaking thick undergrowth. The water is just a few inches short of covering the meadow, and that is likely to change if the snow comes.

"Make it really tight, Redmond," I warn him over the radio. "It has to be impossible to run between the machines."

"I acknowledge, Commander," says Redmond calmly. "Too tight to fit a man between machines."

I turn my attention to the gun, rubbing grease into the slide and checking the hopper for dents. It sways ominously in semi-darkness as I raise and lower the barrel, listening for squeaks.

Boy is watching me with a grim expression. The cat remains asleep at his breast, draping a long white paw over the child's shoulder.

"We eat dinner before sunset," I tell him. "Then it's lights out, and if you have to go to the latrine, keep silent. The sentries have to be alert to the slightest noise."

It begins to snow, with giant wet flakes drifting on the breeze. I stare at it with hatred - fresh snow is the enemy of an entrenched soldier. It hides the sounds of the enemy's approach, and if it is thick enough, it becomes impossible to see, even in daylight.

"Redmond," I say into the headset.

He responds after a few moments, sounding as calm as ever.

"I think it will happen tonight. Prepare mortars for shrapnel fire. Everyone be ready."

"Shrapnel fire, Commander. Everyone is ready."

I lie back, leaving the headset draped around my neck.

"When it starts, keep out of the way."

"Can I be of use?"

I smile and stare at Boy for the final time before turning out the dim light above my bedroll.

"You will be of great use once we train you. I am sorry there hasn't been time yet - but don't think I am not grateful to have you."

"What must I do now?"

"Sleep aplenty. Have you fed Rat?"

"He is stuffed full, Commander - and I had taken him to the bottom hatch for voiding. We are ready."

I smile in the darkness, feeling a wave of warmth I seldom experience.

"Then everything is as it should be."

{}{}{}

I awaken in total darkness, feeling icy air on my face.

I lie still, knowing that it may be the mere discomfort of the cold - but my hands close around the edge of the bedroll, ready to discard it and leap into the gunner's seat.

I begin to listen, but all I can hear is a dense silence. Snow must still be falling, for I can hear no sounds of the forest. The wind must have died down, and that leaves me feeling as if my ears are blocked from rapid descent. I clear them a few times, but all sounds are so dampened outside that I can almost hear the large, wet snowflakes slapping the roof.

I cannot hear Boy's breathing, but a soft snoring sound seems to come from the cat. Every now and again the animal sighs, precisely like a human, shifting in its sleep.

Then he falls silent.

I open my eyes and study its posture - he seems to be listening. As I shift, Rat turns towards me and gently wriggles out of the child's arms. I see its sleek white body glide across the turret in total silence, then it stops beside me and begins to scratch at the floor.

"Clever kitty," I mutter, pushing off the bedroll. I wind open the top hatch and raise the cat to the ceiling. He squeezes out and slides down the side of the transporter in total silence.

I wind the handle to make the gap just narrow enough for Rat to wriggle back in. Then I lie back and begin to listen - whatever Rat is doing on the ground, he doesn't make a sound. Some hunter.

Just as I decide that Rat is stalking some hapless rodent, I hear a muffled gallop that becomes a drumbeat as he runs along the roof. He glides through the hatch in one perfect jump and lands next to me with an angry hiss.

All sleep is forgotten as I reach for the headset.

"Tannis, alert," I cautiously pat Rat in gratitude and rotate the hatch lock shut, sliding into the gunner's chair, the headset over one ear.

I now hear them clearly enough, faint rustle and irregular crackles in the undergrowth. It doesn't sound like very many, but in these conditions it can be hard to tell.

"Tannis," I whisper into the headset. "Flare on my command."

"Flare on command, acknowledged," replies Tannis in a loud whisper.

I pull the slide of the hopper gun as quietly as I can

and listen again. The rustling seems to have stopped.

"Now!" I stare into the bush as a flare shoots upwards, the brilliant orange light highlighting many black shadows. I cut across them with a volley of bullets, shouting in triumph as they are thrown to the ground.

Shots erupt on all sides as the bush is filled with flying metal. There is no way to see through the undergrowth, and the only chance to make a statement is to saturate the darkness with lethal projectiles. I give it a few moments before ordering it to stop.

"Shrapnel grenades, all directions," I tell Tannis.

There are loud taps as mortar rounds are launched from all transporters, and I turn the turret away, just in case. Explosions roar, and a shower of metal shards whistles through night air to clatter against the side of the machine.

"Hold fire."

Tense silence ensues, and inevitably I turn to look at Rat. He sits licking its paw contentedly, next to Boy, who is cowering in the corner. I listen for a long time, longer than I would expect any attacker to bide his patience. There are no sounds in the bush outside.

"Well, kitty," I tell him with respect. "What do you know."

"Are they gone?" asks Boy. His shivering seems to be subsiding.

"They are dead, if that's what you mean," I tell him, rotating the turret to face the outside. Thanks to our white friend, we got them before they had a chance to climb the transporters. That results in the highest kill rate, but we don't usually manage to open fire that soon."

"Did Rat warn you?"

"He did exactly that."

Boy nods his head knowingly.

"Rat does that every time," he explains. "I think the vermin killed his family. I found him near the wall - they killed a lot of people when they managed to get over."

"Well, Rat is welcome in my convoy any day," I tell him. "As are you."

I reach out and shake his tiny hand.

"Will they come again?"

"They are not usually of that habit. In any case, I suspect we killed most of the raiding party."

Boy nods slowly.

"Then we are nearly home?"

"Nearly home. Yes, we are."

{}{}{}

The next day we strike a little luck - the snow turns to rain. We vacate the meadow just as the river begins to flood, leaving many corpses to the mercy of the rising water. The rain soon melts all the snow that fell overnight and we rattle over the ancient road unhindered. There is no snow at the pass either, and we cross to the other side of the range with unexpected speed.

In the early afternoon I make the decision to get to Grey before nightfall. We burn fuel with rare abandon and arrive at the floodplain just as shadows begin to lengthen.

A trailer crammed with refugees gets stuck crossing the river and begins to take water. Two timber tows race from the gates and splash across the river on their great spiked tracks. Everyone works frantically to hitch the trailer to tow chains.

I watch it being hauled out of the river and into town just as it starts to fall apart. The rear wheels collapse, and the tows slow down, just managing to drag it past the gates intact. The rest of the convoy crosses the river and rolls through the gate as afternoon turns to dusk. My transporter stands on guard and is the last to enter town.

It is done. I clamber down the ladder and walk out of the cabin, leaving my things behind. Boy follows me, Rat sitting alertly on his shoulder.

The square is full of people, and a great cheer rises to the purple sky as I walk down the ramp. It takes me some moments to realize that they are cheering none other than myself, and I lift my gaze, acknowledging the cheer with a tired nod. A moment later I change my mind, snap to attention and salute the crowd. The noise becomes a roar as I hold the salute, then abruptly drop my arm.

Trevor hobbles through the crowd towards me. He sees me empty-handed and catches a passing soldier by the shoulder, ordering something curtly. The soldier nods and turns around - I nod too, understanding what Trevor told him.

Trevor waves to me impatiently, and we meet amid the cheering throng of people. He takes both of my hands and clasps them in his gnarled paws, crushing the life out of them for a few moments. Then he slaps me on the shoulder hard enough to make me totter and tells me to go inside and take a bath. I ask, and he tells me that everyone made it down the river without a single casualty.

"Trevor, introductions."

He nods, studying the boy and his cat attentively. I explain who they are and order them to be housed downstairs, next to the furnace. In Boy's hearing I tell Trevor to prepare a warm bed and find Boy some clothes to wear to school. We walk towards the base, the soldier with my kit trailing respectfully behind.

Then I stretch out in the hot bath and fall into a trance. There is no point thinking now - my old world lies in tatters, although my future as Grey's coal supplier does not seem to be dishonourable or harsh. The shape of things to come is entirely unclear, but it seems wise to cross bridges as they are approached.

Trevor refills my mug with hot berry gin twice, then orders me out of a bath into a coarse bathrobe and marches me upstairs. I climb into bed, assailed by the images of a very long day - Rat sliding into the hatch, dark shadows mowed by a stream of phosphorescent bullets, water rising over the meadow as we struggle to manoeuvre our transporters out of the tight formation. Finally, all I see is Rat's sole blue eye.

As I fade into sleep, Rat fixes me with a harsh one-eyed stare. He exudes a profound reproach to myself, the last leader of an idiot species that made such a mess of endless opportunities.

That is something an animal of Rat's intelligence cannot fathom.

{}{}{}

PART II.

It's as if I look on myself from above as I trudge along the street – seeing an old man, his face criss-crossed with scars and burns, a posture bent by a lifetime of heavy labour and a harsh, all-seeing gaze of one who had known too much misery in too long a life.

All of that appears to be correct.

I make my way towards my cousin's foundry works, responding to gushing adulation that is now my constant companion. I am weary of thanking people and shaking hands, exchanging hugs and receiving kisses, so I respond to all expressions of good will with as little churlishness as I can muster - a mechanical smile and a polite inclination of the head. These seem to address most occasions.

Today the wind is low, and the air is heavy with the pungent reek of burnt coal that leaves a bitter taste of acid in the mouth. We learned quickly that coal must be burned in closed boxes as its fumes can kill inside an enclosed house. Normal rules of commerce were suspended as everyone pitched in - my cousin cast the metal boxes and the tall, long flues to take the poisonous fumes higher into the sky. The town supplied labour, and my soldiers tore up a rusting barge to scavenge the metal. Most inhabited houses now boast a brand-new metal coal range that keeps the inside warmer than a steam bath. Babies stopped dying almost overnight - the only price is the stink of coal that pervades the air on still days. For once, we are grateful for stiff breezes that once chilled us to the bone - the still days are rather tart on the tongue.

The refugees from Brana proved their worth many times over. Tough, resourceful people who make it easy to overlook their dour ways. Mind, many of them left the old faith as they left Brana, but they are still a long way off accepting what they call our loose morals, even as they gradually get drawn into town life. The men spend most of their time hunting out of airships, and those who can afford it are now replete with that greatest delicacy of all, fresh meat. The women are adept at all manner of work, from repairing roads to machines in my cousin's works. They quickly formed a large work gang that went through the town repairing run-down houses suddenly filled with new arrivals. I am still undecided about Redmond's suggestion of enlisting a few in The Regiment, just to see how it goes. It is still too much of a change for all of us.

With an influx of new labour we began work on the decrepit ships that could only weigh anchor in calm weather. A few master craftsmen from Brana found their way into my employ, and they proved priceless. Once the spring storms subside, we will let loose the largest whaling and fishing flotilla that took to sea in living memory. By the time they are done with one season, hunger should become a dim, nasty memory. Our children will stop dying, and our lives will no longer be about a daily struggle with the cold. For the first time in my life I see a future for my people.

None of this, however, pertains to myself - I had become a walking corpse, an irrelevant shadow of a man that longs for nothing more than to lie next to Rina in her artless grave. The scarred, hardened body is too stubborn to die, despite having no blessing to live. I blunder along in this state of inertia, but nothing, not even Boy's marvellous progress at school and his insightful pronouncements, so delightful coming from one so young, make the slightest impact on my demeanour. Trevor forces me to eat twice a day, and I have not compromised my duties, which is no more than I owe my men - but I do not even bother to hide a lack of desire to maintain my existence. Rina's death proved a greater blow than I can heal, and I would like to stop suffering as soon as nature permits.

I enter the gates at the end of a long street. My cousin's works are wisely located downwind from the town, on the far wall and next to the wharf on the northern arm of the river that encircles Grey. It's a decrepit building whose only sound part is a tall chimney that now belches a thick column of smoke.

Rendell, his ageing foreman, greets me with a single jerk of his chin, pointing me towards the testing ground. His gruffness reminds me of Trevor, although Rendell has never been a soldier. Another grizzled veteran of the struggle with the elements, outliving most of those he may have cared about.

I nod bleakly in return and walk through the foundry, now a busy, happy place full of metal sparks and loud noises, shielding my eyes against flying metal and welding flashes. We are at the tail end of the production run that supplied the entire town with coal burners, and the last of the stock is lined up against the far wall. Just past that is a small gate that is now wide open, and I enter the testing ground, to be greeted by my cousin Ethel.

We shake hands with genuine warmth - Ethel is a totally decent man, some years older than myself. I had never known him to lie or badmouth anyone, and his blue eyes, now dimming with the passing years, had never but stared straight ahead with a total lack of guile. He stands somewhat taller than myself, a thin man with a trim white beard and long hair tied back in a long tail. Ethel's only weakness is weed, but it doesn't seem to affect his nimble intellect. He, of course, will swear that some of his best designs came to him on the cloying smoke.

With no introductions whatsoever he waves his hand, and one of his workmen spins the flywheel on a machine that looks like a concrete mixer. Its piston wheezes to life and works up a steady rhythm, then Ethel hands me a face shield made of toughened glass. I remove my fur cap and slide the shield over my forehead.

The workman picks up a shovelful of river stones and

drops them into what looks like a hopper. I can hear them gnashing on metal, then a steady stream of stones erupts from the nozzle, arcs through the air and demolishes upright boards, set up as targets at the end of the yard. I nod, and Ethel slides a finger across his throat. The workman shuts down the machine, bows and returns to the foundry.

"That's handsome work," I tell Ethel with genuine admiration. "And you did that in two days?"

"I had some ready parts," he replies modestly. "The mechanics are not hard - but I am still puzzled."

"Gut feeling, cousin," I tell him sparingly. "What about the other?"

"It's almost ready. I can show you something of it now."

We walk inside, and he shows me a wooden mock-up clamped in a large vice.

"The return mechanism needs more work, but this is more or less how it goes," says Ethel. He takes a bundle of wooden rods and loads them into the box on top of the device. I watch with fascination as he works the lever - forward to drop one rod into a slot below, backward to pull the bow string and all the way backwards to release the cocking mechanism. A steady stream of rods drums on the brick wall as Ethel works the lever back and forth until the handle suddenly snaps in his large hand.

"You see what I mean."

"Ethel, you are a miracle worker. Just make the fucking thing out of metal and be done with it. A crossbowman should still be able to carry it over a short distance."

"So this is a defensive weapon?"

"I hope not at all, cousin. All being well, your good work is all for nothing."

Ethel studies me with his blue eyes, frowning slightly.

"Ritter, you make me uneasy."

"I don't mean to. And remember, total secrecy."

Ethel nods his head with an expression of sadness.

"I am worried now, Ritter. You are never wrong."

"I am not saying you shouldn't be concerned, cousin. Just taking sensible precautions. It is nothing more than that at this point."

He shakes his head with disapproval.

"At this point. Right."

{}{}{}

As I leave the foundry gates, a runner approaches and throws off an awkward salute. It's one of the boys we took in after Brana, when a few of my men had left. Many felt that I should have burned Brana to the ground.

It doesn't yet look as if we fed him up - the heavy cloth of the uniform is like a sack on his angular shoulders, and his face still has a hungry, lean look of those we rescued from the streets.

I open the note from Trevor and sigh. Tonight there is singing at school, and I had been nominated as the guest of honour. My men were also there when I found the coal, but only I get a mention. I stare at the setting sun - the concert will begin any time from now.

I dismiss the runner with a careless salute and turn on my heels with a sigh. There is an echoing thought that I could do with some gin as I enter the school, looking up at the new chimneys. The buildings got a new lease of life too, their ramshackle selection of driftwood and recycled planks now neatly covered with a thick, sculptured layer of dry clay. The new roof is lined with rows of shiny iron sheets. I sigh, recalling the buckets that caught dripping water in the classrooms of my youth. We spiced up the proceedings by leaving toads, tadpoles and dead rats in those buckets, for our teachers' delectation.

Further along is the new hall, built by the refugees from Brana. It's an elegant, well-grounded structure with a sloping roof and much glass - a luxury we are now learning to misuse. Personally, I consider glass unnecessary - the hall is mainly used at night, and during the day the students assembled within can do without the distraction of looking out onto the sunshine.

I go inside and see that the choir is in the throes of final rehearsal on stage. The choirmaster, one of the school teachers who escaped from Brana, turns and bows to me deeply. I bow back, suddenly ashamed of my indifference to life.

Mine is the central seat in the front row, and I sit down, feeling sad and anxious. I must survive the performance with grace, regardless of how bad I feel - the children are not to be disappointed.

Boy rushes into the hall and hands me a small backpack. I smile, not only at his presence - the pack contains a few hunks of cheese and a metal flask of berry gin, courtesy of Trevor's worldly wisdom. Boy nods and runs off, taking a vast leap onto the stage, to cartwheel precisely into his place amid the choir. A little bit of warm air wafts past my soul.

People begin to fill the hall, and I sip at my flask discretely, hiding it in my sleeve from the children. Every now and again I return greetings as they turn to stare at me, waving and clenching their fists over the heart in approval. They don't look quite like the same as before - better fed, no longer pale and dressed for the cold in deerskin coats.

However, it is not cold. The corner of the hall next to the stage boasts a coal burner which someone stoked to the full - hot air shimmers above its flat top. There was a fierce debate about the best shape - in the end, we settled for a simple box. The flames hit the flat roof and give it all before curving down - the mouth of the chimney is positioned low in the burner.

The first song brings bitter memories - Mother used to sing it often, that lilting tune about a river flowing through the forest past the dead towns.

Run the river
Past the ruins
Past the forests
To the sea

Through the meadows
In the mountains
All that way
To feel free

She sang it to my older brother when he caught his leg in a boat winch. The leg was cut off by the grim healers, but the rot beat them to it. We buried him three days later, and Mother never sang that song again.

I make the most of furtive sips from the flask as the choir goes through the rest of their songs. I even begin to find it calming, sitting in a comfortable seat in a warm hall, listening to children most of whom would not have survived to adulthood without my coal. It seems a reasonable return on a lifetime of prowling around the forest.

I study Boy's earnest face, and he stares back as he sings. There is no trace of levity - he continues to perform to the utmost, and I almost wish he would run some kind of a childish prank, just once. I nod approval and shift my gaze.

The songs envelop me in their gentle warmth, and I stop sipping gin, feeling a light relief from the black cloud that follows me wherever I go. I think of all the tasks that await me before winter, but all of a sudden life seems almost manageable.

We applaud for a long time, and the choir obliges with more songs until it is truly time to go. I remain in place until the queues at the exits lighten. Boy is nowhere in sight as children rush off the stage to join their parents. I sigh and move towards the doors.

Outside, however, I get a surprise. It is snowing - so heavily that the blizzard has swallowed what was left of the dusk. I blend into the crowd, making my way towards the base. Trevor opens the door as if he did nothing but sat in wait for my arrival. I thank him for the parcel of mercy as he unties my boots. He doesn't look up.

I shower quickly and dress for the cold night, more out of habit than necessity - there is a shimmer around the coal burner in my bedroom, and it is warm enough to sleep naked on the floor. Climbing into a tightly made bed, I stretch the knots in my back and pull the blanket over my shoulders.

There is much to do tomorrow.

{}{}{}

The dream is of a profound, persistent quality - it should wake me up, but I am mesmerized, watching the soldiers from what looks like a sleek, powerful transporter with eight wheels. It is tipped on its side in a steep gully.

There is furious fire, with bullets slashing the ferns all around. I scream at the soldiers to disperse, but no sound comes away from my mouth. The soldiers get picked off one by one, yet someone keeps firing. I throw myself onto the hard ground and awaken, gasping for breath, my heart hammering against the ribs.

There are more shots that sound muffled in the blizzard - but they are indeed gunfire. I count around five, then I hear a thin scream.

Trevor awaits me downstairs, holding my revolver harnesses on outstretched hands. I ram both wrists into the metal circles and let him snap the buckles. He pushes my feet into loose snow boots, and I run out the door, grateful for the thick underwear I wore to bed.

By the lamps that dimly light the market square I begin to make out the wall and two guard towers above the gate. One of them is on fire, with glimmers of flame just visible in the narrow windows. The other tower is immersed in total darkness.

As I run forward, I realize that I am not alone - many dark shapes are dashing around the gate. They want to open it, says the back of my mind, and they don't quite know how.

I run in total silence, my mind now calm and clear, spring both bayonets and approach the enemy under the cover of the blizzard. From somewhere far I acknowledge the bitter cold, the crisp feel of the snow, the icy air that catches my breath. My fingers throb with the cold of the revolvers, and I slow down, crouching through the final approach.

The first few vermin die without even turning around. Heavy slugs pierce hairy backs, slamming their bodies into the metal gate. Others turn on me with not so much as a pause, and I begin to back away, killing the attackers as they rush towards me. I am almost half way across the market when I run out of ammunition and begin to kill with short, quick stabs.

Someone joins me at my side. I don't know the man - he has a timber axe that he easily swings with one hand, using the blunt part to deal skull-crushing blows. We fight facing away from each other, protecting our flanks as more and more vermin leave the gate to mob us.

It is starting to look as if we best turn and run - but a bouncing light pierces the darkness, and I hear a tortured hiss of a cold engine. The hopper gun opens up, slicing into the crowd of vermin just to my right, then a line of soldiers catches up with the transporter, using their revolvers to mop up what the hopper gun had missed. They soon run out of targets; a few try to run, but they are caught and butchered. I turn to shake the axeman's hand.

"Clay, son of Kelvin," says he with a Brana lilt. "It's an honour to fight alongside you, warlord."

I thank Clay as much as words can and turn towards my men. They are dressed much the same as I, but that did not seem to interfere with their aiming.

The burning tower collapses to the other side of the wall, sending a shower of sparks into the dark sky. We climb into the other tower to witness a familiar scene - blood-spattered walls, tatters of body parts on the floor, weapons broken and discarded in disdain. The night crew are all gone, leaving behind two heads that were torn off and discarded on the floor. My men collect them into a sack, which quickly runs with dark blood.

I walk outside, kicking away the broken remains of the door.

"Burn it," I tell someone, jerking my thumb at the tower.

Someone wraps a thick blanket around my shoulders, and I begin to shiver. It is hard to say how much of that is mere cold.

I walk through the door of my home, dripping water from the blanket around my shoulders. Boy sits on the stairs, his usually stern face crumpled with tears. I throw the blanket into the snow outside, then unstrap the revolvers. He comes towards me, and I kneel on the cold stone floor, taking his arms into mine.

"Are they here?" is all he asks.

I stay silent for I must not lie, just staring into his eyes as he cries.

"I knew they would come," says Boy, wiping the tears with the sleeve of his nightshirt. I wait, but he says no more.

"They have always probed our defences," I tell him carefully. "Do you understand what that means?"

He nods once.

"It is true that they come more often than before," I continue, sitting Boy down on the stairs. "But we can and will deal with it. Brana was much smaller than Grey."

He nods and sniffs loudly.

"I am scared, warlord."

"It is only right that you should be," I rest a cold palm stained with gunpowder on his shoulder. "The vermin are a deadly threat, and there are many more of them than there are of us. There is nobody out there to help us. We have to defend ourselves, and it won't be easy. We have few fighters, little ammunition and poor defences. But it can still be done."

I walk Boy to his room next to the furnace, and gently push him through the door. He slides into bed, and I pull the blanket tight over his shoulders. Rat stirs in his basket in the corner, but continues to lie in a tight ball with eyes closed. There is no question that he is wide awake.

I am now warm enough to sit still, and I slide to the floor, wiping my forehead. There is blood on my hand, and I suddenly notice bright stains all over my nightshirt.

"It's not my blood," I tell him.

"You have to stop them," says Boy. He stares at me intently, and I realize that the blood does not concern him. He cares only for what I say next.

"Yes, I will stop them."

"You are the only one who can," says he with force, suddenly not at all like a child.

"That is true. But I am not in charge of the town guard."

"Why not? You are the only one who knows what to do!"

"In our town we have many rules," I reply grimly. "Grey is not my property. I cannot go against something I swore to uphold when I became a grown man."

"That's just wrong. People die, and they don't have to," says Boy, and his face crumples. I look down on the floor to hide my own tears, for I know precisely whose death he means.

"You have to stop it," says he and lies back, closing his eyes and snapping his fingers. Rat unfurls his long body and mounts the bed with a single, precise leap. He pushes his lean backside inside the blanket and gives me a contemptuous stare before resting his head on Boy's shoulder.

I take that as my cue to leave.

{}{}{}

"You killed those men," say I in a cold, menacing voice.

The men of the council stare at me in silence. I stare back into their hateful eyes - they are finally cornered and cannot escape without my consent.

"They killed your men!" I shout into the hall with an entirely genuine fury. A wall of faces stares at me with respect and awe. A lot of heads nod, and I can feel the rush of a hunter who had at last run down his prey.

"There is only one way to protect this town, and these men are not capable of doing it," I say in a calmer tone. "Only experienced soldiers should stand on the wall. We can train the town guard - but later. Right now we must stop the intrusions and the senseless deaths. We must ensure that anyone who climbs over the wall doesn't come back alive, or we will have all of them on our doorstep!"

The day after the attack my men collected the vermin corpses, loading them on a flat sled, pulled by a cargo cart. We opened the gates, drove to the river and reversed the sled into the water. The swift current picked up the vermin and carried them out to sea. I hope that eyes were watching from the bushes.

Little was left of the twelve men who guarded the wall. They were surprised in the towers, where they dozed by the fire. The attackers broke solid wooden doors as if they were made of paper. By miracle someone managed to get off a few shots and wake up the town. Sleeping is not forbidden during the night watch - the noise of someone trying to get through entangled wire on top of the wall is enough to awaken the dead. Or so we thought - I found a crude flax mat draped over the wire. It turned out that climbing over in complete silence was possible after all.

No one wants to contradict me, and I demand a vote. My motion is carried without a murmur. I am now the Protector, solely in charge of every man and woman under arms.

{}{}{}

The day clinic is mercifully quiet, and Wilkins makes his way around large recliner chairs occupied by bearers of cancer. He is in a good mood, dressed in casual trousers of black tweed and a light-hearted tie of blue silk over a simple white shirt. His registrar does his best to keep up, mumbling into his tablet as the graceful brown fingers dance on its grimy surface. The symbol of the healers' priesthood used to be a heavy stethoscope slung around the neck. Technology had now reduced that hallowed device to an ignominiously small, bell-shaped microphone that is bluetoothed to any device with a speaker. The cost is negligible, the quality is perfect, and any tradesman that wants one can buy it for a few dollars. I am not sure if the medical profession can ever recover from such a blow to its mystique.

My visit is blessedly simple. The tests are perfect, and the Hickman's line is removed by a cold-eyed male nurse I haven't seen before. He accomplishes this unpleasant task in mere seconds as Wilkins stands at the door, telling me that he will bring me in for another blast in three months or so. I am a true champion, he tells me.

Because of the small procedure I have to remain in the waiting room for an hour. There is nothing to do but construct a writing desk from another chair and a pile of old magazines, in a corner faintly smelling of dust and human misery.

{}{}{}

It's not the best of nights to be outdoors - gusting wind, sleet and pitch darkness, the moon totally obscured by thick clouds. But I revel in it all - tonight I stand watch with my men, and we are, for the first time in living memory, in charge of security on the wall. Tonight is the first night in my life when I am not falling asleep in fear of what I may awaken to the next day - I can personally deal with whatever happens. The black cloud is gone, and once more I am full of anger and purpose.

Never before had the council allowed The Regiment to gain that much power - setting aside the town guard and taking charge. But guardsmen will only return to the wall once they have been trained, with sergeants from the Regiment to watch over them every night.

We lie under thick sheets of canvas that conceal us well on this dark night. We've strung up warning lines where the wall is easy to penetrate, and a hopper gun has been concealed in what looks like a pile of rubble. A few projectors have been wired to flood the wall with light, and the switch is to be tripped by a man concealed inside a steel cabin that is disguised as a stump of the burnt tower. He will remain awake, sharing the night in short shifts with three others.

We take turns to sleep, which is not overly effective - the ground is cold, and we are alive with anticipation. Tonight is a very likely time, as the moon is ruined by the clouds, and the enemy must feel total confidence.

A young man to my left taps me on the shoulder, and I tense up, beginning to listen. He is not from a good family, and I am still looking for a polite way to explain that he needs to wash. But his hearing is very fine, and I trust him to hear things long before their smell overpowers his. I banned banter and card games - the night watch lies still, silent and camouflaged. You can either listen or sleep. I listen - and catch up on my sleep during the day, which works well.

I am feeling a resurgence of strength as we drift towards winter. The Regiment is busy training the town guard, and the morale is back to normal. My men are deeply respected, and I am gratified to see how hard they work to uphold that respect.

The women from Brana had formed a crossbow regiment. Now, I didn't quite goad them. I merely dropped a few hints about a competition and put up something of an attractive prize. The team training that had miraculously sprung from this event is, not to mince words, military.

The smelly boy taps me again, and this time I hear it too. I nod and tap the man to my right. The alarm signal spreads across the ranks, and I hear just a tiny amount too much clatter as revolvers are cocked all along the wall.

There are a few noisy movements in the grass and heavy, awkward breathing. I make myself loosen up, ready to spring to my feet. There is way too much fog to see what is coming, which is most unpleasant, especially as the moon is now out, pouring light that diffuses in the fog. Not much night vision to speak of.

"What the fuck?" whispers the boy to my right.

I peer hard into the fog and see nothing - until there is an almighty crash, and the barrier of sturdy poles and barbed wire collapses to the ground. I am up on my feet and looking for a target. The fog won't let us see what is coming until it is almost too late.

We all fire into the vast, snarling mouth full of jagged teeth, and the creature deflates and drops on its ruptured belly. Then the big lights burst through the fog, and we can finally see our quarry - a long body with a fat, stubby tail and smooth black skin. The blunt head is large and shaped like a bullet, with massive jaws and a wide mouth. It must weight about twice as much as a man.

"Not something you see that often," I mutter, making my way to the fallen fence.

"What the hell is that?" asks a boy with a Brana accent.

"A salamander, my young friend. They live in the mouth of the river. We call them undertakers because they eat the dead we float out of town. They have been bold of late, on the account of fewer funerals, and they come closer to the wall."

"Are there dead people near the wall?" asks the young boy with a shade of fear in his voice.

"No, it's you," laughs an older man with a harsh Brana accent. "You smell worse than the dead."

I study the scene and return to the tarpaulin.

"Get down, all of you, " I order wearily. "This is a nuisance, giving away our position like that. We should have used crossbows and stayed out of sight."

"It's my fault, sir," says the older man. "I've never seen anything like it before. They did not lurk in the Brana Lake."

"No, I guess they don't live in the mountains," I tell him, cooling down. "The undertakers had been around since my grandfather's time. They are dangerous up close, but seldom come out of the water like that."

In the morning we awaken to the evidence of our butchery writ large. The salamander lies in a vast pool of blood, its muzzle still hooked on the barbed wire. It seems to fix me with black, pebble-like eyes.

I march the patrol out of the gate, and we string a loop around the muscular body to haul it to the river over frosted grass. The stench is spreading - we cut off the rope and use sticks to push the salamander into the icy water. I watch as its body twists in the current and floats away.

Catching the last glimpse of its elegant shape, I suddenly feel a crushing pain I hadn't felt before - the biting regret of a death so unnecessary and so obscenely ugly. I break into a quick march towards the gate to hide from the men, tears streaming down my face. Two images seem to have locked together in my mind - the tortured, tear-streaked face of Dinah, a gaping hole from my bullet amid her chest, and the undead, accusing eyes of the salamander that lies in a pool of blood on the wall.

Once inside the gate, I march straight to the beach and wade into ice-cold surf that laps at my boots, bend down and rinse my face with salt water. It soothes my inflamed eyes as I stagger back onto the beach and kneel before a vast trunk of driftwood. My hand drags the knife out of its sheaf without thought, and I stare at the gleaming blade, then sink it hard into the salted wood, lowering my head to stare at the sun that first ignites, then fades in the watery horizon.

However many hours pass, I don't know, when I resume a march into town, feeling a numbing, punched-out serenity that follows a release of built-up distress.

Trevor stands on the porch, next to the half-open door. He calls me with an impatient wave, and I redouble my pace.

"Trouble, Commander," says he with a frown. "You need to speak with these men right now."

I realize that the choice has been made and bite off the complaint about being awake for so long. There is nothing I can do but nod.

Trevor unstraps my weapons and helps me remove the boots. I unfasten the heavy coat and go to wash my hands. When I return I hear voices in the lounge and walk there slowly. I really have no idea what this could be about.

Most of the men gathered in the lounge are dressed in long black coats, favoured by Brana men for prayer meetings. I recognize the new priest but cannot recall his name. That annoys me, for we were introduced not so long ago. I nod, and he nods back grimly.

I suddenly realize what they are about to say to me, just as he opens his mouth.

"Warlord, we lost contact with Brana."

I take in a sharp breath and lower myself to a seat beside the fire. Behind my back I hear chairs being brought in, and I wait until everyone is seated, marshalling my feelings and gathering my thoughts.

"When?" I turn towards them.

"Two days ago. We waited until the storm was over, but there is still silence. They had never taken that long to fix problems before."

I nod, thinking of the crammed radio room I was shown before departure from Brana. They made five identical units to communicate with their brethren as far away as Karito. It is not possible for everything to break down at once. I also remember the large stack of charged batteries. No, a technical fault is out of the question. I nod, indicating that none of this needs to be explained.

"They've been overrun," I tell the silent gathering in a harsh, slow tone.

The priest nods.

"It looks like you have much prayer ahead of you," I tell him, suddenly feeling deflated. "That much I can tell you now."

"We understand that nothing more can be done," says a short, greying man with a scar across his face. "We only came to hear you say it."

I take my time to reply, studying his calm, steady expression.

"Yes, that is right. Nothing can be done now," I tell him heavily. "There was a choice. They could have come with us."

"That is not in dispute," chimes in the priest. "We acknowledge that they were free to decide their fate."

"Once we departed, father, it was only a matter of time," I speak slowly, struggling to maintain the strength in my voice. "They faced a large force, and they could not keep it at bay forever. Which they all knew."

I study the faces in the room and continue.

"It would take eight days for me to gather a convoy, and it would need three days to get to Brana. If anyone is kept alive, we would need to get to them before their captors kill them, and for that we would need to search the entire town. There will be combat at close quarters, and many lives will be lost. I cannot justify such losses."

"We concur," says the man with the scar. "Thank you for your courtesy, warlord. We know you've been on duty since dusk."

They begin to rise and clear the chairs, stacking and carrying them out under Trevor's directions.

"Wait."

They turn towards me and fall silent.

"I must burn the town."

They stare at me with dismay, but no one says a word.

"The vermin lose their offspring to the cold, just like we do. They cannot build houses, and there are only so many caves. When a town falls, it has to be burned to the ground. They must not be allowed to make use of shelter."

They look at each other uncertainly, but no one replies.

"I need you to tell me how to start a fire in Brana. With three, maybe four incendiary bombs, dropped from an airship."

They stare at me without a sound as I wrestle with fatigue.

"Look, you can take your time. There will be a few days of gusting winds after this storm. Go away, discuss it, pray, then come back. Go in peace."

They start to move towards the door with hesitation. Some time after they are gone, the man with the scar returns.

"I will tell you," is all he says.

"Now?"

"Yes. Now."

I walk over to the writing desk and take a pen, lick its nib and place a few experimental strokes on a piece of blotting paper.

"The mine," he says grimly. "If that goes up, it will burn the whole hill. We were always so afraid of that."

"Where is the entrance?"

He takes my pen and draws me a map with bold, assured strokes. I study it at length.

"Right under the town hall?"

"Well, we didn't know when we built it, you see. It was only when Josiah arrived with the maps that we enlarged the cellar and hit the coal seam. Then we dug a shaft just next to the hall, going straight down. If you drop your bombs into the entrance, the coal will go up, and nothing will ever extinguish it short of a flood. After a while the flames will get to pockets of gas. They will explode, then burn the town right down to the lake."

{}{}{}

Joy to the world - I am, at last, a free man. An hour and a few phone calls later, Helen and I are ensconced in the corner booth of the Chinese restaurant.

Helen seems to have conquered the latest bout of her illness and is appreciative of cuisine that is not especially associated with alcohol. She even dressed like a woman, in a simple white frock with a string of pearls on her sun-damaged neck - the legacy of climbing and glacier skiing when we were young. Her hair is neatly cut, slightly dyed to conceal the grey tips, and her angular cheeks are neatly framed with elegant rectangular glasses.

We sip jasmine tea as she interrogates me. I tell her of my release - until the next dose of poison I am free to do what I like. It is a loaded statement, and I am pleased to see her eyes flash in response.

"Bruce Bay," I tell her. "Just as soon as we can organize it."

Her lips pucker in annoyance.

"Bruce Bay without drink," she says with a frown. "No, can't picture that."

"Well, it doesn't so much matter where."

"I have an idea, she says brightly. "Okarito."

I shrug shoulders. Why there?

"I haven't been to Okarito in ages," says Helen as the first dish arrives. "Wildlife tours and canoeing on the lagoon. Just what the doctor ordered."

"Feeding the wildlife, more like," I ladle her a big serving of satay prawns with broccoli and dump the remainder into my bowl. "I still itch when I remember the last time. Fucking sandflies."

"Can you work?" she asks without warning, wrangling a large prawn with her chopsticks.

"Can and must," I frown at the thought of my finances. "Anything in mind?"

"There is talk of a leadership coup," says Helen.

"Ew, Christchurch. You know how I hate it east of the Alps."

"He who likes yummy food," says Helen, sternly pointing her finger towards the remaining prawns. "Must set pen to paper."

We both smile - none of my commercial writing is ever touched by a pen, from its laboured birth to the moment the article is read on the magazine site. I still prefer to type and collect my thoughts over the keyboard, but our younger colleagues speak into their tablets and even correct the text from hearing it spoken back. They are in grave danger of forgetting the alphabet.

We gorge on the honey pippi, the speciality of the house. The Chinaman brought it out himself, shaking my hand and wishing me good health. Amazing how news travels in this town.

"Take the train on Tuesday," says Helen. "All expenses, three days. Won't kill you."

"Nothing will kill me," I tell her, and she lifts her teacup to toast mine. Tears roll down her cheeks, sparkling like the earth's most precious diamonds in the light that shines gently from the ceiling.

Those sparks keep flashing as we pay, walk across the road through gusting wind and scurry into the lobby.

In the lift Helen grasps the front of my shirt and kisses me hard on the mouth. She begins to cry in earnest as we enter my apartment, and I push her onto the couch. I tear at the dress and enter her with enough force to push the couch along the carpet. She still sniffs and wipes her eyes as I rest on top of her later, kissing her wrinkled, sunburnt neck.

As I withdraw and rise, I see that the couch is a mess that will have to be dealt with later. We walk into the bedroom, leaving behind a trail of rumpled clothes. Helen pushes me down on the bed, clamping a hot

320

mouth to my groin.

Moments later she straddles me and begins to rock gently, her broad hands caressing her breasts. She climaxes first but maintains her thrusts to deplete me once more, then falls on the pillow, stares intently at my face and smiles.

I reach over and wipe her tears one more time.

{}{}{}

The airship executes a ragged takeoff, struggling with the wind that still gusts ten days after the storm. I won the argument with the pilot, explaining the importance of wiping out the shelter before spring, when the vermin begin to give birth. But no doubt - we are risking our lives, flying in this weather with a heavy load.

We are pulled by a stiff breeze towards the sea. When the anchor ropes are at full stretch, the crewman releases the shackles, and we both lose footing as the ship lurches in a gust of wind.

The pilot allows the ship to be carried offshore - there is little else he can do - using speed to gather height. Shore breezes are low, and you can rise above them. That seems to happen but slowly, and I lie still on the planking of the deck, marshalling my thoughts.

We do eventually rise above the wind, and the ship turns to begin its long trek inland. I stare at the mountains and pick out the winding ribbon of the ancient road, which we will follow most of the way. Flying makes appalling mockery of land travel, proceeding with such ridiculous ease and speed. Until, of course, something goes wrong.

After a time that seems far too short I see the familiar outline of the pass. We fly past the saddle, and suddenly the land begins to drop away - then we are over water.

Gliding over the lake, the pilot eases the throttles and lets forward speed fall to almost nothing, to gauge the wind. As I guess from the mirror-smooth surface, there is almost none. The airman and I begin to prepare an anchor line; once over the target, we will drop a heavy stone on a rope into the mine. That will be used to guide the fall of the incendiary bombs.

When the machine hovers just above the water, the airman works the heavy crank to lower the hose into a lake, then he puts his weight behind the lever that tightens the drivebelt of the pump. We used up most of the water during takeoff, and the machine struggles with the unforgiving weight as the boiler is refilled, engine hissing as the pilot winds up the steam, beginning a gentle climb as he gathers speed.

The ship rises with some reluctance as we cross the lake and drop below the ridgeline of the shore, to mask our approach. The crewman slides the door wide-open, and I work the slide on the hopper gun, checking the spring.

The ship slowly covers the last of the distance to Brana. As we emerge above the town from behind the hills, the pistons clatter in full throttle. We quickly clear a short stretch of water - the river I used to evacuate the refugees - and I see Brana beneath me. Its streets are dotted with camp fires, and many of its chimneys belch smoke. A few vermin point to us, begin to shout and run.

We turn slightly and approach the town hall up the slope of the hill. I see the mine entrance and signal; the airman leans out of the ship, his safety line fully stretched. He begins to drop loops of rope one by one, until most of it hangs straight. He then hauls himself inside and rolls the heavy anchor rock towards the exit. I help push it out the door.

The rock hits the ground next to the mine entrance, raising a cloud of black dust. It looks for a moment as if we missed, but then I see it roll over the edge and into mine shaft. The rope follows it down and suddenly stretches tight.

The airman frantically slaps the side of the ship until the pilot reverses the thrust, and we are more or less stationary above the seam. We roll out the barrels, each packed with glass jars containing white phosphorus in oil. The jars will break on impact, and the phosphorus catches fire once in contact with air. The flames reach a very high temperature that sets fire to anything that can burn. The phosphorus globules melt and stick to any available surface, ensuring combustion.

Two tall males rush towards the mine, and I dive at the hopper gun, firing a short volley that throws them backwards into the dirt. We resume our grim task: each barrel is attached to the line with a short length of rope and rolled out the door.

Two barrels smash into the side of the mineshaft, then the wind rises and pushes us back over the centre. Two more barrels go straight down on target, and I wave to the pilot, signalling him to leave.

The airman cuts the anchor line, and we begin to rise. The pilot turns the ship away from the hilltop, then guns all engines to gain speed and height, running towards the lake in a straight line away from Brana.

We are high over the water when a vast tongue of flame rises out of the mine and begins to reach towards us at terrifying speed. The pilot pushes out the throttle, and we only just miss the fireball, but the blast wave arrives and tosses the ship high into the air. Everything inside is thrown against the walls, and I am glad of the thickly padded helmet they made me wear. But my shoulder is mercilessly crushed against the bulkhead, and I shout a curse at severe pain.

The ship rights itself slowly, and I roll back to the deck, my safety line entangled. Growling and moaning with the fire in my right shoulder, I crawl to the door on all fours, unclip the rope and frantically untangle part of the length. I manage to clip the line back in and reach forward, leaning out of the airship to look back.

The top of the Brana hill is engulfed in a sea of white flame. The rest of the town appears to be doomed, as a vast firefront spreads along the streets, houses collapsing as they burn. The ship is now far away, yet even from this distance I feel the heat of the fire on my face.

We spiral, rising higher and higher over the lake. I stare at the wall of flame that leaps from house to house across narrow alleys. Then the pain overwhelms me, and I pass out.

Next thing I sense is the agony of being shaken, which jolts me back to full consciousness. The engines are silent, and I realize that we had returned to Grey. I grasp the airman's wrist with my left hand and twist it away from my broken shoulder, throwing him off his feet. I then rise to my knees, gasping with pain.

Climbing down the ladder from the anchor platform takes forever - I can't seem to use my right arm at all. I am driven back to the house, muttering replies to effusive greetings from the sergeants piled up in the cart. They half-carry me up the stairs and help me remove the flight suit that stinks of sweat and smoke. Trevor shakes his head in dismay, seeing the vast bruise that runs from the collarbone down to the elbow. He gives me some bitter powder after I leave the bath, and I pass out in a warm bed, the pain now a dull sensation I feel from some place far away.

{}{}{}

I get woken up by the jolts as the train pulls into Christchurch. There is little joy to be had from this arrival - grimy warehouses and unkempt fences line the railway track, and the sky is choked with dirty clouds. I stretch hard, then extract my phone and send a short text.

When I step off the train Tavita is there on the platform, resplendent in his blue suit. He stands a head taller than I and about twice the width, his wide Fijian smile glistening with huge white teeth. I feel instant warmth - the man is genuinely happy to see me.

"Made colonel yet, Mr Turner?"

"Still a captain, Tavita. They are afraid of me."

He grabs the suitcase and points me towards the car park. His taxi is a blue van, not overly new or dent-free, but I feel safer inside than I did in an armoured personnel carrier. My fingers are slowly regaining some feeling after his handshake.

We sit in the afternoon traffic as we catch up - the family is all fine, a multitude of names I can never remember. His son is studying to be an oil engineer in America, and the rest are happily ensconced in the miserable suburbs of this city, in mouldy houses surrounded by faded fences. Personally, I would rather be in Fiji - but Tavita's family think they've died and gone to heaven, and if they are happy, I am happy.

He stops at the hotel, and I glance up to see the flagpole, still on a lean after the last quake. The building itself seems to be straight, and I drop off my bag. We drive on to the new town centre, where a vast, squat bunker clad in mirror glass dominates the skyline.

It is more than one's life is worth to go through security procedures in Parliament, and I arranged to meet Roger Stone in a chic café across the road. Tavita drops me off and melts into the traffic. I push past the heavy glass door and survey the combat zone.

The bad news is that I recognize at least four faces at various tables, all functionaries and sundry assistants to politicians. The good news is that all of them look down at their plates in an effort to avoid recognizing me back. They happen to be in luck, for I am loaded for much bigger game.

I am led to a table in the corner, and the dark-haired waitress with a diamond stud in her nose points me to a seat facing the entrance. I sit down, and she spreads a napkin over my lap, then withdraws without a word.

Five minutes later she brings two shrimp cocktails and sets them down on the table. I roll my eyes at the impertinence of someone ordering my lunch, and she walks away just as a large BMW pulls up outside. Two large men in baggy suits emerge, scan the landscape with vigilant stares, then open the rear door of the car.

Roger emerges with some unease - a short man with a mane of grey hair, dressed in his trademark grey pinstripes. He marches through the restaurant, acknowledging a few greetings with what seems a forced effort, and sits at the table, flashing me a perfunctory smile.

"So nice to see you too, Roger. Seems like it's been forever."

"It does. Seem."

He ladles prawn cocktail into his mouth and looks into my eyes for the first time.

"They said you were dying."

It's a deliberate provocation, and I smile back - dangerously and a little too long: dying or not, little man, I can still reach for your throat and tear it away from your spine. Your thugs who stand vigilantly at the door would be shooting at me through your lifeless corpse.

"I can talk about myself all day, Roger. However, I'd rather do that with friends."

He has a few more spoonfuls of prawns in their resplendent sauce, then gulps water nervously. I lift the carafe and refill his glass - slowly, looking into his eyes and stopping just short of the brim.

"Leadership spill, Roger."

He lowers his gaze as if accused of molesting a child.

"Work with us, old chap. The press is like that, you know. We can either help or we could toss you to the wolves."

The woman he molested was far from a child, but her doll face would not play well, not for a future deputy leader. Roger knows that too, and we spend the next hour discussing the coming coup. My article will be three-quarters insightful analysis, a quarter reckless speculation - woven into a long masterpiece and sent across to Helen before I leave the table. The MP's will get advance copies from the proprietor of the magazine site, and their votes will be much attuned to the gritty reality invented by the Fourth Estate.

Democracy is not a good system, said Churchill - but it is the best available. He too was a journalist with a military past. He too was a splendid liar.

As Roger winds down a long story full of half-truths and self-justification, our main courses arrive. I pick at poached fish in a tart sauce, typing along with my other hand. Roger's meal seems to disappear before my eyes, and he eyes my plate with a greedy look. I tread warily, for Roger is a worthy sparring partner - but our meals prove that a sturdy fish on a sturdy hook gets reeled in, sooner or later.

We are almost done when a loud ring emanates from his suit. Roger smiles with relief and reaches inside his breast pocket.

The phone he pulls out is dark and silent, and his expression sours. He pats his side and extracts a much larger unit, which looks a lot more government and much less mistress.

"Make it quick," says Roger, but his tone says: talk slowly, I need a respite.

I rise to give him privacy, but Roger raises his hand and motions that I should stay.

"What do you fucking mean they cancelled?" he asks with what sounds like genuine amazement. "Those talks were scheduled for months!"

I attack the remains of my fish working my mind to tune out the restaurant sounds. Alas, I can't discern the words - being an old hand, Roger set the volume to low, pressing the phone hard against his ear. Many of his colleagues had lost careers and marriages for lack of this simple precaution.

"Quarantine?" asks Roger. "Isolation? Are you shitting me or something?"

There is a lengthy reply from the other end, and I empty my plate as he nods his head with vigour.

"Yeah, I'll come back right now," says he, avoiding my gaze. "Hookup in thirty, right."

He rises to his feet.

"We'll have to continue tomorrow. Sorry, old chap, urgent business."

"Such as?" I rise to my feet and stare at him possessively.

"If you stay quiet for a day or so, you might be in for a nice scoop. There's a good lad."

I dismiss Roger with a lazy wave and watch him leave. The restaurant is otherwise empty, and he scurries to the car without making an effort to hide. I see the big BMW drive away, then sigh and roll up the keyboard.

The young waitress studies me with interest as I ask for another carafe of water. These ladies know politics like any seasoned reporter, and she too is puzzled about what she just saw.

I call Helen and explain what happened. She tells me not to contact Roger - she will anchor tomorrow's meeting herself. I then text Tavita, and he rolls up just as I pocket the receipt for the meal. Naturally, Roger didn't pay a cent.

There is little to do until tomorrow, and I spend the rest of the day walking the shoreline. It never recovered from the big quakes, and much of the beachfront had never been rebuilt. It remains a pile of sickly plank houses, a theme park of a dowdy urban past, whose crooked fences are drowning in weeds. I am glad that nothing so ugly remains in Greymouth.

I end my walk with a bus ride back to the hotel. I can't be bothered with anything exotic and order room service, a steak with a bottle of red wine. The latter is a blessing, for the former is a tasty, but tiny offering out of proportion to its price, camouflaged by soggy vegetables and watery peppercorn sauce that offer little consolation.

{}{}{}

I move stiffened limbs and become aware of a dull burning along my right side, then wriggle fingers and toes - they all appear to work.

"The bone setters came in the night," says Trevor gruffly.

I open my eyes and swivel towards him with great care. My right arm is encased in a wire contraption that is joined to a wide belt around my waist.

"They said you broke everything you could," says Trevor. "Get up, hero. As if there were no younger men to do a simple job."

I had to go, I am about to tell him. Only I could destroy the last memory of Rina - but I know Trevor would scoff at the idea. He is, of course, right. There is no room for sentiment in the present reality.

"Their lives are just as valuable as mine."

"Don't embarrass yourself, Ritter," he supports my right side as I swivel the leaden legs out of the bed. "Without you we are all just corpses, floating in the river on the way to the sea."

It doesn't feel good being up, but I struggle to the toilet and relieve a bursting bladder. When Trevor helps me back in bed, he hands me a spoon full of white powder. I shake my head.

"The healer said you have to take this and move your shoulder. Otherwise it will become stiff and useless for life."

"In a moment," I tell him. "First I want to know what you mean."

His dark eyes flash irritation, but he sets down the spoon on the bedside table and lowers his crooked body into the chair. We both turn to stare at the glowing coals in the grate. I had Ethel make me a door out of thick glass.

"You know what will happen next," says Trevor. I am startled by his tone - harsh, yet resonant with sadness I had not heard before.

I inhale to speak but decide to keep my peace for the time being.

"People say you should not have burned Brana." says Trevor. "Of course you should have. They would come for us anyway."

I nod in silence.

"The winter is coming," continues Trevor. "The mountains will soon fill with snow, and the vermin will take their time. But in the end, it isn't much of a choice for them. No one in their right mind will shiver under a log in the forest when you could occupy a warm, dry shelter and chew on the previous tenant."

I reach over and pick up the spoon. The powder tastes vile, but the pain begins to dull as soon as I toss the empty spoon on the bed. Trevor hands me a mug of water, which I down with haste.

"I say you have about three moons," he tells me with force. "You must get over this love nonsense and begin planning as soon as you damn well recover. We are not ready."

"That's the truth," I tell him weakly, my head beginning to spin from the powder. I begin to flex the muscles of the right shoulder, wincing with pain. "We only have enough coal for a few moons, and we will lose the mine as soon as the siege starts. There is no ammunition and little food. Our wall is useless, and we have few soldiers."

"I will tell the sergeants," says Trevor. "Maybe the day after tomorrow you will be awake enough to give the first orders."

{}{}{}

"So what was it this time?" I wiggle in the armchair, shifting the weight off the aching shoulder.

"He teased me," says Boy matter-of-factly.

"Truly? And you what - hit him and threw him through the window because he teased you?"

"That is what I did."

"But... He is double your size! How did that happen?"

Without a change in sullen expression Boy demonstrates a hard punch to the midriff, followed by a slick throw over the shoulder. Yes, I can easily see how an opponent three years his senior would find himself flying through the window.

"And if you injured him?"

"He earned it. He said that children without parents don't deserve to be citizens."

I shake my head in disapproval, feeling colour rise in

my cheeks. I could have thrown someone like that through a solid wall - after beating him to a pulp first.

"It's an embarrassment to The Regiment. You know how much trouble I take to stop my soldiers getting into fights."

"I am not a soldier yet."

"But I am already disappointed, Boy. You will be no mere soldier, you know that. You have to lead by example. That means showing restraint."

He jumps to his feet, and I can see a glimmer of welling tears. But duty is duty.

"What am I supposed to have done?" demands Boy, his voice close to breaking. "It's easy for you to say - but everyone is afraid of you. I am nothing!"

"Sit."

He shakes his head in mute anger.

"Sit the fuck down!"

Boy studies the chair as if it is smeared in mud and perches himself on the edge, staring out of the window. I allow that, as a small concession.

"In ascending order of importance. Not everyone is afraid of me. My soldiers, for instance, respect me. They are not afraid to tell me what they think when I am wrong. That's one."

There is no visible reaction - he doesn't move a muscle.

"Yes, most people are afraid of me. I fought for them all of my life, and I will not tolerate disrespect. There is nothing wrong with that - it is proper for a man to be treated with the dignity he had earned. That's two."

Boy nods imperceptibly.

"Three: you are not nothing because you too deserve respect. You have earned it. Now you have to defend it, but not with fists. You cannot command the respect of trained fighters by having fights. They can all fight, and they are not awed by it. You must learn to subdue men with your will."

"I don't know how."

"Neither did I when I was your age. That mutt said that you didn't have parents. What are his?"

"His parents?"

"Yes. What do they do?"

"His father is a loader on the pier. I don't know about his mother."

"So that is what you should have told him. In ten years time you will wear a crisp battle tunic and command the best men in Grey. He will be a loader at the docks like his father, smelling of fish and sweat. If he then attacked, that would give you the right to throw him through a window. He would be in trouble instead of you. Understand?"

Boy turns to me and nods, without looking up. I study him for a while.

"Are the dreams very bad?" I ask suddenly.

He looks up at me with a sudden flash of apprehension, stares for a while, then shakes his head.

"But you do have them?"

He looks up and nods, his eyes locked on mine.

"I do too. I see a warrior from the time of the scourge. What is in yours?"

"The sea, Commander. A ship goes down, and I drown. But it's not very bad."

"How so?"

"It is very cold, Commander. The water doesn't feel so cold, and dying isn't bad."

I digest that in silence, wincing from a sudden ache

in my shoulder.

"Does everyone here have dreams?"

"Not all people, but most. Somehow the horror of the scourge was like nothing else before or after. The feelings of those who lived through it were too strong to die with them."

"I don't like those dreams. Will they ever stop?"

"Probably not. It is best to just let them come. They cannot hurt you in any way. Just echoes of a dreadful cry from the past, is how I think of it."

Boy sits totally still, but I have nothing more to give.

"Enough of that," I tell him. "I've asked Captain Hilliger to take you out next moon. After that the seas will get rough, and the voyage will be too dangerous for beginners."

Boy's eyes light up. Sometimes I wonder whether I can hold him on land. He first set eyes on the sea when I brought him to Grey, and he will be one of those men whose fascination with eternally vicious, clamouring depths is never sated.

"I told him to go hard on you," I add with a smile. "It will be anything but a pleasant cruise, you know..."

We both whip our heads to the door as I hear the

cadence of heavy boots on the stairs, and a young soldier bursts through the door without knocking. I instantly take a dislike to the proceedings - his uniform is in disarray, and his eyes are two lakes of deep blue amid a white face.

"Sir, Sergeant Tannis requests your immediate presence," he gasps, remembering at last to stand at attention and salute.

I rise to my feet and inspect his appearance before returning the salute. He hastily adjusts his attire and clicks his heels, still trying to catch his breath.

We walk down the stairs, and I slide on the boots, tying them loosely. We head for the radio hut, and a sinking feeling is well on the way to knotting my guts by the time we arrive.

There are many men in a small space, crowded around the operator of the shelf of bulky equipment that makes the mountain radio set. As I step through the door, they part, and I see Tannis, his wide face a sickly grey smear. Beads of sweat line his receding forehead, and his posture is pure spring - he appears to be hunched at the bench without touching his chair.

"Convoy One, repeat," he barks into the microphone. His hand is poised over the paper with a stubby pencil.

I march up to the bench and flick the speaker switch. The room fills with the wail of a weak signal amplified to the hilt.

"Convoy One, answer," orders Tannis.

I await the reply, but none comes. I push him away and lean to the microphone.

"Convoy One, this is Grey. I am Commander Hans Ritter. If one of you is still alive, you will answer immediately, or you will regret being alive if you return."

A few moments pass, and I begin to sweat. That annoys me, as I was not planning on showering before bed. I turn to Tannis in annoyance.

"So their radio is down. What is this circus about?"

Tannis rises from the chair and takes time to remove the headphones, adjust his tunic and salute. I return it with a stony expression, trying not to wince from the lancing pain in the shoulder.

"Commander, the duty operator was raised by Convoy One shortly before you were summoned. The lead sergeant shouted something about vermin. He made no sense."

"Is that all?"

"More or less. He said they were almost surrounded."

I nod in thought. In that case, things look rotten - it is close to sunset, and they are miles away, caught on a narrow road with long trailers and few men to defend each machine. We will not get there until this time tomorrow.

"Grey, this is Convoy One," crackles Solly's voice. Tannis and I nearly collide as we rush to the microphone. Tannis retreats with an apologetic expression.

"Convoy One, there better be a good explanation for your silence."

"I am sorry, Commander. We had to run and lost the signal in the shadow of the ridge. We are past the saddle now."

"Yes, you are loud and clear, Convoy One. What is going on?"

"Vermin, Commander. They are here."

"Sergeant, get a hold of yourself and report as your rank requires. What about vermin?"

"Many, Commander."

"How many?"

"All of them, Commander."

Tannis and I study each other's faces, and I begin to breathe hard. With a shake of my head I exhale, sit down at the bench and position the microphone in front of myself.

"Sergeant, if you cannot control yourself, hand the headset to someone who is able to report."

A few moments later I hear another voice, and I recognize a man I had failed to promote once too often. That mistake is destined for an instant correction.

"Commander, this is Private Fest. Are you receiving me?"

"Loud and clear. What is happening, Sergeant Fest?"

"I salute you, Commander. We have sighted the enemy in very large strength travelling down the river valley. We are probably forty miles from the coast."

"Are you under attack?"

"Negative, Commander. I don't think they even saw us. We are well above them, and the wind is very strong."

I loosen in slight relief. The vermin have not been sighted since I burned Brana, and one expected something this bad when they eventually regrouped.

"Then what is the big deal?"

"Their strength, Commander. I had never seen anything like it,"

"Estimate how many."

"I am sorry, Commander," Fest pauses and clears his throat. "I can't do that."

"Why on earth not?"

"I have never seen so many."

I shake my head in anger.

"Listen, Sergeant. You are just off the ridge and on my side of the saddle."

"Affirmative, Commander."

"If you look to your right, you see the river valley. About five miles of it, below the road."

"Affirmative, Commander."

"Tell me how much of the valley is filled with vermin."

"All of it, Commander."

I hear sharp intakes of breath and look around in anger, tapping my mouth with a gesture of silence. Then

I turn to the set and carefully study its dials to collect my thoughts.

"Are there any vermin above the river?"

"Negative, Commander. They are travelling in a very large convoy along the river bed."
"Which direction?"

"Towards the sea, Commander. Towards Grey."

"What is your speed?"

"We are travelling at maybe forty miles a day, Commander. The trailers are full."

"Fine. Sergeant Sollard is relieved of command and demoted to private. You are now promoted, as stated, and you are in charge."

"Affirmative, Commander."

"Maintain present speed. Do not engage unless attacked. Get here as fast as you can and stop only if it's completely dark. Resume travel at first light and at all possible speed."

"Affirmative, Commander. Maintain speed and return as fast as possible."

I turn to Tannis.

"Get the mine."

He raises his hand and turns a few dials, then nods.

"Coal, this is Grey. Reply at once."

"Commander, we have monitored your exchange with Convoy One. "

"Enemy contact?"

"Negative, Commander. What are your orders?"

"Load all remaining transporters and evacuate the mine at first light. Excavators too, one convoy. Work through the night, leave at dawn. Do not engage unless attacked and do not stop until you see my angry face. Contact every two miles."

"Affirmative, Commander. See you tomorrow evening."

I stand up abruptly.

"Double the guard tonight," I tell the duty sergeant. "Get three machines with hopper guns to the south wall. Light lots of fires. Go."

He salutes and runs off.

"Tannis, maintain contact with Convoy One. All night. I don't want anyone to sleep."

He merely nods, but I choose to ignore the lapse in protocol.

"Town meeting. Soldier to my left, call the bell man. Soldier to my right, sound general alarm."

{}{}{}

I awaken with an unfamiliar sensation - the sun floods the hotel room, and I do a few push-ups on the hard carpet that smells strongly of detergent. I am used to the sunrise being behind the mountains and awoke annoyingly early.

Deciding to skip breakfast, I dose up on cheap percolated coffee in my room and hit the phones. During the next five hours I make few friends and influence no people, but a couple of calls that are returned provide valuable material. I assemble a neat conclusion to yesterday's article; as soon as I send it across, Helen calls.

"Roger has gone to ground," says she without introduction, as is her way.

"Want me to try from here?"

"Neh, useless. An urgent cabinet meeting. The fuckers are sharpening their knives."

"Hels, you might be wrong. He could be telling you the truth."

"That'll be a first."

I tell Helen about Roger's phone call. She listens carefully, then thinks it over in silence.

"If it's important, we'll know soon enough. Come home. Sorry, have to go - I am in the middle of a meeting."

"Roger said he might be ready to talk in a day or two."

"We. Have. Things. To. Do. Here," enunciates Helen emphatically. I smile - that perfect choice of double entendre tells me that she's well and truly back on top of her game. In more ways than one.

I glance at the watch.

"I missed the train anyway. Give it till tomorrow morning."

"Done," the line goes dead.

I sit back on the hard hotel sofa and take stock. The job is sort of complete, and I can let go with a clear conscience. What doesn't please, however, is my state - I am much too tired for this early hour. It doesn't seem to be a fever, but there is wool my head, and I feel like returning to bed.

Get a hold of yourself, soldier. It is far too early for a

relapse. Surely: I felt fine only yesterday, just out of shape. Hospitals are like that - everything gets done for you. Even a vile ordeal like chemotherapy is something you take, not something you do. Once back in the real world, it is hard enough to boil an egg.

I resolutely decide against going back to bed and wonder out in search of a good restaurant. As usual, the best guide is smell. After a walk of no more than two blocks from the beach, I am seated behind a table in an Italian trattoria, run by real Italians for the past sixty years. The original restaurant was condemned many quakes ago, but the family relocated to the building on the edge of the new wetlands, where the business district once bustled in all its ugly glory, unaware of the faultline under its dowdy landscape.

Now you can sit here on the deck and watch birds rampage in the primordial wetland as you munch on your pasta. As I do with great pleasure, sinking into a mire of house wine, flirting with the plump waitress, belabouring the dessert tray and leaving a generous tip as I wallow out the door.

It is not even cold, and I elect to walk to my hotel, whose silhouette I can clearly see above the shoreline. I walk with my leather jacket undone, sweating out the wine with a firm infantry stride. The fatigue seems to have left me, and I am greatly relieved.

Cancer is like that - beating it is half the battle. The hard part is to live your life without looking over your shoulder. You have to keep telling yourself that you get tired and sick for other reasons. You address the obvious causes, make room for fatigue and minor illness, do all you can to drive away the fear. Otherwise, it's not worth being alive.

I pass a few groups of mean-looking youths who cast suggestive looks at my leather jacket. But instincts serve them well - they observe a respectful distance, and I arrive to the hotel unmolested.

{}{}{}

"Well, dear citizens," I begin with a sarcastic smile, swivelling my gaze from left to right across the hall. "The vermin hadn't forgotten us after all."

I study the sea of pale faces that now peer at me with intense concentration.

"It's your damned fault, Ritter!" cries a young-looking woman in a once-white cloak. "You should have left them Brana!"

There is an ugly murmur of voices, and I raise my hand to still the noise.

"I expected some foul wretch to bring this up, and I am not disappointed," I tell the hall. "Let's get it out of the way. We always burn ruins to stop the vermin sheltering their young from the cold. If we hadn't burned Brana, they would come a few winters later, but in much larger numbers. Please do not bring it up again."

I scan the crowd as its murmur falls silent.

"I am in charge of all defences, so let's make it clear. Disobedience is going to be punished. Anyone who endangers our survival will be dealt with harshly."

"You are declaring martial law," says the blind man from the front row.

"I am, your honour," I tell him with deference. "You must agree that circumstances leave me no other choice."

He thinks for some moments and nods.

"Speaking of defence, dear citizens - you are now at one with my men. Each and every one of you is now a soldier. You do not need uniforms, but if you can carry a weapon, you must do so. If you can't, you will fight lying down. We cannot spare any hands."

I pause to wipe my forehead with a handkerchief and catch my breath.

"I will outline the plan as it stands now. We will lay an ambush at the mouth of the river and kill as many as we can, then return by sea. I am planning to have a long siege to cull as many vermin as we can. If we break their will to fight, they will winter on the shore and die in great numbers from cold and disease. Maybe it's even a good thing that they are coming. Maybe we can even finish it once and for all."

"We need to dig a moat and reinforce the wall in the south with timber. They will not be able to cross from the north or the east because of the river. The south wall is the main problem - the south arm of the river is shallow, and we cannot dam it because it will flood the town. The existing wall is too low, as you are well aware."

I stop and scan the crowd again. They appear to be with me - intent, with just the right proportions of fear and determination.

"All free hands will help dig a moat on the south wall, starting at dawn tomorrow. At dawn, citizens, not at morning tea. Anyone who can use a shovel is to assemble at the south gate. Others will report to the foundry for light work. We have to increase our stocks of ammunition. Ethel!"

My cousin stands up at his seat calmly. His deep eyes stare at me intently, and he has a pen ready.

"Dear cousin, we need those rock catapults up on the wall," I tell him. "Then we need to make as many crossbows as you may manage, with bolts of each and any kind."

"No problem," he says simply. "The good people from Brana will be most helpful, I am sure."

"Sea and air captains, you will see me tomorrow at dusk," I issue the final order. A few heads nod in the hall, and I acknowledge them with a wave of the hand.

"So, fellow soldiers. We are fighting for our lives."

There is more, much more to say - but something tells me to cut my oration at that point and fall silent.

A few perfunctory questions are asked, then the meeting is declared closed as the first night of martial law settles over Grey. My citizen army files out of the hall in total silence.

{}{}{}

"I think you deserve this, Commander," Rendell hands me a mug of foaming beer. Ethel brews his own in the foundry, for consumption by men who spend the entire day around metal furnaces.

I heft the mug with my good arm and salute him in silence, down half and set the mug down. I can feel the grease and the grime on my face, but my hands and clothes are even dirtier, all of which will have to be tolerated until tonight.

"Amazing what you can do with your back to the wall," I tell Rendell between sips of beer. "Three hundred crossbowmen armed in two days, from scraps of waste materials."

"Too true," he replies, downing his glass. "Same tomorrow and same the day after."

After much discussion we made bolts with stone tips. They shatter on impact, preventing the bolt from being reused by the enemy. Brana people showed us exactly how it should be done - the shooters line up in threes. One shoots as the other two reload, putting out a constant stream of missiles. I almost look forward to the battle.

After finishing the beer I drive myself to the wall, where the timber fence is being coated with mud from the river. I was told that at Brana the vermin dipped their javelins in some kind of flammable tree sap and lit them before throwing, starting numerous fires.

The moat is not quite finished, but we have plenty of time. We are digging a wide trench that takes part of the flow from the river, strong enough to float away the corpses. Otherwise disease will get us first.

As I finish my inspection of the wall - now a convincing barrier to men and spears, with a rampart along entire length - the coal convoy appears from the forest. Tow transporters race out of the gate to meet them.

The vehicles appear to be none the worse for wear, although I don't look forward to seeing poor Solly. I watch as the heavy machines clamber through the river and begin to struggle up the bank, dragging their trailers through water. The second machine sinks into the tracks made by the first and gets stuck on the near bank. Men spill from its cabin to stretch cables to the awaiting tows. Hopper guns swivel towards the forest, and gunners stare into the dense greenery, ready to fire at the first sign of movement.

The transporter is pulled up the muddy bank without incident, all three machines making their way to the gate together. The shackles are detached, and the tow transporters return to the river, trailing thick cables on the ground. The remaining trailers come through the water and manage to maintain their speed up the bank until they are safe on stony ground. I watch as the last of the trailers enters town. Sentries frantically work the handle, and the gate closes with a heavy clang.

We are under siege.

{}{}{}

"Captain Turner?" asks a young female voice.

I am still half-asleep and fumble for the switch in the unfamiliar room. My eyes gradually adjust to the darkness, and I find it above the head of the bed, then squint against the miserable brightness of the bedside lamp.

"Is that you, Lindy?"

"Captain Turner, I am Corporal Standish. You are

activated."

I sit up in bed and rub my eyes.

"What time is it?" I ask irrelevantly.

The girl is somewhat flustered by the question.

"It's zero four thirty-three, sir."

I am now fully awake, and a rush of adrenaline subsides. I get to my feet, naked apart from a skimpy pair of briefs and the phone in my hand.

"Identify yourself properly."

"Corporal Shirley Standish, zero-nine-four-eight-one-five, Grey HQ."

"Acknowledged."

"Are you Captain Nicholas Turner, zero-two-five-six-one-seven?"

"I am."

"Sir, you are activated."

"Listen, young lady. I am under treatment for a life-threatening cancer. Until further notice I am exempt from all drills."

There is a long silence on the line, and I can hear loud voices in the background.

"Sir, this is not a drill."

A drop of sweat runs down my forehead, and I wipe it away with the free hand.

"I will speak to your commanding officer."

"Sir, he is very busy right now."

"That was an order, Corporal Standish."

"Yes, sir. I will ask him to call you as soon as he can."

The line goes dead, and I tread to the bathroom. My bladder is full to bursting, and I only just manage to press the flush button when my phone shrills again.

I snatch it up from the basin table and close the door on the burbling toilet.

"Captain Turner."

"Nick, this is Colonel Styles. Remember me?"

"Sir."

"Look, I am sorry. Of course you are listed as inactive - the army is even paying for your treatment."

"Yes, sir."

"I apologize if this seems insensitive."

"Of course, Colonel."

"But I need you back, Captain, right this fucking minute."

I stare at the city lights below as blood drains from my skin.

"What is happening, Colonel?"

"Doesn't anyone watch the news?"

"Sir, I was busy with a work trip."

"Shit. Where are you?"

I run over to the TV and flip open the hotel folder.

"Sixty-four Key Avenue, Colonel."

"What, you are in Christchurch?"

"Sir."

"Stand by. I will call back."

The line dies, and I put down the phone, looking

around.

The remote control is next to the bed, and I turn on the news channel. The screen is flooded with images I know all too well.

The Indonesian jungle is again in the news. There are familiar piles of bodies, but I struggle to discern the cause. They do not look like victims of violence.

The phone shrills, and I grab it with all speed.

"Turner, you will be picked up, in ten minutes outside the hotel. I know your health status, but I have no choice. It's bad, Captain. We are stretched real thin."

"Am I being deployed to Indonesia?"

"I wish. No, this one is here. Be outside in ten minutes. You will be supplied with a uniform and gear. Out."

I soon stand outside the hotel lobby, chilled to the bone by a damp Christchurch dawn. On the twelfth minute precisely an army truck roars up the driveway and doesn't quite stop. The driver jerks his thumb backwards, and I run behind, throwing in my pack. Hands reach out as I mount the step, and I am thrown more than helped inside. Someone thumps the side with his fist, and the driver guns the engine.

There are three privates and two officers, one

infantry and one attack helicopter pilot, already kitted up. I am tossed a uniform and change, doing my best to cope with the rocky ride. Someone shines his tactical torch so I can do up the boots, and I stow my civilian gear in the backpack, hoping to put it on one fine day.

The web belt comes with a holster. I open it, seeing a standard-issue Blazer inside. I take it out, check the magazine and replace the machine pistol back in the holster, then gird the belt. It does not feel good to be in uniform and armed on the streets of the capital.

The others remain completely silent, and I decide not to ask. We arrive at what looks like a rugby oval, jump out of the truck and run to a waiting cargo helicopter. The turbine begins to moan as soon as the last of us is inside, and the machine swings away from the ground. It seems to settle on a course away from the tentative sunrise, and I soon realize that I am going back to Greymouth.

{}{}{}

"Pay out the cables and let the surf carry the platforms to the shore," I tell Redmond. I don't trust any of the seamen with my life, and he accepted the short straw - staying aboard to keep an eye on things.

"Red flare is your signal to retrieve the platforms," repeats Redmond for the fifth time. I nod.

The ship is our largest trawler, towing three fishing

platforms that will be used to launch the attack. We are turning around to let them float up the river on the tide, to where the platforms will be anchored. The edges of each platform are lovingly covered with freshly cut bushes to make them look like natural islands.

I shake Redmond's hand and move towards the gangplank with my crossbow slung over the shoulder. I managed to learn how to pull the string without using my right arm. As instructed by the veterans of Brana, each crossbowman has a hook on his belt - which allows the crossbow to be pulled by straightening the knees. We decided to go for the single-shot type, rather than repeaters, whose range and reliability still leave a lot to be desired.

I banned all firearms - the vermin must forget that we have them. We will use crossbows unless things get desperate, a decision that did not sit easily with my men. Fortunately, they found the crossbows a joy to use - they lack the rate of fire of revolvers, but each man can carry many more bolts than we ever issued ammunition. In any case, that's a moot point - there isn't enough ammunition to go around.

My troops are all women from Brana. They shoot just as well as the men, and their discipline is possibly better. They had been steeled in the long siege, and I wonder, looking at their matter-of-fact expressions, whether my soldiers will fare as well through what is to come.

The incoming tide is most cooperative, and all three

platforms float swiftly, right into the wide river mouth. We did our best to time our arrival to the ramshackle march of the vermin towards the coast, but it is clear that they won't arrive until morning. There should be just enough depth in the lagoon at low tide to keep the platforms afloat.

There is little banter, just curt orders and replies as the crossbow lines are formed up. We sit amid sacks containing bundles of crossbow bolts, on short logs that will hopefully float if we capsize. Most of my troops can't swim.

I suddenly feel a wash of calm, realizing that what I feared all my life has happened, and I had done all in my power to prepare for it. It's as bad as it gets, so there is simply little left to fear.

There is nothing to do for the first time in many days - I take in a lungful of air and let it out very slowly. Then I move the right arm in a circular motion from front to back, in what has become a reflex action whenever I sit down to rest. I managed to retain full movement in the mangled shoulder, but strength is something else altogether.

Then I realize that I revel floating up the river, smelling its stale odours and the faint perfume of the women, who washed and dressed in clean clothes before we set out.

The half-moon rises in the cloudless sky, and only a

slight breeze blows from the sea as the sun sets. It is not very cold, and we are quite comfortable in the middle of the wide river, away from the insects that would make life a misery on the beach. Most of the women wrap themselves in cloaks and promptly fall asleep. I have no inclination to do so just yet.

"Warlord."

I turn to face a woman I had noticed a few times, her fine features and perfect skin catching my jaundiced eye. Her short hair is kind of white or grey, despite a youthful face, and a long scar runs the width of her left cheek. She carries the crossbow with practised ease and seems to enjoy some kind of authority among the women of Brana.

"My greetings, Lady," I tell her in a low voice, as we are not meant to make noise. "May I ask your name, since you know mine?"

"I am called Celia, warlord. I want to say that I am honoured to fight alongside you. Your townsmen don't value you - but I wish you were there to defend Brana."

I feel a sudden pang of hurt and raise my face towards the moonlight, inhaling deeply.

"I too wish that, Celia. But good wishes cannot change anything now."

"That is so, warlord. I also want to say that I knew

her, and she did not deserve you."

I grow perfectly still except for a flash of anger that erupts from my eyes. Celia is not at all intimidated. She places her hand on my forearm, squeezing with surprising strength.

"Precious are the memories of those we loved," she whispers, staring into my eyes. "But you must not go through life thinking that you lost her. She could never be yours. It was very wrong of her to have given you hope."

I inhale deeply and hold my breath, forcing myself to mouth what Celia just said until it sinks in: Rina could never be mine, and it was wrong of her to give me hope.

Rina could never be mine, and it was wrong of her to give me hope.

Rina could never be mine, and it was wrong of her to give me hope...

"Why?"

"She was dying, warlord."

"Of what?"

"Please keep down your voice. May I call you by your name?"

I nod, fighting to keep angry tears out of my eyes. They had become an annoying habit since I shot Dinah.

Celia sets her weapon on the deck and takes my wrist with both hands. With no warning she presses my palm against her heart, pushing through the soft pliancy of the breast until I feel a strong beat.

"Hans, none of you knew. Things went bad in Brana as soon as we arrived," she whispers into my ear. "A disease began to run through families. All children born to sick parents had it too."

A flash of recognition sears my conscience, and I recoil, tearing my hand from Celia's grasp.

"Like Josiah?"
She nods just once, and I see her eyes well up with moisture in the moonlight.

I shake my head in residual disbelief, but I know it to be the truth. I closed my eyes to Rina's rages and rants, but in the end they could not be dismissed. That was the guilty feeling of relief I tried not to feel when we parted.

"Insanity ran in all descendants of her grandfather," says Celia softly, taking my hand again. This time I close my palm around her slender fingers, revelling in her warmth.

"Josiah's father?"

"Yes. All is fine until maybe thirty years of age, then the rot sets in. Rina knew what will happen to her."

I nod acceptance, my mind whirling.

"She loved me."

"She did, and that broke her will. Maybe she still bore hope until Josiah went insane. He was very clever - everyone was stunned when he told people what he had done. That was insane too - he was almost killed on the spot."

"Pity they refrained."

"We let him die on the wall. At least he went to his Maker like a man should."

"It's a lot to take in," I whisper, staring past Celia towards the dark sea.

"Hans, I am so sorry. But I didn't want to go into battle without telling you. One never knows what may happen tomorrow."

I squeeze her hand lightly, and she reciprocates.

"I better say my thanks before the battle as well."

She smiles and grasps my hand with both of hers.

"Promise that when it's all over you will thank me

properly," she whispers. "Will you do that?"

I nod my acceptance. She continues to stare into my eyes, but suddenly their strength is drained, her features showing only fatigue.

Bereft of words we lie on the rough-hewn deck, and Celia presses her head into my chest. She is asleep within moments, her breaths turning deep and slow. I dare not move and stay on my side, staring at the half-moon until the rhythm of Celia's breathing carries me away to a deep, dark crevasse in which I feel no pain.

{}{}{}

I awaken at dawn, cold, numb and stiff in the same posture, even though Celia is gone. She left me a short time ago, something I know from the warmth I still feel on my stomach. I stretch and clamber to my feet, to make my way past the makeshift curtain that marks the latrine on the corner of the platform.

When I emerge, she is there, with a flask of what looks like berry tea. I take a long sip of the hot, sweet liquid and return it, mouthing my thanks.

"So you have slept," says she with approval.

"I am grateful for what you said, Lady. And for what you will say next."

"Then I will save it for later," she replies, a

conquering smile creasing her cheeks and dimpling the long scar.

"Are there any news?"

"The scouts have spotted smoke from cooking fires just beyond the bend in the gorge. We should be in business before midday."

I nod and stretch my limbs once more.

"Is everyone ready?"

Celia nods with a sad smile.

"Don't worry about my women. They've had much worse."

I inspect the troops, now grouped in threes on the edge of the platform. A few bolts are fired at the shore to check the range in the strong breeze that is now blowing offshore. Weapons are checked and checked again, and I inspect the flare gun, replacing it in the holster at my side.

The river had dropped overnight, and it seems as if we will be at low tide just as the enemy arrives. I can see the weeds on the bottom through murky water, and it seems as if we are barely afloat. Worst come to worst, the ship will have to drag us along, although we will be lighter once we fire our bolts.

The ship itself is hidden from view by a low knoll. To tow us out it will need to steam back to the mouth of the river and race against the incoming tide, hopefully dragging three platforms into deep water and out of harm's way.

The vermin scouts appear as the sun stands at noon. They emerge from the bushes on the distant shore and study the landscape with care. They give our camouflaged platforms a long stare, and I begin to wonder if they can smell us.

But that cannot be. The wind blows in the opposite direction, and there are too many competing smells in the river estuary. I force myself to loosen up and relax the sweaty grip on the roughly whittled stock of my weapon.

As shadows begin to lengthen, the last of my doubts are dispelled. We remain hidden as weary arrivals begin to crowd the distant shore, hauling animal skins filled with some kind of belongings. They look young and strong, yet exhausted by an arduous journey. I see profound weariness in their movements - they must have been on the march for a good moon or longer.

It is clear that they await the low tide. Water begins to ebb from the river mouth, and our platforms sink into the foetid weeds. The decision is made for me - we will have to get towed out soon. We can only kill a few that commence the crossing, maybe a few hundred more that are too slow to flee from the shore.

I sigh in disappointment and exchange looks with
Celia. She nods her understanding with a frown - our
hopes of inflicting a significant setback are dashed.

I point at the sun and signal the angle at which I
expect the crossing to commence. She nods and turns
away, checking her weapon for the final time.

The vermin line the lagoon at least twenty deep as
the tidal outflow slows to a trickle. They see that right
away and begin to wade into the water. The scouts
gingerly pick their way through soft mud, laying the
best trail through knee-high water.

I rise up above the camouflage, push the crossbow
into my left shoulder and fire. The bolt takes one of the
scouts through the chest, and he is thrown back with a
short scream. Mud spreads in the shallow water as he
thrashes his way to death. The rest stare in horror as a
red streak drifts along the sluggish current.

The river erupts in an uproar as vermin raise their
spears and toss them across the water. None manage to
span the distance, and I calmly drop the crossbow to the
deck to pull back its string, drop an arrow into the slot
with one smooth motion and raise the loaded weapon, to
fire again.

The platform rocks as women jump to their feet and
begin the dance of death - one fires, one loads and one
gets ready to fire, sending a constant stream of bolts into

the shore. The ranks of vermin literally melt under the onslaught, and those further back turn to run. Many fall before they reach the forest as our bolts continue to hammer the retreat.

I reach into the holster at my side and launch a flare towards the sea. We clear the platforms of camouflage to lighten the load and continue to fire off occasional bolts to keep the enemy in the forest.

The anchor ropes are cut - we begin to drift up the river on the hesitant current that marks the coming of the tide. But tow lines grow tight just as the vermin begin to poke their heads from the bushes. Some rocks reach the rafts, and I see a few women collapse with blood on their heads and arms. We reply with a fresh barrage, and the rocks stop coming.

My platform jerks, throwing us off our feet. One woman ends up overboard, and I rush over, extending my crossbow towards her. She grasps the end, and I drag her to safety just as the platform begins to gather speed in the opposite direction, towards the sea. I look over - the ship billows smoke from its stack as it struggles against the tide.

We fire the last of our bolts with little effect - but in truth, we are now safe from the stones, moving rapidly downstream. The platforms drift towards each other and collide. We exchange ropes to tie them together and drop to the deck, ready for the rough surf line. A few weapons end up overboard in the heavy swell, but then we level out in deeper water.

The tow line is wound in until we moor alongside the ship and evacuate the rocking platforms with haste. I ensure that Celia doesn't leave my sight until we climb up the steep gangplank and step onto the metal deck.

There is a storm on the way, we are told as we unstring the crossbows and stow the remainder of ammunition. Crossing in the shallows is out of the question, and the captain has charted a longer course that will take us further out to sea.

Celia and I stay together as we pile into the smelly cargo hold, holding cloaks to our faces to blunt the stench of stale fish. We feel the ship starting to pitch on the rising waves, but it is no longer of any account. Celia and I grasp each other with the desperation of near-dead and collapse into a deep, exhausted sleep.

{}{}{}

"Here's what it's all about," says Styles. He flicks on the screen, and I see the scenes from the TV - bloated bodies piled up in what looks like the edge of a tropical jungle.

"Began a month ago in Sulawesi," says Styles. "Some new fucking variant of the plague. Four days of fever, then septic shock, collapse and death. Antibiotics are not very effective, and it survives in many critters - insects, fish, rodents. Spreads easily through air and water."

He looks around the briefing room, satisfied that every officer is suitably appalled.

"A week before the outbreak the Indonesian troops raided an Al Shabbab camp in deep jungle. They found a lab, and the soldiers took little care when they searched it, looking for drugs they could put in their pockets. They were all dead inside a week."

He stares above us in silence, gathering his thoughts. I empathize - I am certainly having trouble gathering mine.

"Cases began to show up in Europe and North America last week. The spread has a definite pattern - warmer places do much worse."

He switches slides, showing a map of the world covered in red splotches.

"There is panic in many cities. People are running any place they can."

"Any cases in Aotea?" I hear myself ask in a hoarse and hollow voice.

"None, and this is why we are here," says Styles. He switches to the next slide, and we see a road map of Aotea. "It may be stopped by simple means, boys and girls - if people stop travelling for a week, the infected ones will all die, and no one else will get sick. But we know that other animals die of it - it is possibly that some will carry it forever."

I brush aside the last thought and study the map to see what Styles has in mind.

{}{}{}

The pain in the shoulder jolts me awake, and I move with an involuntary moan.

Celia mutters something incoherent, and I look up. She is fast asleep, but her lips are moving in some desperate recitation, a stream of tears running into the pillow.

What I am yet to get over is Trevor's reaction. By the time we returned from the port, we were soaked from the rain, still stinking of stale fish. I expected him to size her up with the usual sneer he reserves for women. But that was not to be - instead, Trevor stared at her for a few moments and bowed deeply. He helped us undress without a word and hung up our crossbows on the same hook.

As if summoned by that thought he knocks on the door, and I bid him to enter.

He has brought two mugs of berry tea with a few fish cakes for breakfast. Celia awakens and pulls a sheet over her naked shoulders.

"Good morning, honoured Lady," says Trevor in a tone I barely recognize. Apart from Father, he has always treated everyone as disappointing failures. I finally tumble to the answer.

"Do you two know each other?"

"Of course," says Celia. "My mother and I helped Trevor recover when he fell under the transporter. My mother taught me the art of healing."

"I travelled to Brana," says Trevor. "The healers at Grey told me to curl up and die. Those two put me back on my feet, as much as was possible. They were famous."

I nod, somehow not surprised. There is much to Celia that doesn't meet the eye - that was obvious straight away.

We breakfast with the sergeants and take stock of the attack. The enemy sustained only modest losses, but the trial of crossbows was a success. Lined up along the length of the south wall, they should mow down any attack, firing not as fast, but with greater range and accuracy than revolvers. This is good news.

"What is the story with oil?" I ask Redmond.

"Not a lot to report, Commander. The sons of bitches are stuck on their tune - we pay the blood debt for the captain, or they won't trade."

"What do they want?" asks Celia.

"A whole shipload of iron," explains Redmond. "We cannot spare such a fortune."

"Very well," I say after some thought. "We make do with what we have, for now. Ten thousand rounds, did you say?"

"Just over."

"How is the town set for food?"

"No problem - good catches of late. The ships are in good order, too."

"What is the enemy up to today?"

"As of this morning, they remain at the river after the assault, Commander."

"They are eating the dead," says Tannis with revulsion.

"That's right," replies Celia. "The more we kill, the stronger the survivors. We know this from our siege."

"Foul creatures," says Redmond. "I guess we never fought them like that. It was always on the run, in the forest."

A soldier appears at the open door, and I nod for him to enter. He salutes and hands over a note.

I study its short contents and look up at the silent room. Their faces all ask the same question, and I merely nod.

"Scouts were seen on the far bank after dawn. We need to prepare."

{}{}{}

It snows gently from the light-grey sky, and there is even a hint of sun over the mountains. The ramparts along the wall are lined with soldiers, with the town guard stationed along a steeper section that is less likely to be breached.

The vermin are crossing the river in a steady march, and I can already see that we are in trouble. This is no pack of inhuman rabble but a disciplined, well-trained army, marching in long ranks three or four deep. The front rank is carrying large shields made of thick bark; even from this distance they look solid enough to stop crossbow bolts.

We have an answer for this too - as they come into range, Ethel's catapults begin to toss stones. They first land short of the mark, and the crews raise the angle of fire. Heavy stones the size of a large fist now land in the enemy ranks and disrupt the shield line. I raise my crossbow, and it begins.

The crossbowmen fill the air with bolts, and the enemy ranks grow thin from the toll. But instead of retreating, they break into a run towards the wall. Our fire is no longer effective against fast-moving, scattered targets, and the vermin begin to climb the earthen bank. Bolts kill them at point-blank range, but they keep coming, with shields and without.

The first of the crude wooden poles are thrust over the timber parapet, and I see the first of the enemy bolt over the wall and into town. I have never seen that done before - the leading end of the pole, carried by many running men, is thrust into the ground, letting the other end soar into the air, mounted by the last man that carried it. He is catapulted over the wall and begins to swing his spiked club onto the heads of the defenders even before he lands.

One of the catapults is upturned, and the line of crossbowmen breaks up, men trying to use their crossbows to block the blows of clubs. My men wear helmets and armour, and some survive the initial assault long enough to spring their blades. The swirl of combat becomes chaotic, with vermin climbing up the poles to join the jumpers.

The wall has been breached.

Town guards maintain frantic fire into the wave of vermin coming over the wall, but more keep appearing.

An icy fear grips my stomach as I signal to Redmond.

He fires a flare, and three columns of men armed with spears rush up the parapet. I chose them myself, selecting the largest and the strongest. I armed them in a manner of a Spartan phalanx, with shields, helmets and long, heavy spears. They only had a few days to train, but the ancient system proved itself yet again.

Redmond begins to blow his whistle frantically, and all of the defenders retreat from the breached wall. The spearmen rush forward, form a semicircle and crash into the vermin, who bunch together and swing their heavy clubs. They are no match for the spears - the first assault leaves most of them dead, and the spearmen move in close, stabbing anyone in the way. Their only casualties are broken spears, whose neighbours take over the killing.

The onslaught is broken - all attackers are now killed as soon as they climb over the wall, then the spearmen move in and toss the climbing poles into the moat.

To my dismay, the vermin react to the setback as a professional, disciplined force. They break off the attack and reform a wall of shields that protects their retreat. Within moments they are no longer in range and wade through the water in a leisurely manner, disappearing into the undergrowth on the other side.

Redmond joins me on the walkway and studies the battleground thoughtfully.

"You were right, Commander," he says haltingly, his voice sounding choked. "The moat is too narrow."

I turn to study his face - he is pale and wide-eyed. I put my hand on his shoulder and steady my own breathing before replying.

"No plan survives the first shots of battle, my old friend."

We fall silent and stare at the muddy ground in front of the wall, littered with bodies. I know it looks more than it really is. We killed, maybe, a few hundred. What Solly saw in the gorge was probably more like ten thousand. A heavy feeling begins to form in my chest.

"Now the dull stuff, I suppose," I tell Redmond. "Clear the bodies, get rid of those poles, reform the lines. I will go to the infirmary."

"That can wait, Commander," says Redmond grimly. "There were no wounded - only the dead. Those damned clubs leave no survivors."

I shake my head in disbelief.

"Red, we haven't done well. In Brana it took them weeks to even get up the wall. Here they've come through on the first day."

"Our wall is not up to the job, Commander. Brana

was ruled by strong men from the beginning. We had fucked around for too long."

I stare at Redmond in surprise, for he does not often swear. His pallor is now gone, and his mouth is set in a vicious grimace. He is staring at the pile of enemy bodies that marks the breach. The breach we barely turned.

"I am open to all suggestions."

"We have to widen the moat, Commander. It's too late to rebuild the wall."

"Yes."

"We need to set charges in the night and sink the other bank of the moat. Make it into a lake."

"Do it now."

Redmond looks up in surprise.

"That was just our defence being probed," I explain curtly. "The real attack will come tonight."

"You think so?"

"That's what I would do. Maybe tomorrow night. Maybe the one after. I would not attack during the day again. You get to work on the moat, and I will take care of the men."

{}{}{}

I roar into Arthur's Pass in the GTO, some half-hour ahead of the column. All the jeeps were taken, which was just as well - I craved to ride my black predator before everything hit the fan.

I brief the local businessmen on the dismal developments and advise them to leave. Nowhere is safe, I tell them, but the further away from large roads, the better. The highway is already cut off to the west, but I have no orders to lock them up here - they can go down to the eastern plains and find shelter in the small towns nestled in the foothills. That message is to be passed on to all visitors still in the village, with my compliments, for I do not want them under my feet.

The column I am to command arrives to Arthur's Pass mid-morning. There is very much for them to do - first I despatch two squads to shut down the railway that links east with west. At this stage we don't want to do much damage - I tell them to find some machinery and park it across the tracks.

I quarter my soldiers down the hill in Otira, a small settlement once built around a coal mine. Most of the houses are long-deserted and have just about fallen down, but some are still used as baches and offer acceptable shelter. We don't have time to waste on tents and latrines.

I choose a bridge over a deep stream just west of Arthur's Pass as a fallback point. It's a difficult spot to bypass - the deep ravine cuts a steep hill and runs into a cliff above the river. The hill can be climbed, and I station a squad a hundred metres above the bridge, with a machine gun, mortars and much insect repellent.

I leave the armoured personnel carrier on the bridge and drive to where a road block is set up on the other side of the village. We allow the last of the traffic to leave, then one of the trucks returns from the forest, towing a huge log. We lay it out across the road and put up bright warning signs a short distance ahead.

After that I really have to sleep. There is too much noise at the roadblock, and I retreat to the village, where a motel now stands empty. The owner had kindly left all rooms unlocked, and I pick one with the least musty smell.

Sleep does not come easy, and I drag the mattress off the rickety bed onto the floor in front of the fire, cover myself with a blanket and curl up, thinking of Helen. She stayed till mid-morning, and I can still see the radiance in her eyes as she kissed me one last time and headed for the lift.

{}{}{}

As per my own orders, I go to bed after a big meal. Celia takes a long shower and slides into bed beside me.

"We have to sleep," I tell her immediately.

Her hand stops her downward slide on my stomach, and she laughs. I open my eyes and study her carefully.

"You seem none the worse for wear."

"Of course. We had many moons of this in Brana, before you kindly arrived and sprayed the vermin with bullets."

I grind my teeth at the mention of ammunition. The whalers' demand is pure blackmail, and we cannot pay it, especially now. An angry thought nags at the back of my mind, but I set it aside for the time being. The idea is, for the time being, unthinkable.

I mull it over as Celia goes to sleep on my shoulder. Then I nod off too, blocking all further thoughts, breathing in the aroma of her skin, feeling the air of her breathing on my aching shoulder.

A deep boom shakes the windows, and Celia sits up in fright.

"What the devil was that?"

"A little landscape work."

She sighs raggedly and rubs her eyes. After a few moments I feel that she is shivering and reach up, grasp her shoulder to turn her towards me.

Her eyes are very swollen, and tears roll down her tall cheeks.

I nod in understanding.

"Hans, what I dreamt was very bad," she whispers, latching onto my hand. "I was being raped by many men. I think they were dying, Hans. I was right here, on the beach. Raped by dying men."

I stare in silence and wait.

"Right here, in the shadow of this mountain," Celia's voice cracks, and she begins to sob again. "Hans how could they do that if they were already diseased?"

"It was a time of great savagery," I reply heavily. "Many sickening things had happened. I am sorry that you got to see it."

Celia wipes her tears with her sleeve.

"It is truly regrettable," I tell her. "It seems all too senseless but cannot be stopped. Did you not have dreams in Brana?"

"Nothing like this," says Celia, shaking her head. "This must be the worst place of them all."

"Well, this is where all the survivors ended up," I tell her. "Makes sense. I never thought about that before."

"What do you see?" she asks suddenly.

"One man. Only him, nobody else, and only his last hours. He must have been a soldier, one of those who defended Grey. I know nothing else, but he feels very much like myself."

She lowers her head slowly, as if afraid that her vision may return. I settle into the pillow and embrace her firmly. She sighs, and within moments her breathing becomes even and deep. I slide into a contented sleep beside her.

Father often said that life takes with one hand and gives with the other.

{}{}{}

After some debate we decide to leave the lights off. As a compromise, I station three transporters with hopper guns on the wall. There is very little ammunition, but only they can make a difference if an assault succeeds in darkness.

We had reinforced the wall with metal spikes and wire, and Redmond's explosives team did a very nice number on the moat - it is now a deep, wide mire that cannot be breached on foot. The sluggish current from the river seems to have joined our cause, eroding the bank even further and flowing through the moat at some speed - so much so that the corpses from the morning battle seem to have floated away without intervention.

There is nothing I can do to increase firepower. There are only so many men I can pack on the rampart - more would merely interfere. Four instead of three crossbows firing as a team seems to have made no difference - lack of space prevents them from engaging properly. As the sun begins its inevitable fall towards the sea, the troops reassemble at the wall.

I am pleased with their demeanour - there are no nervous looks or long silences. They calmly go about the business of stringing their crossbows - for most that still takes two people to do - and checking the bolts they pick from the boxes placed along the length of the rampart. I sigh in relief - we seem to have met the first challenge and are ready for more.

Ethel's men are adjusting the catapults. They are ill-tempered, as I prohibited them from fighting - they are far too valuable to lose. I ordered both catapults to be angled so they toss stones along the wall, hopefully collecting anyone trying to climb it. They didn't help much when fired into the running crowd - maybe they are more use that way, firing smaller stones at bunched-up climbers.

So we meet the sunset, wrapped in groundsheets against cold and damp, amply supplied with fish cakes and berry tea. I passed on the word that the attack may not come at all - we could be here for many nights, and we have to be ready for anything. From Brana's experience, it could be any time, anywhere, anyhow. There could be a massed attack on the wall in pitch darkness, or it could be fire arrows in broad daylight. We must take it as it comes, or it plays havoc with our heads.

Noise is prohibited, and the sentries have a small fire at each end of the wall, leaving the middle ground invitingly dark. The breeze is blowing steadily from the sea - hopefully, they cannot smell a large number of men and women I have hidden behind the wooden parapet.

I shift in discomfort and stretch my back on the cold ground, then roll over onto where the ground sheet is doubled. Rina is not so much on my mind these days, although I am still having trouble taking in the story of her family. One generation of inbreeding too many - and a world that survived tortuous centuries is on the verge of collapse, at the hands of one man. Just as it was on the verge of a resurrection, at the hands of another.

I grit my teeth and order myself to hope. The winter is not far away, and the vermin we don't kill at the wall will drop like flies from the cold. With any luck, we can reduce their numbers to a point where it will be possible for them to disperse back into the mountains and stay in the forest for a few more winters. By then we will make full use of the coal, facing the enemy in numbers and with weapons they will not dare oppose.

The soft murmur of voices slowly fades as the long night rolls along its dark, cold path. I give up listening to the sounds around me, contrary to habit: there is a wide stretch of muddy reeds that the vermin can probably traverse in complete silence, their backs camouflaged with clumps of long grass. There is little more to do unless the lights are lit, for we are no match for the enemy in darkness.

I had dozed for some time. My joints are stiff with cold and immobility, and the awakening feels especially vile. But once I peel my eyes, I squint at the bright lights that shine on the flood plain.

The crossbows are not yet ready for sustained fire, as the targets are few and seem hard to distinguish from the grass in which they crawled almost as far as the moat. Only movement gives them away, and they are hit by a few arrows at a time.

"This is not the main attack!" I shout at the men around me. "Stop firing! You are wasting arrows!"

They obey, and I peer into the space outside the wall, beginning to breathe hard. Everything seems to freeze; if any vermin are left on the far bank, they stay perfectly still.

The darkness suddenly erupts in shouts, as a long row of the enemy rises from the near edge of the moat and rushes the wall, protecting themselves with large shields. I can immediately see a change in tactic - the shields not only protect the front row but are carried by the further rows above their heads. Our arrows embed themselves in the viscous bark without doing harm.

The catapults begin to rattle just as the tight formation of shields reaches the wall and tosses the first attackers across it. The spearmen are ready, dispatching the leading climbers. They retreat a step and wait for the next assault, their spears bristling from the shield line - but the next assault doesn't come.

I cautiously lean over the wall and see that my catapult placement was the magic ingredient. The stones broke through the shield formation and felled the attackers just as they tried to wade across the moat. The crossbows had little to do, merely chasing a few targets that retreated into darkness.

The rattle of the catapults ceases, and Redmond comes across to me with a big smile on his face, wiping sweat from his brow.

"That's more like it," I tell him, removing the gauntlet to shake his hand.

He grins.

"I was starting to get a little worried yesterday," he tells me in a tired, happy voice. "This is a relief."

"We should get these people home," I say, staring over the wall. "I don't think they will try again tonight. Leave a guard formation."

"I'll ask for volunteers," replies Redmond. "Forgive me if I am not one of them, Commander. I had not slept for days."

"You have done enough, old friend," I clasp his shoulder. "Take the next day off, and the one after."

He nods and turns to walk away. I look over the wall at the mound of corpses - work enough for tomorrow. I am tempted to get the night guard to stay awake by clearing the moat, but give up the idea as far too dangerous. It is just too easy for the enemy to span the distance from the river.

I pour myself a mug of berry tea and screw the tap home with some force. There it is - something they had not thought of in Brana. I ask myself what I would do to protect myself against a shower of stones the size of a child's head - the answer doesn't come easily.

The next day I allow Ethel the entire morning of rest and call on him when the sun begins to descend. He looks a little worn, but a smile plays on his gaunt features.

"Ritter, you old beast," he gives me a vice-like hug. "That was one hell of an idea. What would happen without those catapults?"

"We would have to fight on the wall," I tell him gravely. "There would be heavy losses."

"I will build more," says Ethel quickly. "We cannot afford to have them break down. The hopper mechanism, you see - it will wear out quickly."

I nod.

"Also, you need to send a few crews to the northern beach," says Ethel. "They need to gather the right stones. We are asking for trouble, shooting random shapes and sizes."

I make a note of that.

"Now show me the crossbow."

He leads me to a corner of his workshop, where a large device is worked on by three men.

"We are going to have it finished by tomorrow," says Ethel. "All it needs is a pivot, and it is ready.

I study the metal bowels of the device, marvelling its simplicity. We copied the design from the Brana model, and it still amazes me with its cleverness. Human mind is truly a powerful weapon.

The workmen take a break, and Ethel loads the box on top of the device with crossbow bolts, carefully arranging them in rows. One turn of the crank pulls the string backwards, to the firing position. As it reaches the back of the stock, the crank pulls a lever, dropping an arrow from the box above into the shaft. Once tensed fully, the string slips off the crank, bursting forward. The bolt sprints across the length of the workshop and embeds itself in a thick wooden stump.

Ethel continues to turn the crank, and the cycle begins anew. He fires a few more bolts into the stump, then motions for me to try.

I find the crank surprisingly easy to turn and cautiously increase the speed. The device continues to respond, and I brace my legs to turn it with both hands as fast as I can. A steady stream of metal erupts across the workshop, and I continue to turn it until Ethel puts a restraining hand on my arm. I see that I had run out of bolts.

"You need another crewman to load," he explains. "That way the operation continues until you exhaust the supply. A third crewman will pivot the breech up and down and from side to side to aim."

I nod and turn to inspect the stump. The impact of the bolts almost split it in two. Each bolt seems to have penetrated the damp wood almost a third of its length. It is clear that if the target was human, it would be skewered through.

"How many can you make of those?"

"The bolts are the main problem," explains Ethel. "It's like with hopper guns - you go through ammunition so quickly. There is no point in making more of those until we make a decent mill."

"I will send our mechanics to help," I tell him. "We will tear down a few old ships to get metal. This is crucial, Ethel - if they come full-on, we cannot get enough men on the southern wall to provide the right rate of fire."

Walking back to the barracks, I notice that the streets are as live as usual. It's as if people refuse to cower, and they are out and about, doing their usual business despite lack of sleep. The hugs and handshakes are replaced with salutes when I walk by. Even young children stretch themselves at attention and greet me in crisp imitation of their elders.

I return those salutes with particular flourish.

Redmond walks out of the coal store, looking a little worse for wear. I salute him first, and he returns it with a tired smile.

"Could you not sleep?"

"I might try for some more now," he admits, rubbing his chin, covered in grey stubble that I don't seem to remember from before. "I admit, it's hard to calm down after combat."

"Only natural," I tell him. "What's with the coal?"

"Just finishing the measurements," he tells me. "It looks like we have enough for the winter, if it is not a very cold one."

"Well, we can't fetch coal in the snow anyway," I say hopefully. "It should be just like we planned before the siege."

I tell him about the crossbow machine, and he makes a note to detail men to help Ethel.

"It is not as if we need to service the transporters," he says. "They look like they are out of business until spring. The pilot is just back from a flight over their camp, Commander. They blocked the main road with trees."

"What about the back road?"

Redmond shakes his head.

"They haven't crossed the deep stretch of the river. Not yet."

The back road is in poor condition, and it is much longer, connecting with the main route over the mountains at a high pass. But much of it lies in grassland, where ambush is much harder, with no trees to hide behind or block the road. It is possible to reach the mine that way, after a lot of work that cannot be done over winter.

"Something I need to discuss," says Redmond.

I stop and turn towards him respectfully.

"Father Elwood is ill," he says.

I nod without comprehension.

"The healers think he is going to die of a growth in his insides."

"I am sorry to hear that. He is a good man."

"Yes, sadly. I am to be the replacement."

I stare at Redmond in amazement.

"Are you of the old faith?"

"I am, Commander. Like all my family."

"Why have you never mentioned it?"

"There was no cause, Commander. It is not as if I had any sympathy for Josiah and his rabble. You see, not all of us are willing to use the faith as a tool to gain power. Some of us actually believe what it stands for."

"I don't believe I can succeed without you," I tell him earnestly.

"I am not going to leave until we lift the siege," says Redmond. "Our faithful will have to make do with what time I have available. And, of course, any time you need me in the future, I'll be there, no question."

"Well, that's some relief," I smile. "I never had a sergeant retire like that before."

At that point many little things begin to flow together. Redmond had never showed his faith, but he never violated it either. I now recall that he was always a modest drinker, and he always made himself absent from our romps with women. He showed disrespect for neither, managing to steer a middle course between the stern ways of his ancestors and our ramshackle denials of reality.

We turn to walk towards the barracks in total silence. I want to tell him how much I respect and admire him, but somehow my fatigued brain cannot quite come up with the right words, and we part in silence, with a long handshake. He turns towards the sergeants' quarters, and I trudge to the house to get some rest.

{}{}{}

"Well, they didn't want to keep us waiting," says Redmond, peering at the line of vermin that forms up at the far bank of the river.

"Especially after a gentle prompting," I reply.

Two days before we took advantage of a still day to fly over the vermin camp - a long, wide valley that is now denuded of all vegetation and is, instead, dotted with countless shelters and fires. We scattered incendiary bombs whose detonations sprayed phosphorus over the semi-naked bodies. Burns that turn to rot are as good as a bolt in the chest - except less work and risk.

This time around the enemy is not keen to rush forward and offer their bodies to the crossbows. They shout and shake their maces, but there seems no desire to consummate the intent.

Redmond suddenly grasps my arm, and I turn towards him. He is staring at something in the distance, then begins to pull me away from the parapet.

"Commander, we need to get to the hopper gun. Come quickly."

We run to the nearest hopper gun, guarded by a single soldier. At Redmond's gesture he pulls off the waterproof cover and steps aside.

"Commander, you are the best marksman among us," says Redmond. "I am going to call a target, and I need you to hit it with a volley."

"One of them?" I frown, staring along the sights of the rifle. "I am sure I only need one shot."

"Please don't fuck this up," hisses Redmond sharply, and I look up at him with surprise. "This is of utmost importance. Do not play now."

"What has possessed you, old friend?" I frown,

sliding the ratchet back and forth to spread the grease.

"Look over there, Commander."

I look along the barrel and see a large, powerful figure in a short tunic made of many animal pelts. He shouts at the crowd, swinging a huge mace above his head as if it were a matchstick. His gestures leave no doubt as he points in the direction of the wall with the other hand.

"He is working the crowd," I tell Redmond.

"Yes, Commander. But that's not all. Look at him carefully when he turns this way."

We fall silent, watching the figure for a few moments. Finally, he lets out a long shout and turns to us, pointing his mace towards the moat.

"Scarfoot," I breathe out. "Red, that's our friend. He looks like he is running the whole show."
"Exactly, Commander. He thinks he is out of range. I need you to take him with a volley. Slice that son of a bitch into ribbons. You won't get another chance."

I nod and begin to line up the shot.

"Volley," hisses Redmond.

My finger slides across the lever and locks it firmly to the near side.

"I can take him with one shot, Red. If I miss, I can still get off a volley."

Redmond sighs in reply and falls silent. I begin the ritual of a long distance shot, beginning to steady my breathing and relaxing the body. Scarfoot finishes his fiery speech, his final shout echoing across the river, and he turns away, bends down and presents us with a fine view of his hairy backside. I can see vermin laugh as he straightens and raises his mace in the air.

I squeeze the trigger gently, and the hopper gun jolts in my arms. A jet of flame erupts from the muzzle, and time grows still as I look up at the target. At this distance you actually have time to reload before the bullet completes its flight.

My aim is a little off - instead of taking him in the back of the head, the bullet enters the neck just above the shoulders. Tissues explode in a red burst, tossing the head high into the air. The body lurches forward in an awkward misstep and sprawls on the ground. The head lands in the mud a few feet away.

The vermin fall silent as they stare at the headless corpse, none of them moving. I wait for a few moments, then complete the slide of the ratchet and flick the lever to automatic fire.

After crossbows it feels good just to let go. I raise the barrel slightly and shred the enemy rows with heavy bullets, each piercing a man to kill another behind.

Other hopper guns join me without command, and we mow the far bank of the river with abandon.

The vermin charge.

It takes me a few moments to accept the fact of their reckless courage, but then I come to and begin to shout. The crossbows begin to chatter, the machines and men churning out a dense stream of bolts into the sky. The runners begin to fall, but their numbers appear to swell as more rush from the undergrowth towards us. We are clearly in for the worst they can do, and I signal to the soldier beside me.

He fires a red flare into the sky.

The mortar crews get themselves ready. There are twenty of them - that was all we could scavenge from transporters and stores. Each weapon is served by a crew of five: one man turns the screw to raise the barrel, and four others stand ready to drop one mortar each, getting four shells into the air before the first lands.

The human wave reaches the moat and begins to ebb across, braving the flying stones as they cling to the wall and clamber up. The plain is still dense with their bodies - it is clear that they saved everything for that one assault, which is to either succeed or fail.

I nod to the soldier, who fires the green flair.

We dive to the ground as mortars begin to fill the sky,

whistling their deathly song across the plain. I press my hands to my ears as hard as I can.

The ground shakes hard enough to loosen the timbers of the parapet and toss my body into the air. I land painfully, trying to protect the damaged shoulder without letting go of my ears.

The blasts leave me a little numb, and it takes a while for that feeling to wear off. When I judge it safe, I rise awkwardly, take time to steady my balance and stagger to the sagging wall. I may be forgiven for this gesture of child-like curiosity - but I am the first general to witness such a sight in centuries, and, who knows, I may be the last.

The mortars worked as intended, the shocks from each blast colliding like waves in a pond, shredding all solid matter between them. All the way from the wall to the river the ground is thick with a coat of shredded remains, from which a few intact bodies protrude.

There is no sound, save a whisper of the breeze and the ragged rhythm of my breath.

{}{}{}

I manage to sleep into the late afternoon, then I get up and drive the GTO back to the road block. As predicted, my soldiers are entirely unemployed. There has been no traffic and no one to stop, at either end.

They survive an inspection without a single murmur on my part, and I tell them to get some music and practice a bit of dancing. They are somewhat taken aback by this incongruous suggestion, but I explain that it's not a bad way to keep fit - and all this could last a long time.

With so little to do I decide to move everyone up the road from Otira. The move proves popular, for Otira's sewer had seen better days, and it seriously ruins the ambience on windless days. The trucks quickly ferry everyone to Arthur's Pass, and I join in as they set up tents on the grassy knoll next to the town museum.

My mood goes south when I check the encrypted bulletins. The news is so dreadful that only a part of my brain, the officer one, registers its full extent - the human part simply turns off.

Air traffic is grounded all over the world, and most of the transcontinental cables are down. There are no figures on the extent of the disaster overseas, but "order yet to be restored" coming from most of the large population centres says it all.

Aotea is holding up so far. Fortunately, we are a food producer, although fuel is more of a problem. We can thank the environmentalists for that later - for now all non-emergency vehicles are ordered off the streets. The petrol stations have been shut down, with only essential vehicles permitted to buy fuel. I am glad I filled the GTO as I was leaving Grey.

The Air Force had to shoot down a civilian plane that refused to return to its origin in China. That is sad, and the grim reality is that they probably used the last of their fuel to do it. I can easily see how a unit like mine can end up requiring air support, and it is not a happy thought.

I hear a loud squawk and reach for the microphone pinned to my lapel. The quartermaster, a burly sergeant in his fifties, radios me to advise that we have enough fresh food until the end of the week. After that it's dry rations, he says curtly.

"Ah well, sergeant," I reply lightly. "We'll use less toilet paper that way."

His reply is distinctly non-regulation, and I put down the microphone to return to the bulletins. I scan them quickly to weed out the relevant parts - all four roads leading to the West Coast remain sealed. It is so quiet, in fact, that the high command is fielding accusations of an over-reaction.

Obviously, the overseas bulletins remain secret.

{}{}{}

We settle into a new way of life under siege. It's a reality of gross discomfort that consists of being on constant guard. Sleep is snatched in short stretches, and we awaken drenched in sweat, grasping our weapons and listening for any sound that might separate a bad dream from true terror.

We got lucky three days after my massacre. A vast snowstorm came from the sea as we shivered under the groundsheets on the wall. The vermin failed to take advantage of the blizzard - they were too busy nursing the survivors and feasting on the dead. We did our best to replenish the mortar supplies - I detailed all of the available men to Ethel, who turned away half, saying they can't fit into his workshops. A modest volley was ready by the time the snowstorm abated, leaving the banks of the river with cover that was almost a man's height. I relaxed the guard on the wall, as the snow blocked all meaningful movement.

Once it began to melt, our next blessing became apparent. The river swelled as we watched, burst its banks and began to lap at the wall. The wells flooded in town, and the streets turned into mud pools. Some houses became waterlogged, but none of that mattered - what we all savoured was the site of the massacre under two feet of swiftly flowing water.

It lifted the frozen corpses and took them away. I prohibited clearing them as the task looked hopeless - a field strewn with slippery offal that would have taken days of hard work on open ground, under the watchful, hungry stares from the bushes. The stench just began to rise as the melt waters carried the horror of war to the eternally accepting sea.

The vermin no longer attack but merely menace.

Every now and again they appear at the edge of the forest and shoot their crude fire arrows over the wall. Their range is impressive, but even so, few reach inside, landing harmlessly on the sodden ground. Every now and again they clear the parapet, but their momentum is largely exhausted by poor fletching, which makes them wobble in the air.

The vermin hadn't moved camp, and the main road remains blocked. I sent a work party on two heavily armed transporters into the foothills to clear the landslide at the start of the old road with explosives. They returned, reporting success. I decided to let the winter arrive in earnest and do its work on the enemy before attempting a trip to the coal mine.

Father Elwood died, and I released Redmond to his new life without accepting his resignation. He still makes a point of wearing his uniform, now adorned with a large brass cross on a chain around his neck. He is easily the most respected man in Grey, and I admire him greatly for his quiet courage.

Celia has returned to her calling. At great risk, she sailed north and landed in a swamp with an escort of fifty men to replenish her supply of healing herbs. I see her only late at night, as the demand for her services is unending. She has lost much weight but appears to be happily fulfilled.

Boy has grown another foot, and he stopped fighting at school. This is no feat of self-control on his part -

quite the opposite, he simply became too fearsome for other children to challenge. I spend most of the evening on his homework, my shoulder facing the coal grate to ease its tiresome ache.

The snow settles, and we raise an airship to overfly the vermin camp. To my dismay, it is full of life - hot fires, dancing and sturdy shelters of wood and woven grass, coated with clay. They are dressed in crude flaxen rags, which, despite ridiculous appearance, seem to keep out the cold.

Days filled with long, exhausted sleep now follow, and I lost count. The winter grinds on, but overflights of the enemy camp show no change.

On the day when we dare to send a fishing fleet back to sea, a fire arrow attack succeeds in setting fire to the roof of a house close to the wall. A whole cluster of them lands on the same roof, and the firemen fail to get to it in time. I grind my teeth as I inspect the scene. We are almost out of white phosphorus, and a revenge attack is unlikely to take place.

A few days later the vermin appear at the far bank of the river and launch a barrage of flaming arrows that appear to be the next generation of the craft - long, carefully balanced shafts with heavy stone tips. They easily span the distance to the wall and set fire to a few houses.

A few of the arrows land short of target in a puddle. I

walk past one of them and stop, for my eye latches onto a small detail. I tug on Redmond's arm and lead him to the puddle - he follows my gaze and nods. I pick the arrow out of the water and study it with care.

It has a long shaft of hazel, with heavy spiral fletching at the nock. The arrowhead is a razor-sharp piece of flint, inserted into the split shaft and secured with flax and sealed with resin. Just behind the arrowhead is a strip of bark with dry moss, tightly wound around the shaft. It glistens in the sun - that same oily rainbow I saw on the surface of the puddle.

Redmond smells the bark gingerly and frowns.

"Solly," I call out. "Come this way, could you?"

Solly climbs down from the catapult mount, where he is helping one of Ethel's men to replace the broken hopper. We test the machines every second day, and one of the tests went wrong, throwing a stone back to mangle the feeder. There was little left to do but replace it.

He rushes over, eager to please. I restored his rank after Redmond's departure, which had the effect of shaming him even more.

"Smell this, damn it."

He studies the arrow, takes it from my hands and raises the tip to his nose.

"It's whale oil, Commander. No doubt."

"Fresh, do you think?"

"Oh, no. At least two winters old. It's the shit stuff they keep for lighting. It's not good enough for the generators."

"So what do you say happened here?"

"No doubt of that either, Commander. The fuckers had sold whale oil to the vermin. Nothing is sacred to them."

{}{}{}

"I won't do it," repeats the air captain with exasperated patience.

He is a small man with thin shoulders, but I have to respect his courage. He speaks as if I am a whining child.

There is an uneasy murmur from the sergeants seated around the walls. They tense up, and I play on their minds by placing my hand on the holster at my side.

"You've heard the evidence."

"I have, and I believe it. But I am not bombing innocent people. Show me the culprit who traded with vermin, and I shall strangle him with my bare hands.

But I am not dropping phosphorus on the whalers from a safe sky."

"You realize I can have you shot? This is wartime."

"I have the general idea, Ritter. You seem to have lost sight of who you are of late, but I am not going to do that. A soldier has to have a conscience."

"Being responsible for the survival of our entire kind does things to a soldier," I tell him coldly. "For one, I cannot afford the luxury of taking chances. As we speak, for instance, a new shipment may be on the way to the vermin. Also, if you care to look at this, don't you think it looks familiar?"

I rise and proffer the arrow to the flier. He examines it carefully and nods.

"It does look like a whaling harpoon," he admits. "But I am not changing my mind. If you want to charge me, I demand a public trial."

"I am not obliged to give you one," I tell him curtly. "But we will do this without you, weakling. Be gone from my sight before I change my mind and shoot you myself."

He turns and leaves without his customary salute. I wait until his light footsteps fade on the stairs and look around the room.

{}{}{}

It takes a week to get the ship ready, then the weather turns bad. I grind my teeth, worried that the mutiny may spread from the fliers to the sailors, but that doesn't seem to happen. There is no love lost between whalers and my fishermen.

We sail out on a cold, still morning, sliding along the river in light fog. I spend most of the trip checking the weapons for the final time - we mounted three mortars on the prow of the ship that reeks of fish and coal. The men are in an uneasy mood, and I do nothing to dispel it. We are at war.

When we are two thirds of the way to the whalers' flotilla, I raise them on the radio and present my demands. A few moments later their new leader graces the airwaves with a hoarse voice.

"Ritter, you rabid swamp rat! Have you gone insane?"

"Simple answer. Yes or no."

"If you attack us, we will be your enemies forever. Don't you have enough trouble on your hands now?"

"I have," I feel a rush of anger and let it rise in my voice. "And more, thanks to you. You sold oil. You are teaching them to make weapons."

"You have to prove it."

"It's proven," I stare out over the deck. The flotilla settlement is now in sight, and I can smell the sour reek on the breeze. "You are almost out of time, mermaid."

There is no reply over the radio, but we all hear a distant explosion, followed by a loud whistle. A massive steel harpoon arcs over the sky and misses the ship by only a few feet.

My captain reacts instantly, shouting down for all speed, and my men ready the mortars. We turn sharply, presenting the portside to the distant gunners, then turn again when they fire. We are not so lucky this time - one of our lifeboats is smashed into splinters, and the harpoon embeds itself in the side of the ship not far from the waterline.

We rapidly close the distance, and I give orders for the mortars to fire smoke bombs. Acrid stench spreads over the sea as yellow smoke obscures our view. We make another sharp turn just in time to evade two more harpoons that would have otherwise smashed up the bridge.

I give an order to the mortar crew, and they fire off a rapid volley of six shots. We are well within range, and the mortars land on the flotilla.

Flames erupt in the wake of the explosions, and I see that no more harpoons come through the smoke. We traverse the smokescreen and slow down, drifting through stinging fog, coughing and sheltering our eyes.

A few bullets whistle past my head, and everyone drops to the deck. We send another volley of mortars at the enemy, and the flotilla is now on fire, men screaming and launching themselves into the water.

I nod to the mortar crews, and they adjust the distance, showering the rest of the target with incendiary bombs. The ship turns to circumnavigate what's left of the flotilla. We run out of bombs, but there is no doubt that everything is on fire or soon will be. It is clear that anyone who survived will die in the water, yet I feel nothing but burning rage.

Anger leaves me abruptly when we turn towards the shore, and my men stow away the mortars. Numb and suddenly cold, I speak to no one as I stand on the stern, staring at the pillar of smoke that reaches up to the sky beyond the roiling water.

{}{}{}

They don't call it the witching hour for nothing.

I awaken with a feeling of dread and rise to my feet with unease. The fire is dead, and the room is obscenely cold. I can't feel the tips of my fingers in the left hand, which I draped over the empty side of the mattress.

I get up, mumbling a few soldierly words, pull on the

boots and trudge outside. The moon is full, and the shingle drive of the motel is brightly lit. I fumble with the zip and anoint the ground, stretching to work the painful stiffness out of the back.

It is not quite midnight, and I decide not to try for more sleep just yet. It is probably not worth messing with the fire, but some more writing may be in order.

There is no more room for doubt – the remission is over, with everything that implies. I have no energy, and my body is racked with throbbing pain that I get whenever there is fever. I am slightly sweaty, and my throat hurts just like it did before chemo.

I take a sip of lukewarm tea from the thermos and open the bulletins. It usually takes some minutes to download and decrypt them, and I begin to reconsider the fire. Deciding to act, I set the phone back down on my pack, and it makes a triumphant chirping sound.

Aware that the download and decryption could not have taken place that quickly, I grab it and tap the screen to bring it to full brightness, then touch the secure email icon.

The bulletin rack is empty.

I tap the inbox icon to refresh, and the whirling symbol flashes in the middle of the screen. I stare as it disappears, and the chirp is heard again, with the title displaying a single word:

"SYNCHRONIZED"

There is nothing more to do but reset the phone and begin again – same result.

I go outside to run cold water from the flask over my face and rethink the situation. Then I take the phone from my tunic pocket and send an encrypted email to the HQ. There is no immediate reply, and I decide to work on the fire to pass the time.

Soon there is a homely warmth, and circulation has been fully restored to my hands when I hear my phone ring. The number is not shown.

"Captain Turner."

"Styles here, cap. You awake?"

"What is the sit rep, Sir?"

"Things are not good, Turner. Hope you are sitting down."

"Yes, Sir."

"There is an outbreak in Nelson."

"How?.."

"Probably a boat sneaking into the sounds. A small plane. Who knows. So far we have it contained."

"I hope so, Colonel."

"I am alerting all the unit commanders in the northern sector. We are shutting down the cell coverage at zero-four-hundred. We need to contain this information."

"Acknowledged, Colonel."

"Communication by satellite phone only. Essential traffic only. You to HQ and back. "

"Got it, Sir."

"You are to take personal possession of one satphone right away and remove batteries from the others. Immediately."

{}{}{}

"They wanted a trial," says Redmond, stretching his hands towards the fire. "Oh, they wanted it so very badly."

I stare into the flames and choose to remain silent.

"Then the old judge told them that the law cannot apply outside the city wall."

"That could not have doused the blood lust. What a shame."

Redmond turns to me with a stern expression. He shakes his head adorned white temples that I don't seem to have noticed before. Maybe his hair is longer.

"Hans. What you did was thoughtless."

"I don't dispute that. I acted in anger, but instinct is usually right."

"See, an ancient philosopher said that you must guard against becoming a monster when you fight monsters. We must not let that happen."

"Well, I always thought quite the opposite, Red - you must become a monster to fight monsters. Anyway, what did your ancient know of fighting? Their wars were sporting contests in comparison with ours. They could simply run away. Where do we run now? When the survival of our kind is at stake?"

"Maybe. But we have a standard to uphold. Precisely because so few of us are left. Precisely because each man alive today is the forefather of great multitudes that will one day reclaim the world. When God wills it."

Never before have I heard him speak of God and look up with interest. I respect Red too much to run the kinds of edgy debates I had with his predecessors, which is too bad. They did much to sharpen my thoughts on many matters.

"God clearly takes His time," is all I allow myself to

say.

"Indeed He does, my old friend. Many generations will continue to struggle for survival, even after the menace we face now. There will be many challenges and many temptations to cut corners. We must be on our guard against that. What you did to the whalers was pure abuse of power."

"No more oil will be sold to the vermin. I will live with the blame."

"But the disquiet you created wasn't worth it. Men are afraid of you now. Fear has replaced respect. Can you not see the damage that does?"

I nod once. It is pointless to deny it.

"Do you have anything by way of a suggestion?"

"Yes. Step back a little. Reduce your presence. It is not as if you care much for the town anyway. We are are yet to train our new men - busy yourself with that for the rest of the winter. "

"Who will run the wall defences?"

"Give that to the sergeants. There won't be anything happening for a while. The enemy is in the depths of winter's hardships. Leave them to butcher their dead and fester their wounds."

"I could start on the back road."

"Even better. Restoring the coal supply will do much to put this behind you."

I nod again.

"What of Celia?"

"Of that I am not hopeful," says Redmond with genuine discomfort. "She can't accept it at all. She is a healer. She spent her whole life easing suffering and restoring broken people. You just went and burned an entire people alive."

I shake my head grimly. Redmond is right - the consequences of my action are going to mount up for some time to come.

"Very well. Thank you for your trouble."

"I am truly sorry, Hans. She is very shaken up. I don't think she will ever be able to put it behind her."

"Well, I do regret that," I tell him harshly. "But I still say it had to be done, one way or the other. I possibly did it the wrong way, but I got it done. I am a soldier, and I will pay the price."

Redmond nods his head sadly.

"And I am your friend," he tells me. "I stand with

you, for better or for worse. Just to know where it all stops... How many more nightmares, Hans? How much more blood? Sometimes I grow so weary."

We stare at the flames for a while. I dry logs in my cellar, to burn in the open fire for special occasions, and they crackle with delight. Redmond gets up and replenishes our gin mugs.

"I don't know what to do, Hans. I know you don't either. We can't go on like this."

I frown and grit my teeth.

"We can go on, and we will," I say after a short period of thought. "What we need is coal. Maybe a taller stockade and a wider moat. They are no great obstacles."

"The coal part is dangerous. Once they find out what we are up to, they will be all over that road."

"So we drop all the trees ourselves. Shove them over the side and make it impossible to ambush the convoy. Run scout transporters ahead of the loaded trucks. Shoot everything that moves. Stage ambushes on the trails. Take up an airship and check the entire road before we go. Make a kind of crane to lift obstacles off the road without reversing. We can do all this, Red, and do it we will."

He doesn't turn around. I can't see his eyes, but can

420

tell that he is frowning.

"It's a race," says Redmond slowly. "Whenever they stop moving around, they run out of food. But they can come and go - that is the problem. So long as they maintain any presence near town, they force us to live off fish - and our babies will start dying again."

We lapse in silence, staring at the flames licking the last log. It breaks in two and collapses into the ashes, then firelight begins to retreat before the darkness of late winter.

{}{}{}

As soon as the snows recede we mount the most dangerous mission for some time. Six transporters packed with explosives and logging equipment slip out of the city along the northern road, and we begin the slow task of restoring our access to coal. We wind the first few miles across the floodplane in an uneasy silence, watching the dense treeline approach through the portholes. The engines are the only happy presence among us, gurgling and hissing with delight. There is no comparison with the kind of fuel we used to burn before coal.

The hard work starts as we enter the forest. All trees that may be dropped onto the road have to come down. One crew fires arrows with strings into the canopy, using the thin string to pull heavy ropes over high bows. The second team attaches those ropes to a heavy winch they anchor to other trees and tensions the ropes to set the direction of fall. The third team labours on the heavy, tripod-mounted chainsaw. As soon as the second team is out of the way, they make the cut and drop the tree to the ground. The first team is already busy on the next tree.

We make remarkably quick progress up the first ridge, where we camp among fallen rimu and totara. It is not all waste, I think to myself, inhaling the rich odours of their sap. In a few years this is going to be a treasure for timber harvesters. If all goes well, these logs will crackle in the grates of many houses, and their owners will take pleasure from the wonderful, dry heat as they finish big meals or entwine sweating bodies on rugs in front of the fire.

My jaws clench like a vice at the thought of how much responsibility rests on my scarred shoulders.

The entire moon is spent on clearing the lower ridges. As we get to the treeline, the canopy becomes less dense, and there are fewer large trees that can threaten the road. Our pace quickens, and we begin to load our equipment back onto the cargo tray as we move from tree to tree. After running through the treeless pass, we go downhill and find ourselves back in the forest where the task begins anew - except we are now expert at the job, slashing through a few miles every day. The vermin singularly fail to appear, and all seems well. Convoys come from Grey to resupply us with food, swap a few men who wore out their shoulders on the chainsaw and take back a few letters. I turn away when the letter bag is passed around. I thought of writing, but then thought better of it.

The snows melt on all but the highest peaks as we work our way up the last hill towards the coal mine, past the wreckage of Father Simon's convoy. The side of the hill above the road is very steep, and we opt for explosives, rather than risk labouring on the slippery slope with chainsaws. Before long the road is buried in fallen trees, and we have to devise a pulley below the road to winch them downhill.

At long last we begin to clear the track leading to the mine. I order the men to cover the offal pit in which Father Simon ended his days with a mound of loose soil. I notice that one of the men wears a small metal cross around his neck, and I delegate him to make a large cross of wood, which we affix at the top of the mound with heavy rocks.

The mine remains much as we abandoned it at the start of the siege. There is no sign of vermin even passing through, but we still cut down a few trees that cover the slope leading to the river. I look at the river with a particular longing - if only it was just that little bit deeper, we could float the coal to the sea... I dismiss the thought with an angry shake of the head.

Because we evacuated the coal digger at the start of the siege we have to use the last of the explosives to blast a large mound off the side of the seam, then shovel it on the flat cargo platform. We hastily build sides out of tree branches and tie them down over the mound of coal, to secure the placatory gift to Grey for the return journey.

But there are no signs of welcome as we cross the flood plain the next day. The gate slides open without a single word of greeting, and we grind our way down the street towards the barracks.

The news came through the day before. A raid left thirty men dead, and I have ordered all of the soldiers back to the wall, to stand constant guard until I arrive and take my measure of the disaster.

Judging by the empty streets and the way the fish vendors turn away from my gaze, the raid had a severe impact on morale. I opt not to return to my house but drive straight to the wall after arrival.

The cause of the breach is not difficult to discern – an exuberant growth of spring grass left the southern arm of the river flanked by thick vegetation that is almost waist-high. The whole Regiment could crawl from the river to the wall in broad daylight without being detected.

After a few frantic days Ethel knocks together a kind of a grass slasher, which we mount on a trailer and attach it to a cargo cart. Under the guns of three transporters stationed on the bank of the river, the cart is driven up and down the flood plain until all the grass is slashed to a short length from the ground.

The dead are floated on logs into the river as soon as the job is done. I do not attend the funeral, on Redmond's advice - the ugly undercurrent against me is not going away. If anything, it seems to be getting stronger, and I am not sure that I can do much to stem that flow.

It seems to be noting more than an outlet for anger that has been building up over three generations. There are a few people in Grey who had connections with the whalers, but not many. If asked beforehand, the good people of Grey would probably approve of my actions.

I simply became a scapegoat and lost my good name.

I am not certain if the inhabitants of Grey realize it, but using me that way is playing with fire. I feel my patience beginning to fray like a cable under excessive load. It is best to be somewhere else when it snaps.

{}{}{}

Information containment is never especially effective. No news is instantly assumed to be news of the worst kind, and the men changed once they realized they are being kept in the dark. I went from a much-respected leader to an untrustworthy figure in under the hour that it took to have breakfast. By the time the last of the porridge with cheap honey went down their throats, I begin to feel dagger looks at my back.

I gather the sergeants and tell them everything except Nelson - the bulletins of the last few days, their disappearance and the order to remove the satphones from general access. You can't argue with direct orders, boys - or I certainly won't. Not without a good reason, I add.

As I dismiss them, I am left with a distinct feeling that I just made the problem worse.

I decide to liberate the last keg of beer in the antique café adorned with ski memorabilia from the time of settlement. There is even a little gourmet food to go with the drink - crackers, dry cheese and a few slices of hot sausage.

The mood is slightly improved, and I chalk that up as the first victory in days. We organize a friendly volleyball contest between four squads. Men strip to the waist and shout, more than play, their opponents. Things are almost back to normal when I declare the winners and advise everyone to get a good wash. The forecast is unavailable, but it seems unseasonably warm, and I am expecting a sharp southerly change some time soon. Washing in the river is going to be somewhat less sporting if it snows.

Enlarging on that thought, I order the sergeants to prepare for bad weather. On the crest of a creative wave I take two trucks twenty clicks east, to the vast bridge across the Waimakariri river.

I establish a forepost on our side of the bridge: two trucks with a machine gun and a few sniper rifles. We tow a large log out of the river and block the narrow bridge on the other side, hammering one of the road block placards to its middle. This disposition seems better than allowing someone to just emerge from behind the bend of the road in the village - the bridge is nearly a kilometre of straight, narrow killing zone. Right now the river is a little low, but that won't be a problem after the storm. The forepost also affords a good view of the road on the other side of the bridge.

I tell them to sight in the sniper rifles and supervise the young men as they fumble with scopes. After a few clips they get it pretty right, smashing away the stones I left on the log. I warn them to keep a sharp lookout and to keep the trucks out of sight on the bank, below the bridge. I am sure a few panicked refugees do not require any of these precautions, but somehow I am relieved once the trucks are parked below the road, and the sniper is positioned under a camouflaged tarpaulin with powerful binoculars and a.50-calibre rifle.

I give them the last admonishments about keeping warm in the trucks without resorting to fire, search the vehicles for alcohol and drive back in an open jeep that smells of tobacco and diesel. About half-way back to the village I stop to check their radios. They respond promptly and even somewhat enthusiastically.

The feeling of impending doom is a little assuaged. I return to the camp in time for dinner, check the radio channel once more and sit down to a meal of fatty tinned beef and reconstituted peas.

What a man will do for his country.

{}{}{}

I wake up instantly, breathing hard and sweating. Not yet realizing what is happening, I sit up in bed and listen - hearing only silence.

Suddenly, there is a soul-rending yowl, and I hear Rat screaming at the top of his voice, as if he is being hurt. I am out of bed, hurtling downstairs with a pistol in my hand. I am nearly across the lounge when Rat screams again. I throw open the door to Boy's room, and that's when it happens.

A vast, booming rumble begins somewhere deep under the floor. It hurts my ears, and the darkness turns bright with a green glow. I get thrown off my feet and just manage to avoid slamming the bad shoulder into Boy's bed.

"Get the fuck under!" I hear myself scream, and he obeys instantly, rolling over the edge and scrambling beneath the heavy iron bed. I drop the pistol and manage to squeeze my bulk next to him on the dusty floor. The shaking now begins in earnest, with the bed being thrown into the air and dropped onto my shoulder blades. I concentrate on pressing my head to the floor and extend the right arm, ignoring the piercing pain in the shoulder, to hold Boy down as low as possible.

There is a sickening creak of timbers as the upper floor gives way, and I feel, more than hear, the collapse of the ceiling into the lounge. There are loud thumps as the furniture falls to the floor in what remains of my house. A heavy book cupboard near Boy's bed is lifted into the air before my eyes, and I brace myself for the impact as books are thrown right across the room, a few landing onto my feet.

It stops as suddenly as it began, although the air is now alive with shouts. I clamber out and push against the window. It is stuck - I order Boy to stand back and fire the pistol at the lock, point-blank.

We climb outside - Boy leads and I follow, with Rat clinging to my shoulder with claws deeply embedded in my nightshirt. The ground is still shaking, making it hard to balance. We run towards the parade ground, crouching and stumbling.

The barracks look intact from the distance, although a few chimneys are tilted at considerable angles. Men are spilling outside, dressing on the run. Tancred runs towards me barefoot, holding his boots in one hand and the tunic in the other.

"Get the fire carts ready!" I shout with full might.

My next task is to find Trevor. I order Boy to sit next to the flagpole and run back to the house.

I manage to open the front door after kicking in the lock. The hallway is blocked by the metal staircase, forced into available space by the weight of the upper floor.

"Trevor!!!"

There is only noise from outside. On a wave of anger I rush into the parade ground and shout that they all shut up. I return inside, raise my leg and kick the twisted metal stair, then scream at the top of my voice in frustration.

There is no reply, and I stand still, struggling to catch my breath. Then I run outside, willing myself to calm down. It is now quite light.

The parade ground is packed with soldiers who form neat platoon formations and await orders in what appears to be relative readiness. I run up to the first platoon and issue a string of orders. Two men run off to get gloves, axes and ropes, and the rest follow me back to the ruined house.

Three men link their hands and lift the fourth over the twisted wall, where he begins to climb broken beams like limbs of a sick tree. He soon reaches what was once the central roof beam as the cart arrives with equipment.

I throw him the heavy rope, which he carefully lashes to the beam, then begins to climb down. I tie the rope to the heavy tow hook and order everyone to stand back.

The driver reverses, and I shout for him to slow down as the entire roof is dragged onto the ground.

As soon as the dust settles, the climber is again lifted over the top to find the next sturdy beam. We do this three times before it is possible to gain entry to the lounge, push past the broken furniture and get to Trevor's room. It is empty, and his bed is unmade.

On instinct, I climb down the short stair into the basement. Trevor lies next to the smoking furnace, dark eyes staring angrily into heaven. An empty bucket lies next to him on the floor - he managed to douse the flame, to prevent escaping embers from setting fire to the house.

Trevor's right temple is swollen and dripping a little dark blood. A broken stone from the chimney lies nearby.

As if in a trance I slowly sink to my knees and bend down to close his eyes.

{}{}{}

"So that's that."

We edge away from the cliff - a raw, muddy gash in the hill – once the road to the mine we worked so hard to clear. The quake dropped hundreds of yards of the slope downhill, taking our labour with it.

Redmond and I stare at each other - I had never felt such hopelessness in all my life.

"Stop right there," Redmond places a hand on my good shoulder and squeezes with all his strength. "There is always a way forward."

I take a deep breath and raise my eyes to study the mountain above the broken slope. It's a rise of at least five hundred yards. It is probably a mile wide and a mile long – who knows. We have to fly over it or return in much larger numbers - the vermin could arrive any moment.

"It would take all of the summer to build a road to the other side," I say slowly, keeping my tone neutral. "We will run out of coal long before that."

"That's right," replies Redmond in the same tone. "We only have a moon or so left. Then we start to scrape the bottom."

"Not that we would be left to build it in peace. We would have to clear a wide path through the forest and probably fight for every bend. Red, we do not have the resources to do this."

"Well, Hans... That or something else - there must be a way."

I turn away, feeling tears form in my eyes - I am just so dead-tired. It begins to rain, and I welcome the icy bite of the raindrops on my close-cropped head.

"You know that we are the last ones?"

"Apart from Bruce and Karito."

"After us they will be next and last. They can only resist a few local gangs. Not this army of hungry man-eaters."

I begin to feel dizzy and sit down on the wet road, dangling my feet off the broken stony edge. A little waterfall runs down the mountainside into the gap, washing away the newly exposed earth. I follow the stream with my gaze, right down to the edge of the landslide, where the water meanders into a meadow of broken trees.

There are no answers anywhere in this landscape.

I rise and back away from the edge with some caution, for the stones become slippery with rain, and it's a long way down.

Redmond patiently listens to what I have to say, then shakes his head abruptly.

"Red, you are not my nanny," I tell him with a smile.

"Except, dear Commander, you appear to have lost your mind."

"Possibly."

"Explain this to me again."

"I want to drive up to this mountain from the other direction."

"By yourself?"

"By myself."

"Why, exactly?"

"Because I had risked enough lives as it is."

Redmond studies me intensely, like a deadly threat he cannot comprehend. He stares deep into my eyes, and I stare back calmly. I focus on a bush a few yards behind him and follow the droplets that drip from its branches. It works - Redmond looks away, shaking his head. He possibly does know that I had lied, but still has no idea why.

We drive back down to the flood plain and part within sight of the gate. I shake hands with Redmond and salute the men, who salute back, their faces frozen in a kind of wonder.

Then I walk into the command transporter and turn the crank.

The rear door rises from the ground and gradually

blocks the view of the convoy. When metal hits metal I latch it and walk to the front of the machine, sinking into the driver's seat.

It's the most alone I've ever been in my life.

{}{}{}

The snow starts as a few furtive spits of moisture that sting my neck. There is an instant outbreak of expletives - at no time in history had an infantry man applauded bad weather. The circle of logs near the fire empties as men remove themselves from the mercies of the sky.

I stay put, throwing the hood of the anorak over my cap and thrusting hands deep inside its pockets for warmth. I have gloves in my pack, but it's a long walk to the empty motel, and I would rather not make that trip just yet.

The leading edge of the front dumps a short, sharp shower into the narrow valley, and the air turns bitterly cold. The fire still burns brightly, but it is only a matter of time before we are in the clutches of winter. I sigh with relief - a good dump of snow will make my job almost redundant. No one but the army will be able to move in the mountains.

The thick army anorak is still holding up as the air around me turns white with vast, Antarctic snowflakes that gently coat the ground. The wind then settles, and the blizzard gently obscures my vision. The sounds of voices, generators, clanging cutlery and the whoosh of zips sliding along canvas begin to fade, and soon I am left all alone at the bottom of an ocean of falling snow.

I raise my face to let the snowflakes wash away the dismal grime of the last few days, then begin the long walk to the motel. It is time to pay homage to a single malt that is hidden in the boot of the GTO, for I have every guarantee of being left in peace tonight. It is not even possible to raise me on the satphone.

{}{}{}

This is the hard part, I tell myself. It's a freezing night, and every sound carries from here to the sea.

It's been some years since I did anything of the kind, but everything seems to be working just fine. I am crawling along the forest floor, taking great care not to make a single sound. I had washed in the ice-cold river, from which my skin still tingles. My uniform has been soaked in mud for hours, then washed in the river to get rid of all smell. The boots are caked in dry mud, and the small pistols have been scrubbed clean until their barrels began to shine. My face and neck have been rubbed with pungent fern fronds.

I make my way towards the vermin camp, step by step. I have until dawn the next morning, and I must not make any noise that may frighten my prey. I decide to take all the time before midnight to get into a good position.

The night is cloudy, and there is little to see. My night vision is not bad, but it is nothing compared with vermin. Only a lifetime of experience gives me any kind of chance.

I manage to get so close to the vermin that I spy on them as never in my life. They huddle in front of the fire, chewing on something that is thankfully too indistinct to see. They begin to sing a primitive tune that consists of a few notes, to which they swing their bodies, swathed in what looks like cloaks of bark, interwoven with grass.

I have to relieve myself, which is a dangerous moment. I undo my clothing and rise just above the soil, waiting for the bladder to relax. I stop breathing as the vermin stop singing, but one of the begins to wail another tune, and the rest join in.

I crawl away arm over arm, thinking ahead of each movement, adjust my tunic and resume my watch.

The vermin begin to leave the campfire just as the moon begins to break through the clouds. They crawl inside low shelters that dot the floodplain all the way to the sea, leaving their fires to die down. I stare at the eerie glow, flanked by a few silhouettes that still huddle around the embers.

I flex my hands and form fists, squeezing as hard as I can. Then I bring them up to my head and squeeze the angles of the jaw with my thumbs, with pain shooting through my skull. Fully awake, I adjust my posture so I can pump both calves in total silence and continue my watch.

Two figures slip away from the fire, and I study them intently. They seem young and lithe, nimbly stepping over the obstacles in the dark as they move towards the tree line.

I tense up, realizing that the moment of truth is nearly upon me. They approach and pass me by - I see that one is a powerful male with a mane of tangled hair. His companion is a young girl, whose breasts distort the outline of the rude cloak. She moves as if she had just given birth, and I sense that her child had not survived, for the moonlight catches an etch of sadness on her grimy, angular face.

They make their way up the hill, careless and making much noise as they move through the forest. I turn around and begin to follow, taking steps in rhythm with theirs, stalking the couple up the hill through thick vegetation.

Once they clear the camp by a few hundred yards, the male grasps his companion from behind and runs his tongue along her neck. She arches her back in rapture and extends her arms backwards towards his groin. He makes hungry, growling noises as he raises her cloak and pushes her to the ground. She lands on all fours and thrusts her backside into the air.

I drop to the ground and begin to crawl in total silence, each step synchronized with the noises of their coupling. I reach them just as the girl begins to make cat-like sounds, and her companion intensifies his thrusts. I span the last two yards with a running jump and plunge a blade into his back.

He gasps, spasms and collapses on top of his companion, driving both bodies into the ferns. I hold onto the dagger and pull gently, making it slide out of the corpse.

The girl makes a giggling sound and moves her hips in invitation. Then she tries to turn over, fails under the dead weight and says something. Not getting a reply, she makes a sudden effort and flips over, throwing the body off her back.

She sees me staring at her face and opens her mouth to scream. I swing my leg to kick the back of her head, and she collapses without a sound.

I sit next to her on the ground and catch my breath, waiting for the dizziness to settle. There is a heavy pain in my chest like I never felt before, my left arm tingling and numb. I wait for it to pass, watching the girl intently.

The pain forces a change of plan. Instead of dragging the girl up the hill, I turn her over and tie both wrists behind her back. A dense ball of moss is pushed inside her mouth, then I cut a strip from her companion's cloak and tie the gag in place.

She begins to stir as I secure the last throw of the knot, then she tries to move her arms and freezes in terror. She tries to scream, but the gag stays in place. I flip her over and point the dagger at her eye. She falls silent.

I rise to my feet and tug on the rope - she looks up but stays on the ground. I raise my foot and land a light kick at her side, then tug the rope again. She clambers onto her knees and slowly rises to her feet. I pull on the rope to lead her uphill.

She walks beside me with no resistance, and I guess that kidnapping young women is not a rare thing among her kind - she is not anticipating a great change in fortune. But once we reach the transporter she squeals through her gag in sheer terror and tries to run. I jerk the rope to drop her to the ground and put my foot on the middle of her back.

She struggles with all her might, but I manage to remain in the same position, increasing the pressure on her shoulder blades. She squeals again, and I smell the sour reek of her bowels. There is nothing else to do but to lean down and crash the pommel of the dagger over the back of her head. She drops to the ground and stays still.

I slash her soiled cloak from top to bottom, tossing it into the bushes by a clean end. Then I have no choice but drag her through the last yards to the transporter.

I slide under its cold metal belly, unlatch the bottom hatch and climb in, then wind down the rear door. There is enough water in the canister to splash my captive's nether regions until the stench goes away.

She comes to her senses and tries to bolt, but the rope jerks her back. She falls to the ground, staring at me in terror. I wait for her to dry, then haul her inside. She makes no effort to resist as I push her onto the floor and tie her to the wall before removing her gag. She doesn't make a sound but merely watches me with huge eyes full of terror as I wind up the door.

Success.

I toss her a pile of old blankets and tilt the near-empty container to pour water into her mouth. She drinks every last drop and accepts a fish cake. Then I push her down to the floor with my boot, to indicate that she must sleep and cover her with a blanket from head to toe.

Sliding back in the driver's seat, I inhale deeply and hold my breath, finalizing my decision and gathering thoughts.

I ask myself for the last time whether I have the right to do what I am doing.

No new thoughts come to mind - all I see is an unruly

jostle of images from the past, mainly faces of the dead that stare at me in distress and call for justice. When Rina's eyes become more real than I can bear, I bend down and light the furnace, staring at the nascent flame as it spreads over dry logs. I shut the door as the coal begins to smoke and revel in the spreading warmth.

The girl screams out in terror as the engine hisses to life. I turn on the headlight and gently pull on the throttle. The piston dances its frantic jig, then the machine jerks and engages the sprockets. We begin to move forward, throwing off the leafy branches with which it was covered, to build up speed. I turn into the hill and feel the still-cold engine struggle up the grassy slope, towards the road of the ancients.

The ambush point is reached just as it gets light. The vermin had dropped trees on the road, but, in truth, they failed to tax their customary skill. I push the first trunk to the side without effort and climb over the rest. The ambush could have grounded the coal trailers, but my nimble machine gets over with little grief.

I hear shouts as attackers spring from the bushes, and a few rocks smash into the sides. The girl begins to scream something to her people, and I accelerate, bouncing over the last tree and running uphill with considerable speed. This was the last machine I had built before the siege, and it was made with a larger boiler than ever before.

It easily accelerates past running speed, and the

vermin begin to fall behind. Someone continues to thump on the roof with what sounds like a club. I decide to let them continue, driving as fast as I can. The thumping eventually stops - I suspect that the roof riders jump, rather than take chances with my destination.

I race towards the saddle and negotiate the light snow with relative ease. Enjoying the smooth ride, I even take pleasure from the view of the entire mountain range. It's just what I wanted to see before I die.

Stopping often, I take my captive outside, teaching her not to void in the cabin, without untying her hands. She shows less and less fear, studying me intently from her pile of rags as I drive.

{}{}{}

The fire dies out in the night, leaving the motel room ice-cold by dawn. I awaken with a full bladder and a taste of stale whiskey in my mouth. There is a slight headache and more than a bit of nausea that are expected from sampling a fine single malt without the benefit of real food, and I reach over, snag the water flask by the strap and tip its entire contents down my throat. A few minutes later it definitely pays to be up, as the bladder begins to scream its protest.

What awaits me outside is sheer disappointment. The snow did come - but nowhere enough to make the highway impassable. The snow forecast would not have been a deterrent because no news is being broadcast.

Driving slowly and carefully, most vehicles can get across The Alps in a few hours - which sadly means that I am back in business, hangover, fever, fatigue, desperation and all.

Removing my tunic, I harvest snow from the bushes and rub it into my chest. The shock gets the blood moving, and the nausea goes away. A few paracetamols wipe out the headache, and I am almost back in shape as I start the GTO. It doesn't care for the snow, wide tyres spinning on the slippery road - I even manage to fishtail before gathering speed.

Predictably, my men are cold and grumpy, doing their morning push-ups in the snow with the usual chorus of curses and grunts. I arrive and crack a few jokes they probably haven't heard, but fail to liven the mood. The smell coming from the kitchen trailer entirely lacks inspiration, and the sky is threatening to open with rain, rather than snow. The day is off to a lousy start.

We consume our lumpy porridge, a few snowflakes fluttering in the rising wind. The coffee is warm, if dreadful in its instant flavour, and the conversation is held to a minimum. I too eat in silence, furiously thinking of ways to give structure to the day. Nothing clever springs to mind.

The radios erupt in a cacophony of squawks. I hastily swallow a mouthful of glue and put down my bowl, unbuckling the microphone from the lapel.

"...Under attack!"

"Captain to forepost, say again. You are breaking up. Over."

"Sir, we are under fire!"

"From, over?"

"Army!"

By now all men are on their feet, ready to react to orders. I hold up my hand, palm open.

"Sergeant, explain clearly. What is happening, over?"

There is a hiss of static, then we hear gunfire over the radio. It sounds like a short burst of automatic weapons.
"Get the APC!" I shout to no one in particular.

"Sir, we are attacked by uniformed soldiers, about two squads," crackles the radio. "They are armed with personal weapons only. Repeat, personal weapons only. They are attempting to cross the bridge on foot."

"Fall back to the treeline. Cover with machine gun fire. We are coming to get you with the APC. ETA ten minutes. Out."

The ground begins to shake as the APC roars through the village. There is no time to grab my gear, and I run towards the road, diving through the rear doors as it slows down. The driver guns the engine and takes off, throwing the heavy machine around corners.

I give orders to the young boy manning the heavy machine gun and crawl forward to speak to the driver. He nods when I explain what I want him to do. I grab the handles of the light machine gun and get ready.

We emerge from the last bend into the floodplain of the great river, and I size up the scene. There are bodies littering the bridge, all infantry, heaven help us, and my men are huddling behind a large rock a little further back, still firing busts into the riverbed. All of the enemy who crossed the bridge look like they bought it - except our truck is on fire, belching black smoke as if hit by something like a rifle-launched grenade.

"Sergeant, cease fire," I yell into the radio. The forepost squad turn around and cheer our arrival. We race to the bridge, and a few barrels spit fire directly at me. I flinch, hearing the bullets drum on the light armour.

The boy on the heavy gun opens fire, and the enemy position erupts in fountains of red. The flashes disappear, and we stop on the edge of the bridge.

The opposition had arrived in a number of army trucks. Four – no, five - I can barely see, with bitter sweat running into my eyes. We killed maybe half of the opposing force, and the rest stand next to their vehicles on the other side of the wide river, awaiting further developments.

I give orders, and the heavy gun starts streaking bullets to the far bank. Their trucks begin to move, but too late - the first is cut in half and disappears in a bright flash, as ammunition - maybe anti-tank rockets - detonates in its tray. The young boy on the gun thinks well, shifting his fire to the last truck in the convoy, trapping the middle ones between two burning wrecks. He then destroys the rest of the convoy methodically and ceases fire straight away, cool as a block of ice - as if he won a round on his game console.

{}{}{}

At dusk I stop at the edge of a long, treacherous descent that leads towards the plain. I can see a wide, treeless expanse, whose horizon is obscured by low cloud. I peer at it with a soldier's gaze, appraising the enemy before my last battle.

The enemy, however, is invisible. I sigh and retire inside.

The girl accepts a fish cake and the last few strips of dry meat, which she gulps without chewing. After eating she rises on her knees and turns away. I watch with disbelief as she thrusts a pale backside into the air, displaying her thick lips, sparsely covered with red hair. She tenses her stomach to make them part and shows off her middle, startlingly pink amid filthy skin.

I shake my head to ward off temptation and put my boot on her rump, push her to the floor and cover her with a blanket. She turns to stare with what looks like disappointment, but I put my head to my shoulder and close my eyes, signalling that she must go to sleep.

As I lie back in my bedroll, I wonder if that was even the right thing to do, given that she only has a few days to live - as, for that matter, do I. But the risk is simply unacceptable - she can, no doubt, overpower me in a straight fight. I dismiss the entire subject and begin to dream of Grey, imagining it a few hundred years from now.

I see a stately city with tall stone buildings hugging the beach. They are protected by a great wall, studded with machine gun emplacements. Children romp in a playground near that wall with not a care in the world. A deep port, crammed with large, powerful ships, has been dredged in the mouth of the river, and a vast field with many airships occupies the swampy plain next to the beach.

The next day I awaken to a miserable sight of fog and lashing rain. I drive down the steep slope without breakfast and without looking back at the girl.

The descent to the plain is uneventful - the transporter rumbles along the road with little effort, as the surface is in excellent condition. I steer through the last steep bend with a flourish and grind on, feeling brave and numb.

We stop at a stream to eat and to void, and the sun burns off the last of the fog, letting me see a long way ahead. This is a different world - the grass is short, leaving no means of concealing an ambush.

I tie an extra loop of rope around the girl's neck with a slipknot to secure her in the cabin, then go outside to fill the boiler from a roadside stream. I've used more coal than expected and decide to slow down.

Later in the afternoon, the sun hanging low over the mountains, I reach the first ruins on the poisoned plain. I slow down to a crawl as the road takes me past wooden buildings erased by time, leaving only stone foundations covered in orange moss. A few brick chimneys remain upright amid the rubble, showing what centuries had made of human pride.

I finally see it next morning - a vast lake that once watered ancient crops. It had long eroded its banks, spilling over the road. I am, I know at once, in the right place - the water's edge is strewn with skeletons of birds and small animals that craved its waters, burning with the thirst of their final hours.

From here on it is all destiny. I act as if I become a machine, stopping just short of the water on my inevitable course. I tie the rope that loops around the girl's neck to a long metal pole, kept in the cabin for pulling chains around fallen trees - and lead her outside.

She doesn't protest until I point the pole towards water, then she struggles as the rope tightens around her neck. Her eyes open wide with terror, and she gurgles a scream as her face begins to darken.

I keep pushing down, and she collapses into the water. I sink the end of the poll, forcing her head under the dark surface covered in green scum. She loses her struggle, and her face disappears under the surface - and that is that.

I pull up the end of the pole. She thrashes in the soft mud but manages to get up, gasping for breath and spluttering liquid, choking, retching and finally screaming at the top of her lungs.

I don't suppose it matters what I do now, but out of sheer instinct I avoid the water and wait until the girl is dry. I then lead her back into the cabin. She looks so exhausted that I decide not to tie her to the wall, leaving her free to flop onto the rags, the loosened rope still around her neck.

Feeling a strange, serene fulfilment, I let out the throttle and race back towards the mountains. Darkness catches me half-way up the rise, and I slow down, driving by the dim glow of the headlight, rather than stop and wait until dawn.

The headlight burns out in the middle of the night, and I am forced to halt. I take the girl out to void, then sleep a while, letting the fire die down. A gusting wind awakens me shortly after sunrise, and I throw a shovelful of coal into the burner, to resume our race towards death.

{}{}{}

I shift most of my men towards the western side of the village, leaving a picked crew at the advance roadblock on the other side.

I tell everybody that at all costs we must not enter close proximity to the attackers, dead or alive. Assuming the worst, they are running away from an outbreak of disease, and some of them are already infected.

We abandoned our forepost and returned to the town, for what I hope is not our last stand. There weren't enough explosives to take out the bridge, which is just as well - anyone laying the charges may be infected and would have to stay on the other side indefinitely.

The satellite signal is faint, and there is no answer when I dial any number I know. I am on my own.

I take stock of the situation. I am in charge of seventy-four men, having lost six. I have six anti-tank missiles, eight machine guns, around two hundred thousand rounds of ammunition and a hundred and twenty hand grenades. We have personal rifles and side arms, for what they are worth. We have three trucks, an APC, two jeeps and my GTO.

There is no reason why that can't hold off the very forces of hell.

We drag fallen trees across the road just outside town and form another barricade a little further up, still retaining the commanding view of the road. I am convinced an attack is coming, and if I break it, there won't be others. I know that, somehow.

To my astonishment, I am right, at least about the first part. In mid-afternoon another convoy runs past the cliffs on the other side of the valley. I study it in my binoculars and order an retreat.

They have three fucking tanks.

{}{}{}

The girl refuses food as we struggle through deep snow on the third day. She gulps all remaining water, and I have to stop by the stream at the top of the pass. I try not to notice anything about myself, but I am beginning to grow tired.

She spends the rest of the day huddling inside the blankets, drinking ravenously and sweating out what she drinks. As we approach the ambush, she begins to shiver.

I stop to give her a handful of purple berries in a drink, and she looks a little better. We resume our journey, drop down from the ridgeline, race around the final corner before the ambush and slow down to crawl over obstacles.

The vermin react, but this time their actions look somewhat devoid of passion. They throw rocks, but seem reluctant to climb the transporter, and I clear the ambush with very little delay. I race a short distance to get clear into the next valley, then stop to replenish the water tank.

The girl is now quite ill. I see that she had retched up the berries and decide not to give her any more. It no longer matters - I am that close.

But it is well past midday when I race the transporter right into the vermin camp, using my free hand to shovel the last of the coal into the furnace. Without slowing down I carve a wide semicircle to attract attention. I am soon chased by a crowd of angry creatures, whose shelters I just crushed to splinters.

I let the machine slow down, point it uphill and rise from the seat. Still bumping over shelters and fireplaces, I pull on the blanket, struggle to open the bottom hatch and push her out, head-first and still tangled in a dirty blanket. The girl is barely conscious and makes no effort to resist - her body flips through the hatch, and the last thing I see is a mud-caked foot that lingers in mid-air. She then disappears into the broken grass – and it is done.

Slamming closed the hatch, I run back to the driver's seat and gun the throttles, feeling the transporter weighed down by many bodies on the roof. There are angry screams as the machine lurches forward, and some of the would-be assailants fall off. There is heavy pounding above; I throw an abrupt turn, which appears to dispose of the remainder of my passengers.

The transporter huffs along superbly, outrunning the last of the pursuers up a steep hill. Once on the ridge, I ease back the throttle and settle into the seat.

I can now admit that I am very tired and more than a bit cold, but my joints don't ache, and my breathing is not laboured. My remaining task is to get further away from Grey - ideally, I should return to die on the poisoned plain, but there isn't enough fuel to do that.

Instead, I decide to drive the transporter over the cliff that is not far ahead. If I reach full speed, it will hopefully become airborne and plunge deep into the chasm. By the time it might be found, rats will have taken my bones. The would-be rescuers will be safe from the horror I brought to our broken world.

I am not quite through that thought when the engines sputter and begin to slow. I throw open the furnace and curse at the sight of an empty pan. The machine comes to a halt on a steep hill, rolls backwards a short distance and stops for the last time.

I sit down on the floor, staring at the empty furnace, then kick back its door with a grim smile. There are no hard feelings - I had accomplished what I set out to do. I lean back and rest my forehead on the cold wall of the machine that is going to be my grave.

All in all, that does not displease me.

I put a tentative hand on the holster, but instantly decide against a quick death. I hadn't valued my life for some time, but there is a sudden desire to hold on a little longer, think a few things through and make peace with ghosts. I eat a handful of purple berries and wash them down with the last of the gin from the first aid kit.

It is hoped that Redmond will obey and keep the town sealed until next spring. My strict orders were not to come looking for me and to make absolutely certain that the wall is not breached. He promised to do his best and to pray that no vermin get inside.

Let his prayers be rewarded. If not, everyone I am dying to defend will soon join me. I struck fate a bold, stinging blow - but fate is more than capable of striking even harder.

Was there another way? Who knows - I surely do not. Only one thing is certain - what's done is done.

{}{}{}

I move the rest of the force back to an even tighter choke point on the other side of the village and return to the new forepost, where we used the APC to pull tall trees out of the ground, to drop across the road. We secure them together with a heavy steel cable, and I sent men up the steep, heavily wooded slope with anti-tank missiles.

All this is accomplished at frantic speed - just as well, as the tanks rumble along as soon as we are done.

The lead tank brakes clumsily, then edges towards the fallen tree. The turret turns sideways, and the tank bumps the obstacle, trying to push it out of the way. The trunk slides a few metres, then the steel cable is pulled tight and gives no further.

The tank reverses. Its engine roars, and the machine slams into the tree with full force. The left tread mounts the trunk, but the right doesn't, and the machine roars in frustration, sliding sideways and tilting at a precarious angle. The driver drops into neutral and lets the tank slide back, taking a long time to straighten it before he can reverse.

Moving back about twenty metres, he turns the turret and lowers the barrel. There is a bright flash, and a deafening explosion covers the road in smoke. When the breeze carries it away, I can see that the barricade is shattered. My ears still ringing, I hear the tank roar as it crashes through the splintered remains, pushing them off the road.

I raise the microphone to give the order, and a missile streaks down the hill into the tank's rear, igniting the fuel. I drop to the ground and wait for the huge explosion, which rocks the ground exactly on time - the ammunition detonates before the crew could escape.

The other tanks are stuck behind the ruin on a narrow

road. They fire furiously but at random - shells land in the bush without harm. The missile squad is long-gone, now hidden behind the curve of the hill.

Well, the next fallback position is the steep gorge on the other side of the village. We race back to the bridge and wait for the enemy to close the distance. It has to be assumed that a much larger force will follow behind the tanks, maybe most of the garrison from the capital. I assume that they are running from the outbreak - and so long as I am alive, no one will get past. Everyone I love is behind my back on the coast, just down the road.

There is no sight of the enemy for over an hour, and shadows begin to lengthen. We do not move from our ambush positions, peeing where we lie and keeping our heads low. The weather plays along - it is cold but not windy. There is good visibility, and, crucially, we can hear from far away.

It is beginning to get dark when two remaining tanks make their way down the road, having managed to push what is left of the third out of their way.

My men fire two more missiles from the slope, and both tanks explode. There is, alas, little time for celebration - we hear many engines, and soon the valley is alive with enemy vehicles, jeeps, APC's, trucks, even quad cycles. They turn off the road into the riverbed, to bypass the burning tanks. Most get stuck in the soft shingle, and the valley is now dotted with men dismounting and advancing inexorably towards us. I will be lucky if we even have enough ammunition, let alone men, to stop them.

I pull the microphone to my chin and order everyone to pull back across the bridge. We race for cover just ahead of our pursuers and fire backwards as we retreat, with enemy bullets whistling all around. My men manage to traverse the bridge without losses, and we are finally in a good place - a steep drop to the river flanking our left, with a cliff on the right. A stream that is now our forward perimeter runs down the cliff in a deep gully, spanned by a narrow bridge at the road.

We wait for the first enemy vehicle and detonate the bridge with our last missiles. The APC collapses into the stream below, rolls downhill and comes to rest on its roof amid vast, moss-covered boulders.

We come under intense, vicious fire. The ratio of forces is about right - about three of them for each of us. We shoot them as they try to clamber across the deep stream, and they pick us off as we fire. Men die around me, but we stop the onslaught and the shooting begins to slow down.

I lie behind a log, totally still, watching for any sign of movement in the undergrowth on the other bank of the stream. I am down to my last clip and out of grenades, but there is lots of ammunition on the dead. Acrid stench of cordite drifts on the breeze, and someone is moaning in the bushes just below.

I pick up a used shell and throw it at the man on my left. He looks up, and I gesture him to collect the wounded, adding, with a tap of my eyes, that I will cover. He nods, and I raise the rifle, making a point of staring through my sight at what was once the bridge.

A few minutes later he emerges from the ferns beside me, dragging a Maori boy with a scarf tight around his thigh. The scarf is scarlet with blood, but the boy's face has reasonable colour. I am relieved that his eyes are wide and alert.

I put my hand into the tunic pocket and extract the keys to the GTO.

"Drive him to Greymouth and report our situation. Go."

They crawl away as I turn to cover the retreat. But there is no movement, not even as the V12 roars into life. I smile and wince, hearing it screech around a corner on the damp road.

At dusk the last wave of the attackers arrives with two more carriers. We scramble to hide behind the largest boulders we can find, as heavy machine guns open up across the stream. The air overhead is alive with whistling lead, and fountains of rock fragments erupt all around me. I begin to feel more than hear - then the barrage stops abruptly.

I push aside the ferns to see the carrier's exhaust

belch black smoke. The machine begins to move forward and plunges into the stream, grounding its nose. Its wheels spin and spit stones, but the carrier seems firmly stuck.

The second carrier guns its engine and runs over the first, attempting to use it as a makeshift bridge. This almost works, but then its stern starts to slip, and it tips sideways, collapsing into the stream and overturning.

Enemy soldiers rush from the rear doors, and my men open fire, decimating the attack. A few manage to get across the stream as we run dry, and we meet them in the undergrowth with side arms and bayonets. I plunge my combat knife into the chest of an older soldier with frantic blue eyes, who rushes blindly up the hill, seemingly too crazed to stop or defend himself.

We go down together, and I lie on top of the dying man, holding on to the knife as his eyes fade. He struggles all the way to the end, and I don't react as I should, to ear-popping thumps of a mortar barrage.

There is a shattering thunder behind, and I am tossed into the air, slamming into something hard. Everything goes blank.

When I regain consciousness, I lie on my stomach, with face buried into the soil. I feel dirt in the mouth and gag – and become aware that something is dreadfully wrong.

Rolling over on my side in a strange daze, I rise on my elbow and see that my right leg is soaked in blood. I spring the knife and cut the tattered cloth to see a thick, wedge-shaped rock embedded in my shin. When I reach over and tug, it comes away with no pain. There is a glimpse of white bone in the ragged wound before my poisoned blood wells up and runs onto mossy ground. I chuckle at the thought of leukaemic cells dying in the soil, suddenly nothing more than food for harmless scavengers.

I call for help in a voice I cannot seem to hear, yet my men appear in numbers. They lift me out of the undergrowth and carry me around the bend of the road, past the smoking ruins of our trucks. I am laid down on a bed of roadside moss, and the wound is dressed as well as it can be, whilst my hearing gradually comes back.

One of them takes the satphone from my ammo pouch. He turns it on and tells me there is still no signal. I reach to take the phone from his hand and toss it into the ravine.

With the last of my strength I tell him how it is. After close contact with the enemy, we might all be infected and must be isolated for many days. The survivors must stay put and kill anyone else who may come from the east. I order them to gather ammunition from the dead, to go easy on whatever food is left in the village. They are to barricade the road in both directions: if Greymouth sends relief, it is to be turned away, well short of contaminated territory.

My final order is that they leave me and return to guard the ruined bridge. They snap to attention, salute and disappear with looks of guilty relief. That done, I lie back on the soft moss and stare into the darkening sky.

Well, well – so it won't be leukaemia after all. Truly, I couldn't imagine a better end - a crucial victory, well worth the price of a fatal wound. Instead of moaning and puking my way to the ancestors from a hospital bed, I will greet them like a man, in blood-soaked camouflage, weapon in hand.

I let out a long sigh of relief and lie back with a smile. On reflex I raise my left wrist, but drop it back before I get half-way, realizing that time no longer matters.

On impulse I take the diary out of my pocket and undo the seal of the heavy plastic envelope. The story is not quite complete, and I prize the short tactical pen from my sleeve pocket to fill the last pages with my final thoughts.

After I run out of words I reread what I had written. No doubt, it is the finest of my works, an exhortation to successors, whose future is sadly tainted by the present failure - one I am pleased to have exonerated with my blood.

Then I look around, see a hollow between two large

boulders, crawl over and work the knife until a shelter of small stones can ensconce the last six months of my life in the safety of a rock shelter. That gives me a comfort I cannot even describe. I mark it by sinking the combat knife into a gap between the boulders and take my time to crawl back to the soft moss, my last mission fulfilled.

Dusk gives way to darkness, and sparse warmth gives way to the chill. I stare at the star-studded sky, no longer warm or cold, feeling only the glow of final triumph. Occasionally I hear gunfire that never seems to last. It sounds as if deserters are still arriving, but my men make short work of them every time.

A gentle touch caresses my grimy forehead as I feel Helen's weight on my pelvis. She lowers her breasts to my tunic that is stiff with dry blood, reaches out and closes my eyes with a warm hand.

I awaken in agony at dawn, throbbing pain tearing at the wound just as the sky grows light. I breathe hard, clutching my rifle and grimacing through the agony, fighting back nausea and the urge to scream. I don't want the men to return and clench my jaws tight, willing myself to overcome.

The heart begins to thump against my ribs. It gallops and protests with all its might, rattling the entire body with desperate effort as everything begins to fade. Its sounds take on a deafening clarity as other feelings begin to drain from my body. My entire being is reduced to a thundering drum within the chest, and I revel in the defiance of its rhythm.

Suddenly I hear it stop with no warning and begin to drift into the void, leaving millions of cancer cells to their just fate.

One last thing in the seconds that remain – I must not let go of the rifle.

{}{}{}

Two days later I run out of food and begin to search the transporter, but soon give up - my appetite has faded, and I begin to cough. There is a constant throbbing in my joints, and breathing is laboured when I move. The transporter has long cooled down, and it feels even colder inside than out.

The last of my strength is used up on a short walk, to refill a container from the waterfall next to the road. Not bothering to shut the hatch, I wrap up tightly into the bedroll and let the daze take me.

I come to in short snatches, jolted by a painful, racking cough that turns moist some time in the night. There is blood in my mouth by dawn, and I try not to soil the transporter by retching, splashing my burning forehead with ice-cold water and chewing on the remaining berries.

When I awaken it is light, and I am a overtaken by a craving to see the sky for the last time. It takes me a long time to reach the hatch, drop to the ground and crawl from beneath the machine.

I manage to reach a puddle on the side of the road and drink from it greedily. It tastes of ferns and fresh earth, and I lower my fiery cheek into the water, revelling in the caress of the mountain frost.

Then I smile in recognition - this is the very spot I had seen in my dreams. I rise on my hands and knees and study the mossy rocks in front of me. It couldn't have been a coincidence that I ran out of fuel on this very bend – something is gleaming in the rocks.

The magic metal of the ancients that resists rust hasn't failed despite the passage of time. I climb the slippery boulders and crawl up the waterfall, to retrieve what awaited my arrival all these centuries.

Once I pull out the knife I see a thick sheaf of paper inside a clear pouch that turned yellow and crumbles under touch. I cannot read the spidery writing on the paper, but retrieve it with great care and gently push it inside my tunic pocket. The vicious-looking combat knife finds a home in my boot. Then I slide back down and manage to return to the transporter.

An overwhelming fatigue mercifully lowers me into oblivion, towards all who await me.

Father is pouring over maps as grandfather looks over his shoulder with a heavy frown. I see myself as a child, standing nearby and watching them with awe.

Then Rina's face appears amid a glowing white light. The mountain wind rifles her hair as she beckons me out of the darkness.

Trevor bars my way, standing before me in full uniform and ramrod-straight, no longer a mangled cripple. His scarred face is set in a grim, grudging expression of approval. I return his salute, then throw my arms around his rock-solid torso and stream bitter tears for all that we had to endure.

I am in an airship, drifting above the empty vermin camp, a meadow strewn with white bones that glisten in the resurgent grass. The breeze takes us over the ocean, and I look down to see what remains of the whalers' flotilla - but there is nothing below except heaving swell. I can just make out a dark shadow that lurks under the water, waiting in vain for the corpses of starved children.

I see the remains of my house being pulled apart, board by broken board, as Redmond carefully retrieves my possessions from the rubble. I can see tears that streak down his wrinkled face as he and Celia wrap things in cloth and place them in a carved wooden chest. Celia says, her melodic voice hoarse and choked, that every generation must remember what I had done.

I stretch out my hand, for I suddenly stand beside her, opening my mouth to protest: I do not deserve honour, I who took the survival of my kind into my hands and gambled so wantonly with fate - what I deserve is to be cursed and forgotten by all, whose fortune it is to survive my reckless deed.

After that there are only blurred glimpses - combat, pain, coupling with Rina, a one-eyed stare from Rat, the acid taste of burning coal, a thundering explosion in the cave. Father Simon stands at the door to the baths, the empty sockets of his eyes staring at me with despair. A legless and armless Dinah gives birth to a vermin baby, blood sloshing inside a vast bullet hole amid her breasts. I feel the childhood pain of a rat bite and see my swollen foot, dripping pus onto white sheets. Then I am kneeling on the shingle next to a beached log, stabbing it with my knife.

I next roll down the steep slope with a dead soldier clinging to my back. There, lying broken and defeated at the bottom of a steep ravine, I see the dead eyes of the salamander that clambers towards me from the ferns. Its pupils suddenly gape to reveal a brilliant yellow glow, and the beast straddles me with an unbearable weight, opening a mouth full of uneven, peg-like teeth.

But all I feel next is a sudden, piercing breeze. There are many stars in the vast sky, and I can see them with remarkable clarity. I am floating just above the icy ground, swinging gently to the rhythm of someone's steps.

"Watch your feet," I hear Redmond's voice that

seems unusually harsh. "We must not drop him. He is very cold, and a jolt could stop his heart."

I realize that I am carried on a blanket by four men whom I cannot see. A hammer blow of realization makes me rise, but an arm I cannot resist pushes me down and gently restrains me from trying again.

"Commander, you are very ill," says Redmond, his voice cable-tight with tension. "You could die - please refrain from all movement."

I raise my hand towards him and start to speak, but there is no breath in my lungs, and no sound comes from my parched mouth. Instead, I break into a coughing fit that ignites my chest with searing pain.

Stars grow dim as I lose command of my body and drop back onto the blanket, entirely defeated. They will take me back to Grey, and that will be the end of all, for I am too weak to do anything to stop it.

"Don't slow down," rasps Redmond, his voice floating somewhere above my head. "Watch the ground and keep up the pace, boys. Don't think about anything except what's in front of you."

There is nothing else to do but die before I reach town. Who knows, maybe that can prevent the spread. I take a final glance at the stars and close my eyes, willing myself to drift back into the darkness, where the salamander calmly awaits my return.

That all-knowing patience is quite beyond any endurance. As I fade out, such acceptance of fate terrifies me more than anything I would want to survive.

{}{}{}

Epilogue

It's a warm enough day, and I elect to ride on the roof, with my legs inside the hatch. The convoy is rumbling south - we are in the third day of a long trek to Karito. Our cargo includes the most precious of possessions - smoked meat and clean grain.

They carried me back to Grey, a hairbreadth away from death. My lungs were full of filth, and no one expected me to live through it. But that turned out to be my old friend, the lung rot - not the vile plague of the ancients.

The healers spent many moons nursing the near-corpse, but I surprised everyone by rising from my bed as the buds of spring began to open. I had lost most of my weight; my arms have little strength, and I can only walk a short distance.

But that is only a matter of will, I told them, as I went about urgent business.

By the time I was back from the brink, the vermin had disappeared. There were no bodies at the camp. We made a few cautious trips to clear the old road and collected coal. There was not even a hint of their presence - it's as if they were swallowed up by an angry earth. We flew over the mountains and even landed in Brana - still finding no trace of vermin, dead or alive. We now ride the ancient roads with our guns stored in lockers.

Well, there probably are a few survivors, but that matters little now. Within a few winters I will have everything to repel them, maybe even hunt them down. There will be many young men with guns, airships and transporters. There will be a vast stone wall that cannot be climbed.

Men replete with grain and fresh meat will stand watch day and night without lapsing into exhausted sleep, and bright lights will keep away any menace that lurks in the darkness.

I lean forward and touch the terrible scar on my right shin, then drop into the hatch, favouring the left side. The healers say that a bit of lung rot might have entered my leg through the bloodstream. But I remember how I came to have that wound all too well.

At first his presence was nothing but glimpses, flashes of poignant clarity that came upon me as I read what he wrote. I had read much that was written by the ancients – but that warrior's diary entered my soul as nothing before, as I fought off death, in and out of a twilight filled with quivering shadows.

Then glimpses of a better man began to merge, and one day I finally comprehended his destiny – to take over mine.

I welcomed that at first, clutching at the spirit of a man who thirsted to be. He died long before his thirst was quenched, as he gave up his life without hesitation.

Before he died, he made it so very clear why I must go on, fight regardless of odds as an inexorable duty to my people, for a warrior has no higher purpose than to protect the weak and no alternative but to win.

I only wish he took the trouble to sign his name, lost forever on the winds that hammer the snow-clad peaks.

I rebounded with force, attacking reality in his presence even before I could walk - the modest, relentless soldier would not want me to snivel. There is far too much to do, and I am not in the best condition to make it all happen.

What I cannot do is tell anyone what I had done, nor can I live with that knowledge. Not quite to the point of rupture, it constantly gnaws me from within. That horror and I are quite alone.

I suspect that Redmond knows, for he never speaks of it either. Everyone else continues to bow before me as if I was Jesus returned to earth - but there is no hiding from the warrior who died on the side of the road in damp moss, clutching the sleek black rifle.

His silent, sturdy stare wills me to protect those in my charge, to do my duty. I tell him what I had done instead, how I want to die of my shame - but he shakes his blood-spattered head with a gentle smile and orders me to remain at my post.

Celia somehow found it in her heart to go on. She

cares for me deeply, but knows much that makes her wary. She won't fall asleep under my roof, and sometimes her loving gaze turns to tears when she stares deep into my eyes.

It's almost as if she can see him. I can't tell her, torn by guilt and fear.

Every time I see someone fall ill, I break into cold sweat and begin to spy, not at all afraid of being intrusive. Sometimes sick people die, and I cannot sleep for days, staring at others, reduced to near-panic whenever they gulp water or appear insensitive to the cold.

Then nothing happens. After the terror subsides, I spend many nights and days sleeping a fitful, exhausted sleep of a guilty man.

The dread pervades all my being. It taints hope and fouls my dreams. That fear is with me now, inside the turret, as we grind away the miles to rescue the hungry people of Karito. The victory is all mine, but I will never get used to juggling bright hope with the worst fear.

I awaken at dawn of each unwanted day, allocate its tasks and force myself out of bed with a great effort of will. There is very much to build and many worthy successors to prepare.

Many horrors lie in wait as my people struggle back from the brink.

I drive my shrivelled body by whispering the words that end the nameless diary. I say them again and again, rekindling the desire to fight in the sickly, aching remainder of myself with the ancient truth.

ONLY THE DEAD
HAVE SEEN
THE END OF WAR

IBE 1982-2015

www.ingramcontent.com/pod-product-compliance
Lightning Source LLC
Chambersburg PA
CBHW051938020726
47501CB00001B/183